the
sun gods

CHIN MUSIC
PRESS

PUBLISHED BY
Chin Music Press
1501 Pike Place #329
Seattle, WA 98101
USA
WWW.CHINMUSICPRESS.COM

PRINTED IN CANADA BY Imprimerie Gauvin
COVER ART & BOOK DESIGN BY Dan D Shafer
ILLUSTRATIONS BY Deborah Bluestein
TEXT SET IN Elzevir and Brandon Grotesque
Library of Congress Cataloging-in-Publication Data is available.

the

A NOVEL

ミネドカ イリゲータ 100 01

sun

gods

JAY RUBIN

CHIN MUSIC PRESS   *Seattle, Washington*

CONTENTS

PROLOGUE:
1953

AFTER ANOTHER TENSE SUPPER, Bill slipped out to the garage and sat in his father's Chevrolet, shifting gears. Then he went up to his room. Instead of doing homework, he stared out the window, through the peeling madrona trees that lined the bluff and across Puget Sound. A few specks of light distinguished the shadowy mound of Bainbridge Island from the dark surrounding water. The jagged edge of the Olympic Mountains cut across a torn red sky. Above The Brothers' double peak, three bombers in formation descended southward toward Boeing Field. The thin cry of a seagull pierced the rumbling darkness.

The next morning it was cold and drizzly—classic Seattle weather. Bill wore his yellow poncho when he left for school. Bainbridge and the mountains were hidden behind a wall of fog. The wrinkled face of the Sound glowed silver-gray in the filtered morning light.

A dark green DeSoto was parked across the street at the edge of the bluff. With two short strips of chrome on the fender just behind the front wheel well, it had to be a '49. Four years old, the car looked brand new, its shiny skin covered with a fine layer of rain drops. Bill glanced back at it once or twice as he hurried down the street along the bluff. It was probably Mr. Elwyn's latest purchase. Their neighbor always bought nice used cars, and he knew how to take good care of them.

Bill stood at the curb, hoping that Jeff would drive by in his Ford before the bus arrived, but after a minute or two, the green DeSoto came cruising in his direction down Magnolia Boulevard. The car edged toward the curb and stopped directly in front of him. Through the foggy glass on the passenger side, he saw an arm reach across to crank down the window. Mr. Elwyn was going to offer him a ride.

Bill bent at the waist to peer inside, resting his hand against the door. But when the glass came down, he caught his breath.

The driver was a grim-looking Asian man in his early thirties. His dark, narrow eyes glared at him from beneath the brim of a brown felt hat. Neither the man nor Bill said a word.

They stayed like this for a long time. Bill hoped the man's anger was not meant for him, but he sensed that it was.

"Billy?" the man asked, as if demanding a confession. "Billy Morton?"

Bill nodded. Did he know this man?

"I ... wanted to see you ..." The voice was deep and calm.

The eyes seemed to burn less fiercely now. Before Bill could speak, the man reached out again, and the glass began to rise. That was when Bill saw it: the man had no left arm. The sleeve of his beige raincoat was folded up and pinned at the shoulder. The rain-streaked glass came up, transforming the man into a ghost from another world.

The car turned sharply from the curb and sped away. A city bus pulled up to take its place. Bill stepped aboard, sliding into a window seat near the back. The bus lurched into traffic with a roar. Bill looked out across the Sound at the gray, rain-filled sky. A gull flew parallel with the bus, its beak wide open, but he could not hear its scream.

PART ONE:

1959

PLATE NO. 13

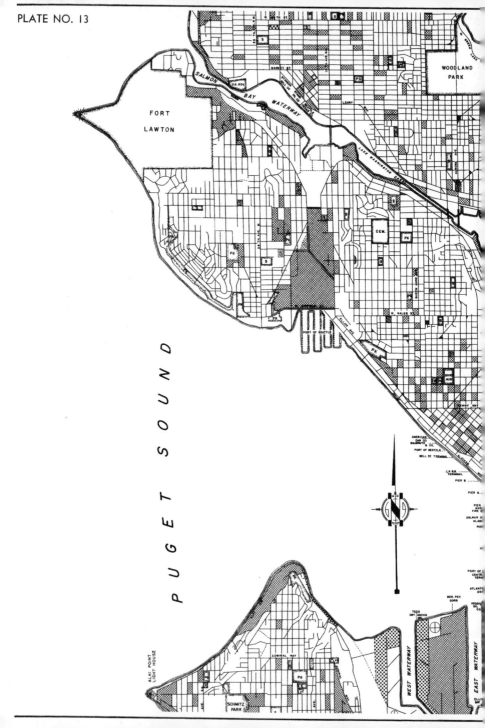

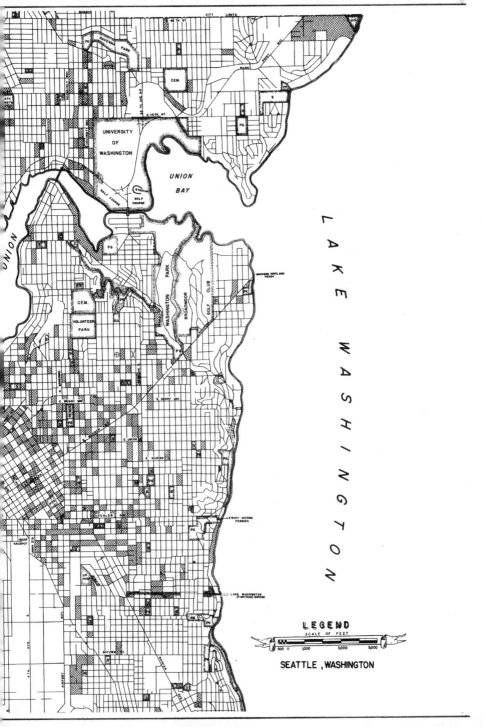

LAKE WASHINGTON

UNION BAY

UNIVERSITY OF WASHINGTON

LEGEND
SCALE OF FEET

SEATTLE, WASHINGTON

1

EVEN WITH HIKING BOOTS ON, Clare's legs were gorgeous in shorts, and, watching them move, Bill kept tripping over the underbrush that lined the Issaquah Creek trail.

"Lord, give me strength," he muttered.

"What's that?" she called out.

"Let me go ahead, Clare," he said. "You're blocking the view."

"What view? Just trees?" She stood aside.

"You'll see," he said, pecking her on the lips as he passed by. "We'll get to the shallows soon."

He jumped over a large rock and took the lead with long strides.

"Slow down! And why do *I* have to carry the pack?"

"You wanted the full experience," he said with a laugh.

Clare trudged along behind him, her heavy boots crunching on the gravel by the stream.

"Bill?"

She sounded serious. Maybe she didn't think it was as funny as he did. Maybe he should have offered to take the pack.

"Yes, Clare?"

"You've got great legs."

He whirled around, mouth agape.

"I mean it," she said. "You're beautiful."

He fluttered his eyelids and touched his hair, but she was not amused.

"Go on, keep walking," she commanded.

He forged ahead.

"Think of it," she said. "There's not a *girl* in the whole college half as nice-looking as you, let alone a boy."

"Come on, Clare, this is embarrassing."

"No, really. I know girls who'd kill to get that shade of reddish blond.

You probably never had a pimple in your life; your eyebrows don't need tweezing; your big, luscious eyes would look good on Rita Hayworth; and you're built like Tarzan."

"Well, that's a relief," he said, fanning his face and grinning. "At least I'm not built like Jane."

"Don't you see what I'm getting at? I don't deserve you. How can a man like you marry a girl like me?"

"That's enough, Clare. You almost had me fooled …" He turned and pointed to the water. "Look at the stream now. You can see them swimming. Hundreds of them."

"Where? I don't see—Oh my God!"

Down in the surging darkness of the stream, long shadows moved. In threes and fives and twos, they glided past, their flared tails waving gently as they propelled themselves against the silent flow.

"So many!" she whispered, as if they had stumbled upon a secret ceremony.

"Wait. This is just the beginning."

He pushed a drooping branch aside and motioned her ahead.

The stream level was dropping quickly now, and the large, dark patches were no longer deep pools of water but swarms of fish—huge Chinook salmon, two and three feet long—massing together, poised in equilibrium against the flow.

"They swim in from the Pacific to the Sound," Bill said. "Through the ship canal. And they just keep coming."

"But the canal only leads to Lake Washington. How do they get way up here? We're practically in the mountains!"

"I'm not sure," he said. "Lake Washington is connected to Lake Sammamish, and this stream feeds into Lake Sammamish. It's incredible how they know the exact route."

Ahead, jutting rocks broke the smooth surface of the creek, and a sudden flutter sent up a spray of water. A salmon surged across the gravelly shallow stretches of the stream, its gleaming, dark body exposed to the air, tail churning the water like a small motorboat. Nervous seagulls stood in the shallows, hopping away whenever a thrashing salmon came too close.

Lone salmon, some with dead white scars where rocks and predators had gouged out their reddish-black flesh, lay on sandy pockets of the creek bottom. They latched their fiercely hooked jaws upon any other fish that happened to stray into their territory. Pink spheres of salmon eggs littered the stream bed, and the gray, rotting bodies of huge fish lay upon the banks, crows pecking at their bleached guts.

"This is it?" she asked. "They just lay eggs and die?"

Bill had come year after year to witness the fall salmon spawning, drawn by the fatal sureness that brought the fish back to the waters of their birth. He decided not to show her the hatchery, where workmen slashed open the bellies of the females, disgorging thousands of orange-red eggs into big buckets, then fertilized them with the thick, white milt they squeezed from the bodies of the males.

They continued up the creek to a small, sunny clearing. Moving in behind her, he lifted the pack from her back.

"That feels good!" she said with a sigh.

Bill sat cross-legged on the warm ground and opened the pack. She followed his lead, sitting opposite him, her knees touching his, and took the water bottle he handed her. She drank her fill, then closed her eyes as she leaned toward him, and their lips met, softly.

"Which reminds me," she said, pulling away. "How *can* a man like you marry a girl like me?"

"Don't be ridiculous," he said. "You're absolutely beautiful. But what matters most is our love of God and our love for each other. If we're going to spend our life together, spreading the Gospel, we need to have complete faith in each other, right?" His father would be proud to hear him say that, he thought.

They joined hands, resting them on his bare knees, and looked into each other's eyes. The only sounds were the gurgling of the stream and the sighing of the wind in the trees. To these were added on occasion the squawk of a bird among the branches, followed by the beating of wings. The breeze was a little cooler than Bill had expected for mid-September, but warm sunlight flooded down on the grassy clearing.

"Let's go farther upstream," he said at last.

"Oh, Bill, not today. I'm not that crazy about dead fish."

"I'm glad your campers can't hear you. Even I could hardly keep up with you this summer! Anyhow, it's too early to go back to campus."

"We can stay here and talk, can't we?"

"Give me my jacket, then," he said, pointing toward the pack behind her.

They lay on their backs, side by side, looking up into the circle of sky fringed by swaying tree tops.

A strong gust of cool air swept over them, and Bill drew his knees up.

"It is a scar, isn't it?" Clare said, pointing at his right thigh above the knee.

He glanced at the scar and looked away. "Uh-huh. It's an old one."

"Well? Aren't you going to tell me about it? It was obviously pretty bad."

"Yes, I suppose it was."

"It looks as if an arrow went right through."

A huge, empty feeling of night came to him, and he was running.

"I'm not sure what happened," he said. "I was only four or five."

"I remember lots of things that happened to me when I was four or five."

"I don't know, my father told me it was some kind of hunting accident. I was staying with my aunt's family in Kansas."

But even as he spoke, images of gigantic, black houses loomed up inside him: a huge dining hall crowded with Asian people shouting at each other; sand in his mouth and eyes; and the wind screaming like a train outside the room. Another monstrous chamber full of steam and water sprays and laughter and naked women.

"Bill? Can you answer me?"

"I'm sorry. Did you ask me a question?"

"You haven't heard a word I've said! You do that a lot, you know."

He sat up and touched her shoulder. She ignored him.

Large patches of cloud were blowing out of the west, and the clear blue of the sky was filling up with gray.

"We'd better go," Clare said.

They barely spoke during the return hike and the ride back to the city.

He thought of that strange rainy morning when he was still in high school. A one-armed Asian man had glared at him and spoken his name. Somewhere out there were people who knew him, who knew more about him than he himself did. And they were not his color.

"Where do you go when you get all quiet?" she asked when they were waiting for the light to change at Rainier Avenue.

"I don't know," he mumbled. His hand crept down to his bare knee, and the fingers began to trace the scar.

All these years, he'd been living inside the mind of a child, accepting anything he was told about who he was and where he'd come from. Here he was, a twenty-one-year-old man, standing on the verge of independence, thinking of marriage, and he hadn't had sense enough to bring his grade school geography lessons together with the living truth in his heart.

Whole cities filled with Asian people in Kansas? And which of those people could have been the "aunt" he was staying with? Was it the one called Mitsu? Was she really his mother? But wasn't his mother dead?

Somewhere nearby, car horns were honking.

"Bill! The light's green!"

He gunned the engine and peeled away from the intersection.

"Why can't you tell me what's bothering you?" Clare said when they pulled up to her dormitory. "You make these pretty speeches to me how we have to trust each other, but you have a problem and you shut me out. It's the same when I ask you about your family. When are you going to introduce me to them? You say you've got a father, a mother, and two brothers, but for all I know, you might as well be making them up."

Clare was right. There was a part of him he didn't know how to share with her yet: a dark void that he had scarcely glimpsed himself. He knew he needed to explore those depths alone at first. "I'm sorry, Clare," he said. "I can't explain it."

She sighed and shook her head, then got out of the car and walked away.

2

AFTER HE HANDED in the assignment for his 9:30 class Monday morning, Bill found the thought of sitting indoors, taking notes, intolerable. His first impulse was to throw his hiking boots in the car and drive out to Issaquah to see the salmon again, but that would solve nothing. Should he visit his father at the church? Maybe now was the time to ask about those murky years between the death of his real mother and the arrival of his stepmother. The topic had never been part of life in the Morton household.

He got into the Chevy and started to drive before he knew where he was going. Soon he realized he was headed toward Chinatown. He pulled into an Esso station, and while the attendant pumped a dollar's worth of regular, he went inside and found a street map in a wire rack. As well as he knew Seattle, the oriental neighborhood was an area into which he had only strayed once or twice with some of the other students. Certainly his father had never taken him there.

Working his way along the ship canal, he turned south onto Aurora past the rows of billboards to downtown, then struggled through the traffic toward the white prominence of Smith Tower. It seemed like a gateway to a world beyond.

He turned onto Jackson Street and found himself in foreign territory, where all the shop signs were half in exotic characters, half in nearly-as-exotic transliterations: Ming Hing Grocery, Asahi Printing, Chong Wah Gift Shop, Chung Kiu Company, Nakazono Produce, Higo 10¢ Store. Wads of newsprint drifted along the street in the wakes of the passing cars. Green and white shards of glass littered the asphalt. They called this blighted area "Chinatown," but some of the names here must certainly be Japanese. Chinese people had names like "Chang" and "Wong," while Japanese names were more like "Yamamoto" or "Tanaka." "Mitsu" had to be Japanese. He turned down 8th Avenue and drifted up King Street, looking at the restaurants and at the markets with ducks and sausages in the windows.

A pang of hunger reminded him of the time. Clare would soon be looking for him at their usual table in the cafeteria. He hated to disappoint her, but he would not be going back.

He pulled up to the curb and started down King Street on foot, scanning the stores for a Japanese-sounding name. He passed the Wah Young Grocery, one window of which contained garish red porcelain cups, the other metal strainers with bamboo handles. In the next window hung headless chickens, their darkly roasted skins glistening.

At the corner of Sixth, he looked to the right, beyond Jackson and part way up the hill, where there was a sign that had to be Japanese: "Maneki," it said in red letters above a smudged, gray area. That rhymed with the notorious General Tojo's name: "Hideki."

Not until he was standing beneath it could he make out the foggy lower portion of the sign. It was the badly weathered figure of a seated cat holding its left paw up as though taking the Boy Scout oath with the wrong hand. The picture seemed both bizarre and oddly familiar to him.

The restaurant itself did not look promising. Behind dust-smeared panes of glass were some sort of bare wooden lattices that prevented any view of the interior, and the gold letters on the door had flaked away almost completely, but the small sign on the door frame said the place was open. He gave the door a push.

The first thing inside was a black wooden display shelf with various knickknacks, the center piece of which was a foot-high porcelain version of the cat with the upraised paw. Now there was no doubt in his mind that he had seen something like this before.

"One?" asked a slim, graceful Japanese woman who had come up beside him.

"Yes, I'm alone."

She turned silently, and he followed her to the left. The restaurant was shaped like an L running along two sides of a long rectangular structure, a kind of house-within-a-house that had its own shingled roof beneath the shop's high, brown ceiling. The crashing of pots and clash of glass came from a small window in the side of the "house."

The left wall of the restaurant was lined with eight or ten booths, all having bright red imitation leather backs. The waitress gestured for him to take a seat in the one unoccupied booth, and then she glided away. One other waitress—a plump woman in her thirties—scurried between the window and the booths.

His waitress returned with a dented aluminum kettle, from which she poured some greenish water into a squat cup that had no handle. The green leaves in the fluid sank languidly to the bottom. The woman pointed to the other end of the gray Formica table and said, "Menu." He took one of the plastic-covered folders from behind the napkin holder and opened it while she stood over him.

"This might take a while," he said to her, but she merely smiled and waited. He let his eyes wander down the menu, the four corners of which were decorated with drawings of the cat. The terse English explanations of the Japanese items were not much help when it came to choosing one dish over another. The woman's presence made it difficult to concentrate, and so did the noises from the kitchen. There seemed to be two cooks at work in there, one of whom yammered endlessly in Japanese, the other responding sometimes with grunts, sometimes in a form of English.

Near the bottom of the second page, one word struck him as familiar: *O-nigiri*. The menu described o-nigiri as rice balls wrapped in seaweed, which sounded anything but appetizing.

"I'll have this one: o-nigiri," he said to the waitress, who giggled and bit her pencil.

"Is something wrong?" he asked.

"I surprise. You say word so nice. Not many *hakujin*s—I mean, white people—know o-nigiri."

"I really don't know what it is. I'll try it, though."

For a moment, she looked puzzled. "Oh, I know," she perked up. "You study Japanese at U.W. *Konnichi wa. O-genki desu ka?*"

She cocked her head, obviously waiting for some response from him.

"No, I don't know any Japanese," he said, smiling weakly.

"You sure you want o-nigiri? I don't think you like. Sukiyaki has beef."

"That's all right. I'm just experimenting."

She smiled and started to move away.

"Wait, just a second," he called. "I want to ask you something. What is this cat? I mean, why is he holding his paw up?" He pointed to the drawing in the corner of the menu.

"Oh, that *maneki-neko*, like Maneki Restaurant," she said, smiling, as if no further explanation were called for.

"Yes?"

"It mean welcome. Cat go, 'Come here.'" She made a pawing motion with her left hand.

"It looks as if you're waving goodbye."

"Oh, no. Japanese people wave like this mean come here."

She left him to place the order, and he tried sipping the contents of his cup. It was bitter but not unpleasant. He drained the cup, being careful to avoid swallowing the leaves at the bottom, and poured himself another. The stained, yellowish aluminum kettle had the words "Made in Occupied Japan" stamped at the base of the handle.

Accompanied by a small, covered bowl, from which steam was escaping, his plate arrived with three thick, triangular wads of rice, each sandwiched between paper-thin sheets of blackish-green stuff.

"How do I eat this?" he asked the waitress.

"Just pick up and—" she chomped at the air in her hand.

She went off to another table, and he took the wad on the right. The black stuff crinkled as his teeth tore through it, and suddenly his mouth was filled with secret delights long denied. He had eaten this! He had enjoyed this penetrating, salty, sea-like flavor, but along with the pleasure, it brought back an ancient fear: a monster would find what he had inside his stomach and rip it out of him.

3

BILL FOUND A NOTE in his dormitory mailbox. Clare wanted to know why he had not met her for lunch. He was not ready to explain his excursion to the Japanese district, but by the time he found her in the library, the best excuse he could come up with was that he had taken the car to the gas station—which, in a sense, was true.

"You're keeping something from me, Bill. I know it. Do you have another girlfriend?"

"Absolutely not. I swear to God. It's nothing like that."

"So there *is* something going on. Why can't you share it with me? I'm going to be your wife, aren't I? Who else can you share your problems with?"

Who else? There was only one person he had to share his problems with at this point: his father. But he needed something to talk to him about. When Clare hurried off to her European history class, Bill went to the college's Office of Missions for the umpteenth time. He didn't have to search long before he found a newsletter from an organization called the Evangelical Alliance Mission. The Japan branch was run by an Englishwoman named Irene Webster-Smith, who described her experience of finding Tokyo in ruins after the war. Now she had an office near a big student center, where she concentrated her efforts on bringing the Gospel to Japan's new generation. This would be the perfect thing to talk to his father about.

Bill sat in the phone booth in the dormitory lobby, fingering the pebbled metal surface of the wall with one hand while the other played with the nickel in his pocket. Finally, he dropped the coin in the slot and dialed the number of his father's church.

Thomas Morton seemed to be in particularly fine spirits, and he readily consented to have a talk with Bill about his missionary plans. He had some ideas on the subject himself, he said, and he could spare an hour at two o'clock tomorrow afternoon if Bill would come to the church.

Even in first gear, the Chevy barely made it up the roller coaster slopes of Dravus St. the next day. As much as he still loved the old car, Bill half wished it would break down then and there. The closer he came to his destination, the more he dreaded the moment when he would open his mouth to speak of what had never been spoken between them. The car whirred and chugged its way past the tiny, boxlike houses to the summit of Magnolia, where wood frames suddenly gave way to brick and stucco, and the roof lines soared upward, above them all the red brick steeple of his father's church, glowing in the light that filtered through the dense gray clouds.

He parked out front and sat for a moment, staring at the white letters on black felt backing, announcing next week's sermon. "The Reverend Thomas Morton, Pastor." Those words stood out from the others, reminding him of his own special relationship with God through his father, who seemed simultaneously to be pushing him toward the holy gate and also standing before it, challenging his right to enter.

He glanced at his watch. The time was exactly one minute before two. His father expected him to be punctual.

Thomas Morton welcomed Bill into his sparsely decorated office and invited him to sit down in an armchair by the side of his dark, heavy desk, turning in his swivel chair to face him. The ceiling lights reflected momentarily on Tom's octagonal wire-frame glasses. Rather than a son wishing to speak with his father, Bill felt like a member of the congregation who had come to see the pastor about a personal problem.

"You know I've been thinking for some time of missionary work," Bill said.

"Yes, of course," Tom replied, smiling and clasping his hands together atop crossed knees. Tom wore his skin like a firm leather covering stretched tight over the square jaw bone. It seemed to match the strong, almost radiant voice that Thomas Morton always projected, though it made him appear somewhat older than his fifty-one years. The impression of age was especially noticeable these days when he had his thirty-nine-year-old wife by his side.

"I think you know I've been seeing someone steadily since the beginning of summer," Bill added.

"Well, I have had the impression that there was one particular girl, but you've been pretty vague on that topic."

"We're, uh, thinking of getting married."

"Oh? Not right away, I hope. Marriage is too serious a matter for young people to rush into."

"I've been planning to bring her home and introduce her to you and … to both of you." He hesitated to use the word "Mother" for Lucy.

"Good. What's her name?"

"Clare. Clare Korvald."

"Ah, a Ballard girl, no doubt!" The deep slash of a smile cut across Tom's leather visage. Ballard was the sprawling Scandinavian neighborhood north of the ship canal.

"Of course," Bill said, trying to smile back. "Her parents are from Norway."

"Which means they're Lutherans."

"No, surprisingly, they're Baptists. I think that's one of the reasons they left. Her father works for Boeing."

"And she goes to Cascade-Pacific with you?"

"That's right. We're planning to do some missionary work together for a year or two after graduation and before I enter seminary. Clare wants to go to Norway."

"Sounds perfect. Is she pretty?"

"I think so. Very pretty."

"Well, what are you waiting for? How about this weekend? I'd love to meet her."

Bill was not quite ready to make firm plans. "Actually, I wanted to talk about … Norway," he was surprised to hear himself saying. His father looked just as surprised.

"You probably know more about the country than I do," Tom said.

"Well, I mean, I don't really want to talk about Norway."

"Oh. You *don't* want to talk about Norway."

"I mean, I'm not too crazy about the idea of going there."

"Well, where would you rather go?"

Bill hesitated a moment. Then he looked directly into his father's eyes and said, "Japan."

Tom's leathery jowls began to darken in color, almost to a brownish-purple, and his eyes turned to glass. "You don't want to go there," he said with such absolute finality that it seemed unthinkable there could be any divergence between his own determination and Bill's.

"What's wrong with Japan?" Bill asked as innocently as possible.

"What's right with it? Heathens, all of them. Look at what happened at Pearl Harbor."

"Which is precisely why they, above all, need to hear the Gospel of Our Lord. I think this country has a moral obligation to bring the healing words of Christ to those people after what they've been through."

"You mean, after what they put themselves through."

"That's not a very—"

"Christian?"

"Not a very forgiving attitude. I've been reading about an Englishwoman doing missionary work in Tokyo who—"

"She's wasting her time. And you will be, too, if you go there. There's no such thing as a Japanese Christian."

"How can you say that? Thousands are being converted every year."

"Lies. Deception. That's all it is. Not one of them knows how to take Christ into his heart."

"How can you be so sure?" Bill pressed.

"Believe me," Tom concluded. "I know."

"How do you know?"

Tom was now shifting in his chair, the muscles of his jaw working.

"Are you questioning me?" he bellowed. "You don't know anything. You're barely out of your teens. I have lived. I'm talking from experience."

"And that's exactly what I've come to you to learn. Teach me from your experience! Show me the error of my ways!"

"How can I if you won't listen to me!"

"But I am listening. Tell me why I shouldn't go to Japan. Tell me what you have lived through. Why have you written off an entire people as heathens beyond redemption?"

Tom glared at Bill and said nothing.

"All right, then, let me ask you this," Bill went on, emboldened now by the emotional upheaval he had caused in his father. "Who was this so-called 'aunt' I was staying with in Kansas after my mother died?"

Bill knew that he was unleashing a bomb, and it had its intended effect. Tom rose to his full height, towering over Bill, who sat gripping the arms of his chair. Tom raised his fist, then slumped back in his chair, arms dropping limply by his sides.

"Why don't we ever hear from this 'aunt?'" Bill continued. "Why aren't there any letters? Why aren't there any photographs? What was her name?"

"What does all that have to do with missionary work in Japan?" Tom spluttered.

"I don't know," Bill answered truthfully. "That's what I want you to tell me."

"The two have nothing to do with each other. They're completely separate."

"It's not true! You're lying to me! You've always lied to me about that!"

"Do you know who you're talking to, you young fool!"

"Yes, of course! You're my father, and you're not telling me the truth! I want to know about Mitsu—who she was to me and to you!"

"Get out!" Tom shouted with such force the windows rattled. "Get out!"

Suddenly, it was as if Tom's energy was spent. He turned his face away and waved feebly toward the door.

Bill pried his fingers from the arms of his chair and struggled to his feet. He dragged himself across the office and closed the door behind him.

PART TWO:
1939

4

BILLY CHEWED ON the end of his little brown necktie as Tom struggled to pull the groggy boy's coat on. Five months past his first birthday—the first anniversary of Sarah's death—Billy was becoming increasingly difficult for him to deal with alone.

Tom had to be at the Japanese Christian Church on Terrace Street an hour and a half early to address the older congregation. His own sermon for the English-language service was ready, but he needed at least ten minutes with Pastor Hanamori before the *Nichigo* service.

Billy rubbed his eyes as Tom placed him in the back seat of his Hudson Coach and headed from Summit Avenue down Union to Broadway. The main thoroughfare was so much more pleasant on Sundays without the long lines of black, boxy, frog-eyed cars. On Sundays you could see people on the sidewalks instead of rows of horse-drawn wagons overflowing with fruit and vegetables. Even the usual mounds of horse manure had been cleaned away, as if in deference to the Lord's day.

The gigantic white cone of Mount Rainier towered over the city like a hill of freshly ground grain. To Tom, there was nothing beautiful about Seattle's most famous landmark. He had spent endless hours under the blazing Kansas sun grinding grain for cattle feed. Whenever he saw the mountain, he could almost feel the grinder's white dust caking his sweaty arms and face.

The car's engine shuddered and coughed as he pulled up in front of his red brick church. Only a short way down the block from Broadway's bustling traffic, the place seemed closed off from the rest of the world, especially now, as the spring leaves of the oaks lining both sides of the narrow street cast their shadows on the brick facade and on the concrete stairs.

Tom carried the sleeping Billy inside, surrendering his bundle to the hands of the aged Mrs. Uchida. Her skin of wrinkled parchment drooped from every skeletal protuberance, which gave her face the appearance of having been formed of capital "U"s. Tom climbed the dark stairway to the second-story office of Reverend Hanamori, where the Japanese books were crammed into shelves from floor to ceiling and there was an ever-present smell of damp paper.

The diminutive, gray-haired Japanese pastor greeted him with the benign smile he showed to all the world, wrinkling the large, brown mole on the side of his nose.

"Good morning, Tom," he said softly. "You are here early."

Just as Tom had expected, Reverend Hanamori had forgotten.

"The outing," said Tom.

"Yes?"

"Today's outing, Reverend Hanamori. I want to invite the Nichigos myself."

The old Japanese pastor's perfectly round face slowly lit up with recognition.

Was it just the difference in language that caused this inevitable delay in communication every time? The gap between the American-born generation—the Niseis—and these native Japanese was enormous in so many ways! He had learned long ago that, whenever he spoke to the Nichigo congregation, a good deal of preliminary coaching would be necessary if his remarks were to be translated into Japanese accurately. Too often, he had assumed his words were getting through, only to find out afterward that all of the Nichigo choir members had shown up at the wrong time for practice, or that only the ones with children attending his own worship service had managed to find their way to the outing on Hunt's Point.

Oh, those children! What a God-given blessing and inspiration it was to see their hopeful faces turned up to him on a Sunday morning! He blushed to think of the resentment he had felt when he had been sent to shepherd an all-Japanese congregation. Now, each day, he thanked the Lord for the great harvest that it had been given him to reap.

After repeating to the elder reverend his mission this morning, Tom followed him down to the gloomy narthex and into the sanctuary with its three high windows. He watched the gaze of the congregation move from Reverend Hanamori and up his own tall frame to meet his eyes. They never seemed to have grown accustomed to the piercing blue of his eyes, the wheat-field yellow of his hair. He felt to see that his suit coat was buttoned and his vest straight.

Standing beside Reverend Hanamori, listening to the staccato syllables of his Japanese, Thomas Morton allowed his gaze to wander. There was Paul Morikawa, his skin blotched and sagging from years of work under the sun. Not once had the long trek and ferry ride from his Eastside farm prevented him from attending Sunday worship. The widowed Mrs. Tamura: the picture brides she had taken in after their arduous crossing from Japan were still a matter of legend, fifteen years after the floodgates had been closed by the Immigration Act of 1924. Mr. and Mrs. Nomura, among the most youthful and vigorous of the elderly Nichigo congregation: in their zeal for Christ they had boosted Sunday school enrollment to more than four hundred after the retirement of Miss Tessie McDonald, the missionary who had founded the school upon her return from Japan. Mrs. Nomura was wearing a large hat again today—her personal trademark.

The woman sitting next to Mrs. Nomura also wore a broad-brimmed hat. She seemed to be reading something in her lap, and the brim obscured her face. Just as Pastor Tom was about to look away, the woman raised her head, and he felt his legs grow weak.

She was stunning. Her eyes lingered on his for a moment, and then the wide brim of the hat came down, obscuring her face again. He had seen enough to realize that there was a strong resemblance between the woman and Mrs. Nomura. They both had prominent cheekbones and full lips and the double-fold eyelids that he preferred to the narrower single-fold kind. But where Mrs. Nomura had begun to show a middle-aged pallor, this woman had the glow of youth. Even now, with her head bowed, the thrust of her shoulders bespoke a kind of energy that had long since spent itself in the others assembled here. The original Seattle Japanese were in their fifties, the young ones usually in their teens. But this was a woman. She might be twenty-five, or possibly a little older. She was part of the missing generation, the great age gap that had been created by the immigration law.

"...welcome Pastor Tom," he heard Reverend Hanamori saying, as if from a great distance, and he turned to see the reverend looking up at him expectantly.

He knew he must speak, but for the moment, he had forgotten what it was he had planned to announce. "Dear beloved brothers and sisters of the Nichigo congregation," he began with practiced sonority, "today I bring you a message of the love of God."

Now, if only I could recall that message!

"In Psalms 126:3, we read, 'The Lord has done great things for us; whereof we are glad!' and how can we be anything but glad when we think back on our rich heritage? On May 28, 1900, with the Reverend Kenji Ishihama as pastor, our little church was founded, and a long and rich history of thirty-nine years witnesses to a great heritage."

Why can't I stop repeating myself?

"It has been a rich heritage indeed, as we remember the sacrifice and faith of those early immigrants who became Christians."

Lord God, he prayed, *lift the scales from my eyes and let me see.*

"It is difficult to imagine that out of their meager means and trying circumstances, these early Christians purchased land and built buildings. Their zeal for Christ and their love for their fellow immigrants impelled them to reach out over a hundred-mile radius from Seattle, even as far as Vancouver, British Columbia."

Pastor Tom's panic began to lessen somewhat as he saw the looks of satisfaction among the congregation. All you had to do when you talked to the Nichigos was invoke the struggles of the Isseis—the first generation Japanese immigrants—and they would go with you anywhere. "In time," he continued, "this permanent sanctuary was erected, and their faith was translated into the solidity of honest red brick. More amazing, they had the foresight to include a gymnasium in their plans—the center for all the youth activities of the Japanese community."

A gymnasium! That's it! The athletic meet and picnic this afternoon!

"Indeed, they left a legacy of untiring devotion and practical service for Christ. The challenge now is for the present generation to take up this rich heritage to ensure a glorious future."

Look at them beaming. I could call for $100 donations now and they'd come flocking up here.

He saw the Reverend Hanamori looking at him oddly. Tom had made a point of defining precisely what his little message to the flock was going to be, and now he was wandering all over the landscape. "How my heart is moved by the love of God when I stand before you like this, and I know that you are the very chosen people who were there when it all began!" And, in fact, he *was* moved. What would these people have done? Where would they be today without the love and concern of God Almighty? Would they be kneeling before a golden idol? Prostrating themselves at the feet of some dreaming Buddha, damned forever to the fires of hell? How much more satisfying it was for him to work amid this benighted flock than among people of his own race, to see, in their very difference from himself, the souls that he had won for Christ. He felt the tears begin to well up, and he could feel the waves of emotion rushing toward him from all corners of the sanctuary.

"Good people," he went on, his voice husky now. "Forgive me if I have gotten off the track. Whenever I see you, I can't help but think of those pioneer Isseis. They gave so much of themselves that we may have this abundant life, as God gave His only begotten Son that we may have everlasting life." He drew his handkerchief from his back pocket and, chuckling and hanging his head, he wiped his eyes behind his spectacles, then looked up, glowing and triumphant. "Please, Reverend Hanamori," he said, his voice ringing, "please explain to them how important it is to me and to all of us in the English-language congregation that all of our Nichigos be with us this afternoon in Jefferson Park. If there are any without rides, we will provide them. Let them come to see me, personally, after your service, and even if it means delaying the start of ours, they will be provided for."

Pastor Tom sent his smile once again to all in the sanctuary, and this time he saw the woman with Mrs. Nomura looking at him with intensity. He strode down the aisle and out through the door.

Ordinarily, while the Nichigo service was in progress, Tom would be in his office, polishing the details of his sermon, but today he paced restlessly back and forth in the broad narthex, greeting the members of his congregation as they began to arrive. When that became tiring, he headed for the darkness of the back corridors.

"Daddy!" he heard Billy's squeaky, little shout as he passed the choir room. His son came running out with Mrs. Uchida close behind.

"He's quite a handful for you, isn't he?" Morton said to the old woman as she picked Billy up.

"Oh, no, Pastor Tom," she puffed, the enormous bags under her eyes seeming to sag more than usual. "Come, Beelee."

Billy squealed and reached out for his father.

"You must learn to behave yourself," said Tom, starting to walk away.

"Pastor Tom, we go with you?" asked Mrs. Uchida.

"Well ..." Tom hesitated. "All right."

"You not busy?" she asked.

"No, not today. Not until the service begins."

"Come, Beelee," she murmured again, walking ahead of Tom down the hall.

Billy loosened one arm from around Mrs. Uchida's neck and put a finger in his mouth, rolling his eyes up as if in deep thought. Then, his forefinger glistening with saliva, he pointed down the corridor, smiling.

"Wah-tah!" he demanded.

Tom knew that his son loved the drinking fountain in the narthex and would pester anyone in sight into lifting him up to it over and over again. Poor Mrs. Uchida had probably brought him to the choir room just to get away from the fountain.

"Wa-*ter*," Tom corrected him. "Wa-*ter*!"

"Wa-*ter*," mimicked Billy.

"That's it," Tom said, pleased. Mrs. Uchida's influence on the boy's pronunciation would probably not be permanent, but he wished he could find a young Nisei member of the English language congregation to take care of Billy.

Mrs. Uchida continued on down the corridor with Billy pointing the way and squeaking, "Wa-*ter*, wa-*ter*." In the narthex, she bent to let the boy slurp loudly at the arc of water. When Billy was satisfied, she made a circuit of the narthex, then let him take another drink.

Just then, the doors to the sanctuary opened, and the Reverend Hanamori came out. He stood in the front entrance, bowing and shaking hands as the Nichigos filed past him. Taking Billy from Mrs. Uchida, Tom joined his fellow pastor at the door.

"Remember what I said," he announced to no one in particular, "anyone who needs a ride this afternoon, just talk to me. And be sure to come!"

Several of the grey-haired churchgoers bowed to him as they passed, murmuring things in Japanese. He recognized the words "*fukuin,*" meaning "gospel," and "*kokoro kara*"—"from the heart"—among the syllables that Shinichi Kawamoto directed to him, but the rest of it passed him by, and Reverend Hanamori was too busy chattering with other Nichigos to translate for him.

Billy demanded "Wa-*ter*" a few times, but when he saw that he would have to wait for his next drink, he wrapped both arms around his father's neck and laid his head on his chest.

"Pastor Tom," he heard a soft male voice saying to him, and he turned to see the grey temples and round spectacles of Mr. Nomura. "I want you to meet my sister-in-law."

Now the woman was standing close to him, her high, clear brow conveying a serenity that only added to his unease. She looked straight at him, the hint of a smile on her full lips. At this point, Mrs. Nomura took over. Her English was much better than her husband's. "This is my sister, Mitsuko," she said, pronouncing the name "MEETS-ko." "She's visiting us for a while from Japan."

"Oh, I see," said Morton, reaching out to take the woman's hand. In doing so, he jostled Billy, who lifted his head and again called for "Wa-*ter*," turning to point toward the fountain. When Billy caught sight of Mrs. Nomura's sister, however, he wrenched himself away from his father and all but threw himself into her arms.

"*Abunai!*" several Nichigos shouted in unison: "Watch out!"

Mitsuko herself almost lost her balance as Billy came hurtling toward her, but she managed to catch him, and the cries of alarm turned into peals of laughter.

But Tom Morton did not laugh. He saw his son clutching at this woman with mysterious tenacity, and he wondered what it meant. "Bad boy," he said at length. "You almost hurt the lady. Come away, now."

He reached for his son, but Billy pressed his face against the woman's throat and held on with increased determination. Again the others laughed, and Morton heard someone saying "*skee*"—Billy likes her. Mitsuko held the boy close and began pacing around the vestibule, rocking him gently and singing in low tones, her mouth next to his ear.

Morton turned back to continue his conversation with Mrs. Nomura, but there was nothing he could say when he saw the look on her face. She was watching Mitsuko with Billy, her eyes full of tears. Even Mr. Nomura, usually a stolid sort, seemed moved to see his sister-in-law and the child. Mrs. Nomura looked at her husband, the two nodded almost imperceptibly to each other, and she stepped closer to Pastor Tom wearing a doleful expression.

She spoke in a quavering whisper, and Morton had to bend down to catch her words.

"My sister lost a child last year. When I saw her holding your son, I …"

But she was too overcome with emotion to go on. Tom put his arm around her shoulder and said soothingly, "I'm sorry to hear that." And, in fact, he was sorry, in a way that he himself could not quite have expressed.

Again he turned to watch Mrs. Nomura's sister with Billy. The tension had left the boy's little body. Before long, he was asleep in her arms.

Mitsuko shifted Billy until his head was cradled against her left arm. She smiled at him tenderly and brought him to his father.

"Excuse me," she said, her voice soft but clear.

"There's no need for you to apologize," replied Tom. "It's my fault. I should make him behave better."

She smiled and shook her head as she placed the sleeping little boy in his father's arms.

"He is very beautiful," she said.

Tom wanted to say "So are you," but that was out of the question. Neither could he bring himself to respond with the reply that had become almost automatic whenever anyone complimented him on Billy's good looks: "He takes after his mother." He did not want to talk about his dead wife just now.

"Thank you," Tom said finally.

Mitsuko turned to her sister and said something in Japanese.

"Well, then," said Mrs. Nomura, her usual cheery self again, "we must go now. See you this afternoon, Pastor."

"Wonderful," said Pastor Tom. "You'll all be there?"

"I think so," she replied, looking at Mitsuko, who again spoke to her in Japanese.

"Are you bringing Billy?" asked Mrs. Nomura.

"Well, of course! You know how he loves to play with the other children!"

"Then we will all be there," she said.

5

THE NUMBER OF WORSHIPPERS was small at today's English-language service. Most of the girls were home, helping their mothers prepare picnic lunches for the afternoon potluck outing. Even some of the young men who attended most faithfully were absent, no doubt running last-minute errands. This led to an abnormally high proportion of squirming boys to listen to his sermon, "God's Ultimate Love and Justice." He himself was hardly listening as he concluded, "We strive toward that day when we will finally be all that Christ saved us for and wants us to be because of what he did for us."

It was still a few minutes before noon when he pulled out of his parking space in front of the church. Mrs. Uchida had offered to take Billy with her. Tom would pick them up and bring them to Jefferson Park after changing clothes. Driving up Broadway, where worshippers returning from the white churches were being accosted by Indian panhandlers, he silently thanked the Lord for having blessed them with such a lovely spring day.

Tom had always enjoyed these outings, but last year's, without Sarah, had been something of a trial. Today, he felt a new kind of excitement as he imagined the crowds of laughing children, the proud parents urging them on to victory, and ... yes, he had to admit it to himself, Mrs. Nomura's sister, Mitsuko. Would her husband be with her? Why had he not attended the service? How long would they be staying in Seattle?

At home, he shed his dark suit and changed into light cotton pants, a check shirt and a windbreaker. He packed a small duffel bag with some extra diapers and a fresh pair of coveralls for Billy, and he also threw in a sweater for himself, just in case. Seattle weather in May could be unpredictable.

A few minutes later, he was driving among the decaying buildings on the waterfront edge of Japantown, heading for the old Carrollton Hotel at the corner of Main and Occidental where Mrs. Uchida lived. He had difficulty locating a place to park. The Ace Café next door seemed to attract a large lunchtime crowd on Sundays. He left the car in front of a small cigar store a block away at the corner of Washington and walked back to the hotel, trying not to look at the two drunks—a man with a black beard, a shabby woman with spindly arms—sprawling in the doorway of a shop that sold deep-sea fishing gear.

Mrs. Uchida had lived here ever since she lost her husband. She had found the room through connections in the Japanese community. Several of the older hotels in the waterfront section were run by Japanese. The Carrollton was owned by a Mr. Itoi, who attended the Methodist Episcopal Church at Fourteenth and Washington. What a catch the Itois would have been for his congregation!

"Good afternoon," he said to the slim Japanese girl at the front desk. He imagined she was about eighteen or nineteen. "Could you ring Mrs. Uchida's room for me, please? Just tell her Pastor Tom is here to pick her up."

The girl nodded and made the call, speaking in Japanese.

An awkward silence followed. He had hoped the girl would ask him about church activities, but she started shuffling papers on the desk. Tom glanced around the dingy lobby. A massive man with a scruffy, red beard and wearing the checked shirt of a lumberjack was sitting in a faded, pink armchair in the corner. The stuffing showed through a tear in one arm of the chair, and the man appeared to be asleep. Tom was about to ask the girl her name when an elderly woman poked her head out of a side door and called to her. "Sumi-*chan*," she said, and continued with a stream of Japanese. So the girl's name was Sumi.

Mrs. Uchida was taking a very long time. Tom had become seriously hungry. Suddenly Billy ran up behind him and latched onto his leg. Tom turned to see poor, old Mrs. Uchida huffing and puffing with the strain of carrying a picnic basket the size of a small bathtub.

"Praise God, Mrs. Uchida! How many people are you planning to feed?"

Mrs. Uchida bared a mouthful of crooked teeth.

"Here, let me help you," he said. He should have known that she would bring far more than necessary. Everyone always did.

He left Mrs. Uchida and Billy on the sidewalk with the basket and went for the car. High overhead a white gull floated against the blue sky. After squeezing the enormous container into the trunk, he settled in behind the wheel for the long ride down Rainier Avenue to Jefferson Park. The closer he drew to the park, the more unsettled he felt. Again and again he found himself having to back off on the accelerator.

Soon the grays and blacks of the city were replaced by the green lawns of the Jefferson Park picnic grounds and the golf course across the road. No longer obstructed by the downtown buildings, a breeze blew in from Puget Sound, straining against the park's tall, pliant poplars, and sending cool gusts in through the car's open windows. Tom was glad he had brought a sweater—until he left the car and discovered how hot the sun was on this uncommonly clear day.

Everywhere he looked, the green grass was dotted with the glistening, black heads of his congregation. The playground equipment was literally swarming with children. Many of the families had already spread their blankets and straw mats and were busily emptying the contents of their picnic baskets onto the row of tables that had been set up for the potluck. "See, Pastor Tom?" Mrs. Uchida said, laughing. "Not so big."

And indeed, by comparison, the basket she had prepared for them was quite modest. While Mrs. Uchida unpacked, Pastor Tom circulated among the colorful squares and rectangles on the ground, greeting his flock and noting the foods they had heaped on the tables. There were round disks of rice pressed together with green and pink stuffing in the center and greenish-black seaweed wrapped around the outside. They called this *maki-zushi*, and they included it in any packed lunch without fail. He recalled how the flaky seaweed had stuck in his throat the one time he had tried it.

The Miyamotos proudly pointed to some oozing red objects that looked like the vital organs of a toad crushed on the highway. Thank God for the fried chicken, and for the potato salad, ham sandwiches, and hard-boiled eggs that lay there among the more forbidding concoctions. And fortunately he would be able to have lemonade instead of green tea, which reminded him of the bitterness of aspirin.

Since the announced starting time had come and gone, and it appeared that almost everyone—except the Nomuras—had arrived, Pastor Tom led grace and the eating commenced.

Tom had lost his appetite. He returned to Mrs. Uchida's blanket, but he remained on his feet, fidgeting and watching for more cars to pull into the park. He would know when the Nomuras arrived: their blue Buick was the most luxurious automobile in the congregation. But fifteen more minutes went by, and still there was no sign of them. Maybe they had just been giving polite answers at the door of the church this morning. More than once, Mr. Nomura had chosen to attend functions at his bank over church activities. There was no questioning their devotion, but still ...

Pastor Tom's inner debate came to a halt when the Buick pulled into the park and came to a stop. As one of the last to arrive, Nomura had few parking spaces to choose from and the car was more than a hundred yards from where Tom stood. The glare of the sun on the windshield prevented him from seeing how many passengers there were inside, and it seemed to take forever for them to alight. Eventually, all four doors opened, and he thought he saw a silhouette emerge from each of them. Then the trunk lid went up and the activity was concentrated at the rear of the car. Finally, when it closed, and the shadowy passengers began to walk this way, there could no longer be any doubt: there were four of them.

Mr. and Mrs. Nomura formed the vanguard, and a rather tall man was walking behind them with the sister. Tom squinted in the glare of the sun, trying to focus on the face, which he soon came to recognize. It was old Paul Morikawa, the Eastside farmer. What was he doing with the Nomuras? Just then, the farmer drew to a halt and, shading his eyes, began to survey the crowd. From far off to the left, shouts arose, and Morikawa waved in that direction. He turned, bowed to the Nomuras, handed the bundle he was carrying to the sister, and hurried over to join his family. Of course! Instead of taking the ferry back to Bellevue, he had gone home with the Nomuras, and his family had come over with the food.

Pastor Tom felt glad and confused at the same time. The Nomuras were a trio again, and they were in need of an open patch of ground. No one else here seemed to have noticed the double load that the sister now had to carry. Without thinking, Tom bounded over to them. Mr. Nomura was a step ahead of the women, an expensive-looking camera dangling from his neck.

"Welcome! Welcome!" Tom cried. "Here, let me help you with those," he said to Mrs. Nomura's sister, Mitsuko, taking two large cloth-wrapped bundles from her hands. She nodded silently and gave them up. Once his hands were full, Tom noticed that Mrs. Nomura herself was struggling with a much heavier burden, but by then it was too late. "Come," he said, "we've got plenty of room over here."

He led them to a spot near the blanket that he and Billy were sharing with Mrs. Uchida. A delighted smile on her face, the old woman was tearing strips of white meat from a piece of fried chicken and handing them, one at a time, to Billy, who was too busy eating to notice the arrival of the newcomers. Tom helped Mrs. Nomura spread their blanket, then withdrew to his own. Mrs. Uchida proceeded to offer Tom one food after another, but he had still not found his appetite. Pretending to survey his flock, he stood and scanned the broad picnic grounds, allowing his gaze to drift back to the neighboring blanket as often as possible.

In a simple blouse and skirt, Mitsuko looked even lovelier than before, her slightly tawny complexion radiant in the glow of the sun. Her hair must be very long, he thought, seeing her large chignon. There was a vital fullness about her, a glow that set her apart from the others. Only after Tom's eyes had made several circuits of the field did he think to check the third finger of her left hand. It bore no ring. He felt his heart give a thump. But what did it mean? Maybe in Japan women didn't wear wedding bands. Maybe they wore them on their right hands. Mitsuko's right hand was turned away from him, holding a piece of *maki-zushi*. She smiled and nodded to her sister, who was yammering in Japanese a mile a minute. But Mitsuko herself did not speak.

Soon Billy finished eating and began rolling around on the blanket. Tom wondered what Billy would do when he saw Mitsuko this time. Mrs. Uchida was teasing the boy with a ball on an elastic band, and he never turned in the Nomuras' direction. They, instead, were attracted by the child's lively movements and began to laugh each time he giggled. Mr. and Mrs. Nomura had no children of their own, which was perhaps what made them such enthusiastic supporters of the Sunday school.

Finally, Mr. Nomura seemed determined to join in the fun. "Hey, Billy," he called, "Look at this!" He held up his camera as if it were something that Billy could have.

Billy turned from Mrs. Uchida, intrigued, his blue eyes sparkling, his platinum blond hair pointing off in all directions after his energetic roll on the blanket. On all fours, he began to crawl toward the wide-eyed Mr. Nomura, but just as he was about to reach out for the camera, Mr. Nomura grabbed him and began tickling him in the ribs. Billy laughed at first, but soon was squealing in agony. Tom glanced uneasily at Mitsuko, who had stopped smiling and was trying to catch her sister's eye. But Mrs. Nomura was laughing as hard as her husband. With knit brows, Mitsuko looked at Tom, but when he did not move, she stood and snatched Billy from Nomura's hands. Immediately, Billy wriggled loose. As he ran to his father, he turned to glare with tear-filled eyes at his torturer.

Seeing Mitsuko, he stopped in his tracks. Then, as if it were the most natural thing in the world to do, he walked back to her, took her hand, and pulled, indicating that he wanted her to sit on the blanket. She obeyed, folding her legs beneath her, and he calmly sat on her knee, still holding her hand.

"*Maki*," he commanded, which caused the adults around him to exchange puzzled looks—all except Mrs. Uchida, who retrieved another *maki-zushi* from the basket and handed it to him. He tore into it. Everyone laughed, and Mr. Nomura snapped a picture of Billy in Mitsuko's lap.

Tom went off to oversee the church Boy Scout fellowship hour, and later he helped Reverend Hanamori with the devotional songfest. Then the children's athletic events could begin.

Midway through the three-legged race, Tom realized what an easy time of it he was having. He had not seen Billy since leaving him with Mitsuko. Ordinarily, the boy could abide Mrs. Uchida just so long, after which he would become restless and start crying for his father.

As the poplars began to stretch their long shadows over the field and the breeze turned from cool to chilly, the festivities closed with a brief service of praise. "Look to the Lord for guidance," Pastor Tom concluded before the hushed crowd. "We have to live day by day more like Christ so we can be closer as the people of God; sharing, caring, and bearing one another's burdens. Praise the Lord that we all will have a part in His vision."

"Praise the Lord," echoed several of the congregation, and the cry was taken up by all: "Praise the Lord!" Hands touched, heads bowed. In the deepening dusk, Tom saw golfers across the road, men of his own race, peering at this gathering of Japanese with expressions of open disgust. Looking down upon his close-knit community standing here in the shadows, Pastor Tom knew once again that it was for them, these special people, that he had been called by God.

The crowd then turned to the final cleanup. They folded blankets, and a crew of men went into action, ridding the tables and grounds of whatever scraps of paper or food had been left behind. Even Mr. Nomura, who usually kept aloof from such lowly tasks, rolled up his sleeves and helped. Mitsuko and Billy, holding a grocery bag between them, were picking up stray scraps and tossing them in.

"Thanks for watching Billy today," Tom said to her. "It was a great help."

She bowed and said with a clarity that surprised him, "I enjoyed myself, also."

It was the most he had ever heard her say at once, and her English sounded fine.

"Where did you learn English?" he asked.

"At mission school," she replied.

"Well," he said, searching for more to say, "we must … talk some time."

"Yes," she answered with a faint smile. This woman possessed a deep calm that seemed to radiate from somewhere behind her eyes.

"All right, young man," he announced to Billy. "Time to go."

Still clutching the paper bag, Billy simply ignored his father and went on hunting for trash.

"Billy …"

Billy shook his head.

"We've got to go now, son. Say goodbye to—"

Tom realized he didn't know what to call her. "Mitsuko" would be too familiar, and he didn't know her last name.

Billy was not going to give him the chance to find out. "No! Pick up more."

"Let's go, son," said Tom, kneeling to lift the boy in his arms.

Tom easily scooped up his little body, but the child would not release the paper bag, which tore, spilling its contents on the ground.

"Sorry," said Tom, putting Billy down again and gathering the scraps. "I hope to see you next Sunday."

Mitsuko nodded silently.

Tom picked Billy up one more time and took a few steps in the direction of his car, but there was an explosion of kicking and screaming in his arms.

"Hold on now, Billy." Tom's voice deepened in anger. He grabbed Billy by the armpits and shook him. "Stop it!"

The boy's hysteria only increased. "Mitsu!" he screamed. "Mitsu!"

Before Tom realized what was happening, Mitsuko was by his side. She reached up and pulled the boy from his hands.

"That's very kind of you, but he's got to learn not to act this way."

Tom reached for his son, but Mitsuko turned her back on him and began walking slowly in circles, cradling the boy and singing softly to him.

"Really," said Tom, following after her helplessly. "I'll take him home now."

Mitsuko turned and looked at him intently. "I will come," she said.

"What?"

"I will ride your car. Billy will sleep."

"But …"

"Please wait." With Billy in her arms, Mitsuko hurried off to where the cleanup crew was working. Tom could make out Nomura's white shirt in the gloom. A moment later, she was back. "He will follow us."

"No, really," insisted Tom. "It's too much trouble for all of you. And Billy should learn not to behave this way."

Mitsuko smiled knowingly. "Tomorrow teach him," she said. "I take care of him today."

Her upturned eyes caught the fading glow of the sun. He seemed to feel the light from her eyes entering his own. There was nothing more for him to say.

Billy was quiet now. Mitsuko put him down and they proceeded to gather together the remaining scattered bits of paper. Tom thought of joining the men's cleanup crew, but they were stuffing the last of the trash into barrels and beginning to disperse into the darkness. Nomura saw him and came running over.

"We take Billy home now," he said.

A few minutes later, Tom was driving up Rainier Avenue, Billy asleep in Mitsuko's arms in the back seat and Mr. and Mrs. Nomura following in their blue Buick. Tom glanced into the rear-view mirror and saw how tenderly Mitsuko looked down at the sleeping child.

"Before," he said, breaking the silence. "I mean, when I was telling Billy to say goodbye ..."

"Yes?"

"I didn't know what to call you."

"I am Mitsuko."

"Yes, yes, of course," he said. "Billy can call you that."

"Yes," she said.

She was being no help at all.

"What I mean is, what is your last name?"

"Ah, I see. My name is Fukai."

"Good. Then I can call you Mrs. Fukai."

She said nothing in response.

"Is that all right?"

Still she said nothing. Billy moaned, and she began singing to him again in a near whisper.

Tom stopped for the traffic light at Dearborn. When he checked the rear-view mirror, he found Mitsuko's eyes looking into his. He averted his glance, but when he looked again, her eyes were still there.

"I am not Mrs. Fukai," she said. "I am only Mitsuko. I have no husband."

6

PASTOR TOM COULD HARDLY wait for the Sunday school committee meeting to end. In the three days since the church picnic, Billy had been making life miserable both for him and for Mrs. Uchida, and he hoped that Mrs. Nomura could help them.

But on and on Mrs. Suzuki whined about textbook repairs, reading her report word-for-word and biting her lip whenever anyone asked her for a clarification. Finally, when it was over, Tom asked Mrs. Nomura to remain for a few minutes and showed her into his office.

Yoshiko Nomura eased her plump, little body into the yellowing wooden armchair facing his desk and looked at him expectantly.

"Now that I've asked you in here," he began, "I'm not sure I know how to say what I want to say."

"What is it, Pastor Tom?" she asked, her dark brows drawing together.

"Well, it's about your sister," he replied, watching her reaction through his wire-rim glasses. "Is she busy? I mean, how is she spending her time in Seattle?"

"Well," Mrs. Nomura began hesitantly, "we took her to see the Pike Place Market, of course …"

Tom smiled, wrinkling the leather of his cheek. "Wait. I'm not putting this very well. You know how much Billy seemed to like her."

"Yes, and she likes Billy very much."

"I could see that. She—what should I call her? She told me that her name is Fukai. Miss Fukai?"

"Well … yes, I suppose so. I never thought about what to call her here. She's Mitsuko—my baby sister, Mit-chan."

"You pronounce it MEETS-ko?"

"That's fine, Pastor Tom."

"You mentioned something about her having lost a child." The words came out more easily than he had expected, but now he turned his gaze to the black canvas roofs of cars trundling past on Broadway.

"Yes," she said uneasily.

"If you'd rather not talk about it, we can stop."

"It's very painful, Pastor Tom."

"Well, then—"

"But that's probably why I ought to talk about it. I don't know, I haven't even said anything to Reverend Hanamori. I shouldn't be like that. This is my church, after all."

"Indeed, it is. But any time you're ready will be soon enough." He watched her eyes grow moist even as she fought back the tears.

"I'm ready now," she said. "I want to tell this to you."

She emphasized the "you."

Tom folded his hands on the big, square blotter that partially hid the stained and pitted desk.

"Mitsuko was married five years ago, in 1934, when she was twenty-two," Mrs. Nomura began, her soft voice barely audible above the putt-putting of the cars outside. "It was an arranged marriage, of course. Almost all marriages in Japan are arranged."

"Yes, I know," Tom answered softly.

"Her husband was from a samurai family. Their ancestors had been warriors for many centuries, and the son went to the military academy. He was an officer, one of the elite. The Fukais—our family—were not poor, but we did not have that kind of history. My parents thought it was a great honor to have a daughter marry into such a family."

"And your sister?"

"She did as she was told. In some ways, it was a very good match. Her husband was an extremely handsome man, and after one look at Mitsuko he insisted on marrying her. If it had been just the two of them, the marriage might have worked, but there was a lot of pressure on Mitsuko. Her husband was the family's only heir, and he had to have a son. Even better, he should have many sons to carry on the family's military tradition. Mitsuko was treated very well for six months, but when it became obvious that she was not going to have a baby right away, things started to change. The mother had always felt their family was too good for the Fukais, and her pride began to win out over the son's enthusiasm. Japanese mothers-in-law can be very cruel, you know."

"Yes, I know," Tom said. "And they do not have to be living in Japan. I have had to counsel many families here."

"It's a shame. Even with the love of Christ ..."

"Were they a Christian family?"

"No, that was one of the problems. Like me, Mitsuko went to the mission school from the time she was a little girl. Our whole family embraced the Gospel when I was twelve. But when she did not have a baby, the mother-in-law began to scream at her every day to abandon Our Lord. She said it was because of the evil Western religion that Mitsuko could not give her a grandson. She used to beat her. She often wouldn't let her eat. Mitsuko practically turned into a skeleton."

"And the son let his mother do these terrible things?"

"He was usually away with his regiment. He argued with his mother whenever he came home and he tried to protect Mitsuko, but then he was sent to the China front. That was in July, the year before last, when the fighting started. He came home for a few days' leave at the end of the year, and that is when Mitsuko finally became pregnant."

"At least the beatings must have stopped," Tom said.

"Well, the mother left her alone, but when the son came back from Nanking, he was not the same man."

"You mean, he was one of those animals who raped the city?"

Mrs. Nomura sighed and hung her head. "But almost no one in Japan knew," she said. "The censorship is so strict. Mitsuko only found out the truth about Nanking when she came here. Then she told me she pitied him for what he had done to her."

"What did he do?"

"Well, by the time he came back, Mitsuko was five months pregnant, but he began to beat her."

"I don't understand. He should have been thrilled."

"It didn't seem to matter. All he did was drink and shout, and if she said anything, he beat her bloody."

"My God!"

"The baby was born prematurely after one of those beatings. It was a boy. The family's dream had come true, but the baby was too weak to nurse. It died on the third day. Poor thing, it never tasted its mother's milk."

Mrs. Nomura dabbed at her eyes.

"How she must have suffered! But at least she had proved she could give the family an heir."

"Yes, that's exactly what her mother-in-law said. From now on they would treat her well, she promised. They would send her to a hot spring resort to regain her health. They would let her go to church. For two whole years they had not allowed her to worship Our Lord. But Mitsuko said no, it was enough. She would not stay in that house anymore. In Japan, a woman cannot divorce her husband, but she left his house and swore she would never go back. They had no choice but to divorce her."

Pastor Tom asked, "Where did she go after that? What did she do?"

"All that time, Mitsuko had never told my family of her suffering, and they were shocked when she came home. In Japan, there is much shame when a daughter returns to the house of her parents. But they welcomed her with open arms. They showered her with love and understanding."

"Praise the Lord!"

"They tried to make her whole again. Oh, Pastor Tom, I am so proud of my parents and my brothers! Their love for Mitsuko was such a great expression of their faith in God, a true witness of His love and justice. Their strength was in the Lord. In Him they found the strength to defy the hate surrounding them."

"And all this happened just a year ago?"

"It's hard to believe, isn't it?"

"Lord, yes. You can see it: the light of Grace shines forth from her eyes. She is a true child of God."

Mrs. Nomura's own eyes were shining.

"There, now," said Pastor Tom. "Aren't you glad you shared your burden with me?"

"Oh, yes, yes, I am. Thank you, Pastor Tom."

He reached across his desk and placed his hand atop hers. "It does my heart good to hear you say that. But now," he said, sitting back in his chair, "after the suffering you have described to me, I'm almost embarrassed to tell you my problem."

"I'd love to help, if I can," she said.

Tom hesitated.

"Well, it's Billy. All he does now is ask for 'Mitsu.' He can be a very stubborn little fellow when he wants to be. He's not satisfied with Mrs. Uchida anymore. Besides, he's too much for her: she never intended to put in such long hours."

Mrs. Nomura looked at him, her black brows arching.

"I was wondering," he went on, "if she has some free time ... do you think she would be willing to do some babysitting? I'd be glad to pay her—"

"Oh, no, Pastor Tom—"

"Ah, that's too bad. I suppose she's very busy, but it wouldn't have to be more than a few hours a day."

"Oh, no, what I mean is you should not think of paying. I'm sure she would be glad to stay with Billy. It would be good for her, instead of the consulate."

"The consulate?"

"She has a kind of job there. It's not really a job. And she doesn't have to go very often."

"I don't understand."

"It's the only way we could arrange for her to stay here a long time. U.S. immigration laws are so harsh. She had to come as an employee of the consulate. My husband had to pay a lot of money ..."

"A bribe?"

She nodded and lowered her eyes, but then she faced him with a look of determination. "When I heard what they did to Mit-chan, I was so angry! I wanted to save her. I wanted to bring her to this land of the Gospel. It took us a year to arrange, but we did it and I'm glad."

"I'm sure the Lord forgives you," said Tom. "He knows what was in your heart."

"Yes. I believe that, Pastor Tom. I really do. And it's working. She has been here only three weeks, and I can see the difference already. She wasn't ready to meet anyone at first, but now she loves the church and is looking forward to the next service."

"Wonderful. I hope we see her often. And," he added, smiling broadly, "I hope that we can arrange for her to spend some time with Billy."

"Yes, I'll talk to her about it as soon as I get home."

———

Ah, the smell of fresh-brewed coffee.

Even before he opened his eyes, Tom Morton knew that this was going to be a special day. What a luxury to have a full night of unbroken sleep! Sarah had taken care of Billy during the night, and now she was playing quietly with him in the—

Sarah?!

He sat bolt upright in bed, and a chill ran through him. Sarah was dead. The thought struck him like a boulder crashing down a mountainside.

But, undeniably, he could smell fresh coffee. And he could hear Billy jabbering and laughing down the hall.

Mitsuko must have made the coffee. In less than a month she had gone from part-time to full-time baby-sitter to live-in governess. And now she was also turning into a housekeeper, unless Billy had suddenly learned how to use a percolator.

Tom rose and showered. By the time he came out to the kitchen, his hair still wet and shirt sticking slightly to his hurriedly dried back, Mitsuko was at the range, frying eggs and bacon. She wore a dark blue apron, and her rich hair was fastened at the back of her head in a swirl.

"Good morning," he said.

Mitsuko bowed slightly, smiling.

"You really don't have to be doing that," he said. Her full lips moved with the struggle to suppress a smile.

"Daddy, Daddy!" shouted Billy, running over to him and waving a wooden cross. "Tumble! Tumble!"

Mitsuko pronounced the word for Billy slowly and clearly: "*Tom-bo. Ta-ke-tom-bo.*"

"Tombo! Fly tombo!" Billy shouted, handing the thing to his father.

The flimsy object, somewhat larger than Tom's outstretched hand, was shaped more like a T than a cross. The upright member was a kind of narrow skewer and it was fastened to a flatter, twisted piece of the same material: bamboo, probably, judging from the straight lines of the grain.

"Fly tombo," said Billy.

"Fly?" asked Tom, looking at Mitsuko. Wiping her hands on her apron, she approached Tom and took the "tombo" from his hand. She pressed the skewer-like part between her palms and gave one quick rub. The T flew up to the ceiling, where it struck and fell to the floor.

"Wheeee!" screamed Billy, handing the thing to Tom again. "Fly tombo!"

Tom tried to duplicate Mitsuko's method, but the crosspiece smacked him in the wrist. The second try caught him in the thumb, but the third sent the "tombo" to the ceiling and the floor again.

"Fly tombo!"

"You try it," said Tom. "I have to eat breakfast." But the simple maneuver was still too much for Billy.

"I am sorry," apologized Mitsuko. "I should have maked something for his age."

"You made it?"

She nodded, smiling. "I mean 'made.'"

"Well thank you, Mitsuko, thank you very much. I didn't mean to be correcting your English."

He looked more closely at the simple toy. The curved propeller had been carved with great precision and fitted exactly to the vertical shaft.

She started to return to her work at the range, but Tom stopped her. "Somebody has to fly that thing for Billy," he said, smiling. "I'll serve myself. Thank you for making breakfast."

She nodded and backed away.

From the kitchen table, he watched as Billy scrambled after the "tombo" each time it clicked against the hard ceiling and ricocheted off the enameled walls. Sitting on the floor with the boy, Mitsuko seemed to have endless patience. Billy's delight was infectious, and Tom found himself smiling and he listened to Mitsuko teaching Billy the full name of the toy.

"Ta-ke-tom-bo."

"Ka-ke-kom-bo."

"Ta-ke. Take is bamboo. Say 'Ta-ke.'"

"Ta-ke."

"Tom-bo. Tombo is dragonfly. 'Tom-bo.'"

"Tom-bo."

"Taketombo."

"Kakekombo."

Mitsuko laughed aloud and held the boy close, chattering to herself in Japanese. Tom recognized "*kawaii*," the word they always said when they were excited about children.

"Fly tombo!" Billy started up again, and another round of flights followed. For Tom, the novelty had worn off, and he was becoming annoyed. Mitsuko, too, seemed to be wishing for some relief. She tried suggesting that Billy find another toy or a book, but the child insisted that Mitsuko fly the taketombo for him. Tom wondered why she didn't just take it away from him, as he himself would have done. He concluded that she must be waiting for Billy's father to back her up with a show of authority.

"Bil-ly," Tom growled, letting the word rumble in his chest. "Enough, now."

Billy ignored him.

"Billy," he barked. "I said stop."

What was wrong with Mitsuko? She should have chimed in and told the boy, "Listen to your father," or "Don't make your Daddy mad." But she just kept sitting there with him, letting him get away with murder.

This had gone on long enough. Tom started to push his chair back, expecting the noise to alert Billy to his last chance to avoid the strap. Instead, it was Mitsuko who looked at Tom. She said nothing, but she wore a grim expression and slowly shook her head from side to side.

"The boy must be disciplined," he said to her, still in his chair.

Again she shook her head. Then, turning back to Billy, she put a hand on his shoulder and looked him in the eye, her face suffused with a deep, quiet sadness.

Billy dropped the toy and put his arms around her neck.

Mitsuko picked him up and glided from the room.

7

AT CHURCH TOM FOUND it difficult to concentrate on his work. His mind kept wandering back to his little apartment on Summit Avenue. *It's two o'clock, Billy's nap time. Mitsuko must be singing him that Japanese lullaby and patting him on the stomach in rhythm as he falls asleep.*

He tried to recall the melody she always sang to the boy, but its twists and turns were too strange; no matter how many times he heard it, he could never anticipate the next note. All he could bring back was the sound of Mitsuko's voice, soft and slightly breathy, caressing.

Going home at the end of the day was more and more an event to be anticipated and savored. Not even the long days of early summer could keep him in the office much past four o'clock.

Mitsuko and Billy would greet him at the door. Despite his protests, she would help him out of his coat and hang it up for him. "It is the Japanese way," she explained. But when she went so far as to bring his slippers to the threshold, he found it embarrassing. For one thing, it made him uneasy to think of her rummaging around in his bedroom.

"Really, Mitsuko," he said, "I asked for your help with Billy. I don't expect you to do so much for me. And please don't tell me 'It is the Japanese way.'"

Her only response was that same sad look she gave Billy to make him behave. No matter how many times he asked her to stop the special service, she was there with the slippers and the sad look.

Finally one day, with more of an edge to his voice than he had intended, he said, "From now on, I expect to find my slippers in my room."

The next day, when he opened the front door, he found a brand new pair of slippers waiting for him. Her determination was incredible! He tried to ignore the things and put on a stern face, but in the end he couldn't help laughing.

"All right, all right," he said at last. "If you insist on acting like a servant, there's nothing I can do."

She did not reply, but from that day on it became his habit to change into his new slippers as soon as he entered the apartment.

"You really should talk to that sister of yours," he said, smiling, to Mrs. Nomura at the next Sunday school committee meeting. "She has too much of the old Japanese servility. We have to work on making her more American."

"It is not servility, Pastor Tom," replied Mrs. Nomura.

"No? What is it, then?"

"Simple cleanliness."

He looked at her.

"In Japan, we make a firm distinction between the inside and the outside. A Japanese person would no more wear shoes in the house than an American would walk on the dinner table. I am always amazed to see Americans with their feet up on furniture—even beds—wearing the same shoes they walked in where people spit and dogs and horses foul the streets. I have lived here for many years, and still I cannot get used to it."

Tom blushed and found himself at a loss for an answer.

———

That Thursday, a grim-faced Mrs. Nomura met Tom when he walked into the apartment.

"It's Billy," she said before he could speak. "He has a high fever."

"Did you call the doctor?" he asked, hanging his coat in the front closet and changing into his slippers.

"Yes," she said. "Dr. Wallace is with him now."

Despite the warm June weather, he found Billy lying under blankets. The window was closed, and the room smelled of sweat and fever. There was some kind of contraption on Billy's forehead. Dr. Wallace, a grey-haired man with ruddy complexion, was kneeling by the crib. He closed his case and stood to go.

"Thank you for coming, Doctor," Tom said, shaking the doctor's hand. "How is he?"

"He has a bad summer cold with a high fever," said the doctor. "He will be okay, but you better watch him, Reverend. Give him plenty of fluids, aspirin. Try to keep the fever down. He should be all right if we can control the fever. That ice bag's just the ticket. Couldn't have done better myself."

Tom glanced at the device on Billy's forehead.

"Your housekeeper rigged it up with a piece of oil cloth. Neat idea hanging it from a stick like that. Takes the weight off. Anyhow, let me know if the fever doesn't break by tomorrow or if it goes any higher. It's up around a hundred and four now. Keep an eye on him."

"Of course."

Tom showed him to the door.

"Thanks again," he called as Doctor Wallace headed down the stairs.

"Excuse me, Pastor Tom," Mrs. Nomura said, squeezing past him at the doorway. "I have to go cook dinner. My husband will be home soon."

"Yes, by all means. Thank you so much, Mrs. Nomura."

"Let us know how Billy is doing," she said as she hurried downstairs.

He closed the door and started for the bedroom but decided to stop by the kitchen for a drink of water. Perhaps Mitsuko could use one, too. While the water was running, he noticed that the kitchen table's scratched white porcelain surface was exposed. So that was what Mitsuko had used to make Billy's ice bag. Very resourceful, he thought.

He walked to Billy's room holding two glasses of water. Mitsuko was sitting on the floor by the bed. She looked up when he entered. There was a film of sweat on her forehead and upper lip, and a few strands had come loose from the tight bun in which her hair was always tied. He held out a glass to her, and she accepted it, but she waited for him to drink before bringing it to her lips.

"I am sorry," she said after the first sip. "I will pay for the table cloth."

She recited the words with touching simplicity, as if she had been rehearsing them for some time.

He could not help smiling.

"Never mind," he said. "It was for a good cause."

"Cause?" she asked.

"It was for Billy," he explained. "Besides, it was old."

"But it was still good. I put it in the drawer by the sink."

"Put what in the drawer?"

"The rest of the oil cloth. Not to waste it."

She was so serious about a scrap of oil cloth, he wanted to give her a hug. She must have been frantic, and yet she had had the presence of mind to cut the table cloth and put the rest away. Instead of a hug, he patted her hand that was resting next to Billy. She did not move it, and gave him a glance before smiling a little.

Several times that evening, Tom suggested to Mitsuko that she let him watch Billy in her place, but she relented only long enough to cook a simple dinner for the two of them and to take a quick bath. She bathed every evening, never in the morning. As warm as the weather had become in recent weeks, she was apparently still taking scalding hot baths, judging from the steam that filled the apartment. The gas and water bills were up, too.

He went to bed at ten, setting the alarm for midnight. When it woke him, he put on a robe and walked into Billy's room to spell her, but she refused to budge.

"His fever is still very high," she explained.

"That may be so, but I can sit with him as well as you. Get some rest for tomorrow."

"I will stay here," she said. The day's sunny warmth had dissipated, but she wore only the thin cotton kimono she always wore after the bath.

"At least put on a sweater or something. You'll catch cold yourself. You're not used to Seattle summer weather. It gets chilly at night. That kimono is not enough."

"This is not kimono. It is *yukata*."

"Whatever you call it, it's thin."

"I am fine, thank you."

There was no point in arguing. He would get his rest tonight and stay home from the church tomorrow, when she could sleep. He went back to his room, though he doubted that he could fall asleep again. Still dressed in the robe, he lay atop the bed, reading.

At three a.m., he woke with his magazine on his chest. The night was silent, but after he had lain awake for some time, he heard a distant cry.

It seemed to rise and fall with the wind. But there was no wind. And the sound was not coming from the distance. It was here in his own apartment.

He tiptoed to the door of his room and listened. It was Mitsuko, singing her lullaby, but her voice was barely above a whisper.

If she was singing, Billy would be awake; perhaps his fever had broken. Tom edged to the door of his son's room and peeked inside. Her back to the door, Mitsuko sat on the chair beside the crib, yukata open and dropped to the waist, holding Billy in her arms. Even in the dim light, he saw her flesh, glowing like the sun in its full glory. Tom watched the top of Billy's head moving as he sucked at Mitsuko's left breast. The boy's little moans mingled with the unearthly sound of Mitsuko's clinging, insinuating lullaby. Tom turned away and hurried back to his room.

He could still hear the song as he sat trembling on his bed.

How could this be happening? *Was* it really happening? Or was it an apparition sent by the Devil himself?

Yes. Let it be that. Let it be a vision of sin with no more substance than a nightmare.

But no, he knew that it was real, and it was evil. Un-Christian. He should rush back in there now. He should cast her out, send her back to the land of darkness.

But he was paralyzed. All he could do was listen to the sound of corruption and know that, even more than to rid his home of this abomination, what he longed to do was to see more.

The shame of it was overwhelming. He clamped his eyes shut and felt his heart pounding. He groped for the lamp on the night table and pulled the chain. A comforting blindness enveloped him. He stretched out on the bed and fought to calm his breathing. Taking deep, regular breaths, he brought at least this much of himself under control. The heart was less obedient, but before long the pounding in his ears diminished. And, finally, like a gift from God, blessed sleep came to rescue him.

A sharp sound brought Pastor Tom into the daylight.

He heard it again. A kind of slapping sound.

He sat up and looked at the empty white walls, the somber face of Jesus over the bed. After a moment's hesitation, he stood and walked quickly to Billy's room.

Another slap resounded as he turned into the doorway, and the summer morning sunlight flooding through the open curtains almost hurt his eyes. Silhouetted against the window stood Mitsuko, in a dress now. She was facing the light with head bowed and, it seemed, her hands clasped in prayer.

She heard him enter and turned with a radiant smile. "The fever has broken!" she proclaimed joyfully.

Sure enough, Billy lay there awake, slowly turning the taketombo in his fingers. As Tom approached the crib, he could see weariness in Billy's little face, but the boy's eyes were clear.

"Thank the Lord," he muttered, trying not to look at Mitsuko. He knelt by Billy's crib and put his hand on the boy's cheek. It was cool. Billy smiled at him. Still holding the toy in his right hand, Billy stretched his left toward Mitsuko, who sat down on the other side of the crib and took his hand.

Tom could feel the warmth of her body across the narrow crib. He finally looked up at her, afraid of what he would see, but discovering in her eyes only joy, the joy of love and thanksgiving. Her gold cross hung outside the collar of her dress. He sensed that she had been touching it as she stood at the window in prayer. But what could that slapping sound have been? He bowed his head and intoned, "We offer our thanks to thee, o Lord, who hast seen fit to look down on us, His humble servants, and to shower upon us His redeeming love and grace through Jesus Christ."

"Amen," responded Mitsuko, her voice trembling.

When she raised her head and looked at him, so openly expressing the joy she felt at the recovery of his son, he could not find blame in his heart. "Thank you," he said humbly, "for helping him pull through."

She bowed her head slightly in acknowledgement, but her face told him that something was troubling her.

"What's wrong?" he asked.

"I'm sorry," she said. "What is 'pull through?'"

Tom could not help smiling. "'Pull through' means 'to get better,' 'to recover from an illness.'"

Her face brightened. "I see. Thank you." She paused. "I wish I could speak English better."

"Your English is excellent," he said. Indeed, it was, what she knew of it. The mission school had taught her grammar very well, and even now her pronunciation was far better than that of her brother-in-law, who had been living here for twenty years or more.

"Please teach me," she said.

Her simple words touched his heart. "Yes," he said, "I will teach you." And, speaking only in his heart, he added, *I will teach you the true Way to Christ. I will bring you out of the shadows that remain upon your soul and I will purify you. I will show you the glory of God as you have never seen it before.*

8

TOM FOLDED HIS NEWSPAPER when he heard Mitsuko leaving Billy's room. Without a word, he followed her to the kitchen and closed the door. The hiss of sleet against the window pane seemed worse on this side of the apartment, and the bare walls and white enameled cabinets only increased the winter chill. They knew from seven months' experience that this was the one room from which their voices would not keep Billy awake.

Two Bibles now stood on the shelf by the kitchen table. Tom took his and sat on one of the hard kitchen chairs. He placed his Bible on the lace table cloth that Mitsuko had bought and opened it. "Exodus, chapter 31."

Taking her seat at the opposite end of the small, rectangular table, Mitsuko reached for her Bible, but instead of opening it, she placed it in front of her and folded her hands atop it.

"Pastor Tom," she said, looking at him, "tonight could you please help me with pronunciation?"

He smiled and closed his Bible. Her hair seemed more tightly pulled back than usual tonight, the normally serene brow slightly tense, a touch of color in the cheeks. "Did you have trouble again?"

"Only a little trouble," she replied. "If I am not very careful, I say 'z' or 's' instead of 'th.' Today when I asked for moth crystals, the drugstore man thought I was asking for something to kill moss. He told me to go to a garden shop. And when I asked at the garden shop, they told me to go to a drugstore. It was very confusing."

"Listen to you now. You're doing just fine."

"That is because I am being careful. I need practice."

"All right. Say 'mother.'"

"Mother."

"Father."

"Father."

"Now, that did sound a little like Fah-zer."

She blushed and looked at her hands.

He thought for a moment. "Say 'Our Father.'"

"Our Father," she responded, looking up again.

"Good. 'Our Father.'"

"Our Father."

"Which art in Heaven."

"Which art in Heaven."

"Hallowed be thy name. Oh, there are lots of tee-aitches in this!"

"Hallowed be zye—"

"Thy—"

"Thy name."

"*Thy* kingdom come."

"Thy kingdom come."

"*Thy* will be done."

"Thy will be done."

As Mitsuko worked with fierce concentration to produce the dreaded "th," Pastor Tom watched her mouth with equal intensity. Each time the pink tip of her tongue found its proper place between her straight, white teeth, he felt a little thrill. But when he intoned, "And lead us not into temptation," the words nearly stuck in his throat.

As Mitsuko's full lips formed the word "temptation," it seemed to take on a whole new, physical meaning.

"But deliver us from evil," he implored, wondering what the words could mean to her as she spoke them. Did she know, in her heart, that the kingdom, and the power, and the glory were indeed God's for ever? Or were these only sounds to her in a pronunciation practice?

"Amen," concluded Mitsuko, looking at him expectantly.

But instead of giving her an assessment of her language skills, he asked, "Do you understand the Lord's Prayer, Mitsuko?"

She hesitated before answering. "I have known it all my life."

"But do you really understand it? Do you understand what it means by asking the Lord to lead us away from temptation?"

"I do not understand your question, Pastor Tom."

"Of course you do," he insisted. "Tell me, Mitsuko, why do we pray to the Lord to lead us from temptation?"

"Why are you asking me this?" she pleaded.

"You tell me," he demanded. "You *must* know why I am asking you this." He wanted her to see it herself. He wanted her to recognize her sin and confess it openly before God. Surely she could come to know the true Christ only when she had abandoned the twisted ways of her benighted country.

She heaved a long, long sigh, and bowed her head before him. But when she raised her eyes again, they were shining with conviction.

"Then I will say it," she declared, her voice barely rising above a whisper. "The Lord is tempting me now," she said, looking at him hard. "You are my temptation, Pastor Tom."

Her answer struck him like a blow to the forehead. He had been preparing to lecture an innocent, childlike creature on the profoundest meaning of prayer and redemption, but she had proven herself to have a woman's understanding, and now he did not know what to say.

"I have seen you look at me," she said. "I was a married woman. I know. And I have been looking at you."

He felt his face growing hot, his heart pounding.

"I love to be here with you," she said. "I love Billy. I pray to God every day that we can stay like this forever. I was never going to tell you what I feel. If you are strong enough to fight temptation, I am also strong enough. I can be your sister until I die."

Her hands, still folded on the Bible, were trembling slightly. Her eyes were moist, but they were looking straight at him.

He had to turn away. Pushing his chair back noisily, he nearly stumbled as he rose. Mitsuko's eyes dropped to her hands, their smooth skin now streaked with tears. Tom lurched out of the kitchen and into the living room, where he slumped onto the couch.

He stared out into the night with empty eyes, his mind as chaotic as the sleet that swept past the window pane in heaving gusts: Sarah, in a long yellow dress, running to him through the shallows of a rock-filled river. A room full of flowers—masses of red and white and pink and yellow—and Sarah in her coffin, in the hearse, in the grave. Billy, bruised and hairless, cradled in his arms and sucking greedily on a bottle. The curve of Mitsuko's bare shoulders sculpted in a maternal embrace, and eyes looking down in adoration.

A thin thread was running through these scenes, stretching from the distance and weaving its way closer. It was a thread of sound, a cry he seemed to recognize. Tom looked at his watch: the hands pointed to 10:15. Billy always woke at 10:15, as if he had a tiny alarm clock set inside his head. Tom heard Mitsuko padding from the kitchen, through the hallway, to Billy's room. She was going to pick him up and walk with him, as she always did at this time, despite Tom's protests that she was coddling the boy.

And then she began to sing the lullaby whose melody he would never grasp. Tom listened for some hint that it was different tonight, some indication that Mitsuko's declaration had shaken her as deeply as it had shaken him, but on and on it droned, unchanged from yesterday, or the day before that, or the weeks before that. Eventually, as always, Billy fell asleep again and Mitsuko tiptoed from his room. Tom heard her go to her room, then the bathroom, as she always did after this little ritual, and the bath water started running exactly on schedule.

He wondered if she would emerge in her Japanese robe, bow to him in the door of the living room, and withdraw to her own room after wishing him a good night as always. Rather than waiting to find out, he shut himself in his bedroom, changed into pajamas, and made sure that he was in bed with the lights out before she had finished her bath. He heard her walk toward the living room, and his heart began to pound again when it sounded as if her footsteps were coming this way. But no, they continued past his room, and after her door closed, there was only silence.

He slept fitfully. At one point during the night, he sensed that Mitsuko was in Billy's room. Staring at the dim light seeping under his door, he considered looking into his son's bedroom, but he was afraid of what he might see.

Pastor Tom had to drag himself out of bed in the morning. As always, he dressed to the accompaniment of Billy's laughter and the sounds of cooking in the kitchen.

"Good morning," he said as he stepped onto the linoleum floor. Mitsuko responded with her usual "Good morning" and little bow and smile. Had it all been a dream? Had she not spoken words that could alter their lives forever?

Over the next five days, he made a point of continuing with their Bible reading as though nothing had happened, questioning her to check her understanding of difficult passages, answering her inquiries on doctrinal interpretation, even correcting her pronunciation. He found in her only flawless self-control. Perhaps they could go on living this way, as mutually supportive brother and sister. Perhaps nothing had to change.

Tom was impressed with the eloquence of the sermon he composed on Saturday, and the passion with which he delivered it brought numerous compliments from the departing worshippers the following morning. His heart still seemed to echo with the strains of the choir as he watched the last of his congregation file out into the soft February sunlight.

It was one of those glorious, cool, spring-like days, the kind that occurred with increasing frequency once the gray pall of the Seattle winter had broken. Taking advantage of the weather, the three of them had walked to church this morning, bundled up, cheeks glowing, breath white in the chilly air, he and Mitsuko taking turns carrying Billy whenever his little legs became tired.

Now, bundled less tightly under the noonday sun, Pastor Tom and Mitsuko and Billy retraced their steps up Broadway, pausing to admire the crocus shoots in one front yard, stopping to examine the buds of a plum tree and trade guesses on when it would burst into bloom, praising the dome of blue that arched over the city and the delicate wisps of white cloud floating within it. The street was quiet today without the long lines of chugging automobiles.

As they neared the corner of Cherry Street, Tom noticed a man lurking in the shadowy entrance of a furniture store. He moved away from the curb side of the sidewalk to place himself between the man and Mitsuko and Billy. He pointed to the fresh spring green of a willow tree on the other side of the street to distract their attention.

Surrounded on three sides by store windows, the black and white tile floor of the entrance was littered with newspapers. The man wore a tattered brown overcoat and black felt hat that had long since lost its shape, as had his gray, grimy face. He clutched a bottle to his chest and stood glaring out at the world through bloodshot eyes. He seemed ancient, but the closer Tom studied him, the more he realized the man could not be much older than himself, certainly no more than forty. Then it struck him who this was: Manfredo, the farmer who used to park his horse wagon on Summit Avenue each week to sell vegetables and fruit until two summers ago, when he had been replaced by Noboru Shimozato from Tom's own congregation.

Tom felt moved to speak to the poor fellow, but just as they approached the entrance, the man fixed his wild eyes on them and released a foaming, white gob of spit that grazed Tom's pant leg and dribbled onto his shoe.

"Jap bitch!" he yelled hoarsely. "Go back to Japan, bitch! And take your white Jap husband with you!"

Suddenly Tom was a seventeen-year-old Kansas farm boy again, and he whirled around to confront his attacker.

"What are you gonna do?" the man sneered, "hit me with your Bible? Goddam white Jap, I'll kill ya!"

"Pastor Tom! No!" cried Mitsuko, and Billy started to shriek. Mitsuko pulled on his arm, and he backed away from the man, who laughed with flaring nostrils and spit on the ground again.

Mitsuko grabbed Billy and hurried on ahead. The man's derisive laughter echoed from his glass cage as Tom followed after her, feeling angry but also disappointed in himself for having forgotten the lessons of the Gospel so easily, if only for a moment.

"Mitsuko, wait," he called to her. They had put a block or more between themselves and the drunkard. Holding Billy, she whirled around to face him, and when he came up to her, their clouds of steamy breath mingled in the chill air.

"We shouldn't let a poor soul like that ruin everything," Tom said. "It's still a lovely day."

She glanced back down the street, and Billy began to struggle in her grasp. He wanted to walk again.

They resumed their leisurely pace, but Mitsuko was no longer smiling. "On this day of all days," Tom said, "we must try to understand the suffering of a poor man like that. The evil words he speaks are not directed at us; they echo from the pain he feels in his own heart. These are the times when we are called upon to turn the other cheek."

She nodded to him, but her jaw was still firmly set.

Even Billy seemed subdued. Tom pointed out more signs of spring growth, but his heart was no longer in it. Soon his attention was shifting from the flowers and trees to the people on the street. Thank goodness, there were no more angry drunks, but now Tom became aware, as if for the first time, of the glances sent his way by other well-dressed folk. And many of them were more than glances. One middle-aged couple holding Bibles glared openly at them as they passed within inches of each other.

White Jap.

The words began to echo in his heart.

He gazed at Mitsuko, whose eyes were fixed on Billy. She watched nervously as the boy wandered too close to the curb, and her relief was obvious when, after examining the contents of the gutter, he came running over to her again.

What a loving child of God she was! Couldn't these bitter people see that? Couldn't they, for once, open their eyes and hearts and see the love that she poured out endlessly upon his own blond, blue-eyed little son, a child who was not even hers, who was born of another woman's flesh? Did this young woman want to hurt them? Kill them? To take from them what was theirs? No, all she wanted was to love and be loved.

To be loved.

Suddenly Tom's face was burning.

To love and be loved.

His whole life seemed to fall into place. God had sent poor Manfredo to give him a message: he, Thomas Morton, was to be the White Jap. Until now, he had stood upon the heights, surveying his flock from afar, concerned only that, as shepherd, he not lose any of his valuable sheep. But now the time had come for him to descend into the valley, to be among them himself, not merely to guide them but to shower them with love as a sign to the world. Now, for the first time in his life, he knew for certain what it was that God had called on him to do. He knew now why the Lord had taken Sarah from him, why Billy had been left alone in the world. Oh, the wonder of God's mighty deeds!

Tom stopped and turned toward Mitsuko. Her eyes rose toward his, and he perceived the amazement in her face when she saw his exultant smile. He took both her hands in his hands.

"It's true!" he announced.

"Pastor Tom, please!" she cried, struggling to free her hands from his grasp.

"It's true!" he repeated. "I *am* a 'white Jap!' I am *the* White Jap!"

At home, Tom strode triumphantly back and forth in the living room while Mitsuko prepared their lunch.

"What is it?" she asked with a mystified smile each time she looked at his beaming face during the meal. But he would only smile more broadly.

After the meal, Mitsuko took Billy to his room for his nap. Tom waited, sitting, standing, pacing, looking out the window, and when, finally, Mitsuko entered the living room, he insisted that she sit on the couch next to him.

"Mitsuko," he said, taking her hands, which, this time, she surrendered less hesitantly, "I have seen the ultimate plan of God almighty—the building of His kingdom on earth as it is in Heaven."

He paused to drink in the wonderful look of expectation she wore. How she would rejoice with him!

"I want you," he said, as calmly as he could manage, "to be my wife."

Then, as her eyes widened in amazement, he told her of the many truths that God had given him to know over the past week, culminating in the moment of enlightenment this morning.

By the time he was finished speaking, her eyes were full of tears. She bowed her head and let them flow freely. But when she looked at him again, her head was moving almost imperceptibly from side to side.

"No," she whispered. "I am afraid."

"Afraid? Afraid of what?"

"I am not strong enough."

"We will be each other's strength. The Lord will be our strength."

"But there is so much hate."

"I know," he said, almost joyfully. "And that is exactly why we must not hesitate. We will conquer hate with love. I will show my people that to be a 'white Jap' is to walk in the footsteps of Christ."

"If your people were the only ones with hate, I would not be so afraid."

Her words brought him up short. "What do you mean?" he said, his exultant smile fading.

"Do you think the Japanese have no reason to hate?"

"Of course," he said, "there has been great injustice, but those who have embraced Christ—"

"—are still yellow, and you are still white."

"But my congregation, my flock—"

"—are still yellow, and you are still white."

"No!" he shouted, gripping her hands until she winced in pain. "Mitsuko! Do you love me?"

She fell to her knees before him, bowing her head and sobbing. Her whole body shuddered as she fought for breath. "Oh, God!" she gasped, "I do love you! Please believe me. I would die for Billy and you!"

"Thank God almighty!" He placed his hands gently upon her head and waited patiently, smiling again, until she had cried herself out.

"I am still afraid," she whispered, raising her tear-streaked face. "If we marry—"

"*When* we marry!"

"What will the congregation think? What will they say?"

"They'll be thrilled, of course!"

"I am not so sure."

"You'll see, I promise you. I'll tell them next week."

"No," she said, with quiet determination. "Do not tell them."

"But that's impossible," he said. "We could never hide our marriage."

"I do not mean to hide it. I mean do not *tell* them: *ask* them."

She was right. If they were to have any hope of fulfilling the life he had planned for them, it would have to be with the support of the people in his ministry. He was certain that, if he bared his heart to them, they would respond with love. He cradled her face in his hands, and for a long while they looked at each other silently. *Here*, he thought, *within my hands is the woman the Lord has chosen to be my wife*. But when he bent to kiss her on the lips, she turned aside.

"I will be yours, my Pastor Tom, when we both know for certain it is what we want."

"I know for certain now."

She looked at him deeply, without speaking for several moments. "Until that day," she said, "let us continue to live as loving brother and sister."

Her intense gaze moved him profoundly. "I swear I will," he said, "as God is my witness."

9

TOM AND MITSUKO were at the dinner table in the Nomuras' cozy house on East Olive Street. The childless Nomuras lived well on Goro's salary from Nichi-Bei Bank. A modest but handsome chandelier hung from the dining room ceiling, and the walls were covered with colorful Japanese prints. On the mantelpiece stood the foot-high porcelain figure of a cat.

"We must be realistic, Pastor Tom," Goro said, peering through his thick glasses. "The people of this country can be very cruel about matters of race."

"How well I know that, Goro!" Tom responded with feeling. "But we must not allow the worst in our brothers to shape our lives."

"And you, Mitsuko," Yoshiko said, her hair parted in the center like her sister's. "Do you have any idea how difficult marrying Reverend Morton will be?"

"I know," Mitsuko said, "but my love for Pastor Tom and Billy is like nothing I have ever known before."

Yoshiko glanced uneasily at her husband.

"Believe me, Goro, we have thought out everything carefully," Tom insisted.

"I hope so," Yoshiko responded. "My sister has already suffered much in her young life."

"Never again," Tom said. "With the Lord's help, I can promise you that much. Never again."

———

By mid-week, their plan was ready. Tom would first confer with Reverend Hanamori and ask his blessing. Mitsuko would come with him to be certain there were no language difficulties. That hurdle crossed, Tom would ask the reverend to announce only that Tom had a message he wished to deliver to a joint worship service of the entire congregation. The announcement of the time change could be made at both the Nichigo and English-language services this weekend, and the following Sunday they would hold the special service at 10:30, a little late for the Nichigos and somewhat early for the Niseis. Tom would present their case in the form of a sermon, and Mitsuko would rise at the end to join him in their petition. This would be the correct way to proceed, even if the process were a time-consuming one.

But the first hurdle proved unexpectedly high. The Reverend Hanamori greeted their solemn plea with equal solemnity. Did they realize the suffering they surely had in store for them if they took this momentous step? he asked. They assured him they did, but even so he asked for time to think it over. One Sunday went by, and then another.

To Tom, each day seemed twice as long as the one before, but Mitsuko went about her domestic duties with the same cheerful efficiency and tried to comfort him with protestations of her belief in the elder cleric's wisdom.

Finally, after two weeks, through Yoshiko, the reverend gave his approval. The following Sunday, a special "Service in Unity" was announced for the week ahead, March 3.

Tom spent the intervening weeks writing his special sermon, polishing it, memorizing it, and practicing his delivery. As the day drew near, the intensity of his anticipation increased, and rumors that both segments of the congregation were looking forward eagerly to the special service confirmed his feeling that this was to be the most important performance of his life.

His heart was pounding as he stepped to the podium that Sunday, but when he saw the smiling faces turned to him in communal joy, a feeling of serenity overtook him, and he began to speak with calm confidence.

"My friends," he began, pausing, and allowing the truth of even this simple phrase to permeate the sanctuary, "I come before you today to tell you that 'His Love is One.'"

Already, his eyes were gleaming, and he looked from face to face as the Reverend Hanamori translated for the Nichigos. "His Love is One!" he repeated more forcefully. "Oh, my wonderful Nichigo brothers and sisters! If only I could speak to you in your native tongue. If only my words could embrace you as my arms have embraced you and as my soul now embraces you.

"And you, my English-speaking flock. Week after week, month after month, I have stood before you with the word of God and pretended to be one of you. That's right! Pretended! And I confess it to you, here and now."

He paused to let the meaning of his words sink in.

"Look at me! Look at this white skin, this yellow hair, these blue eyes. Think back, my children, think back to the countless times your minister has come to you and professed to understand your suffering, and to preach to you the love of God, and never once has he—have I—mentioned these things. It is as if you and I have been sharing a secret of which neither of us has dared to speak. But today, in God's Truth, I dare to speak of it. I dare to proclaim openly before you that you and I are different. We are not the same."

By now, the confident smiles of the congregation had been replaced by furtive glances, as he had known they would be.

"Does this disturb you, my children? Does this make you uneasy? It should not. It is the truth. The truth is something you should welcome. The truth is always good. The truth is always God's truth. And you shall know the truth, and the truth shall set you free.

"My people, my beloved children of God, let us together recognize that you and I are different, because that difference tells us of the glory and majesty of God. His Love is One! Do you hear my words? Do they penetrate to your hearts? His Love is One. What a blessing and a miracle this is. God's love is so great and all-embracing that it brings all of us into His bosom, whatever the color of our skin. To other men, we are irreparably parted: they look at you and see black hair, they look at me and see blond, and they think that because of these differences, we are forever doomed to be sundered in two.

"But not God! God's Love is One. If all of God's children were the same, what miracle would there be in his loving us equally? But, my beloved brothers and sisters in Christ, the great, the awesome miracle is that He loves us all the same. Look at this! Look!"

Pastor Tom suddenly pinched the flesh of his cheek and began pulling and stretching it.

"Look at this ugly, white stuff. No, it isn't even white: we who have it like to call it white, but what color is it, really, this rubber or leather or whatever it is? Can you believe it? Can you see what I mean when I tell you what a miracle it is that God can love *this*?"

Tom's antics were easing the tension in the congregation, and laughter rose here and there in the sanctuary.

"Yes, it's funny, isn't it? Of course, God doesn't love *this*. He loves *this*." Tom pointed to his heart. "God's Love is One because he loves the hearts and souls of all his children, and he doesn't care *what* those hearts and souls are wrapped in."

He could feel his audience opening themselves to him, and he waited for the wave of amusement to quiet down.

"Now," he continued, returning to his subdued tone, "there is something else I must confess to you. What I want to confess is that I never realized any of this in the years I have been your minister. I have stood up here—yes, *up* here, above you, feeling I was closer to God than you, and delivering to you His holy message, the Gospel of Our Lord Jesus Christ. I hope and pray that some of His truth made it through to you, and I believe that, if you let me, I can truly be your minister of God in the years to come.

"Now, you may be wondering what has opened my eyes in this way. You may be asking yourselves, 'How comes it that our minister has suddenly seen the light?' Well, I am proud to say that the agent of God was one of your very own."

The eyes in the sanctuary shifted to Reverend Hanamori, who began to fidget and to wave feebly as if to sweep away the misdirected admiration.

Beaming, Tom held his hand out to Mitsuko, who was seated today in the front row with Billy in her lap. Having heard Tom's rehearsals, she rose on cue and, leading Billy by the hand, she walked to the podium, where she stood beside him, head bowed.

"By now, you all know Mitsuko, the sister of Mrs. Yoshiko Nomura. God, in his infinite wisdom, drew to her my little son, Billy, who has never known a mother's love. Those of you who were there on the day the Lord brought them together cannot doubt that it was, indeed, a miracle. They have been inseparable ever since. Dear Yoshiko made it possible for her to come and live with us, and as Mitsuko cared for Billy, I have tried to teach Mitsuko to understand more fully the words of the Gospel in English.

"I say that I have tried to teach Mitsuko, but in comparison to what she has taught me, I cannot claim great success. For she has taught me everything that I have said to you today. It was from Mitsuko that I learned the truth of today's sermon: His Love is One. It is a truth which, I hope, you will all feel in your hearts. I say this because today I am going to ask you to act upon that truth and to share its glory with Mitsuko and Billy and me."

By now, he could see, the point of his talk had dawned on some of the members of the congregation, and they did not look pleased. Still hopeful, he continued.

"The three of us wish to become a family." He paused. "I have asked Mitsuko to join me in holy matrimony, and she has accepted my proposal."

A few of the younger worshippers clapped their hands in joy, but the faces of the Nichigos were grim.

"But this miracle can only happen with the blessing of our brothers and sisters in Christ. We stand before you today as a witness: His Love is One. We have experienced this truth in the profoundest depths of our souls, and we humbly pray for you to experience it with us. We know all too well that those outside our church will continue to see only the outward differences that separate us, but I believe—and Mitsuko believes, and surely, when he is older, Billy will believe in his mind as he now so clearly does in his heart—that the Love of God binds us together as one, and that, in this Unity of Love, I can be one with you as never before."

Tom paused.

"We will go out now," he concluded, "and I have asked Reverend Hanamori to lead you as a community in deliberating on our solemn petition."

Tom turned to Mitsuko, who bowed to the congregation and spoke to them in Japanese. He was taken aback when she stopped speaking after only a sentence or two. Now there was nothing left but for the three of them to withdraw from the sanctuary and wait.

No sooner had the door closed behind them than Billy ran to the water fountain. Mitsuko went to lift him up to the stream.

"Why didn't you say more?" Tom asked her while Billy drank.

"I asked them for their good will—*yoroshiku*. They could understand. I am only a woman. They would not want me to say too much."

"Still ..."

But there was no point in talking about it now. For the next hour, they walked up and down the hallways of the church, listening to their own footsteps echo off the floors and walls.

When Reverend Hanamori came to call them into the sanctuary, his expression was blank. As he walked ahead down the center aisle, the congregation did not look at them. When they reached the center of the sanctuary, the reverend spun on his heels, and, with a broad smile, he proclaimed something loudly in Japanese. Tom recognized the syllables, "*o-medeto*"—"congratulations," and the entire congregation converged on the trio to offer handshakes, bows, and good wishes. Only a few of the older members seemed to be hanging back, but Mrs. Uchida was not one of them.

"Beelee, Beelee!" she cried, pushing her way through the crowd and sweeping the little boy up in her arms. "You so lucky! Now you have mommy!"

Billy grabbed the nose of his old baby-sitter, which brought a roar of laughter from those nearby.

The modest wedding took place six weeks later, in April. The Fukais in Japan and the Mortons in Kansas allowed the event to pass in silence. Neither Tom nor Mitsuko felt a honeymoon to be necessary or appropriate. Mitsuko said she had no intention of leaving Billy for any length of time, and, although he said nothing about it, Tom had no desire to encounter any angry Manfredos on the road.

After the festivities, Mitsuko gave Billy his bath and sang him to sleep while Tom sat in the living room, reading and half-listening. Instead of taking her own bath, however, Mitsuko came to him and suggested that Tom bathe first.

"In Japan," she explained, "the master of the house should be the first to enter the bath."

Instead of complying, he merely looked at her and said, "Come here."

When she was an arm's length away, he took her wrist and pulled her down onto his lap. She let him kiss her mouth, but she did not return the kiss, and she stood up as soon as she could regain her footing.

"Please," she said, gesturing toward the bathroom.

Tom sighed and went to the bathroom, where Mitsuko had prepared everything for him: fresh soap and towels and even a new bathrobe. It was a light kimono with a gray sash.

When he was through washing, he lay in bed, feeling the crisp cloth of his new sleeping robe and listening to the sound of the bath water. It was the same splashing he had been hearing for nearly a year, but tonight it sounded different. Tonight, his new wife was in there, preparing herself for him. The bare walls of the bedroom were lighted only by the small oak pull-chain lamp on the simple nightstand that he and Sarah had brought from Kansas. When, at last, he heard the bathroom door open, he looked up, expecting to see Mitsuko enter his room in her usual bluish-grey kimono. Instead, the room's shadows seemed suddenly dispelled by a burst of gold and red from the doorway. She stood before him now, as if swathed in the burning red of the sun, its golden rays spilling in all directions, long and sinuous.

Mitsuko's eyes were fixed on his, but when she neared him, she lowered her gaze and knelt beside the bed. He could see that she had been planning this moment, carefully preparing the words she would speak to him.

"I gave my heart to you long ago," she said in a voice little more than a whisper. "Tonight I give myself completely. Please love me as I love you."

Again she raised her eyes to his, and as she stood, she loosened the sash that held her kimono together. He could not take his eyes from her, dreading the inevitable moment when, like Sarah, she would ask him to extinguish the light. Instead, the sash fell away, the edges of the silk robe fell open slightly of their own weight, and still the words did not come.

She sat upon the edge of the bed, and the opening widened, and now he could see that the tawny gold of her skin lay just beyond the borders of the robe. Her hands began to move, slowly, gracefully, upward. She wore her hair up, as always after the bath, but in profile now he saw that its folds and twists were more elaborate, held in place by combs with sparkling edges. First one, then another she removed, and the shining black strands of her hair fell past her shoulders.

His eyes began to ache, and the thought of extinguishing the light himself momentarily flashed through his mind, to be followed immediately by the fear that the sight would actually vanish.

He reached up and touched her cheek, then pulled her face down toward his. This time when their lips met, she was with him, and her whole body began to glide toward him, slipping under the covers. He closed his eyes tightly.

Now her robe was open wide, and he felt her working at the knot that held his sash together. His hands moved down, inside her robe, and he felt her shoulders shift to help him slip the silk from her body. Here, in this golden twilight, all he could think of were the dark gropings he had known with Sarah, who had made him struggle every time for each square inch of flesh. The unashamed luxury of this woman was overwhelming, almost frightening. He knew that he could look at her, and that she would let him, but he was not sure he had the strength to look.

His lips caressed her cheek, her ear, her neck, and she softly moaned with pleasure through parted lips. She pressed against him tightly, willingly offering the warm, soft mounds of her breasts. He had longed for and dreaded this moment ever since that shocking night in spring when he had seen her with Billy. He had kept that frightening image of her locked away in some remote corner of his heart. But now he had to see, to behold the flesh his hands and lips had discovered before his eyes dared to learn the truth.

He drew back to survey the glowing skin, the dark V below, and he felt that he was seeing a woman for the first time in his life. She was real. She was here. And now, she was his.

They joined together in the light. Her body clung to his, and sunlight seemed to flow from her, darting and streaming inside his flesh, flowing out again through him to her, then back again, a long, shuddering, frightening spasm. He would not relent, he would not relent, he would not give his eternal soul to this, he would not plunge into the darkness beyond, he would not, he would not.

He heard a slap that drew him out of the darkness.

Mitsuko stood at the window, facing the morning light, her hands seemingly clasped in prayer. But then he saw the elbows of her robe move, and the sound came again.

"Mitsuko, what are you doing?"

She turned, her palms pressed together, lips in a gentle smile.

"Praying," she said. "Praying that the sun will give us as wonderful a day today as he did yesterday."

The simple beauty of this woman standing before him stirred his soul to the depths.

"The sun?" he asked. "You mean Our Lord God Almighty?"

"The sun is God's sun," she said, slipping under the covers again and looking into his eyes.

There was danger here. He would have to teach her soon. But now he wanted only to hold her close again.

10

THE WEATHER WAS GLORIOUS again this year for the spring outing to Jefferson Park. Everything else was the same as well—the families, food, races, prizes and prayers—and yet, for Tom, the world was a whole new place. Not only was it the first year of the forties, it was a new age with a new wife by his side.

The day after the picnic, a cable arrived from Japan. Mitsuko's brother Jiro would be coming to spend the month of June with them as the family's "official representative."

As stiff as the words sounded, Jiro turned out to be even stiffer. When his ship docked in Seattle, he walked down the gangplank in a tight-fitting suit, looking as if he had a steel rod for a spine. He bowed to his elder sister, Yoshiko, to Yoshiko's husband, Goro, to his younger sister, Mitsuko, and finally to Tom. His thick, black eyebrows and grim face gave him a forbidding air. He seemed to have left his youth in a far more remote past than should have been possible for a man of thirty-two. To Billy, however, he offered a limp hand in what he apparently conceived of as an American handshake, and he came close to smiling.

On the way to the Nomuras' house, where Jiro was staying, Tom felt like a chauffeur. The hushed conversation was entirely in Japanese, and no one ventured to translate for him. If he turned to look at the others, he could see them, and they could see him, but he might just as well have been on the other side of a thick pane of glass.

When they were alone later, Mitsuko explained to Tom that her family had taken some time to decide what to do about her marriage to an American. Yoshiko's letters had helped to soften the initial shock, and of course her parents had been partially mollified by Tom's being a minister. But Ichiro, the eldest, was still feeling bitter, and Jiro was at best ambivalent. He had married a non-Christian woman and was indifferent to religious matters. Finally, they had decided to send this younger brother to investigate.

Jiro lived in Tokyo, far from the family's rural home, where he worked as an engineer. The family decided that he could take off from his job more easily than Ichiro could be spared from overseeing the tenants who worked their farmland, and since Tokyo was so convenient to the port of Yokohama, Jiro was the logical one to make the two-week crossing. He had surprisingly little trouble obtaining a leave of absence and travel documents.

"Why was that surprising?" asked Tom.

"I am not sure I understand exactly," replied Mitsuko, fidgeting with the doily on the arm of the sofa. "He needed permission from the Army."

"Is he in the reserves?"

"I don't think so. It has something to do with his age. He can be … what do you call it …?"

"Drafted?"

"Yes, that is it."

"His company was willing to let him go just like that?"

"I think so. I am not really sure."

Tom had little opportunity to find out more about Jiro, who seemed to have remarkably little interest in his newly married sister and her family. He spent most of his time on his own, touring the area by bus and cab, though he apparently visited none of the usual tourist spots.

Tom again played the chauffeur when Jiro suggested they drive down to nearby Tacoma. They drove with windows closed in spite of the warm weather because of the foul-smelling industrial flats on the south side of Seattle. Near the Boeing plant, Mitsuko said that Jiro wanted him to stop the car.

"Here?" Tom protested.

Yes, Mitsuko said after checking with Jiro, there was no mistake. As soon as Tom pulled up to the curb, Jiro leaped out and stood clinging to the chain-link fence by the sidewalk, surveying the vast empty spaces surrounding the plant. He had never shown half as much interest in Mount Rainier or the Olympics as in this bleak stretch of concrete.

"I think my brother is only interested in his work," Mitsuko said to Tom that evening.

"I should think so," replied Tom, "if factories excite him that much.

What kind of engineer is he, anyway?"

"He works for an airplane company."

"So this was a real busman's holiday for him," Tom remarked.

"No, he does not drive a bus," Mitsuko said.

Tom laughed out loud and explained to her the meaning of the expression.

―――――――

Tom was far from laughing when he saw the headlines that Thursday. The Japanese air force had bombed Chungking, the remote site of the Chinese government, which had fled there from its temporary refuge at Hankow, keeping just ahead of the Japanese invaders. Most of the people had taken refuge in the rock caves beneath the city, but the vicious attack had destroyed the homes of 150,000 people.

"What kind of planes does your brother Jiro's company make?" Tom asked Mitsuko at dinner in the Nomuras' house.

"I am not sure," she said without looking at Tom.

"Why don't you ask him?" he pressed.

There followed a good deal of Japanese buzzing, after which Mitsuko told him that Jiro's company made small planes.

"Are they the kind of 'small' planes that just bombed Chungking?" Tom asked, staring at Jiro, whose dark brows hung over his eyes like two storm clouds.

Jiro spoke in Japanese, his eyes never wavering from Tom's.

No one translated.

"Well?" asked Tom, his eyes still fixed on Jiro's. "What does he say?" Mitsuko, Yoshiko and Goro discussed this with a perceptible note of tension.

Goro was the first to speak. "I am sorry, Pastor Tom, but Jiro is a very proud man. He says he cannot tell you about his planes, but they are the best in the world, much better than the planes that Boeing makes in Seattle."

"That doesn't surprise me in the least," said Tom, gritting his teeth. "Tell him that Boeing's planes are made for transportation, not for killing."

"Please, Pastor Tom—"

"Tell him, Goro. Tell him for me."

Still Goro said nothing. Mitsuko began to speak, slowly, in Japanese. As her words filled the small dining room, Jiro's black brows seemed to bristle, and his face was distorted into a horrible grin. No sooner had Mitsuko finished speaking than Jiro's mouth opened wide, the red gash in his face reverberating with a hard, derisive noise that sounded more like rusty farm machinery than human laughter.

"Let's go, Mitsuko," said Tom. "I don't think I want to stay in the same house with your brother."

"But Tom—"

"Now!"

Mitsuko rose slowly from the table, mumbling apologies to the others. Gathering Billy's toys, she took her little blond son by the hand and followed Tom out. Jiro was speaking angrily as they stepped into the fading summer light.

———

Yoshiko called two days later to say that Jiro had decided to return to Japan early. Tom felt some satisfaction at that news, but the reports that came in the paper each day were increasingly harder for him to deal with.

At the end of June, the Japanese foreign minister proclaimed his country's wish to unite all East Asia and the South Seas under Japanese control. A few days later President Roosevelt declared that no American soldiers would be sent to war, which sounded more like wishful thinking than an unshakable commitment. A new Japanese cabinet was formed in July vowing to "enhance" the spirit of the empire. On August 15, all political parties but the Japanese militarists' ruling party were dissolved, and on the twenty-second, Japan recalled most of its diplomats serving in the United States. By mid-September, Roosevelt signed a bill authorizing a military draft. Less than a week later Japanese troops crossed the northern border to attack the French defenders of Indo-China.

None of this found its way directly into Tom's sermons, but there was a new intensity each time he spoke, a new sense of urgency, as if he had to help his flock understand more clearly than ever the gospel of Christ. Only he, standing in the pulpit, could insulate them from the evil influence of their yellow brothers in Asia. Only he, stretching forth his protective embrace, could shield them from the rising tide of resentment here at home. Carried along on the current of his own words, he felt the truth of his mission with absolute certainty.

If only he could find a way to make this feeling last outside the walls of the church! If only he could find a way to forget that his wife was the sister of a man whose very hands might have worked on the planes that were raining down the manna of hell upon the heads of the helpless Chinese!

The wind was tearing Seattle apart on Thursday morning, November 7, but Tom found the thought of staying home all day unbearable. Increasingly, his little office at the church had become a refuge for him. He loved his wife, of that he was certain, but the sight of her, the touch of her, the sweet ecstasy she gave him with her flesh, seemed to undermine everything he had always been. He stood at the window, watching the rain sweeping horizontally past, the wind carrying with it tree branches and sheets of newsprint, shreds of hay, tumbling signboards and umbrellas and hats.

"Why don't you stay home today?" Mitsuko said, coming up behind him. He had been thinking the same thing, but the caressing, velvety sound of her voice convinced him almost instantaneously that he must do exactly the opposite. With hardly a word to her or Billy, he left the apartment.

The wind turned out to be less devastating than it had at first appeared to be, though traffic was slowed by horses pulling their tarpaulin-covered loads with heads drooping.

Once he had closed himself in his office, Tom continued doing what he had been doing at home, standing at the window, watching the storm. He had needed desperately to get away, and now that he was away he needed just as desperately to go back.

Shortly before noon, the power failed, and Tom wondered if everything was all right at the apartment. He lifted his phone, but it was dead.

The streets were strewn with sodden pine branches as he made his way back, and in the short run from the car to the front entrance of his building, his coat became drenched.

"Daddy! We're having a picnic!" Billy squeaked when Tom walked in. His mouth was ringed with rice grains, and he clutched a glob of rice in both hands.

Mitsuko had shaped her leftover rice into triangular lumps topped with the flaky dried seaweed that had almost choked Tom the first and only time he had tried it.

"Do you have to feed him that stuff?" Tom grumbled.

Mitsuko explained that she had been unable to shop because of the weather.

"Well, you could have found something else ... peanut butter and jelly ..."

"But he likes o-nigiri," she replied.

"I know, maybe he likes it too much. Don't feed him so much Japanese food. It's not good for him. It's not good for anybody."

"Tom, what is wrong ... ?"

"Have I made myself clear? I don't want to see that stuff around here anymore."

Billy was crying, and Tom realized he had allowed his voice to rise to a near shout. He had been looking forward to joining them for the afternoon, and now he felt there was no place for him here in his own home. He spun on his heel and stomped to the front door, where he had thrown his wet overcoat on a chair.

"Tom! Where are you going?" Mitsuko cried, hurrying after him.

"Out," he muttered between clenched teeth. "Just out." He slammed the door behind him.

Tom spent the rest of the afternoon in his church office, going through his files and filling several waste baskets with useless papers. After a while, he could no longer concentrate on even this busy work, and when the power was restored he switched on the radio for the latest news. With professional calm, the announcer reported that the new Tacoma Narrows suspension bridge, the world's third longest span, had collapsed that morning. The winds had reached no more than forty miles per hour, but the bridge's oscillations became so wild and powerful the bridge ripped itself apart and plunged into the tossing waters far below.

Tom was still not ready to go home when dinner time came. He could only drive up and down the streets at random, staring at store windows and the big, round headlights of oncoming cars. The air was filled with clouds of exhaust that flowed and shifted each time a car plunged through.

Suddenly, the glowing marquee of the Roosevelt Theater lit the night. *Little Nellie Kelly* with Judy Garland was playing. Now he was sorry he had not thought to check the show time of *Gone with the Wind* before he left the office. It had first appeared about the time he met Mitsuko and won the Academy Award for Best Picture of 1939. A year and a half later, it was still playing to packed theaters. He hadn't seen a movie since before Sarah became pregnant, and at this rate he wasn't going to be able to go out with Mitsuko until the Japanese were pushed out of China. A movie alone was exactly what he needed.

Parking near the Roosevelt on a Thursday night was easy enough. He paid his thirty cents at the box office and had time for a hot dog and Coke before *Little Nellie Kelly* started. He was not really in the mood for such silly shenanigans now, though, and he hoped the second feature would be better.

First there was an intermission to sit through, and previews, and finally newsreels. The first news story showed representatives of Germany, Italy and Japan signing a 10-year military-economic-alliance pact in Berlin. Then came the drawing of the first numbers in the new national military draft followed by President Roosevelt promising not to send "our boys" to war. Another Roosevelt clip showed him denouncing the Republican National Committee Chairman for inciting a whispering campaign that he intended to commit an act of war against Japan immediately after election day. There was some respite from the subject of war with "Grieving Dog Flown to Master" and "Beauties on Display," but then came Interior Secretary Ickes intoning solemnly into a microphone, "We should supply instruments of war to those who are fighting for our Christian civilization." Next were shots of Japanese troops marching into French Indo-China and capturing several thousand French legionnaires. This was followed by a cartoon titled "Jap in the Box," which showed a hand labeled "Hitler" pressing the button on a box from which popped a bespectacled, mustachioed, buck-toothed Japanese face wearing an officer's cap.

This was more than Tom could bear. He tramped out of the theater and sped all the way home.

11

"**MITSUKO, LISTEN TO THIS,**" Tom called from the living room. "Mitsuko! Shut off the water a second."

The noise of the washing of dinner dishes subsided, and Mitsuko came to the door of the living room, wiping her hands on her apron.

"Look," Tom said, showing her the paper. "I'm on the front page of the *Star*."

A wooden crash echoed from the kitchen, complete with Billy's vocal sound effects. He had been playing on the floor with the toy cars Mitsuko made for him. He had a large collection now, and he enjoyed knocking down piles of them.

Tom ignored the noise and read from the paper slowly, enunciating so that Mitsuko could catch every word.

"The headline is 'CHRISTIAN ENDEAVOR CONCLAVE,' and here's what it says: 'The Christian Endeavorers of Seattle are planning for their district convention to be held next week-end, March 1 and 2, at the Covenant Presbyterian Church on Queen Anne Hill, Rev. B.A. Hotchkiss, pastor.'

"I met Reverend Hotchkiss last month when I spoke at Seattle Methodist," Tom told her. "A very nice man—very soft-spoken, but a preacher of great authority."

He continued reading: "'Over 500 young people are expected for this convention, the theme of which is "Trust in the Lord." The convention will open Friday evening with a talk by William F. Wilson, for forty years a missionary to Africa in the British Kenyan colony. Dr. Wilson, stopping in Seattle en route to his home in Boise, will also speak Saturday afternoon. Following the banquet a play will be presented entitled *The Challenge of the Cross*, under the direction of Albert Culverwell.'

"Now, here's the important part. 'Another speaker for the convention will be the Rev. Thomas A. Morton, English Language Pastor of the Japanese Christian Church on Terrace Street.'"

"Very nice," said Mitsuko, smiling and raising her eyebrows in anticipation of more.

"Well, that's all there is about me," Tom said, with a wry smile. "They didn't give the title of my talk. I suppose half the audience will think I'm there to explain the latest diplomatic initiative of the Imperial Japanese Government."

"It will go well," she said.

"Yes," he replied. "I always have them eating out of the palm of my hand."

"I wish I could come and hear you," said Mitsuko.

"Maybe sometime," he muttered. "When the war in China is over."

Tom knew that talk of her country's military activities made Mitsuko uneasy. It was the one thing that always seemed to come between them. They could go for weeks at a time without a harsh word, but then Chiang Kai-shek or Madame Chiang would visit Washington to ask for help against the Japanese, the newspapers would proclaim the deep friendship uniting the American and Chinese peoples, and Tom would become short-tempered and sullen. He resented having to defend his flock from the welling tide of anti-Japanese sentiment.

"Oh, Lord," Tom exclaimed. "I spoke too soon. Look at this, right next to the article on the conclave."

"What is that?" she asked, still in the doorway.

"'JAPAN CLAIMS SOUTH PACIFIC.'"

"Never mind," she said, turning back into the kitchen.

"You'd better listen to this, Mitsuko. It's what's happening in the world."

She stopped short. "All they do is make war," she said.

He read on: "'Foreign Minister Yosuke Matsuoka today called upon "the white race" to cede Oceania—the more than 1,000-mile square region of the South Pacific—to the Asiatics.' The fool! Talk like that only makes matters worse. 'Speaking to a committee of the lower house of parliament, Matsuoka said the Western powers should realize that Japan and other Asiatic nations must have some place to send their excess population and that the islands of Oceania are logical places, since they now are largely undeveloped and underpopulated.'"

"I don't want to listen anymore," said Mitsuko, her face flushed.

"It's maddening, isn't it? 'The white race.' What arrogance!"

Lost in his thoughts, Tom realized someone had spoken to him. He looked around the banquet table. "Excuse me, Dr. Wilson, it's so noisy in here."

"I was just saying what wonderful biscuits these are. Don't you agree?"

"Oh, yes, yes indeed, very nice biscuits."

William Wilson, a powerful-looking man with stark white hair, a ruddy complexion, and a generous midsection struggling to pop out of his checkered vest, sat to Tom's right at the head table of the Christian Endeavorers' banquet in the Covenant Presbyterian Church. Holding up a biscuit, he said, "This is what I missed most of all in Africa."

"Biscuits?"

"Biscuits. Dinner rolls. Any decent baked goods. They just don't know how to make anything light and fluffy like this. *White* bread is out of the question. You know, you can only teach them so much."

He raised one eyebrow and peered at Tom through rimless spectacles.

Tom chuckled uneasily.

"Now I know how to get your attention," said Wilson. "Talk about food."

"I'm sorry. Have I been a poor dinner companion?"

"Anyone who can speak with the fire you have at your command ought to be a scintillating conversationalist."

"That sounds a little bit like a compliment."

"It is, my boy, it is! There aren't many speakers like you in Kenya, either. Lord, I'm glad to be back!"

"After forty years ..."

"Incredible, isn't it?"

"You won many souls for Christ."

"I suppose so. But never enough. Never enough."

"You're being modest."

Wilson leaned toward Tom and lowered his voice, using the general hubbub of the banquet to camouflage his words.

"You of all people know that I'm not being the least bit modest," he said, looking Tom in the eye. "You never know what's in their minds."

"I see," Tom answered vaguely.

"I *know* you see. Do you think I'd say this to anyone else?" He looked around warily. "We're in this together, my boy. The Lord has sent us to work among the colored peoples of the world. He's given us a heavy cross to bear."

Just then Dr. Wilson's wife, a tall, gray-haired woman in a blackish dress said from Tom's left in a high-pitched voice, "William, do stop these little tête-à-têtes!"

Wilson looked startled, then bit into his biscuit. Tom found it amusing that such a large, forceful man could be brought to heel so easily by a woman, but she did speak with a commanding tone.

"That was a marvelous speech you gave, Reverend Morton," she said, smiling grandly. "I was deeply moved."

"Thank you, Mrs. Wilson," said Tom. "It's very kind of you to say so."

"Are you here alone tonight?" she asked.

"Pardon?"

"Are you married? Did you bring your wife?"

Now it was Tom's turn to be unnerved by this overbearing woman. "My wife couldn't attend this evening. She sends her regrets."

"What a pity," she clucked. "I would have liked to meet her."

"Yes indeed!" piped up Lucy Hotchkiss, wife of the church pastor. She was a petite, pretty redhead sitting on the other side of Mrs. Wilson. By the way, what is her name?"

Tom's forehead was moist and he wanted to dab it with his napkin. "Her name?" he asked lamely, which brought giggles from the people nearby.

"Surely you remember your wife's name, Reverend Morton," said Mrs. Wilson, which provoked more laughter.

Perhaps Mrs. Hotchkiss really didn't know the truth. Her question seemed innocent. And even if she did know that his wife was Japanese, she probably didn't know her name.

"Sarah," he said at last, grinning foolishly. "Charmed by Mrs. Hotchkiss here, I momentarily forgot."

"Oh-ho!" bellowed Wilson. "There's a man who knows his way around the ladies!"

Mrs. Hotchkiss looked demurely at her plate, and conversation shifted to the fate of the Moral Re-Armament movement, which had failed so utterly to prevent war in Europe.

Mrs. Hotchkiss observed, "The idea of the four principles was a good one: honesty, purity, unselfishness, and love. The problem was putting them into action—how did they used to say it?—'in the home, in business, the village, city, state and nation in order to banish war.'"

"Frightfully idealistic, Lucy," interjected Reverend Hotchkiss, who was seated on the other side of Dr. Wilson from Tom. "And at the same time, strangely lacking in religious values."

A lot of sober nodding followed this remark, and the conversation once again broke up into little constellations. With his previous conspiratorial air, Dr. Wilson glanced in his wife's direction, then bent toward Tom.

"I might not have another chance to talk to you," he said, speaking rapidly, "so let me give you a little advice. You can take it or leave it as you wish, but let me assure you it comes from the heart and is based on forty years' experience. If you're anything like I was at your age, you're convinced of your calling and proud as punch of your abilities to win souls for Christ. Forty years from now, you'll see it differently. Oh, there will be those little victories along the way, and your faith will keep you going. But when you get right down to it, you'll never know for certain if any of those souls truly belong to God or to some black devil they keep hidden in a closet. Now, don't get me wrong. I haven't wasted my life. But I could have done a lot better. And so can you. Find yourself a nice, white congregation and stick with it. Hotchkiss here has the right idea."

Tom was stunned at the forthrightness of the man and at the precision with which he had brought out doubts that had been lurking in the back of his own mind. But surely, he thought, the situations that he and Wilson faced must be totally different. Forty years of struggling against a surrounding black horde could not hope to yield the results that a representative of the dominant white race could expect ministering to a small, vulnerable minority.

Tom's inner debate continued through dessert and was still going strong even after the evening's play began. Less than a half hour into "1941: The Challenge of the Cross," Tom quietly left the auditorium to drive home through a chilling rain.

Things would have to change. Something would have to change. In the ten months since their wedding, he had been telling himself to take charge of his life, to be the master of his fate and of his household. But Mitsuko was always there, increasingly the immovable axis on which the world was spinning: silent, alluring, and drawing him, it seemed, ever farther from his god, ever deeper into darkness.

Find a nice, white congregation, Dr. Wilson had told him. Finding any congregation had seemed like such a victory before. From dirt farmer's son to pastor of his own church, what more could he have asked for? After his initial disappointment, it had not seemed to matter that the Lord had called him to minister to "colored" people as Wilson put it. This was to be his life, and he had been satisfied. But now he saw that there was an opulence in this city of a kind he had never known—and certainly never thought to share in.

The night was piercingly cold, but when he put his key in the lock and opened his apartment door, he was met by a soft, warm blanket of moisture that clouded his glasses.

"I'm back," he called, removing his glasses to wipe them, but there was no answer. He stood there in his overcoat, listening, until he heard splashing in the bathroom tub. Smiling, he hung his coat up and changed into his slippers.

"I'm back," he called again, scuffling over to the bathroom. "Daddy!" called Billy, his voice reverberating off the hard tile walls.

"Taking a bath?" Tom asked, twisting the knob and walking into the billowing steam clouds, but he was not prepared for the sight that greeted him. Mitsuko was not kneeling outside the tub, washing Billy, as Tom had imagined. She was in the water with him, a towel wrapped around her hair.

Billy was straddling her naked thighs and excitedly holding up a homemade sailboat to Tom with one hand, while the other hand was pressed against Mitsuko's breast for support. Both of them were bright red from head to foot, and Mitsuko's forehead was beaded with sweat.

"How long has *this* been going on?!" Tom's voice boomed in the little bathroom. Billy blinked and dropped his boat onto the floor, snapping its mast. "Get out of there *now*!"

Billy clung to Mitsuko, wailing and pressing his head between her breasts. "Mommy! Mommy!" he cried. "No spanking! Mommy!"

Tom grabbed Billy by the arm and yanked him away from Mitsuko. "She's not your Mommy. Never call her that again!" He looked at Mitsuko. "Never let him call you that! I won't have it! Do you hear me? You're not his mother."

Billy's piercing scream echoed off the hard bathroom walls. Tom dropped the boy onto the rug and stalked out, slamming the door behind him. After a while, Billy's crying subsided, and Tom heard Mitsuko lead him from the bathroom and put him to bed. Tom himself prepared for bed while the soft tones of the lullaby insinuated themselves through the dark apartment, and he had been under the covers for a few minutes when Mitsuko came in.

She looked grave and slightly comical with her hair still wrapped in the towel, but the glow of the hot bath could still be discerned on her cheeks, and the V at the neck of her robe was a deep, warm pink.

Standing by the bed, she bowed slightly and said, "I am sorry."

Tom did not speak.

"I know I am not his mother—"

"No, you're not, are you?"

"But I love him like a mother."

"I won't have it," he said.

"Please, Tom—"

"He used to call you Mitsu, and he can learn to call you Mitsu again. His mother's name is Sarah, and she is dead."

"I will not hide that from him. When he is older—"

"Older? How old will he have to be? When he's too old to take baths with? How old is that? Five? Ten? Twenty-one? You are a Christian wife, and you must learn to behave like one! It has been almost a year now, and I see no change."

"Why should I change? I have done nothing to offend God."

"My Lord, listen to the woman! I am a Christian minister, a Christian American, and I must have a wife who understands that. For one thing, you must not flaunt your naked flesh, not to me, and not to Billy."

"But—"

"Do you understand?"

"Yes."

"It is not Christian. It is not American."

"I am not American."

He glared at her. "Are you proud of that? Are you boasting that you are not American? Do you want to bow down to that emperor of yours and sing the praises of his 'sacred' troops?"

"No," she said firmly. "I hate the Army."

"And the emperor?"

She paused. "I do not hate the emperor. But I no longer bow to him."

Tom gave a sour smile. "We have to work on making you more American," he said, his voice softening. "You can't apply for citizenship yet. Maybe we can start with your name."

"What do you mean?"

"We can change your name," he said, "or give you a new one."

"I do not want to change my name."

"Why not? What's so special about it? You're always complaining that Americans never pronounce it correctly. Does it mean something?"

"Not exactly. Mitsu is *hikaru*—to shine."

"What do you mean, 'Mitsu is *hikaru*'? Mitsu is Mitsu."

"It is very difficult to explain. But I do not want to change my name. It is the one I was born with."

"Far more important is that you must take Our Lord wholly into your heart and admit no other."

"But I *do* admit no other."

"Not the sun? Not the Japanese sun god? I've seen you praying to it in the morning."

"That is different," she said. "I do not pray to the sun as I pray to Lord Jesus."

"Then you admit you do pray to it?"

"No. I only ask it to shine on us and make the day good."

"What is that if not praying?"

"It is different," she insisted. "It is very difficult to explain."

"Everything is 'very difficult to explain.' Mitsuko, do you understand what I am trying to say?"

"You want me to be a better Christian wife."

"Yes, it's as simple as that. Shall we work at it?"

She nodded, smiling weakly.

Slipping out of bed, he opened a bureau drawer and handed her a pair of his pajamas. "Wear these until we can get you some of your own."

She took them, not entirely able to suppress a smile, and went to the bathroom to change. By the time she walked back into the bedroom, she was giggling. She had the sleeves rolled up to wrist length, and the pant legs rolled to keep them from dragging on the floor, but the excess cloth could have held another two or three Mitsukos without strain.

"All right," Tom said with a sardonic smile. "You do look funny, but I'm absolutely serious about this."

Determined to resist temptation, he kissed her on the forehead and wished her a good night. Her "good night" to him could not disguise the tenderness of her feelings for her husband, but she pronounced the words solemnly and lay down with her hands close by her sides.

Tom was very pleased with the civility, and his mind filled with the image of those five hundred young people in the audience today, the reds, yellows, and browns of their hair color promising to decorate his dreams like a Christmas tree.

His eyes opened to the deep darkness of night. Aside from the sound of his own pounding heart, he heard only the gentle whish of Mitsuko's regular breathing. He felt as if he were lying in bed with an oven. But what woke him was the pain of his erection thrusting up against the heavy blankets. He pushed the covers aside to relieve the pressure, but his body was still on fire, and the tension between his thighs seemed only to increase. He half believed he could see Mitsuko's naked breasts in the darkness, rising and falling with each breath. He reached out and felt the reassuring coolness of cotton, but his fingertips grazed the upthrusting nipple beneath, and a shock ran through his body.

No. He would not let her do this to him. He lay there as still as possible, but the chill of his perspiration began to make him shiver.

"Mitsuko," he whispered.

The sound of her continued steady breathing brought him escape from his humiliation even as it signaled to him that his agony would not be soothed.

God, help me, he prayed silently, but the more he concentrated on the source of his physical discomfort, the more stubbornly it persisted.

He brought his hand down to the throbbing organ and began to stroke it. Mitsuko shifted in her sleep. What if she awoke and found him in the midst of this perversion? And what would he do with the fluid when he came to his climax? What would she think when she laundered his pajamas and the sheets that he had fouled?

Feeling like a miserable prowler, the Reverend Thomas Morton crept from his bedroom and spent a short but critical interval of the night standing spread-legged before the bathroom sink.

PART THREE:
1959

12

HIS FATHER'S SIN. It was all that Bill could think of as he found his way out of the church where the Reverend Thomas Morton presided as the spokesman of God. The woman named Mitsu had been the object of that sin, or perhaps the cause.

But he found that impossible to believe. The shadow she cast deep within his soul gave him only comfort, warmth and tenderness. The distant reverberations of her goodness reached him the day he entered Maneki, and before the week was out he found himself drawn there twice again.

Back at Cascade-Pacific on Friday, he found Clare in the cafeteria eating dinner with her friends. She smiled at him wearily and excused herself, following him with her tray to an unoccupied table in the corner.

"Do we still have a date tomorrow night?" he asked.

"I don't know. Do you have time for me?"

"I'm sorry," he said. "I know I've been acting strangely."

"That's an understatement!"

"But I do love you, Clare."

He reached across the table for her hand. She turned her palm up to his and clasped his hand warmly. For a long, silent time, they looked into each other's eyes.

"I have something to tell you tomorrow night," he said.

Her brows twitched. "I'm not going to like it, am I?"

"I don't think you will."

She squeezed his hand. "You're going to leave me."

"It's nothing like that. It's just that I've been thinking about our future."

She sat back in her chair, yanking her hand from his. "Why don't you just break off our engagement and get it over with?" Heads turned in their direction. She glanced up and flushed.

"Can we continue this tomorrow night?" he whispered.

"What's the point?" she said, lowering her voice. "I've got the message."

"No, you haven't got the message at all, damn it! Please, calm down and I'll come for you at 7:30 tomorrow."

Bill was nervously straightening the knot of his tie when Clare floated through the lobby door in a sleeveless, pale yellow, flowing dress of a silky fabric that clung and moved alluringly. Her hair was down, falling to her shoulders in billowy cascades, and she beamed at him as if in an unabashed declaration of love. In high heels, she was nearly as tall as Bill. He stood there, stunned. It was as if all the strains of the past week had vanished.

"What's wrong?" she chirped playfully, her blue eyes glowing.

"You look lovely," he murmured, taking her hand.

"Is that so unusual?"

"I wasn't even sure you'd be here."

She smiled, bringing her face close for a kiss.

He planted a warm kiss on her lips and they went out to his car. As Clare snuggled up against him, he asked, "Where would you like to go?"

"To Ballard," she said without hesitation.

"Your home? I wasn't exactly planning to spend the evening with your parents."

"Just for a little while," she cooed.

The Korvald house was dark when they pulled up to it a few minutes later.

"So much for an evening with the folks," said Bill.

"Let's go in anyway. I'm sure they'll be back soon."

Bill expected the warm, slightly fishy smell that always lingered in his future in-laws' house, but today the air was merely stuffy. Clare went around switching on lights and opening windows. The place always struck him as the site of a battle against homesickness, its walls covered with large photographs of dramatic green mountains and sparkling fjords. Next to a modest cross over the mantelpiece hung, almost as if in competition, the blue-on-white cross on the red rectangle of the Norwegian flag. An old framed photo stood on the end table by the blue sofa, showing Mr. and Mrs. Korvald in traditional wedding dress, staring stiffly into the camera, the bride with a wide, flat crown on her head from which hung clusters of metal flowers. Clare had once shown him another photo of the couple. In it, the groom, smiling broadly, was holding a cup carved in the shape of a Viking ship, and his new wife, still in her crown, was drinking from it. This picture was kept in an album and never displayed, Clare explained, because the cup contained beer that had been brewed especially for the wedding ceremony, and her mother did not want to be seen drinking beer.

Bill let himself sink into the deep cushions of the sofa and listened to Clare moving about in the kitchen. By the lamp on the end table stood a balsa-wood model of a B-47. Mr. Korvald had probably made it himself. Boeing employees were nothing if not loyal to the company.

Clare appeared with a tray and set it before him on the coffee table. When he saw the two long-stemmed glasses flanking a plate of cheese, Bill exclaimed, "Not you, too, Clare! It's bad enough your father makes me drink that stuff."

"No one is allowed to leave the Korvald home without having tasted aquavit."

"You mean kerosene."

"Didn't your mother ever tell you it's not polite to refuse what you're offered? Drink up."

"Oh, come on, Clare, you don't like this stuff any more than I do."

She put her fists on her hips and stood over him, tapping one foot like an exasperated mother.

"This is crazy," he said, taking his glass and waiting for her to take hers.

She sat down beside him and grasped the fluted stem in her fingertips, raising the sparkling glass to him.

"Skoal," she said as they touched glasses. A bright flash of red passed through the inverted cone of clear liquid atop the stem, the smile on Clare's painted lips momentarily twisted into a gaping grin.

"Skoal," he replied halfheartedly. He took a sip and felt a jolt as the fiery concoction tore down his throat. The warmth spread immediately and the caraway-scented fumes filled his lungs.

"Now," she said, smiling demurely, "What are these new thoughts you have about our future?"

"I've decided I want our missionary work to be in Japan, not Norway," he said without hesitation.

"You sound very definite."

"I am very definite."

"Without a word to me?"

Clare slowly twirled the stem of the aquavit glass in her fingers, peering down into the little puddle remaining in the cup. Then she set her glass on the tray, and he set his next to it.

"Bill, what's happening to us? We used to talk over everything, and now, all of a sudden, you're acting like—well, like my father! He tells my mother what they're going to do *after* he's made all the decisions. He never even asked her if she wanted to leave Norway."

"I don't mean to be like that. It's just that …"

"What?" she cried. "What is it that's been eating you up so? Why don't you talk to me anymore?"

She reached for his hand and, trying to smile for her, he let her take it.

"I love you, Bill," she said. "I don't want to lose you." She rose up and threw herself against him. "Kiss me. Please kiss me."

His arms closed around her strong shoulders, and she pressed her lips hard against his. "Oh, darling," she moaned, "I'll do anything for you. Anything. I love you so much!"

Her mouth was open now, and her tongue was jabbing at his lips, trying to force its way in. She loosened his tie and sent thrills of pleasure through his body with her lips on his throat, his ears, his face. His hands moved across her back, but when they encountered the zipper there, they hesitated.

"Open it," she urged him.

It came down so easily, and now his hands were touching her where he had always longed to touch her. He pulled at the dress from either side, and it slipped from her shoulders. She moved away from him and let it fall in front. Her breasts were thrust before him, a lacy brassiere all that separated him from them. Her eyes burned like two aquamarine coals.

Just then he heard a car outside. "My God, Clare, what if your parents come back and find us like this?"

"It's all right," she murmured, her breath coming in small gasps. "They went to Poulsbo for the weekend."

The truth of what was happening crashed into him with the chill of an arctic wave. How easily they had forgotten their vows to remain pure until marriage. "For God's sake, Clare. What if your parents hadn't been away? Would you have gotten me to take you to some seedy motel? Or done it in the back seat of my car?"

The look of intoxication she had been wearing changed to one of fear. She collapsed on his knees, sobbing. "I don't want to lose you," she wailed. "I love you so much."

He caressed her hair, trying not to look at the creamy flesh of her back and shoulders.

"No, Clare, this is not the way."

As his own surging passion cooled, Clare's sobbing began to abate, and he gently lifted her from his lap, helping her to slip her arms into her dress. She let him raise the zipper, and then, without a word, she stood and left the room, walking unsteadily on high heels.

A door closed, and water began splashing in the sink. He stood and smoothed his rumpled clothing, straightening his tie and shaking his hair into place. The bathroom door clicked open and the sound of footsteps approached the living room, but Clare remained hidden in the hallway, only the yellow hem of her dress showing past the edge of the door.

She tried to speak, but her voice caught until she had cleared her throat. "Please go."

"At least let me take you back to the dorm," he said to the door frame.

"Please, Bill, just go!"

"Can I call you tomorrow? We have so much to talk about."

"Not anymore."

He knew she was right. Things would never be the same. Drained, he got into his car and headed automatically for the Ballard Bridge. But returning alone to the dormitory was more than he could bear at the moment, and instead of turning onto Nickerson he continued down 15th past the billboards and factories, the armory and the railroad switchyard.

He followed the road to the waterfront and drifted past the dark, hulking warehouses on Alaskan Way, catching glimpses between them of Elliott Bay off to the right, the lights of Duwamish Head glancing across the water's shimmering surface. The car's open window scooped in the salt air, heavy with the medicinal smell of creosote from the piers. He passed under the arching footbridge at Marion Street by the ferry terminal and momentarily toyed with the idea of driving onto Colman Dock for a slow boat trip across the dark waters of the Sound.

The floodlighted white peak of Smith Tower suddenly loomed into view above and to the left. It looked strangely unfamiliar until he realized that he had become accustomed lately to seeing it from the Chinatown side. As he watched it from below, it seemed to fill the night with a huge image of Maneki's white cat, beckoning to him simultaneously from a mysterious past and an unknown future.

13

AS SOON AS BILL pushed open the glass door of Maneki, the two waitresses—the thinner, younger Reiko on the left and the buxom Kumiko on the right—dropped what they were doing and rushed toward him, reaching him at exactly the same moment.

"You look so handsome tonight," Reiko said, "in a suit and tie."

"Prince Charming!" Kumiko said. "*Ohji-sama!*"

Kumiko was the boss's wife. She muttered something in Japanese to Reiko, who sullenly returned to her section of the restaurant, glancing at Bill once or twice.

"Why are you so dressed up tonight, Ohji-sama?" Kumiko asked.

"I was on a date," Bill said. "It didn't end very well. I probably won't be seeing her again for a while—if ever."

There were few diners in the restaurant this late, so when she brought Bill his food she joined him in the booth, settling her plump, little body in the seat opposite his. "Are you sad?" she asked.

"Yes," said Bill, "we were engaged."

"No more?"

"Probably not."

"I'm sorry for you," she said. Her round, little eyes were damp with tears.

In the next moment, he was surprised to hear himself telling this waitress he hardly knew, "I'm having problems at home, too."

"Yes?"

"I had a big blowup with my father. He's so upset with me, I doubt he'll keep supporting me. I think I'm going to need a job."

"Wait a minute," she said, and hurried off to the kitchen.

The noise level in Maneki's kitchen was always high, but the male voice was louder now and growing clearly agitated.

When Kumiko came back, her small face wore an unaccustomed flush, but also a triumphant smile.

"You work here," she announced, white teeth flashing.

"What do you mean?"

"Wash dishes."

The idea appealed to him, but it seemed unlikely that such a small restaurant could afford additional hands. "Are you sure it's okay with your husband? He didn't sound very happy."

"That's all right. You work hard. We only pay minimum wage. Dollar an hour."

He liked the idea of spending more time here—and getting paid for it. Having his own independent income would enable him to minimize his contacts with his father. "Thank you," he said. "I'd love to work here."

Maneki was deserted when he walked in at four o'clock the next day. Kumiko came running out of the kitchen. She pulled him to the back of the restaurant and through the hanging bead curtain into the roofed enclosure. Two men in white chef outfits were busy cutting some brown, spongy stuff. Kumiko introduced him to the one with thinning hair, whom she referred to as "my husband, Kamekichi Nagaoka." She immediately cautioned him to call her husband "Boss-san," which she pronounced "Bosu-san." The "Bosu" looked at Bill's extended hand for a moment before giving it a feeble shake, but the grim nod and deep grunt he offered left no doubt that he was firmly in charge. He was not much taller than Kumiko, but he was built like a wrestler. When he turned back to his cutting board, his white shirt strained across his powerful shoulders.

The other fellow, who was probably two or three years older than Bill, grabbed his hand and shook it firmly. In lightly accented English, he said, "Hi, Bill, I'm Teruo, but everybody calls me Terry. I'm glad you're coming to work here. I hate washing dishes." The boss grunted something in Japanese. Terry stopped smiling and went back to cutting the spongy stuff.

Kumiko gave Bill a white jacket, pants and apron. She said they had ordered large sizes for him from the linen service. Then she showed him the big, gray stone sink in the back corner of the kitchen where he was to wash dishes. There were various stiff, brown-bristled brushes, rags, towels, bottles of detergents, and a large rack where the dishes would drain before he dried them. He was also expected to keep the floors clean with the mop and brooms kept in a galvanized cabinet nearby and he would be in charge of cleaning the small restroom. One thing he would never do, she said, was wash the pots and pans. The boss took care of those himself. No one was allowed to touch them. They had built up a slick, black carbon coating over the years which cooked the food to perfection, and only the boss knew how to clean them.

Kumiko was showing him how to handle the covered soup bowls, the long, narrow dishes for seaweed, and the little, round ones for soy sauce dips, when Reiko walked in, squealing with delight at Bill in his white kitchen togs. Kumiko glanced up at her and went on talking to him as though Reiko did not exist. The younger woman stomped off to the back of the restaurant.

Bill could hardly keep his eyes open when he drove back to his Cascade-Pacific dormitory at one o'clock in the morning. His legs and hips were aching, his hands were sore, and he could smell the fumes of soy sauce and boiled fish flakes clinging to his body. He slept until almost eleven the next morning. Lying in bed, he wondered how he could possibly drag himself to classes at 8:30 on weekdays. But he smiled to think that he had learned a few Japanese words. *Hayaku* meant "hurry," and *dame* meant "stop it" or "bad." He had the impression that something the boss kept grumbling to Terry, *kusottare*, meant "stupid," but Kumiko said only, "I think you don't want to know what it means, I think," and Reiko was laughing too hard to explain it.

As the job went on, Bill found himself able to understand—and even to speak—a surprising amount of Japanese. The more he learned, the more the others encouraged their Ohji-sama, and they even worked with him on learning to read the simple phonetic scripts.

One Saturday night, the big dinner rush was over and the late-night crowd had not yet begun to come in when Reiko invited him to sit in one of the empty booths for a Japanese lesson. She sat next to him rather than on the other side of the table, and she edged closer to him as they traded phrases. He had seen enough now of Japanese feminine behavior to ignore the silly slapping and patting that constituted the greater part of their coquetry, but he was not prepared for the placement of a hand high up on his thigh.

Almost the moment it happened, Kumiko burst out of the kitchen, aiming a machine-gun spray of syllables at Reiko. He recognized the word *guzu-guzu*—"wasting time," but the rest went by too quickly for him to make any sense of it. The intensity of Kumiko's fury was obvious enough without a knowledge of Japanese, though. Reiko jumped to her feet, bringing her broad, flat mask to within inches of Kumiko's little face and matching Kumiko's husky snarling with her own high-pitched squeals. Heads popped up from the two booths where customers were sitting, but the show ended quickly. Reiko tore off her apron and flung it at Kumiko's feet. Then she stalked to the back of the restaurant and returned with her purse. Casting one last, pleading glance at Bill, she rushed to the door and flung it open with a bang, disappearing into the night.

By this time, the boss had come out from the kitchen holding a large, black ladle. "*Dohshitanda*!" he demanded of Kumiko: "What the hell's going on here?" She was too agitated to speak, but stood there, holding onto the edge of the table, eyes moist with angry tears.

Bill tried to explain in Japanese what had happened.

"*Kenka desu*," he said, at which the normally poker-faced boss bared his enormous teeth and threw his head back in reverberating laughter. Even Kumiko was unable to maintain her high level of excitement and began to titter, covering her white teeth with a tiny hand.

Bill looked at them in bewilderment, which prompted another round of laughter. "Too polite," Kumiko said finally when she stopped laughing. From what he could understand of the mixed English and Japanese explanation he received from the couple, he had stepped forward at the culmination of the wild battle to announce in formal Japanese, "It is a quarrel."

Kumiko and the Bosu-san then launched into a serious discussion of whether or not they should bring Reiko back, to which Kumiko was adamantly opposed. When the after-theater-after-gambling crowd began to pour in looking for sushi and *ochazuke*, though, they would be in trouble, he cautioned her. She would find a way to handle it, she assured him.

Even before all the booths had become filled with hungry customers, Bill peeked out from the order window to see that Kumiko's confidence had begun to crumble. Her forehead was beaded with sweat.

"*Oi!*" called the boss, motioning toward Bill. "You go."

"What?!" he exclaimed, incredulous that he, too, should suddenly be fired in the midst of the chaos.

"You go," repeated the boss, this time gesturing with his hands as if holding a pad and pencil.

Incredible—the boss wanted him to wait on tables. He pictured Kumiko and Reiko zipping back and forth in their little ballet between the booths and the order window, and he saw himself as a big blond ox stumbling across the stage, smashing dishes and trampling people's feet.

The boss grunted at him again, and Bill wiped his hands and grabbed an order pad from the pile in the corner. Since Kumiko had been trying to cope with the entire L-shaped restaurant, the clear division between her section and Reiko's had been lost. He simply searched for the booth with the most impatient-looking people, approaching four Japanese men who were craning their necks toward the kitchen and grumbling loudly.

"*Onna wa doko da!*" demanded the fat one in the left-hand corner. Bill hadn't been expecting this. Why hadn't he looked for a booth containing white faces? He turned in search of Kumiko, hoping to trade tables, when he realized with a thrill that he understood the man's question: "Where's the woman?"

All four men had open collars and their hair was slicked back. They slouched in the booth, looking at him with sullen expressions that dissolved into smiles when he replied, "*Ima wa imasen*"—"She is not here now."

It was one thing to parrot phrases from Kumiko or the boss, but the experience of having successfully communicated with a hostile stranger made his heart dance. He wished he could follow it up with something equally impressive, but the best he could do was wave the order pad in their faces and say, "*Dohzo*," which meant "Please."

"*Ore wa katsudon*," said the fat one. He wanted katsudon—a bowl of rice topped with a pork cutlet and eggs. Bill knew the menu inside out by now, and even if he couldn't catch all the words used to order the dishes, he could tell what people wanted. Numbers were a problem, though, which he realized when the other men were specifying how many items they wanted. To double-check, he read back the order to them, holding up the appropriate number of fingers. Sent off with smiles and nods, he had started back to the order window when one of the men called to him, "*Oi! O-cha!*" Of course—he had forgotten the tea!

He managed to serve the meal without a hitch after that, and when the four men left an hour later, he experienced the warm glow of a successful debut. In addition, they had left him a dollar tip. He walked into the kitchen with the four quarters spread out on his palm. "*Doh shimashoh?*" he asked. "What should I do with this?"

Terry, who had been forced to wash dishes again, looked up from the sink and grunted, but the boss said, "You keep!" flashing his big teeth and gesturing as if putting something in his pocket.

Bill's other customers that night were not as generous as the four men, but he came back to the dorm satisfied with an extra $2.80 in his pocket.

The boss was quick to see the commercial potential of having a tall, blond waiter who could speak some Japanese. He gave Bill a black and blue *happi* coat with big, white Japanese characters on the lapels to wear along with a white *hachimaki* headband. Bill was still expected to wash dishes in his spare time, but when word began to spread about the *gaijin* waiter in Maneki who could speak Japanese, he rarely had time for that. The booths were constantly full, and some customers waited for tables to clear in Bill's section of the restaurant rather than have Kumiko or one of the other waitresses serve them.

Soon he began to have regulars, like Seiji Nagahara, a fisheries company executive. All Bill had to do was say "*Konban wa*"—"Good evening"—and Nagahara would gush at Bill's phenomenal linguistic powers. Atsushi Bando never failed to get drunk and tearfully sing "Danny Boy" in impenetrable

English, proclaiming that Bill was his own, personal "Danny Boy," whatever that was supposed to mean. Norman Miki, who worked for Boeing, was Bill's most loyal customer and perhaps the closest thing he had ever had to a public relations manager. Norman never missed a chance to promote his "act." Every couple of nights he would show up with new friends who, he insisted, had to "see this guy." Women customers especially enjoyed calling Bill by his nickname, Ohji-sama, and soon he was permanently established as the Prince Charming of Maneki.

With the aid of a little sake, some of the women would boldly ask him when he got off from work, or they would hand him their telephone numbers scribbled on scraps of paper. Kumiko remained ever vigilant, and when one tipsy woman of middle age began shamelessly propositioning Ohji-sama and yanking on his arm in hopes that he would sit next to her, she slapped the woman's hand and scolded her, provoking tears and apologies.

One cold, stormy Saturday night in the middle of November, Norman Miki arrived at Maneki with two new spectators for the Ohji-sama show, both of them Japanese men in their late thirties or early forties like himself. Bill smiled and bowed and welcomed them with a vigorous "*Irasshaimase*!"—"Come right in!" He gestured toward a table, and the three men began to file past him.

The last of the three was a tall, well-built man with a strong curved nose. Bill guessed he must be a successful executive somewhere: he dressed with an understated elegance that spoke of a comfortable life. But one feature of his clothing took Bill's breath away. The left sleeve of the man's beige silk sports coat was empty and pinned up to the shoulder. Bill shrunk back as the newcomer edged by him.

The man turned, glaring at Bill. In that instant, Bill was fifteen years old again, waiting for a bus that one gray morning when the green DeSoto pulled up. He could feel the cold drizzle and hear the cries of the gulls winging over Puget Sound. He knew, as surely as he had ever known anything, that this man was the driver who had emerged from behind the rain-streaked window and called him by name.

Bill tore himself away from the table and went for the tea. He felt himself moving through the smoke and commotion of Maneki, but he was no longer a part of it. Carrying the tray with the teapot and cups, he was headed down a long, dark tunnel toward Norman Miki and the stranger. When, at last, he stood before them, he saw that the one-armed man was still staring at him.

"Hey, you look a little *hen* tonight, Ohji-sama," piped up Norman, a Nisei who always spoke English peppered with Japanese phrases. "Whatsa matter? *Neko* got your tongue?"

"Aren't you going to introduce me to your friends?" Bill asked, relieved to hear words coming from his mouth.

"Oh, sure. This is Frank Sano," Norman said, cocking his head toward the one-armed man sitting next to him, "and this is Jimmy Nakamura. We were buddies in the 442nd."

Norman had regaled him with stories of his outfit's military prowess, so he knew all about the Nisei fighting unit, the 442nd Regimental Combat Team. Norman always called it "the famous 442nd," and boasted of its many military decorations, but Bill had never heard a word about it from anyone else. There had been many stories of friends lost in action and others wounded, but this was the first time Bill had actually seen someone who had brought home the scars.

He poured the men's tea and took their orders. Frank Sano's eyes were alive in a way that Bill could not define, in a way that was a little frightening.

When he served their food, Norman Miki tried to engage him in the usual banter, but Bill had only one thing on his mind. Finally, when he had a spare moment, he filled their water glasses and said directly to Frank Sano, "Are you still driving the green DeSoto?"

The others looked at Bill, then at Frank.

Frank glanced down at his newly filled glass, then returned Bill's gaze. "No," he said, "I traded that one in a long time ago."

"Hey, what's goin' on here?" exclaimed Norman. "You two know each other?"

Frank snorted once and, looking down, jogged his water glass so that the ice clinked against the sides. "Yes and no," he said. "What time do you get off from work, Billy?"

"Billy?" asked Norman. "Is *that* your name?"

"It used to be," he said, and then looked at Frank. "I'm off at midnight."

"I'll be parked out front. I'm driving a black Chrysler now."

At midnight, the black Chrysler was waiting at the curb, and, without the slightest hesitation, Bill opened the front door and got in.

"We'll go someplace quiet," Frank said, pulling into traffic. "The bar in the Olympic is open all night."

"I don't drink," said Bill.

"Why not? You're legal now, aren't you?"

"I turn twenty-two next month. You know a lot about me, I see."

"Not as much as I'd like to," he said. "Anyway, we'll order you orange juice or something. I don't suppose you're a milk drinker anymore?"

Bill chuckled.

They sat at a small table by the window, the lights of Seattle spread out beneath them and bending away in a long curve tracing the edge of Elliott Bay. A lone piano played quietly at the far side of the plush room, and glasses clinked now and then.

A waitress in a short, frilly skirt took their orders, and when she left them, Bill looked at Frank. "Who am I?" he asked.

Frank smiled and shook his head. "I can tell you who you were for me," he said.

"Fair enough."

"The first time I ever saw you, you were four years old. We were all trying to stuff mattresses, and you kept me busy tossing you into the straw."

"Wait, you've just gotten started, and already you're miles ahead of me."

"This was in Puyallup," Frank explained. "Camp Harmony."

"'Camp What?' You mean the fairgrounds? I've been to the state fair a few times."

Frank looked puzzled. "All right, we weren't in Puyallup very long, but don't tell me you don't remember the camp in Idaho!"

The only "camp" Bill had been to was the Bible camp, with Clare, this past summer. He shook his head.

"You must have heard about the wartime relocation camps, at least."

Again Bill shook his head.

"I guess I shouldn't be surprised," Frank muttered. "No one ever talks about them anymore. It's as if the whole thing never happened. Well, it happened, all right. God-*damn* did it happen!"

PART FOUR:

1941

MINIDOKA RELOCATION CENTER

— HUNT, IDAHO —

— L E G E N D —

M.P. - MILITARY POLICE.
P.O. - POST OFFICE.
G. - GARAGE.
C.S. - CENTRAL SERVICE.
G.S. - GASOLINE STATION.
OFF. - OFFICES.
E.S. - ELEMENTARY SCHOOL.
J.H.S. - JUNIOR HIGH SCHOOL.
H.S. - HIGH SCHOOL
S.D.P. - SEWAGE DISPOSAL PLANT.
B.R. - BUREAU OF RECLAMATION.
S.H. - STAFF HOUSES.

(S) COOP. STORE.
(W) WELL.
(L) LIBRARY.
(N) NURSERY SCHOOL.
(SH) SOCIAL HALL
(A) AMPHITHEATER.
(B) BALL FIELD.
(C) CHURCH.
⊕ WATER TOWER.
🏠 FIRE STATION
(T) THEATRE.

S.P. SWIMMING POOL.

HOSPITAL AREA
M.P.
P.O.
ADM. G.
AREA
S.H.
TWIN FALLS
ROAD TO STATE HIGHWAY No. 25
NORTH SIDE
S.D.P.
C.S.
G.S.
OFF. 22
WAREHOUSE AREA
S.P.
40 ACRES
ZUCCH
CAR

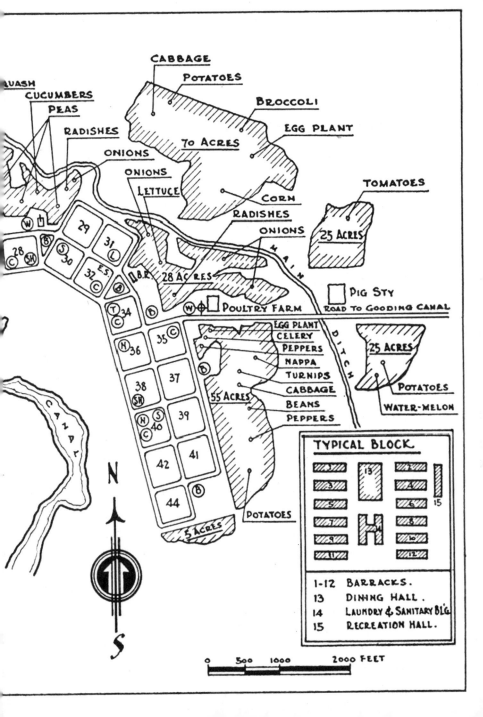

14

MITSUKO HAD BEEN half listening to Tom's sermon on "Strength and Humility," but when he brought the topic around to the present diplomatic crisis, she wished that she had not been listening at all. Could nothing be free from the taint of the Japanese military? Christmas would be here in a few weeks. What a wonderful present it would be to the world if America could convince the Japanese to get out of China.

"Even yesterday," Tom intoned, his voice echoing through the sanctuary, "President Roosevelt showed us that humility can be the ultimate expression of strength. All through November, the militaristic government of Japan presented us with arrogance. First we heard that they were amassing troops in Indo-China, and then, a few days later, that some 30,000 troops were on the move south."

Mitsuko wondered if her first husband, Tadamasa, was among those troops, leading his men on to more savagery. She imagined him as he had been in the early days of their marriage, a dashing sight with his thick moustache and his sword in its gleaming, black scabbard. But that had been before he had seen action; later, she had wondered if the sword was stained with Chinese blood. When he began to beat her, she sensed that it was out of shame for what he and his troops had done to Chinese women.

"Tojo told the world that Anglo-American 'exploitation' must be 'purged with a vengeance,'" Tom continued, "and Togo rejected what he called the United States' 'fantastic' proposals for settling the Far Eastern crisis. But just look at the strength of our good President Roosevelt. Only yesterday, as if turning the other cheek, he made a personal appeal to Emperor Hirohito to rein in his troops, cutting through all the diplomatic jargon to speak simply and humbly, from his heart to the heart of another man, in the hopes of bringing peace to a beleaguered world."

To be sure, thought Mitsuko, the emperor was but another man. She had known that at the age of six when he was a seventeen-year-old prince whose photograph would appear now and then in the papers. She and Yoshiko and her brothers Ichiro and Jiro had been at the dinner table with her parents, answering their questions about school. For Mitsuko, it had been especially exciting, her first day of school ever, and she could still recall the ring of smiles that surrounded her at the table when she recounted the teacher's talk on their future of service to the nation.

"And what do you want to be when you grow up?" her father asked her. Without hesitation, she replied, "I want to marry His Imperial Highness, the Crown Prince, and become the Empress!" Instantly, her father's hand shot across the table and stung her cheek—the first and last time he ever hit her.

"Sacrilege!" he cried. "Never say such a thing again!" She never dared to speak of it again, though when the prince had become engaged the following year, she had been bitterly disappointed.

"In these troubled times," Tom concluded, "we can only pray that more men of strength and vision learn the lesson that Christ has taught us."

Even little Billy seemed to feel something of the gravity of the mood that descended on the sanctuary; he was uncharacteristically quiet as they made their way to the front foyer. Tom solemnly wished the worshippers goodbye, the veins at his temples still bulging with the excitement of the sermon. The tension was evident, too, in the muscular flexing of his clenched jaw.

Tom had a luncheon appointment this week with ministers from some of the white churches, so Mitsuko and Billy drove home with the Nomuras. The December weather was crisp and clear, and the car heater provided welcome relief from the cold.

Luxuriating in the ease of speaking in her native tongue, Mitsuko was reluctant to part with her sister and brother-in-law.

"Come in," she said, "I'll make some o-nigiri."

"Yum!" Billy said. "O-nigiri. Daddy's not home."

"What difference does that make?" asked Yoshiko.

Before Mitsuko could answer, Goro complained, "I can't stay parked in the middle of the street like this. "Let's go in. I like Mitsuko's o-nigiri."

That settled the matter, and he found a place to park his blue Buick.

Goro stayed in the living room listening to the radio while Billy played on the floor and the women got busy in the kitchen. Yoshiko toasted the black-green sheets of *nori* over the gas flames while Mitsuko chopped and sliced the pickles: the deep purple of *shiba-zuke*, the intense green of *shiso-no-mi*, turmeric's muted yellow in the disks of *takuan*.

"You never answered my question," said Yoshiko.

"I was hoping you had forgotten. It's nothing, really. Tom doesn't like o-nigiri, so Billy only gets to eat it when he's away. Of course, he's been away a lot lately …"

"Is it just o-nigiri he doesn't like? Look, don't think I didn't notice Billy was calling you 'Mommy' for a while. He still slips occasionally. Is that another privilege he's allowed only when his father is away?"

Mitsuko concentrated on slicing the translucent amber *nara-zuke* as thinly as possible, and before she could answer, Goro charged in from the living room.

"*Taihen da!*" he shouted, the round lenses of his spectacles shining in the kitchen light. "What awful news! The Japanese Navy bombed Pearl Harbor this morning!"

Yoshiko clucked impatiently and proceeded to fold and cut the *nori*.

"Those poor natives," said Mitsuko, shaking her head.

"Natives?! What are you talking about?" shrieked Goro. "Pearl Harbor's in Hawaii! The Japanese are dropping bombs on America, you idiot! This means war! You should have heard the announcer. He must have been foaming at the mouth!"

Mitsuko looked at her brother-in-law crossly, more annoyed at the tone of voice he was using with her than struck by the news.

"It can't be that bad," said Yoshiko. "Some crazy person set off a bomb."

"A fanatic," said Mitsuko. "They'll catch him."

The women's placid reaction had its effect on Goro, but he maintained— if now in a calmer tone of voice, between mouthfuls of o-nigiri—that they were underestimating the importance of the news.

The more Goro talked about war, the more vividly Mitsuko could imagine Tadamasa wielding his sword. She was glad when he and Yoshiko left shortly after the meal.

The Nomuras had been gone little more than ten minutes when the telephone rang. It was Yoshiko. "Mit-chan, we've been robbed! They tore the place to bits."

"Did you call the police?"

"Yes, just now."

"I'll be right over," said Mitsuko. "I'll take a cab."

She did not even finish putting away the leftovers, but more than fifteen minutes had gone by before she managed to ready herself, bundle Billy into his winter coat, and hurry down to the street. A cab came by immediately, but the driver looked at Mitsuko and sped away. They walked to Broadway, but most of the cabs were occupied, and yet another driver of an empty cab passed her by. Finally, one stopped for her, and more than three quarters of an hour after Yoshiko's call, Mitsuko and Billy stepped out in front of the Nomuras' small frame house on East Olive Street.

A stocky policeman stood in the doorway, night stick in hand.

"Where do you think you're goin'?" he demanded as she approached the front door with Billy.

"I am Mrs. Nomura's sister. She called me about the burglary."

"Burglary? What burglary?"

"They were robbed. Isn't that why you are here?"

"Look, little Jap lady, I don't know nothin' about no burglary. I'm just here to guard the place. Now, you better get goin'."

"Guard? What do you mean? I want to see my sister."

"She ain't here, so get goin' now before I have to arrest you."

Mitsuko knew her sister was inside, but there was no point in arguing with him. She led Billy back down the front walk to the street, from which her cab had long since disappeared. A few cars drifted by, some of the drivers gawking at the policeman conspicuously stationed at the door.

Mitsuko turned to look at him again, and he waved her away with his night stick. All but dragging Billy, she hurried down the street and turned the corner. Down half a block, she came to the fence-lined back alley. At the rear of the Nomuras', she peered through a crack in the fence. Just as she had feared, another policeman was stationed at the back door.

"Billy, let's run!" He scurried after her to Madison, where she found a public telephone. Her breath clouded the glass of the phone booth. She dropped in a nickel and dialed Yoshiko's number.

A man answered the phone, and when Mitsuko asked to speak to her sister, he would say only that the Nomuras were "indisposed" and could not come to the telephone. No amount of explaining seemed to budge him, and eventually he hung up.

She dialed home and Tom answered.

"Mitsuko, where are you?" he demanded. "I've never seen this place in such a mess. That Japanese food of yours is spread all over the place."

"Tom, please." She explained the situation and gave him the exact location of the phone booth. In the ten minutes it took him to drive there, she began to shiver.

They went to the Nomura house, where the policeman was now walking up and down and rapping his hand with his stick in an apparent effort to keep warm. Mitsuko hunched down in the car while Tom stepped out to speak with him. The policeman kept shaking his head. He eventually noticed Mitsuko, and the look on his pink face changed to a sneer.

"He wouldn't tell me anything," Tom growled when he was behind the wheel again. "Except it's got something to do with the FBI."

"What is that?"

"The Federal Bureau of Investigation. The national police."

Mitsuko had heard horror stories involving the Japanese national police, the so-called Special Higher Police, who lurked in every corner of the nation and pounced on anyone who dared to whisper criticism of the emperor or the government.

"I didn't think there was such a thing in America," she said. "But why are they keeping my sister?"

"I don't know," Tom said, "but it must have something to do with Pearl Harbor."

Back home, Mitsuko tried several times to reach Yoshiko by telephone, only to have the same man tell her that her sister was "indisposed." Tom spent the afternoon by the radio. Finally, as the sun was going down, a call came from Yoshiko.

"They took Goro!" she wailed. "They're gone. Please come over."

"We'll be right there," Mitsuko assured her and hung up.

Reluctantly leaving his radio, Tom drove Mitsuko to Yoshiko's, Billy singing to himself in the back seat.

Tom said, "The Treasury Department has impounded all Japanese investments. I wonder what this is going to do to Goro's bank?"

In tears, Yoshiko greeted them at the door. Before they had their coats off, she started telling them what had happened. She and Goro had driven straight home after lunch and found that the house had been broken into. Assuming they had been burglarized, they had called the police, but found nothing missing. The police arrived a few minutes later along with a half dozen FBI men. It was the FBI, not burglars, who had broken into the house while the Nomuras were eating lunch with Mitsuko. Goro had asked indignantly if they had brought a search warrant with them, but they had acted as though they resented such a presumptuous question. A few minutes later, four of the FBI men had taken Goro away, leaving one man to answer the phone and another to prowl around while a policeman guarded each door.

"None of them would tell me what it was all about," said Yoshiko, "but when I asked if it was connected with the bombing in Hawaii, they smiled in a nasty way."

Tom telephoned the FBI, but no one would talk with him. He drove downtown to the FBI office, but he was turned away at the door. It was decided that Mitsuko would spend the night with Yoshiko, and after Mitsuko cooked a simple dinner for them, Tom took Billy home.

The two women were startled when a car pulled up at the house after eleven o'clock at night and the doorbell rang. It was Tom, holding Billy, who was in pajamas and wrapped in a blanket, his eyes red and teary. The boy had been screaming his lungs out for Mitsuko since bed time, Tom said. He thrust his son into Mitsuko's arms and drove back home.

Yoshiko said she could not sleep, and Mitsuko kept her sister company well past midnight, but Yoshiko was up first thing in the morning to wait for the newspaper, and as soon as it came, she began reading the horrifying news to Mitsuko. They learned of the American ships sunk in Pearl Harbor and the loss of life, but it was when she turned to page three that Yoshiko began to whimper.

"My God, listen to this! Someone made a threatening phone call to the Japanese Baptist Women's Home and now the police are standing guard. And someone threw stones through the windows of two Japanese grocery stores. And this is even worse: 'Numerous calls were received by police from citizens who offered their services, some of them volunteers expressing a wish to help intern Japanese residents.'"

She looked grimly at Mitsuko. "They're going to lock us up," she said.

"It must be some crazy people saying those things. The government wouldn't—"

"Here it is!" Yoshiko cried before Mitsuko could finish. "This is about Goro: 'Foreign-Born Japanese Rounded Up.'"

Yoshiko began reading silently.

"What does it say?" Mitsuko pressed her.

"Wait, wait," she said, shaking her head and moaning. "Listen: 'Japanese who have been kept under surveillance—'"

"Under what?"

"Under surveillance: being watched by the police."

"Just like in Japan! But why would they be watching Goro?"

"'Japanese who have been kept under surveillance were taken into custody by police for the FBI. They were taken directly to the immigration station—' That must be where Goro is—'and their personal effects, cameras, Japanese documents, firearms and certain other possessions were held at police headquarters.' His keys! They took his house keys, his car keys, his office keys, even his safety deposit box key."

"I don't understand. Is he at police headquarters?"

"No, it says the people's personal effects are being held there and the people themselves in the immigration station. But why? What are they going to do with them? Send them back to Japan? Kill them in revenge for the men killed at Pearl Harbor? We've got to get him out of there."

"I'll call Tom. He'll go," said Mitsuko, though she was dismayed to find herself wondering if her own words were true.

On the phone, Tom's initial reaction was reassuring. "Of course I'll go," he said. But then he asked, "Will this afternoon be soon enough? I have to go to a meeting of the Council of Churches. It's an emergency meeting, to call for fair treatment of American-born Japanese."

"But Yoshiko is going crazy. And what about Japanese who were not born in America? What about Goro? What about me?"

"Just stay put. I'm sure that everything is going to be all right. Do you have enough food?"

"I don't know. There are plenty of stores nearby."

"No, don't go out. Stay home and listen to the radio. The President is about to speak."

Yoshiko turned on the radio. If the attack on Pearl Harbor had seemed the isolated act of a madman, the intensity of President Roosevelt's thin, sharp voice made it clear that something new and dreadful had begun:

"Yesterday, December 7, 1941—a date which will live in infamy—the United States of America was suddenly and deliberately attacked by naval and air forces of the Empire of Japan.

"The United States was at peace with that nation and, at the solicitation of Japan, was still in conversation with its government and its emperor looking toward the maintenance of peace in the Pacific.

"Indeed, one hour after Japanese air squadrons had commenced bombing in Oahu, the Japanese ambassador to the United States and his colleague delivered to the secretary of state a formal reply to a recent American message."

One after another, the President listed the treacherous attacks that Japan had launched throughout the Pacific. Yoshiko listened in silence, and Mitsuko brought a box of tissues from the bathroom.

Exhausted from last night's crying jag, Billy was still asleep, but soon he was up and hungry. Hurrying back and forth between the kitchen and the living room, Mitsuko fed him and monitored the swift process by which Congress declared war on her homeland.

After his breakfast, Billy wanted to go outside to play, and Mitsuko had to find things for him to do while they listened to the radio and waited to hear from Tom. Yoshiko spent much of the day grabbing things from Billy's hands and putting them up where they could not be broken. Billy seemed determined to touch the white porcelain cat on the mantelpiece. Once, when left alone, he dragged a chair to the fireplace and tried to reach it. Finally, with a nervous Yoshiko watching, Mitsuko put the cat on the floor for him and let him "pet" it.

"Say '*neko*,' Billy. Nice neko."

Billy touched the cat and pretended to shake its upraised paw until Yoshiko could no longer stand the threat to her prized figurine. She snatched it away and restored it to its honored position, which of course prompted tears from Billy and cries of "I want the neko!"

Tom's first call of the day came at 4:30. He had been to the immigration station and argued with officials there for hours but could get no one to admit anything more than that "some Japs" were being held there. He called next from police headquarters, where he had been told that no one knew where any of the detainees' personal possessions were kept.

"It's after six," Mitsuko said. "Yoshiko is making dinner."

"Don't wait for me. I'll see what else I can do," Tom replied.

"Are you sure? Where are you now?"

After some hesitation, Tom said, "I'm not downtown anymore. I had some other business to take care of. I'll call you later."

Before she could say anything, Tom cut the connection. After dinner, Mitsuko and Yoshiko switched on the radio, but it seemed to have gone dead. Tom finally called again after ten o'clock.

"Where are you?" she said. "Billy should have been in bed hours ago, and I need sleep, too."

"I can't get back there tonight. There's a blackout going on. No lights, no driving after eleven o'clock. Everybody's worried about a Japanese sneak attack here in Seattle. The radio stations went off the air, and the buses are going to stop running."

"Can't you get here before eleven? I wasn't planning to spend the night here. I don't have a change of clothes for Billy or myself. I haven't even given him his bath because I didn't want to take him out in the cold afterward. Where are you?"

"I'm up in Mountlake Terrace with some of the other ministers. I can't make it back in time." .

"Are you sure?"

Tom sighed. "Yes, I'm sure."

"All right," she said vaguely and hung up. There was still a little time before the blackout was scheduled to go into effect.

"I'm going home by cab," she announced to her sister, but Yoshiko pleaded with her to spend another night there. If Mitsuko needed fresh clothes, she could borrow some of hers.

Mitsuko pointed out that there were none for Billy. He also needed his own blanket and his stuffed animals. "I'll catch a cab and run over to my apartment. I can be back in fifteen minutes."

"But Tom said not to go out."

"It can't be that bad. There were interviews with Nisei in the newspapers. They're going out." Taking her coat and purse and a scarf, she left the house, ignoring Yoshiko's pleas.

In the darkness, and with the scarf on her head, she was sure she would have no difficulty hailing a cab. She walked to Madison, and the first empty cab stopped for her. Hunching down in the shadows of the back seat, she gave the driver her address. He grunted and stepped on the gas, but he missed the turn and continued on toward downtown.

"Wait," she cried, "you should have turned right on Summit."

"You don't want to go to Summit, lady," he said.

"What are you talking about? Of course I do."

"No, lady, you want to go to Tokyo."

"Let me out of here. Stop the car now."

But the man kept on driving.

"What's the matter, lady? They're havin' a party in Tokyo just for you and all your Jap friends. Then they're gonna come over here and drop some more bombs on us."

She planned to leap out at the next stop light, but all the traffic signals were green, and when the light at Third Avenue started changing, the driver swerved wildly up Fourth. Now he was in heavy downtown traffic, and at last, near the corner of Pike, he had to apply the brakes.

Mitsuko jumped out even before the car came to a full stop, and she heard the driver yelling, "Go back to Tokyo, you lousy Jap!" She ducked between two parked cars and hurried along the sidewalk.

As she passed a clothing store on the corner, the street was suddenly plunged into darkness. The blackout had started, but her eyes adjusted soon enough. The dark night became suffused with a strange green glow. All the people and storefronts and lampposts wore this morbid, new patina.

"Hey, turn it off!" a male voice called to her left.

"Yeah," a woman's screech chimed in, "this is war. Ya wanna show the Jap bastards where we live?"

For a moment, Mitsuko thought that everyone on the street was looking at her, but she realized their eyes were fixed above her on the source of the green light. She stepped to the curb and looked up. "Foreman and Clark," read the huge, green neon sign. It was the only light in the intersection that had failed to go out at eleven o'clock.

Again the woman yelled, "This is war, ain't it? What the hell do they think they're doin'? Tryin' to sell clothes to the Japs?"

This drew a few laughs. Gradually, the number of onlookers began to grow, and the remarks became more resentful and surly. With some difficulty, Mitsuko withdrew her gaze from the dazzling green loops and began to walk into the darkness. Three young, scruffy-looking men blocked her way.

"Hey, will you look at that," exclaimed the one in the middle. "Jap tail!"

She stepped down into the gutter to go around them, but the next thing she knew, two of them had her by the elbows and the third thrust his hand beneath her chin. "It's a Nip, all right," he said. "Chinks' eyes slant in the other direction."

"Let me go," she muttered.

"You speakee English, Miss Tojo?" laughed the one holding her left arm.

"I will scream," she warned.

"Oh, yeah?" the greasy-haired one in front of her said. "Who's gonna hear you? I don't see any cops around. And anyway, right now, we're the only ones who know you're here. You don't want all those other guys to find out, do you?"

"Come on," said the greasy one, "Let's have a little fun." With him leading the way, they entered the dark edges of the crowd that was forming under the neon sign.

Suddenly there was a metallic thud, and something bounced from the sign onto the street.

"Aw c'mon!" yelled the same shrill female voice she had heard before. "You can do better than that!"

"Yeah!" a number of voices responded in unison, and the throwing began in earnest. A brick. A few stones. More bricks. Half the time, the green neon tubes escaped unscathed, but when a missile connected, there was a shower of sparks and the sound of shattering glass. On the far edge of the crowd, someone turned a trash bin upside down, spreading a fresh supply of bottles and tin cans on the pavement. These began to pepper the sign relentlessly, and soon there was nothing left of the green lettering. The mob cheered when the last bit was extinguished.

"Hey, Ernie, look!" said the man on Mitsuko's right. They turned in the direction of an illuminated clock half a block away. The three men ran toward it, dragging her along. The one called Ernie picked up a rock and hurled it at the red neon lettering, "Weisfield & Goldberg's Fine Jewelry," crushing two letters with a single blow. Others in the mob joined in, but the sign remained stubbornly lit. Finally, Ernie himself climbed up the clock standard and, to the accompaniment of cheers, smashed the rest of the neon tubes with his fist.

From behind, Mitsuko heard a police whistle and a voice yelling, "Come on, make way! Get back!" Instead of parting for the policeman, the crowd pressed in to form a protective barrier around Ernie, and as Mitsuko's two captors moved to join them, she wrenched free. Fighting her way through the crowd, she slipped into the anonymous darkness.

Hurrying down Fifth, she returned to Madison and began retracing the route the cab had taken. She walked as quickly as she dared through the darkened streets, which were rendered darker still by the thick overcast that had blanketed the city all day. She had experienced such darkness in the countryside before, but never in the city. Childhood stories of bewitching foxes and badgers flashed through her mind each time some black shape loomed out of the night. More than once, her shin crashed into a fire hydrant hidden in the shadows, and as she rounded the curve at the top of the hill, a car without lights nearly ran her down. A few blocks further, another darkened car sped by, and a moment later she heard a sickening crunch of steel and glass, then silence. She wanted to help, but she was afraid.

By the time she neared Olive Street, a fine mist was filtering through the night air, cooling her cheeks.

"Mit-chan, what happened?" Yoshiko cried when she stumbled into the house.

"I'm okay. Where's Billy?"

"I put him to bed in my room. Where have you been? What happened to you?"

Begging Yoshiko to hold off her questions until morning, she dropped onto the living room couch and sank immediately into a deep sleep.

15

"MIT-CHAN, WAKE UP! Listen to this: 'Enemy Planes Off Coast.' So it's true!"

Mitsuko found herself under a quilt, still wearing her overcoat. Her body ached and her shins were throbbing, and the smell of perspiration lingered about her. When she sat up and her bruised legs slipped out from under the quilt, Yoshiko gasped.

Mitsuko told her about the cab driver and the three men and the riot.

"You were in this?" Yoshiko said, showing her the headline: "Mobs Smash Windows in Riot: Crowd Irate Where Lights Still Show."

As Yoshiko read to her, Mitsuko felt as if she were hearing an account of someone's bad dream. "But what about the planes?" she asked when Yoshiko finished.

"Listen to this one: 'Seattle, which was the first major American city to stage a practice blackout in the current war last March, repeated the performance last night. But this time it was no mere rehearsal. It was in grim and deadly earnest, and the blackout extended all the way from the Canadian border to Roseburg, Oregon, along the strip west of the Cascades. The blackout extended at intervals for the entire length of the Coast. It was the result of persistent—though completely unconfirmed—rumors that a Japanese aircraft carrier was loose somewhere in the North Pacific and might unleash a murderous attack anywhere on the Coast.'"

Yoshiko's face brightened. "'Unconfirmed rumors!' That means it's all a mistake. They know the Japanese planes can't come all the way over here to attack us. They'll let Goro out soon."

"I hope so," Mitsuko said. "But people believe the rumors. You should have seen that mob last night."

"It must have been terrible," Yoshiko said. "Are you really all right? Here, let me give you some breakfast."

"I'm going to look in on Billy and take a bath first."

By the time Mitsuko joined her at the breakfast table, Yoshiko's spirits had improved. "It's not all bad news," she said. "There's something here on that Council of Churches meeting that Pastor Tom went to yesterday."

"Let me see. Does it mention Tom?"

The headline didn't raise her spirits: "Council of Churches Asks Fairness to Jap Residents."

"I like the fairness part, but do they have to call us Japs?"

At least the article itself used the word "Japanese." Tom's name did not appear.

"What is so wonderful about this?" Mitsuko said, then read aloud: "'The council issued a statement to Japanese of the Pacific Northwest expressing sympathy and pledging cooperation with the problems which face them as American citizens.' We are not American citizens."

"Don't be so pessimistic. They will treat us all the same. Look at this one—'Racial Harmony Welded By Resourceful Teacher.' I cried when I read it."

The article told of Miss Ada Mahon, principal of the Bailey Gatzert School, where six hundred Japanese children were enrolled along with one hundred Chinese and one hundred white children. "Well aware how easily ill feeling and strife might become rampant among her pupils, Miss Mahon held a special assembly at the start of the school day. 'I want to tell you a true story,' she said to them. 'While I was downtown yesterday, I saw three little American boys, arms around each other. They were laughing, and as happy as could be. I asked them if they were shopping, and they said they were just looking at the things in the windows. Now of these three little American boys, one had Chinese parents, and the other two Japanese parents. Yet they were Americans and they were happy together. That's the way I want you to be. What has happened in the world outside is not the fault of any one of us here in the school, and we can't do anything about it. So I want you to forget the things that are going on outside, and not even talk about them.' Miss Mahon then faced the flag and gave the Pledge of Allegiance, after which all the children did the same. They then marched quietly to their classes, and everything went on just as before, with no hint of racial feeling."

"It is very sweet," said Mitsuko. "I only wish there were more people like Miss Mahon."

"I have lived here much longer than you," said Yoshiko, "and I have met many white people like her. The Americans are not bad people. As soon as they realize there is no danger of an attack, they will let Goro go."

The FBI did not let Goro go that day, nor the following day, nor the day after that. Mitsuko brought two large suitcases full of clothing for herself and Billy to keep a vigil with her sister. The newspapers were full of reports on the fear of air raids, the establishment of medical centers where local "war wounded" could be taken for treatment, the continuing blackouts, and the deaths and injuries resulting from cars crashing into each other or into pedestrians in the dark. Two Japanese were the first to be arrested for blackout violations, and Japanese-born hotel owners were told they could not legally collect rent from their tenants owing to a prohibition against payments of money to Japanese nationals.

Money was beginning to be a problem for Yoshiko as well. On Thursday, Mitsuko went with her to the Nichi-Bei Bank, the firm for which Goro worked and where most of their money was kept. The doors were locked and a notice from the Secretary of the Treasury was posted outside prohibiting entrance under penalty of law. At Rainier Bank, Yoshiko was told that, as an enemy alien, her account had been blocked and they would not be able to release any money to her until the government had specified the limits they were imposing on withdrawals.

Finally, on Friday, a postcard arrived from Goro in the immigration station. It said only that he was well and that he needed a change of clothes and his shaving equipment. That same day, the decapitated corpse of a Chinese longshoreman was found on the Seattle waterfront, and the police, unable to establish a motive, speculated that he had been mistaken for a Japanese. Within hours, red, white and blue buttons with "CHINESE" in large capitals across the central white stripe were appearing on the lapels of many Asians.

A week later, permission came through for the detained Japanese nationals to have visitors. Tom was out on church business, so Yoshiko and Mitsuko went with Billy to the immigration station. The building was dark and depressing, and their footsteps echoed off the bare walls as they were shown down the corridor leading to the visitors' room.

Goro entered in his shirt sleeves, looking glum and tired. He bowed deeply to his visitors, and they to him. Then he picked Billy up and hugged him tightly.

"I am going to leave here soon," he said when all had taken their seats around a dark oak table.

Yoshiko clapped her hands. "*Yokatta!*"—"How wonderful!"

But Goro did not return her smile. "They are sending us to a detention center in Montana."

To Mitsuko that sounded like the regional "Protection and Supervision Centers" run by the Japanese thought police where "patients" with unorthodox ideas were "treated" until they realized their true Japaneseness.

Yoshiko sobbed into a handkerchief.

"There are nearly fifty of us, all Japanese nationals in important positions," Goro said. "Before that, there will be hearings by a board of review. The immigration authorities, the district attorney and the FBI will decide if I can be released. We must get our white friends to sign letters saying that I am not a danger to the country." He smiled wanly. "If only they had let me become a citizen, I would not be so dangerous to them."

That evening, Tom came to eat with Mitsuko and Yoshiko at the Nomura house. He was withdrawn, and had to be reminded that today was Billy's fourth birthday. Not even that news made him smile.

At the dinner table, Yoshiko said, "Goro has made many white friends in banking. Miss Nelson and the other white ladies who help with the Sunday school will sign, I'm sure. And with an affidavit from you, Pastor Tom, I am sure they will let him out. We'll have him home for Christmas."

"Santa Claus!" shouted Billy, who had been fed earlier and was playing nearby with a new truck that Mitsuko had carved for him. The women smiled at him.

"What do you want for Christmas?" called Yoshiko. "Uncle Goro will buy you anything you want."

"Neko!" he replied without hesitation, pointing to the porcelain cat on the mantelpiece. "I want the cat. I want him to sleep with me."

Yoshiko and Mitsuko laughed heartily at his persistence.

Tom had hardly said a word since entering the house. Now, setting down his knife and fork, he fixed a somber gaze on his sister-in-law. "Yoshiko," he said. "I'm going to ask you something I have never asked you before, and I want you to answer me in absolute honesty."

Yoshiko's eyes widened, and, like Tom, she set down her silverware. "What is it, Pastor Tom? Of course I am always completely honest with you."

Mitsuko looked from her sister to her husband, and a knot grew in her chest.

"With Christ as your witness, can you tell me with total sincerity that you had no idea that Pearl Harbor was coming?"

"Tom!" Mitsuko cried. "What are you saying?"

"Mitsuko, you keep out of this. This is between Yoshiko and me."

Mitsuko pushed away from the table. "How can you say that?"

"Be quiet. Let her speak."

Yoshiko had gone pale. Her head dropped forward, and she pressed her hands against the table top as if to keep from losing her balance. "As God is my witness," she began in a whisper.

"No!" shouted Mitsuko. "Don't answer him!—Tom! How could you?"

"Mitsuko," he intoned, "your husband has commanded you to keep silent. Do you think this is easy for me? The FBI has arrested my wife's brother. There must be a reason for it."

"Are you saying he is a spy?" Mitsuko asked.

"I'm not saying anything. I'm saying I just don't know."

"Don't know? It's Goro, Tom. Goro and Yoshiko."

"I know that, but don't you know what people are saying?"

"Yes, I know what they are saying. Hundreds of Japanese are coming forward and pledging their loyalty to this country. The white newspapers are saying they believe them. And you—"

"I know they're loyal. Who knows the Nisei better than I do?"

Yoshiko raised her head. "But I am not a Nisei?"

"I didn't mean that," Tom said. "I just want to hear it from your lips."

"I did not know," she said calmly.

"And Goro?"

"Tom—"

"Mitsuko, be silent!"

"It's all right, Mit-chan. Goro is very sad, Pastor Tom. He only wishes he could have become a citizen of this country. He loves America as much as I do. He is not a spy."

"Thank you, Yoshiko," Tom said, offering her a comforting smile. "That's all I wanted to hear."

"And now, Pastor Tom," said Yoshiko in the same tone of quiet resignation, "would you please leave this house?"

Tom's blue eyes shone through the transparent reflections of the ceiling light on his glasses. Without speaking, he placed his napkin on the table beside his plate and stood. He looked at Mitsuko, but she folded her arms and turned away from him.

"I see," he said. Leaving the table, he called to Billy on the floor, "Let's go, son. Put on your coat."

The boy had grown quiet and apprehensive. Now he stood and ran to Mitsuko, cowering behind her chair.

Tom glared at Mitsuko, then at Yoshiko. He stood before them, surveying the room as if for the last time. Then, slowly, deliberately, he walked to the front door, turned once more to look at them as he opened it, and stepped across the threshold.

16

*I am for immediate removal of every Japanese on the West
Coast to a point deep in the interior. Personally, I hate the
Japanese. And that goes for all of them. Let's quit worrying
about hurting the enemy's feelings and start doing it.*

— COLUMNIST HENRY MCLEMORE

*The Japanese should be under guard to the last man
and woman and to hell with habeas corpus.*

— COLUMNIST WESTBROOK PEGLER

*Every Japanese alien should be removed from this community.
I am also strongly of the conviction that Japanese who
are American citizens should be subjected to a more
detailed and all-encompassing investigation.*

— SAN FRANCISCO MAYOR ANGELO J. ROSSI

*It seems to me that it is quite significant that in this great
state of ours we have had no fifth-column activities and no
sabotage reported. That was the history of Pearl Harbor. I think
we ought to urge the military command in this area to do the
things that are obviously essential to the security of this State.*

— CALIFORNIA ATTORNEY GENERAL EARL WARREN

*Once a Jap, always a Jap. You can't anymore regenerate
a Jap than you can reverse the laws of nature.*

— MISSISSIPPI CONGRESSMAN JOHN RANKIN

*It makes no difference whether the Japanese is
theoretically a citizen. He is still a Japanese. Giving
him a scrap of paper won't change him. A Jap is a Jap.*

— LIEUTENANT GENERAL JOHN L. DEWITT,
WESTERN DEFENSE COMMANDER

*I am determined that if they have one drop of
Japanese blood in them, they must go to camp.*

— COLONEL KARL R. BENDETSEN,
WARTIME CIVIL CONTROL ADMINISTRATION CHIEF

*The Japs live like rats, breed like rats and act like rats. We don't
want them buying or leasing land or becoming permanently
located in our state. I don't want them coming into Idaho and I
don't want them taking seats in our university vacated by our
young men who have gone to war against Japan.*

— IDAHO GOVERNOR CHASE CLARK

Japanese are in America through fraud, deception and collusion.

— SEATTLE PUBLISHER MILLER FREEMAN

*Being closest to the enemy and a possible point of first attack,
we have a responsibility to our own loyal citizens.*

— WASHINGTON GOVERNOR ARTHUR LANGLIE

*Many of the Japanese who came here thirty or forty years ago are
among our most loyal citizens, but even among American-born
Japanese, some are thoroughly disloyal. The reason there hasn't been
sabotage here is because it has distinctly been withheld by Tokyo.*

— SEATTLE MAYOR EARL MILLIKIN

EXECUTIVE ORDER NO. 9066

Whereas the successful prosecution of the war requires every possible protection against espionage and against sabotage, by virtue of the authority vested in me as President of the United States, and Commander in Chief of the Army and Navy, I hereby direct the Secretary of War to prescribe military areas from which any or all persons may be excluded. The Secretary of War is hereby authorized to provide for residents of any such area who are excluded therefrom, such transportation, food, shelter, and other accommodations as may be necessary.

FRANKLIN D. ROOSEVELT
THE WHITE HOUSE, FEBRUARY 19, 1942

"TOM, I NEED TO see you right away."

"Out of money again?"

"Haven't you heard the news? Please come to Yoshiko's."

"Can't it wait? I've been busy all week and I have only today and tomorrow to work on my sermon."

"Tom, please. This is an emergency. I have done what you asked me to do. I have not told anyone of our troubles. I have gone to church with you every Sunday. But this Sunday is different. You must come."

"Are you threatening me?" he asked.

"Threatening? What do you mean?"

"Are you saying you are going to make me look bad in the eyes of the congregation this Sunday by staying home?"

"No, how could you—"

"Because if you are, let me tell you I'm not the least bit worried."

"Tom, please—"

Before she could say anything else, he cut the connection.

Mitsuko sat staring at the useless receiver. Then she hung it up and called out, "Yoshiko, I'm going to the church to see Tom."

Yoshiko peeked in from the kitchen. "What's the matter?" she asked. "Can't he come over?"

"I have to see him there. Watch Billy for a while."

Mitsuko put on a light raincoat and comfortable shoes. She was prepared to walk all the way if no buses stopped for her.

Walking down Madison, then Broadway, she felt a slight chill in the air, but the sun was shining, and before long she had to loosen the top buttons of her coat. She must have passed half a dozen shops with the same tagboard sign in the window: "JAP Hunting Licenses Sold Here." The words "Sold Here" were crossed out by two printed lines, and underneath it said, "Free!" Americans had such a wonderful sense of humor.

She approached the dark brick church, her house of worship during the past three years, but the promise of serenity it always held out for her had been replaced by a sense of dread. She climbed the stairs to the second floor and walked swiftly down the gloomy corridor. The soft clicking of her heels on the marble floor was the only sign of life in the building. She paused for a moment at the door of Tom's office, listening, but there seemed to be no one inside. At last she knocked.

"Yes? Come in," said Tom in his deep and gentle ministerial voice.

Without hesitation, Mitsuko turned the knob and pushed the door open. Tom sat behind his desk, his back to the window, his pen poised in mid-air above a tablet of lined paper. The light poured in around him, casting him in silhouette, but she could see his jaw set tightly.

"I told you I'm busy," he said.

"There is no time for that," she insisted. "Have you still not heard the news?"

"I don't have time for listening to the radio. I am trying to write, if you wouldn't keep interrupting me."

She closed the door and sat down in a hard-backed chair, facing him. The light from the window was nearly blinding as it flowed in around Tom's shadowy figure.

"General DeWitt made another announcement today. It is even worse than the ones before. Now he says we have only until March 29th to evacuate voluntarily. That's two days, Tom. Sunday."

He looked at her without speaking.

"Don't you realize what this means? If you do not take me away now, they are going to lock me up. We have to leave by Sunday."

"Leave for where?" Tom asked at length.

"Anywhere," she said. "East of the Cascades. As long as we are not in Military Area Number One."

"We?" he asked.

"You and I, Tom. And Billy."

"And Yoshiko?"

"Of course, Yoshiko."

"And all of Yoshiko's friends and relations, and half the Japanese population of Seattle before we get through."

"No," she said. "We will take only Yoshiko."

Warm from her walk, Mitsuko unbuttoned her coat and twisted in the chair to take it off.

Tom raised his hand and said, "Don't do that. I know what you're doing! Because I'm resisting your words, you want to lure me with your body."

She stopped wrestling with her coat and stared at him, openmouthed. "And what if I did? Would that be so terrible? Tom, I am your wife. We have not been together for three months. I want us to be together again. It is our last chance. If we start packing now, we can be ready by Sunday. You and Billy and I can live together as we used to. It is all I want. As soon as Goro is released, Yoshiko will join him."

The veins stood out on his jaw and forehead. When she had first seen him in church, this had seemed to give his preaching a special intensity, but now the bulging blood vessels looked more like worms crawling beneath the surface of the skin.

"What makes you think Goro is going to be released?"

"He has done nothing."

"How do you know that? How do I know that you—"

The tears were running down her cheeks, but she made no move to wipe them away. "Tom, listen to what you are saying! I thought you loved me!"

"Funny," he said with a wry smile, "I thought I did, too."

She sank back in her chair. "And the vows we took in Christ's name? What about those?"

"Don't speak to me of Christ! You have no right to speak of Christ."

She smiled at him sadly. "Are you not afraid for your son in the hands of this devil?"

Tom brought his fist crashing down upon the desk and then he stood, casting the full length of his shadow over her. He walked around to her side of the desk, and she saw his arm reach out. She shielded her face, but the blow did not come. Instead, Tom yanked his coat from the hanger and swung the door open, smashing it into the filing cabinets that stood nearby.

Mitsuko listened to his footsteps receding down the hall and then the stairway, and when the outer door closed behind him, there was only silence.

It was over. She sat there, listening to the emptiness of the building. Tom would need time to pack the boy's things. She was glad she would not be there when Billy was torn out of her life.

More minutes ticked by.

Rising to her feet, she walked slowly through the door and down the stairs. Instead of stepping outside, she turned down the corridor to the sanctuary. The creak of the opening door echoed in the empty chamber. She drifted down the aisle, looking up at the altar where Tom stood each Sunday.

She took a seat in the front row, studying the cross hanging over the pulpit. What kind of wood was it made of? Probably something hard, like cherry. As her gaze traversed the glowing satin planes and sharp edges, she imagined workmen cutting and shaping the wood, gluing together the members, applying the lacquer finish layer by layer, painstakingly rubbing and polishing until the hidden lines of the grain shone forth on the surface. In her mind, the workmen were Japanese, and they performed their tasks with skill and patience, dedicating their hands and hearts to the inner life of the wood.

This cross of wood hung before her, naked and beautiful. Her right hand moved slowly upward, closing around the cold metal cross against her breast. A sharp pull, and the chain on her neck parted. She looked from the wooden cross to the golden one on the living flesh of her hand, the ends of the chain hanging down against her skirt. Slowly, she turned her hand, and she watched the metal object slide inexorably toward the edge of her palm. It did not rise up to the heavens. The pull of gravity carried it over the edge, down to her lap, and as she stood, the cross clattered to the floor like a lost button or coin. Looking once again at the wooden cross, she saw the massive bolts that kept it fastened to the wall. Then she turned and walked from the sanctuary.

17

"PLEASE, MIT-CHAN, I don't want to go alone."

"I will never set foot in church again," said Mitsuko, lying on the Nomuras' living room couch.

"You mustn't say that," cautioned Yoshiko. "Now is when you need the Lord more than ever. We can go to the Baptist Church if you don't want to see Pastor Tom. Reverend Andrews is such a wonderful man."

"The Bainbridge Island Japanese are being taken away tomorrow. What can I do to help them? I want to help."

"There's nothing we can do, Mit-chan, except pray for them—and for ourselves."

"*You* pray," said Mitsuko. "Be quiet and let me think."

Yoshiko went to her bedroom to finish dressing for church. Before leaving the house, she approached Mitsuko. "What good will it do for you just to lie there? It won't bring Billy back."

"I am trying not to think of Billy."

"Maybe I can help," Yoshiko suggested.

"You? How can you help?"

"I will talk to Reverend Hanamori."

"No!" Mitsuko sat up. "You must never mention this to anyone."

"But ..."

Mitsuko stood and laid a hand on her sister's shoulder. "Promise me before you leave the house."

"He can bring you and Tom together again ..."

"Never. If you go against what I have said, I swear to you I will leave this house and you will never see me again."

"Please, Mit-chan, I would be so ashamed."

"Then let me handle this my way."

Yoshiko nodded, biting her lip. Finally, putting on one of her broad-brimmed hats, she left the house.

Mitsuko spent the rest of the morning on the couch. Against the blank ceiling, she could see Billy's clear, blue eyes looking at her with love. This must be what the mother of a kidnapped child must feel. If there were anything she might still be willing to pray for, it was that Billy should quickly become accustomed to living with his father again. A piece had been ripped out of her heart, and the only hope of healing the wound would be some word that Billy had learned to live without her. Once Tom refused to take her away east of the mountains, he had doomed them to separation.

By the time Yoshiko came back from church, Mitsuko had begun to formulate a plan. Pacing back and forth, she announced her determination to go to Bainbridge Island herself and offer her services to those who were being uprooted from their homes.

"But you can't go to Bainbridge," protested Yoshiko. "It's at least eight or ten miles out into the Sound, and we're not allowed to travel more than five miles from home. Besides, once you got there, you'd have to come straight back to beat the eight o'clock curfew. And if they caught you, they would put you in jail."

"Maybe that's where I belong," Mitsuko said. But she resolved that, at the very least, she would be there when the Bainbridge Islanders were brought over on the ferry.

Mitsuko woke early the next day and tried to leave the house before Yoshiko was up. Fearing that she might not be able to find a restaurant that would serve her, she spooned cold rice from the pot on the stove and ate it with a sour plum. She was certain that she had accomplished this in absolute silence, but the moment her chopsticks clicked against the rice bowl, Yoshiko walked into the kitchen in a flannel nightgown.

Yoshiko cried aloud when she heard where Mitsuko was going. "You can't, you'll be risking your life. I heard that some Nisei are refusing to surrender their guns. There might be riots."

Mitsuko found Yoshiko's warning strangely exciting, but nothing about the Seattle waterfront that morning proved her fears true. The big, gray warehouses loomed over Alaskan Way. The chilly air was heavy with the smell of the ocean, and an occasional breeze carried in the cough-medicine smell of creosote from the docks. Gulls circled overhead, their cries clear and shrill.

An almost uncanny quiet prevailed as Mitsuko joined the throng that gathered for the somber parade. Thousands of onlookers jostled each other for a better view surrounding the short route from the Colman Ferry Dock to the switch tracks across the street, where blue Pullman cars waited. The out-of-step, oddly casual marchers in their dark coats and hats crossed Alaskan Way in groups of twenty-five or thirty at a time, many of them smiling sadly and waving to the crowd. Above them arched the high footbridge from Marion Street, the narrow span crammed to overflowing with curious white faces. Only the uniformed soldiers at the head and tail of each docile group seemed out of place. Rifles at the ready, bayonets fixed, a few of these young men had tears in their eyes. From the crowd, Mitsuko heard some of the jeers she had expected, but they sounded strangely hollow amid the overwhelming mood of good will.

Standing on the bumpers and running boards of a car parked in front of the Palace Fish and Oyster Company, a half dozen white boys waved limply to youngsters in the procession, some of whom waved back, while others hung their heads, sniffling.

After the group with their friends in it had crossed the street and climbed aboard a Pullman car, the little gang of boys stepped down from their vantage point and squeezed their way through the mass of people toward the train. Mitsuko tried to follow their progress through the crowd, but she was distracted from them when a tall, blond girl of high school age suddenly broke through the cordon of soldiers and dashed out to the middle of the street. Sobbing uncontrollably, she threw her arms around a Japanese girl from behind, almost knocking her down. The Japanese girl pressed her face in her hands, never turning to look at her friend, and a soldier gently urged the blond girl back to the side of the street.

Still curious about the boys, Mitsuko edged her way through the crush of human bodies toward a point near the train where they should have come through. She found them on the street, looking up at the faces of the reluctant passengers.

The windows of the train were open, and some of the people inside were calling their goodbyes with bittersweet smiles. All eyes were moist but those of a tiny boy whose mother had placed an American flag in his fist and was helping him wave it. Behind them, Mitsuko could see the profiles of other passengers who had taken their seats on the far, shadowed side of the train. They made no attempt to look out, and most sat with heads bowed and shoulders stooped.

"You're still the best hitter on the Island, Tets!" yelled the dark-haired boy standing nearest Mitsuko.

The boy he called Tets knelt on a seat by a window, flexing his biceps and thrusting out his lower lip.

The mugging and the encouraging shouts continued for some time, but a piercing blast on the steam whistle sent a spasm of fright through the crowd, followed by nervous titters, and then, when the train gave a lurch and actually began to move out, a number of gasps and wails. The little gang of white boys began to trot next to the train, running faster and faster as it picked up speed, and finally coming to a halt when it had outpaced them.

The train had momentarily disturbed the waterfront's eerie calm. Now the gulls were crying again, and out on the bay sounded the blast of a tugboat horn.

Mitsuko stood her ground, waiting for the boys to retrace their steps as the murmuring crowd began to disperse. A freckle-faced redhead was talking excitedly about "some neat pinball machines" when he passed her by, but beneath his eyes she saw muddy smears, where he had wiped away his tears with dirty hands.

She had come down to the waterfront today half hoping to see a bloody resistance, and the docility of the Bainbridge prisoners had momentarily filled her with contempt. They had ignored the ugly taunts of certain members of the crowd, seeing only those observers who had come to share something positive with them, and the sight had moved her deeply. There was something of value here, something worth nourishing and keeping.

She did not know what it was, but she was sure she wanted to be a part of it. Her place was with them. Until now, she had feared the prospect of being forced to live inside barbed wire under the threat of the gun, but suddenly something in her heart welcomed it. If she could not have her Billy, if the happiness she had found with him and with Tom were destined to come to an end, there was still something left for her.

When Mitsuko arrived home unscathed, Yoshiko clucked and fussed over her like a mother hen. Mitsuko tried to explain her strangely uplifting experience, but the only thing that seemed to make an impression on Yoshiko was the mention of the armed soldiers.

"What if a *Japanese* girl had run over to her blond friend on the edge of the crowd? Would they have shot her? Mitsuko, I'm so frightened. When is our turn coming?"

"Yes," whispered Mitsuko, "when is our turn coming? We had better not be caught off guard like the Islanders."

"Not caught off guard? Mitsuko, what do you mean?"

"Don't worry," she said with a reassuring laugh. "All I'm saying is that we should begin looking for places to store your property while there is still time. What we can't store, we'd better sell."

"Sell?" Yoshiko looked around in fear and confusion. "I wish Goro were here."

"Goro is not here, so it's up to us. How much do you think this house is worth?"

"No, Mit-chan, not the house!"

"We'll see," said Mitsuko calmly.

The next day, Yoshiko began calling white friends and business contacts who had been willing to sign for Goro's freedom, asking them for spare storage space in their attics and cellars. While she was busy on the telephone, Mitsuko visited neighbors with the same request. A few doors were slammed in her face, but old Mr. Harrison three houses down even offered to care for their garden while they were away.

Hurrying home with the good news, Mitsuko was shocked to see a tiny pair of shoes in the front hall.

"Mitsu!" came the familiar, high-pitched cry, and before she knew it, she was on her knees with Billy in her arms. She held him with all her strength, her eyes shut tight, almost afraid that if she looked, he would disappear again. At length, however, his little body began to squirm in her embrace. She held him out at arm's length, and her heart sank. He was pale and noticeably thinner, and there was a greenish-purple bruise on his left cheek.

She rose to her feet, incensed, looking for Tom.

Yoshiko was standing there, shaking her head. "He dumped him here and left," she said. "He wants you to take him. He said that Billy only cries, and he refuses to eat. Pastor Tom said you put a curse on him. And maybe you did."

"What are you talking about?"

"I almost hate to tell you this," Yoshiko said with the hint of a smile on her lips. "He bit him."

"What? Who?"

"Billy bit him. Hard. I saw the teeth marks on Tom's hand. I think he broke the skin." Yoshiko was grinning now.

"You're kidding," Mitsuko said. "No, you're not kidding, are you? He really did that?" Before she knew it, Mitsuko herself was smiling. The two sisters looked at each other and burst out laughing.

18

ON TUESDAY, APRIL 21, the order came through for the first contingent of Seattle Japanese to report for transfer to the state fair grounds at Puyallup. The Army started with the Beacon Hill neighborhood, where the greatest number of Japanese lived. They gave the people exactly one week to put their affairs in order. Each person would be allowed to bring only two suitcases of clothing and a seabag full of bedding.

Immediately, sidewalk sales began springing up all through the area. Each day, Mitsuko, Yoshiko and Billy took a bus south to Beacon Hill, where they served as babysitters and sales clerks to harried mothers who were trying to sell off possessions they could not store.

The clouds hung thick over the city late in the afternoon of Monday the twenty-seventh, the last day for sidewalk sales. Mitsuko sat in a folding chair by a table—a door on two orange crates—on the sidewalk outside the boxy, little house of Mrs. Ayako Kishi. Mrs. Kishi herself stood by, incessantly yanking at the stray hairs from her big, gray bun. Never very robust, Mrs. Kishi had become a bag of bones over the past week, and each time she lifted an arm to tug at the hairs, the sharp corner of her elbow seemed about to tear through its sallow covering of skin.

A tall, dark-haired white woman with a black hat and pocketbook hunched over the table, fingering a porcelain figure among the piles of dishes that remained on the rickety makeshift table. Almost a foot high, the piece was more a sculpture than pottery, depicting a cross-eyed, smiling little boy bent at the waist and holding at arm's length a bulbous gourd almost as tall as himself. He pressed the gourd down upon the head of a huge, green-finned catfish that wriggled between his wide-spread legs. Decorated with bright red and blue and green floral designs, the fine white skin of the porcelain was crisscrossed by a network of hairline cracks suggesting great antiquity.

"What is this?" asked the white woman, never looking up.

"That is *hyotan-namazu*," replied Mrs. Kishi. "I don't know in English.

Old Japanese saying. Hold down slimy fish with gourd. Can't do it. Can't stop it."

"I'll give you five dollars," said the woman brusquely.

"This very old piece. More than a hundred years. I will sell for fifty dollars, but worth a lot more."

"I don't mean five dollars for the piece," said the woman. "Five dollars for everything on the table." She shot a glance at Mrs. Kishi.

The emaciated Japanese woman let out a sharp, little giggle, her face a contorted smile. Then she turned to Mitsuko, pleading in Japanese, "Please tell her this is a Kakiemon porcelain. We've had it in the family since the time of my great-grandmother. It's priceless."

But before Mitsuko could say anything, the woman piped up, "Come on, I haven't got all day, I have to go home and cook dinner for my husband. You're leaving tomorrow, it'll be dark soon. I'll give you five dollars *now*."

Mrs. Kishi began to shiver as if a cold gust had blown down from the mountains. She looked at the woman, her head shaking almost imperceptibly at first, then violently as she reached out for the porcelain boy with the gourd. Her bony arm went up, and a horrible animal shriek tore from her throat. With all her strength, she smashed the figure to the sidewalk, scattering white shards in all directions.

"No!" she cried. "No! No! No! No!"

In the next instant, her spindly hands fastened on the edge of the door-table and yanked it upwards, sending a cascade of gleaming porcelain crashing to the sidewalk around the feet of the white woman.

"You're crazy!" the woman screamed, stumbling back and nearly falling into the gutter. "I'll have you arrested!"

"Arrested? Arrested?" wailed Mrs. Kishi. "I am already arrested!"

Mitsuko stood and tried to restrain Mrs. Kishi, who bent down, grabbing one unbroken dish after another and smashing it to the pavement. One of her furiously pumping elbows caught Mitsuko in the ribs, but Mrs. Kishi seemed not to notice. Mitsuko stepped back, wincing in pain. She watched helplessly as the lovely dishes turned into white splinters in the waning light.

Again the next morning, Mitsuko, Yoshiko and Billy took a bus headed south, this time to Eighth and Lane, a drab industrial intersection in the Japanese quarter, where the evacuees had been ordered to report by eight o'clock.

"At least the rain has stopped," Mitsuko said.

"Thank God for that," replied Yoshiko.

"Yes, I suppose He deserves some thanks for something."

"Please stop it, Mitsuko! You can't let an innocent remark pass anymore. You have not been abandoned by God, just a man."

Mitsuko was concerned that perhaps the man himself might be among those gathered at Eighth and Lane. She did not want to see Tom if she could avoid it, but she was willing to endure that much discomfort rather than miss the departure of the greater part of the congregation.

She stood in the crowded bus, holding Billy's hand and trying to ignore the ugly stares of the white passengers surrounding her. Why did Goro have to make such a display of his wealth, buying a house outside the center of Japanese life among these hate-filled people? If he had found a home near Beacon Hill, they would have been among the ones shipped out this week, and this dreadful state of limbo would be coming to an end. As it stood now, they did not even know when they would be ordered to register and pack.

Slowed by heavy traffic, their bus did not deliver them to Dearborn Street until nearly 8:30, but as soon as they turned the corner Mitsuko knew they had not missed the departure. Hundreds of Japanese crowded the block of Lane Street. Most had paper tags on their lapels and sat or stood among dark, lumpy mounds of suitcases and seabags, also tagged. A light breeze stirred the tags dangling from the humans and their baggage, but Mitsuko could see that the paper strips bore numbers, not names.

The evacuees wore an incredible variety of clothing: high-heeled shoes and hiking boots, sandals and galoshes; silk slacks, woolen dresses, dungarees and gabardine; cardigans and fur-lined parkas, overcoats and business suits and rain ponchos and parasols.

One young couple standing near them was smartly attired in brand new ski outfits. When Mitsuko pointed them out to her sister, Yoshiko exclaimed, "*Ara*! It's Howard and Linda Domoto. They were just married two weeks ago at the church." She touched the young man on the arm and, bowing, expressed her heartfelt wishes for a good trip. She and her sister Mitsuko would be joining them at 'Pile-Up' before long, she assured them.

The man ducked his head and said, "It's 'pyoo-allup,' Mrs. Nomura. The spelling has nothing to do with the pronunciation. But thanks. I look forward to seeing you in Puyallup, I guess."

"Oh, well," Yoshiko chuckled. "I'll be learning it soon enough."

"Excuse me," interjected Mitsuko, "you and Mrs. Domoto look so handsome in your ski clothing, but …"

Domoto laughed, forming a deep crease in his upper lip. "I'm starting to sweat already. I guess I took them too literally when they advised us to wear warm, sturdy clothes. I wish they had told us where we'll be going after Puyallup."

"You can be sure of one thing," remarked his wife, rolling her eyes, "it won't be Palm Springs."

Car after car of new evacuees and well-wishers drove up to the curb. There were some white faces among them, but fortunately not Tom's. A black man driving a shiny new car deposited a Japanese family and their bags at the curb, hugged each of the children, and drove off shaking his head.

The older people were bowing to each other with great formality, while the youngsters laughed and shook hands and kissed. Most faces wore smiles, some of them more strained than others.

Mitsuko noticed Mrs. Uchida, and she brought Billy over to say goodbye. The woman was as affectionate as ever to Billy, but was distant with Mitsuko. Other women she knew from the congregation also seemed uncomfortable with her, most likely because of her recent absence from the church. Rather than complicate an already difficult situation, Mitsuko held back and allowed Yoshiko to do most of the circulating and talking.

When the goodbyes had gone on for an hour or more with no sign of the promised transportation, the tedium of waiting had many people gazing blankly at the sky or sitting on their sacks of bedding, staring at the pavement.

"Maybe they changed their minds!" piped up a man wearing round eyeglasses, but few in the crowd were in the mood to laugh anymore. Several people warily eyed the press photographers who mingled with the crowd, occasionally snapping pictures with their big Graflex cameras.

Some of the commotion was restored when a convoy of Greyhound buses roared around the corner and pulled up to the curb just after ten o'clock.

"I was kinda hoping they'd forget," said Howard Domoto with a sour grin, but the few chuckles shaken loose by his remark quickly gave way to gasps and grumbles when an armed soldier stepped off of each vehicle, coming to attention by the front door with bayonets held aloft. The news photographers became especially animated, and flashbulbs began firing at several points along the block.

Now most of the action seemed to be concentrated at the lead bus, and Mitsuko brought Billy there, Yoshiko following close behind. A young man with a "JACL" button on his jacket stood by the front door of the bus, officiously calling out numbers from a list on a clipboard.

"Who is that?" asked Mitsuko.

"Jim Shigeno," said Yoshiko. "He is one of the leaders of the Japanese American Citizens League."

"Oh, yes. They are the people who were so eager to be sent away to 'prove their loyalty.'"

Before Yoshiko could respond to this, one of the photographers pushed his way onto the bus and dragged a young couple and their little son outside to pose by the soldier at the front door. Faces bright red, they produced their best smiles to cover their embarrassment, then hurried back onto the bus, the driver closing the door behind them.

"Look!" cried Yoshiko, "it's Reverend Hanamori!" She hurried over to the reverend, who was leaning on his cane and speaking with two tall white men. After some hesitation, Mitsuko brought Billy over to the group. Yoshiko whispered to her that one of the men was the Reverend Everett Thompson of the Methodist Episcopal Church, who spoke fluent Japanese, and the other, the Reverend Emery Andrews of the Japanese Baptist Church.

Each of them vigorously shook the Reverend Hanamori's hand and spoke to him encouragingly.

"I don't know why I'm saying goodbye," said Reverend Andrews. "You'll probably be seeing me every day in Puyallup. I have a list this long of errands my people want me to run."

The two clergymen moved on through the crowd, and Reverend Hanamori turned from them with a broad smile on his face, but the smile disappeared when his eyes met Mitsuko's.

"I have not seen you at church," he said. "You must be having a very difficult time."

Mitsuko flashed an angry glance at her sister, but Yoshiko looked startled and shook her head to deny she had betrayed Mitsuko's trust.

"I thought so," said Reverend Hanamori, looking from one sister to the other. "No," he said reassuringly, "Mrs. Nomura has told me nothing. And let me guess: Pastor Tom has also told you nothing."

"I do not understand," said Mitsuko.

"Pastor Tom has left our church," he said.

"Left the church?" gasped Mitsuko.

"Yesterday. I was just as surprised as you. He has moved to a Congregationalist church in Magnolia. A very rich ... *white* church."

"I can't believe it. Pastor, I wish I could apologize for him. The man is such a ... such a ..."

"Let us just say he is no Emery Andrews. Do you realize that Reverend Andrews is going to follow his flock wherever they go, even after his church is boarded up? Look at him over there, smiling that loving smile of his. You would never guess that his heart is breaking."

Before there was time to say more, Jim Shigeno's hoarse voice called a number that made the Reverend Hanamori perk up. "We'll talk more at the camp!" he said, hobbling over to the next bus after a bow in the sisters' general direction.

Before long, the buses were filled with nearly five hundred passengers, and their engines began to whir. Just then a car screeched around the corner and pulled to a stop. A young Japanese woman holding a yellow bouquet leaped out, wild-eyed, and at the same moment a window on the lead bus flew up. "Minnie! Over here!" shouted the young man who had opened the window. The young woman ran to him, breathless. "Sorry I was late, Henry. Here!" She thrust a bouquet of daffodils into his outstretched hand.

"Thanks," he said. "I'll be seeing you, I hope."

The buses began slowly to pull away from the curb. Sad smiles and feeble waves were sent from the windows to the crowd on the sidewalk. Mitsuko heard sobbing behind her and turned to see a thin, bespectacled white woman with tight, white curls over her ears and a long chain around her neck. Her face was buried in a handkerchief. She held her hand aloft in parting, but obviously she was too distraught to look directly at anyone on the buses.

Mitsuko nudged Yoshiko, who whispered, "That is Miss Mahon, the principal of Bailey Gatzert school. We read about her in the newspaper. What a wonderful woman." Yoshiko herself began to weep now for the first time.

That evening, Mitsuko opened the paper to find the photograph of the embarrassed couple with their little son who had been pulled off their bus by the photographer. The caption under the picture read, "Japs good-natured about evacuation."

Three days later, their own orders to register and evacuate came through, which meant it was time for Mitsuko to stop assuming vaguely that everything would work out with Billy, and to start making plans. First, she had to call Tom to say that she intended to keep his son.

"You'll get no fight from me," said Tom. "It won't hurt him to go to a government camp for a few weeks, or even a few months. I can't handle him right now. There's too much happening in my life."

"That is what I heard from Reverend Hanamori. Aren't you ashamed?"

"Ashamed?! You are the one who ought to be—"

Mitsuko hung up rather than listen to more of his ranting, and he did not call back.

So she was nothing more to him than a convenience, a babysitter. As soon as he was ready for Billy, he would come and take him away. Perhaps it was the best she could hope for. All mothers have to lose their sons eventually;

she would simply have to live more consciously of the day-to-day joys than most. And who was to say that a just god would not strike—

She must break herself of the habit of hoping for divine intervention.

"Maybe we should dye his hair," suggested Yoshiko. "It's as straight as Japanese hair, just the wrong color."

"And what do we do about those blue eyes?" Mitsuko asked skeptically. "Not to mention his platinum eyebrows and white skin!"

"I'm sure if Tom wrote a letter …"

"I refuse to ask him for anything."

"But as a last resort …"

"Only if worse comes to worst."

The night wore on, and still no plan took shape. Mitsuko woke early and watched the sun rise. Almost unconsciously, she bowed her head and clapped her hands together as she stood before the kitchen window.

And then it came to her. She hurried into the bedroom and shook Yoshiko. "Wake up, Yoshiko!"

After struggling to open her eyes, Yoshiko was awake.

"All right," she said. "What is this amazing plan of yours?"

"We don't have to do anything," she said. "We don't have to fool anybody. They're already fooling themselves, those arrogant government officials. They see 'Japs' in every corner. 'Once a Jap, always a Jap.' If I say I'm Billy's mother, he's a Jap! They want to lock up people with as little as one-sixteenth Japanese blood, don't they?"

"But if you're supposed to be his mother, he should be half Japanese."

"I'll say he takes after his father. Besides, registration can be done by one representative from the family. Billy doesn't have to be there."

"But he does have to go with us to the camp."

"By then, he'll be tagged and registered like everyone else."

"I don't know," Yoshiko said.

But Mitsuko was sure it would work.

Instead of registering right away at the Civil Control Station on Monday, they joined the long line at the old Japanese Chamber of Commerce building on Jackson Street for the required typhoid inoculation. The Japanese doctor administering the shots looked up in surprise as Mitsuko shoved Billy's little, white arm in front of him.

"Just do it," she commanded, and she collected the signed card from the nurse with a triumphant smile.

On the following day, she went alone to the Control Station and came back waving a handful of white tags. "Here," she said to an incredulous Yoshiko, "from now on we are Family Number 20710."

19

BILLY WAS ASLEEP when the Greyhound bus pulled through the gate of the Puyallup fairgrounds. Four months past his fourth birthday, he was now a significant armload. Mitsuko had difficulty squeezing between the rows of seats, and she had to feel her way down the steps of the bus. Her right foot came to rest on something solid, but her left foot plunged into lukewarm, sticky mud, and she began to topple sideways. At the last second she managed to shift her weight to the foot on solid planking, and only the left leg and the edge of her skirt touched the mud. Billy was still sound asleep in her arms.

A young Nisei man with a JACL button helped her pull her foot out of the mud and gestured for her to follow the line.

"I want to wash this off," she said, looking down at the grayish slime clinging to her foot and ankle.

"You'll have to register first," he replied. "Just get in line with the rest of your family members."

"But I registered in Seattle."

"You'll have to register here now. Please, other people are waiting to get off the bus."

Pausing every few steps to shake the gray ooze from her foot, Mitsuko followed the planks to the end of the line, above which stretched a cloth banner rippling in the wind: "Welcome to Camp Harmony." The air was filled with the hum of human voices.

Off to the left, beyond a sign reading "Area A," stood row after row of tar-papered sheds next to a tall grandstand.

"What could those be for?" she asked Yoshiko, who came tottering up behind her in high-heeled shoes and wearing a black hat of raw silk. "They're a little too high for chicken coops."

"And they're not big enough for horses or cows. Maybe they're for the sheep and goats at the fair."

"I don't know. They look new ..."

A Japanese woman emerged from the door of a nearby shed carrying a broom.

Mitsuko looked at Yoshiko, who said with a grimace, "They're new, all right. And they're for us."

"Time to wake up, Billy," Mitsuko whispered. The boy picked his head up, blinked once or twice, and stretched his feet toward the ground. Mitsuko set him down and took his hand. He looked up at her with a puzzled expression.

"Picnic?" he asked.

"No, funny boy! Were you dreaming about a picnic?"

"It sounds like a picnic," he said.

The continued hum of voices near and far—the shouts and murmurs of a thousand disconnected conversations all happening beneath the open sky—was reminiscent of nothing so much as the church picnics at Jefferson Park that happened at this time of the year.

"Maybe it is a kind of picnic," she said. "You know how Timmy and Robert went away to camp last summer and they had so much fun? Well, this is a kind of camp. A kind of big picnic."

He looked up, smiled, and, with his free hand, took Yoshiko's hand. Together, the three moved ahead a few inches at a time as the line slowly shrank into a dark shed.

"I hafta pee," announced Billy.

"Can you wait?" asked Mitsuko.

"Okay."

Standing in line, Billy looked uneasily at the armed guards who walked past them now and then. "Mommy, is this a scary place?" he whispered.

Mitsuko tried to smile for him. "It is not such a nice place," she said, "but it is not scary."

"But look," he said, furtively pointing to a soldier. "Who are they afraid of?"

Mitsuko knelt down and hugged him tightly. "Don't worry," she said, "Mommy and Aunt Yoshiko are here." But Billy continued glancing nervously about until something higher up caught his eye.

Mitsuko was horrified to see there an observation post with two guards, a machine gun, and a huge searchlight. The perimeter fence was topped with barbed wire. Was it for keeping hostile whites out or them in?

They had been standing in line for nearly half an hour when they reached the registration desk. Yoshiko, as family head, presented their inoculation cards and filled out forms. Mitsuko asked if there were a place where she could wash her foot, but the tired-looking Nisei woman behind the table told her she would have to wait until they reached their quarters. The same was true of toilets. Billy was dancing in place.

"Only three of you?" asked the woman. "You'll be in Area D."

Yoshiko looked at Mitsuko with a smile. "Good," she whispered. "I was hoping we wouldn't be in those Area A chicken coops."

A Nisei girl in her teens led them out of the registration shack and across a stretch of mud, Mitsuko picking Billy up to keep him from getting too filthy. The girl's shoes were almost as dirty as her own, and everyone else's were, too, some with mud up to the ankles like herself.

They passed through a chain link gate manned by four guards in combat helmets, crossed a paved street, and entered through another guarded gate which bore a small paper sign: "Area D." The ground was not as muddy; patches of grass held the earth together. But there was no mistaking the purpose of the buildings to which they were being shown: these were stables, and they had obviously been here for years, unlike the new tar-paper chicken coops in Area A.

"Which one is yours?" asked the girl.

"It says here 'Apartment 3-II-D,'" answered Yoshiko.

She led them to the second row of stables. "Down there on the left," she said, coming to a stop as if hesitant to proceed any further. "The toilets are over that way," she added, pointing at them and nodding toward Billy.

"Where can I wash this?" Mitsuko asked, putting Billy down and lifting her foot.

The woman shrugged. "You should have done it in Area A. The showers here are no good."

"But they told me at the registration desk I would have to wait until I got to my room."

"They probably didn't realize you were assigned to Area D."

"Now what am I supposed to do?" she demanded, though she knew it wasn't this young woman's fault.

"I'm sorry," said the woman. "Ask one of your neighbors when you settle in." She left them standing there.

They walked down the narrow alley separating the rows of stables and found a door with a black '3' stenciled on it. Clumps of grass prevented the door from swinging out easily. Yoshiko gave it a yank, and the flimsy, white boards flew open, fanning toward them the suffocating odor of horse manure.

"*Kusai!*" exclaimed the sisters together. "What a terrible stink."

"Kusai!" echoed Billy, holding his nose and looking at Mitsuko for the praise he had come to expect whenever he mastered a Japanese word. But this time she was too disgusted to give Billy a glance. She edged toward the opening and peered into the gloom. There were no windows. The only light came from the open door where she stood. The flooring consisted of warped two-by-fours laid directly on the bare earth. The cubicle, no more than ten feet wide and fifteen feet deep, was empty except for a pile of sticks in one corner.

Reaching back for Yoshiko's hand, Mitsuko took one step into their new quarters. Normally, she would have instinctively removed her shoes upon entering any habitation, but there was nothing here to inspire even such well-ingrained impulses. Inside, the smell was overpowering, and she had to make a conscious effort to fight the urge to vomit.

"*Maa, hidoi,*" gasped Yoshiko, holding a hand to her face. "This is terrible."

"Where are we supposed to sleep?" asked Mitsuko.

"On the cots," said a gravelly voice from out of the foul-smelling shadows, frightening the two sisters back into the daylight.

"Pee!" shouted Billy, but by the time Mitsuko turned to him, it was too late. A dark stain was spreading downward from his crotch, and Billy started to cry.

"*Ara ara ara!*" cried the gravelly voice. "*O-shikko shichatta*—He did it in his pants."

A frazzled old woman was standing in doorway number four. She wore baggy cotton *mompe* trousers like the ones used by farmers in Japan. Mitsuko saw her looking back and forth between Billy and herself, the birdlike swiftness of her movements matched by the curve of her nose.

"What's a little blondie like that doing here?" she said.

"It's all right, Billy," Mitsuko said. "It's not your fault. Stop crying. — Where are the bathrooms?"

"You mean the outhouses," the woman cackled. "Too late for blondie, though."

"Don't these apartments have any plumbing?" asked Yoshiko.

"Apartments? That's what the administration calls them," growled the old woman. "Horses don't need plumbing."

She explained that the public facilities such as the outhouses, the showers and the mess hall were behind this block of stables, and Mitsuko hurried down the grassy path with the sniffling Billy. Five large outhouses built of new lumber were lined up in a row. Mitsuko tentatively opened one to find a long bench with six holes cut into it. There were no partitions between the holes, and, despite the shed's newness, it already smelled like an outhouse.

Billy swore that he had nothing more to do. Mitsuko congratulated herself on having stuffed an extra pair of underpants for him in her coat pocket, but now she at least wanted to wash him off before changing him; he would have to keep his present outer pants until the truck arrived with their suitcases. She peeked into the women's bath shed and was appalled to see that it was just one big rectangle with a row of shower heads sticking out of the wall. There were no partitions. The floor, at least, was concrete, and not the ubiquitous mud. The only other washing facilities were outside: three-foot pipes sticking out of the ground with spigots on the end of them. She would be able to sponge him down and rinse the caked mud from her own foot.

She stripped Billy from the waist down and held his underpants beneath the spigot, thinking she could rinse them out and use them as a washcloth to wipe him down with before putting his clean underwear on, but when she turned the handle, only a few brownish drops came out, staining the white cloth.

This was too much! She looked around for someone to scream at, but the area was deserted. All she could do was have Billy put on his fresh underpants and the stained pants. The mud on her foot would have to wait.

Back at their stall, she plunged into the stink to find Yoshiko and the woman from stall four struggling with the objects she had seen lying in the corner. They were camp cots, explained the woman, who introduced herself as Mrs. Sano. She and her husband, both in their middle sixties, were here with their twenty-year-old son, Frank, who had been a student at the University of Washington until the evacuation.

The cots were a confusing combination of canvas and wood, and Mitsuko was grateful they had Mrs. Sano's experience to rely on for unfolding them and making them stay extended.

"Next you have to fill your mattresses," explained Mrs. Sano. "Did you see that big mound of straw by the outhouses? You take these bags and fill them up with that."

"And that's what we sleep on?" asked Yoshiko.

"If you can sleep," said Mrs. Sano, smoothing back her unkempt black-and-gray hair. The smell from her armpits was strong enough to rival the invasive odor of manure.

"I'll be next door if you need me," she said, walking toward the door. She turned right in the rectangle of light, and the rafters above them grew brighter as Mrs. Sano's door opened. Now Mitsuko realized why the woman's hoarse voice had sounded as though it was coming from their own cubicle. The partition between their box and the Sanos' did not go all the way to the ceiling. She could hear every little sound as Mrs. Sano moved about on her side of the partition.

Mitsuko sank down on the opened camp cot, staring at her new home. The cubicle had been whitewashed in obvious haste. Clinging to the walls were the ghostly white corpses of horse flies and strands of straw and cobwebs. From the middle beam hung a bare light bulb on a cord.

"It doesn't work," said Yoshiko when she saw Mitsuko looking at the light. "I tried it already."

"Why did they have to rush us out here like this if the place wasn't even ready?" Mitsuko protested. "There's no water, no electricity. They haven't even—"

Suddenly from the direction of the outhouses came a clanging sound.

"Lunch time!" called Mrs. Sano.

"I want hot dogs!" piped up Billy gleefully. "Can I have hot dogs, Mommy?"

How could he think of food, Mitsuko wondered, when the choking stink of manure had her ready to throw up? But at least this would be a chance to get away from the smell for a while.

The three of them followed Mrs. Sano toward the mess hall. Rounding the corner, Mitsuko saw that water was now dribbling from the spigot which earlier had given her only brown goo, and at least thirty people were standing in line waiting to rinse their hands. The other spigots were not working.

They took their place in line for water, then lined up again for entrance to the mess hall, another slapped-together shed with tar-paper siding. The place seemed to vibrate from the voices within. As they entered the hot, roaring space, each of them was handed a stamped tin plate with dividers, and they walked with these past a steam table. Into one section of the dish were piled lima beans, and next to those, kidney beans. These were soon joined by a moldy slice of bread, on top of which sat two slices of grayish salami. Each adult was handed a cup of yellow coffee, and Billy received a cup of milk.

The sullen workers made some perfunctory comments to them, none of which was audible above the drone of voices and the clashing of silverware against the metal plates.

As soon as they found a place at a wooden bench, Billy gulped down his milk.

"It tastes funny," he squeaked at the top of his voice, but he said he wanted more.

Mitsuko tried to break into the line for another cup of milk, but she was told there would be no seconds.

Billy thrust out his lower lip when he heard the news, and he refused to touch the food on his plate. Mitsuko found the beans the only thing vaguely edible, and while she hated to waste food, there was nothing she could do but scrape the remainder into a garbage barrel on the way out. They had to wash and store their own tin plates and cups.

Mrs. Sano sent her son Frank over to accompany them to the straw pile. Frank was a clear-eyed young man, tall and well-built as so many of the Niseis were, as if the bent bodies of their prematurely aged parents had absorbed all the hardships they had encountered emigrating to America, passing none on to the children. Frank did have one feature he had inherited from his mother, though: her strong aquiline nose.

The main beneficiary of Frank's strength was Billy. While Mitsuko and Yoshiko stuffed mattress cases, Frank tossed him over and over again into the huge, prickly mountain and he rolled down to the bottom, squealing in delight.

At five o'clock the truck arrived with their suitcases and seabags. Frank helped them unload. Mitsuko wanted to wash before changing into clean clothes, but the showers were still not working, so they made do with the dribble from one spigot.

Dinner was a huge chunk of salted liver, its opaque brownness overlain with a distinctly blue tinge. Mitsuko poked at it; its elastic consistency suggested that it might well bounce, but the stomach's digestive juices would have no effect upon it. There was rice this time—one small ice cream scoop full, and it tasted gritty, as though it had been boiled in muddy water. This and the single canned peach half provided for dessert were all that she, Yoshiko and Billy could eat. Billy had another skimpy cup of the funny-tasting milk.

Several times during the meal, a fat man with long sideburns clanged a large triangle and announced to the assembled throng of perhaps a thousand people that the showers in Area D would not be working tonight. All "residents" were asked to forego a shower. Those who absolutely needed to wash would be escorted to Area A in small groups under armed guard.

After what she and Billy had been through, Mitsuko was determined to get clean, and they reported to the Area D gate carrying towels and a change of clothes. Yoshiko preferred to wait until tomorrow.

The guards lined them up, military style, and marched them through the gate, across the street, and into Area A. Just as they had had to line up for the spigot and for the mess hall, they stood in line now again, waiting for a shower.

Mitsuko had seen the interior of the Area D shower, but the sight of such a facility in actual operation was another matter. As they waited at the door for their turn, Billy pressed up against her, giggling, and yanked on her sleeve. She bent down to hear him whisper, "I can see those ladies' *things*!"

Mitsuko was not sure precisely which "things" he meant, but she decided not to pursue the matter, and when her turn came, she had no choice but to strip down like the rest of them. She could not help wondering if there were male eyes affixed to the other sides of the knot holes in the walls.

"Mommy, let's not take a shower. Let's take a bath," Billy grumbled when she undressed him and led him to a free shower head. As soon as the water splashed into his face, he began to cry. The temperature of the shower water alternated crazily between scalding hot and freezing cold. Mitsuko hurried to end the ordeal as quickly as possible.

Hanging on hooks in the shower room, their fresh clothes came out soggy, but they were still an improvement over the musky garments they had shed. A soft cotton yukata at the end of the day was always a source of comfort. There was no way to prevent their feet from being flecked with mud on the way back, but even here, surrounded by soldiers and bayonets in the darkness of a chilly night, cleanliness felt good.

"The horse smell seems to be weakening," said Yoshiko when Mitsuko and Billy walked into the stable to find her huddled on her cot.

"Don't be ridiculous, it's worse than ever," growled Mitsuko.

"Yuck," said Billy, holding his nose.

"Maybe we shouldn't have taken showers after all," said Mitsuko.

By then it was ten o'clock: curfew time, and Mitsuko was only too happy to extinguish their now-functioning light bulb and put an end to this terrible day, though she shuddered to think what kind of dreams she might have, falling asleep with such a stink in her nostrils.

She tucked Billy in and crawled under her quilt, but soon Billy was whimpering and she let him join her on her lumpy straw mattress. The endless moan of nearby voices at last dissolved into silence. Mitsuko was grateful for Billy's added warmth and was beginning to drift off when he said he had to go to the toilet. She dragged herself out of bed, put Billy's shoes on his feet and his jacket over his pajamas. Throwing on her coat, she crept out into the faintly starlit night.

Before they had groped their way past two rows of stables, she saw a few flashlight beams moving through the darkness. Several doors opened, spilling streams of light onto the ground. The number of people moving toward the outhouses was growing, and the silence of the night became filled with voices and slamming doors.

"Hey!" a voice boomed out into the night from on high. "What's going on down there?" and a blinding glare tore through the darkness from the guard tower.

"Get back to your apartments, all of you!" the voice boomed, but instead of turning back, the people around her broke into a run. There was a clatter of metal in the tower, and Mitsuko looked up to see a soldier in combat helmet pivoting a machine gun in the direction of the latrines.

"Don't shoot! We're just going to the toilet."

The huge searchlight swung toward her now, and she held up her hands to block the glare. Billy screamed and grabbed her leg.

"All right," shouted the guard. "Make it fast!"

Mitsuko ran ahead as quickly as she could with Billy, who was wailing. As they stood in line, waiting, Billy said through his tears, "I don't like this place, Mommy. Let's go back to America."

The next morning at breakfast, Mitsuko heard that half the camp had been stricken with food poisoning in the night. Perhaps it had been the blue liver.

———

Mrs. Sano helped Mitsuko and Yoshiko with the rigors of camp life, although it was also Mrs. Sano—along with her husband—who made sleep nearly impossible with their symphonic snoring. The four-foot gap between the top of the partition and the ceiling let in every guttural note. Usually, they would alternate, but sometimes they would breathe in perfect unison, arriving at simultaneous crescendos that could shame the Seattle Symphony for sheer power. Lying awake, the sisters went from frustration to anger to uncontrollable laughter when Mitsuko suggested that Frank could not possibly be sleeping through the racket: he must be standing over his parents, baton in hand, conducting.

———

A week after the move to Puyallup, a messenger arrived from the administration building with a telegram for Yoshiko. It was from the Justice Department detention camp in Montana where her husband was being held. Yoshiko said she was afraid to open it.

"I can't, Mitsuko. What if Goro's dead?"

"Don't be foolish," Mitsuko said, snatching the envelope from her sister, but she could not keep her hands from trembling as she tore it open. The telegram said that Goro Nomura was being released on parole and would be joining his wife in Puyallup tomorrow.

"On parole?" asked Mitsuko. "Isn't that what they do with prisoners?"

"Yes, but so what? He's coming here!"

The messenger came to their room again the next day to announce that Goro had arrived and was now in the administration building. Yoshiko ran out to the Area D gate, but the guards would not let her pass until the messenger caught up with her and escorted her through. Mitsuko tried to follow with Billy, but they were held back. They stayed there waiting for nearly half an hour until Yoshiko returned with a gaunt man in shirt sleeves whose appearance frightened Billy and whom even Mitsuko felt she would not have recognized had they passed on the street.

Goro reported that he had been treated well in the detention camp but that the combination of tedium and bad food had caused him to lose nearly thirty pounds. Distinctly overweight before, he was now almost painful to look at, the waistband of his pants rippling with excess cloth and the end of his belt dangling down.

Goro told the story of his removal to Missoula on an ancient train with hard wooden seats, the cars from Seattle being added to a train that had started its journey in Los Angeles and moved up the coast, growing with its load of "dangerous" enemy aliens, the oldest of whom was eighty-four. They had been forced to keep the blinds drawn and were under constant armed guard. Once they got to Missoula, they were placed in Army-style barracks, thirty to a room, in two rows of cots, and given all sorts of demeaning tasks to do, from cleaning out the latrines to waiting on tables.

With each revelation, Mrs. Sano would pipe up from next door, "*Maa, taihen datta deshoh*—oh, how terrible!" until Mitsuko finally brought her around and introduced her to Goro. After a while, Yoshiko's fidgeting made it clear that Mitsuko should escort the garrulous old woman elsewhere, and it occurred to Mitsuko that she had best vacate the premises herself. Fortunately, Mr. Sano and Frank were out as usual, which made it a relatively easy matter for her to drag Mrs. Sano and Billy off on a hunt for lumber scraps with which furniture could be fashioned for the new inmate.

As the weeks wore on, Mitsuko became increasingly uncomfortable living in such close quarters with a married couple, even if they were her middle-aged sister and brother-in-law. She spent virtually all her time with Billy, carving new wooden toys for him, watching him romp in the mud with other children his age, nursing him through measles and chicken pox when those epidemics tore through the camp, sewing an Uncle Sam costume for him to wear in the July Fourth kiddies' costume parade, and going through the predictable round of meals, showers, trips to the outhouse, and bedtime reading and singing.

At bedtime, Billy would sing the lullaby he learned from Mitsuko: "*Odoma Bon-giri Bon-giri, Bon kara sakya orando ...*," his pronunciation and his feeling for the melody as pure as any Japanese child's, although the words were only pleasant sounds devoid of meaning for him. His favorite book was *The Wonderful Adventures of Nils*. Once, when they were strolling by the camp fence, Billy said, "I wish I had a goose to ride on like Nils."

"Would you fly away without me?" Mitsuko asked.

"I mean a great big goose for both of us."

The predictability of life in the camp made time almost irrelevant, and Mitsuko felt a strange joy in relinquishing her soul entirely to her little blond son. Although she knew that Tom could end their idyll whenever he wished, she immersed herself in the present moment with Billy, a seemingly endless succession of present moments that had the feel of eternity. The ever-present hum of voices in the camp contributed to this sense of immersion in something endless.

An occasional companion on excursions with Billy around the compound was Frank Sano, who could thrill the little boy by hoisting him high on his strong shoulders. Like other Nisei, Frank was a dutiful son, and Mitsuko had never heard a harsh word between him and his parents, but he obviously enjoyed both his time away from the old people and the physical games he played with Billy. He missed his daily workouts with the university swim team, he told Mitsuko. As he tossed the gleeful Billy high in the air, he talked in a free, excited way that she had never heard across the partition.

Only one recurring event seemed to be a reminder to Mitsuko of the passage of time: the strain of Sunday mornings, when Yoshiko invariably attempted to lure her back to worship services. The Reverend Hanamori had been allotted part of a shed in Area A for church activities, and each Sunday morning the members of the congregation who had been assigned to Area D would line up with their passes, be counted by the guards, cross the street, be counted again inside the next gate to make sure that no one had escaped during the thirty-foot expedition, then proceed on their own to the makeshift church.

Mitsuko refused to be a part of this or of anything connected with the church. She had been enormously relieved the first Sunday in camp to learn that the religious activities would be held in Area A, where the old reverend was staying. Then, on a Wednesday in mid-July, a message arrived from the reverend asking her to come see him. She liked Reverend Hanamori and had no desire to offend him personally, but if he tried to persuade her to resume her ties with the church, she fully intended to reveal to him the extent of her disillusionment. She left Billy with his big friend Frank and followed the messenger through the gates.

Only when she saw the reverend's benign smile did Mitsuko realize that she had been walking with her hands balled into fists, and she felt the tension go out of her. No, this was not a man who sought to impose his beliefs on others. He welcomed her with the simple joy of his own convictions, and she read in his eyes the grief of having lost her as a beloved child.

"I wanted to tell you about Pastor Tom," he said, taking her hand, "before you heard it from others."

A thrill went through her, followed by a pang of horror at her own readiness to believe that she was about to receive news of Tom's death. The reverend's words could have meant almost anything. Did she want Billy for herself so desperately that she was willing to bring down death on the man who had fathered him?

"You know, of course," continued Reverend Hanamori, "that he used his contacts with the white churches after Pearl Harbor to obtain a new position. Well, now I hear that he has told his new congregation that he is a widower. He tells people that his wife's name was Sarah—"

"Which it was, as if he never had another wife!"

"—and that his son is now staying with his sister in Kansas."

"Such arrogance! He is so confident his precious white congregation would never have contact with 'Japs.' To think I believed in him."

"We all did." He looked at her tenderly, as if he wished he could bear her burden himself. "Perhaps I shouldn't tell you this," he added. "It's really just a rumor ..."

"But ... ?"

"He seems to be involved with a woman—a married woman. The wife of another clergyman."

Mitsuko hung her head. Her face was burning. Never in her life had she felt so ashamed. How blind she had been.

"Thank you, Reverend," she said, unable to look at him. "I know this has been difficult for you."

"If there is anything I can do ..."

"No," she said, raising her eyes at last. "I am too much in your debt already. There is nothing anyone can do."

She turned and left the shed, knowing it was the last time she would ever cross the threshold of any church.

"Mommy! Mommy!"

Followed closely by Frank, Billy came running to her as she neared the stable. "I can do somersaults!"

"No!" she and Frank cried as Billy was about to put his head down on the soggy earth.

Mitsuko was the first to reach him, snatching him up almost ferociously and hugging him to her. The harder Billy struggled to break free, the more tightly she held him. Hot tears streamed down her face. Frank stood rooted to the ground, his eyes locked on Mitsuko's.

———

From that day on, whenever Yoshiko would gush about the lucky Baptists visited each week by their Pastor Andrews, Mitsuko would feel all the more disgusted with Tom and with the Christian religion as an illusory castle built on a foundation of empty words. If a man like Tom could spout those words—and apparently believe them himself while he did so—then anyone could spout them, and they amounted to nothing. As long as she was able, she intended to protect Billy from such lies.

She found an ally in Frank, who refused to accompany his parents to Buddhist services. They had always been members of the Seattle Buddhist Church on Main Street, only a few blocks—but several worlds—away from the Japanese Christian Church. Frank had lost all religious belief at the university, he said—"in the twinkling of an eye, as soon as I started to think about such things."

Mitsuko, however, was not entirely lacking a sense of reverence; in fact it deepened with each day she was allowed to spend with Billy. Who or what it was that "allowed" her this privilege, she did not know, but almost instinctively, she found herself turning to the sun each morning and evening as it came and went. Puyallup, with its low huts huddled against the mire, provided a greater sense of nearness to the fiery lord of the heavens. In the morning, before the hum of voices began for the day, she would slip out of the stable as the sun came up in the east, and she would bow her head to it wordlessly, offering it only the clean slap of her palms.

Billy would be with her in the evenings, and she loved it when he would stand beside her, sharing in this moment of humility as the day came to an end. For these little ceremonies with him, she felt, words were entirely appropriate, and she taught him to say, "*Kyoh mo ichinichi arigatoh*—I give thanks for yet another day." Never did he ask who it was they were thanking. Had he asked her, she might have told him it was the sun. Yet it was not the sun, not exactly. It was the day, it was the wonder of being, it was the two of them standing here together beneath the sky's red glow. The very fact that he did not ask her about it seemed to confirm her conviction that he knew exactly what it meant and that he would cherish the truth of these moments in his heart forever.

20

"HOW CAN BILLY SLEEP with the wind howling like this?"

Mitsuko could barely hear Yoshiko above the roar. She looked down at the sand-flecked handkerchief covering Billy's face. Nearly twenty-four hours since their jubilant departure from Camp Harmony, the smiles and the exclamations of "freedom" were gone, having been replaced by the air of grim endurance that had become so familiar after three months in Puyallup. At least the Army promised there would be no more barbed wire.

The guards let them keep the shades open during the daylight part of the trip from Washington to Idaho, but the sandstorm had darkened the world outside the train. Inside, the people and bundles and wooden seats were coated with a fine, silty powder.

The train continued to creep through the storm until it pulled into Shoshone, where they were herded onto buses for the last fifty miles to Minidoka. In the short dash between train and bus, Mitsuko felt her eyes burning, and her mouth seemed to be filling up with gritty grains of the streaming sand. The wind stripped the handkerchief from Billy's face, but still he did not wake.

Buffeted by the abrasive gusts, the buses crawled through the yellow-gray cloud.

"They couldn't drown us in the mud," Goro said. "Now they're trying to strip our skin off. Even Missoula was better than this."

The bus droned on through the storm for two hours or more. Then, suddenly, almost mysteriously, the wind let up and the air emptied itself out. The bus shuddered and groaned and began to pick up speed.

The sight of the desert reminded Mitsuko of a slice of moldy bread half-buried in balls of dust she had found long ago the first time she cleaned under Billy's crib. The wrinkled, gray land stretched off into the distance. Rolling through the sunbaked desert, the bus grew unbearably hot, and windows which before could not be shut tightly enough, now could not be opened wide enough. The wind tore inside in pursuit of moisture.

A commotion started among the people at the front of the bus; something had been sighted up ahead. Mitsuko leaned from her window and saw low, dark buildings, a tall brick smokestack, and a water tank glinting in the sun. As they drew closer, she could make out tar-paper-covered sheds like the ones at Puyallup. Sighs and groans filled the bus as it passed through a barbed wire fence that seemed to stretch for miles on either side.

"At least they don't have any guard towers here," a young man's voice piped up, but half-hearted grunts were the only response.

When the bus stopped, she lifted Billy. There was a large sweat stain where he was nestled against her. Moving to the front of the bus, she recalled her muddy arrival at Puyallup. Before she stepped off the bus, she checked the condition of the ground. It looked dry, but her foot sank into the soft sand, and she lost her balance. Billy slipped from her hands, and she cried out as she fell. Coming down on all fours, she saw Billy land squarely on his own two feet. The boy looked around, blinked for a moment, and then he laughed at Mitsuko on the ground.

"Mommy's crawling!" he said, as if he had just happened by there while Mitsuko played in the sand.

Goro helped her to her feet, and with Yoshiko they followed the line of disembarking passengers. The August sun beat down on them as they waited in line to register. All exposed skin seemed to be sizzling under its rays. Mitsuko heard a buzzing inside her skull until, at last, they crept in under the roof of the registration shed.

A pudgy, young Nisei man took their names and asked what seemed like a thousand questions. Mitsuko didn't mind. In fact, the more the better—anything that would delay their going back out into that sun! Finally, the young man handed Goro an instruction sheet and a sketch map of the compound. He said they would have to find their own way to Block 39, Barrack 10, where they were to live in Apartment E.

"Look at the size of this place!" Goro said as they stepped out of the administration building onto the broad, flat stretch of glaring yellow sand. Inspecting the map, he said, "Let's see, we're here, in the middle of the camp, and Block 39 is way down here." He showed them on the map how the road ran eastward and then turned sharply south. Their block would be nearly at the bottom of the road, on the east side—a long walk without shelter from the burning sun.

The camp was built in the shape of a large crescent following the bend of an irrigation canal. As they kicked up little dust clouds with every step, Goro pointed toward the canal far off to the right. "Listen!" he said, "You can hear the water flowing."

In addition to the continuous low rush of water, there was the familiar sound of human voices. Again they would be living with that constant background murmur.

"Those are pretty houses over there," said Yoshiko, squinting in the sun. She gestured toward a handful of new-looking bungalows painted green and blue and yellow. "Maybe all the buildings here will look like that when they're finished."

"I'm sure they will," said Goro encouragingly. But then he consulted his map again and said, "I'm afraid not. That's staff housing. No 'Japs' in there."

Cloth bundles and suitcases dangling from their hands, they continued eastward down the dusty road. The afternoon sun was lower in the sky, and it had begun to cool a little.

"Well, well," Goro remarked as they passed a large excavation on the right just before the first block of barracks. "This is going to be an amphitheater."

"Maybe it won't be so bad here after all," said Yoshiko, but no one answered her.

They passed row after row of indistinguishable tar-papered barracks arranged in blocks separated by a thirty-foot-wide bulldozer scrape. Each block was composed of two rows of six barracks, between which stood two much larger buildings. Goro told them the rectangular building at the center of each block was the block's mess hall, and the H-shaped building behind it housed the laundry and latrine facilities. At the side of each block were "recreation halls." Goro said, "We can spend the war playing ping pong."

After they had passed four blocks, the road curved to the right. The building on the left side of the curve was labeled "Fire Station." On the right was an open field dotted with clumps of dusty grass. They followed the road past five more blocks on the right-hand side and a few others on the left interrupted by open spaces, coming at last to Block 39 on the left. Barracks 1 through 11 faced the road. Their apartment was in a barrack next to the latrines.

"At least it doesn't actually face the toilets," remarked Yoshiko hopefully as they traversed the hundred-foot length of their barrack searching for Apartment E.

Mitsuko said to Billy, "Can you find E for us?"

Billy scampered on ahead, squeaking "A ...B ...C ... D ...E!"

"E" was near the center of the long building. Goro motioned Billy inside, but he seemed hesitant to go in alone. All of them hesitated when they came together in front of the crude plank door.

"I don't know, I'm afraid," Yoshiko said. "This is where we're going to live for—who knows how long? They might keep us here forever."

"Don't be silly," said Goro. "Puyallup was an 'assembly center,' but this is a 'relocation camp.'"

"Don't tell me you believe the government is going to 'relocate' us somewhere nicer. Maybe if we were Nisei, but not dangerous enemy aliens like us," Mitsuko said. She reached out and gave the door a shove. It creaked open, and the four of them took a step forward to the threshold.

Another empty wooden box. It was larger than the Puyallup box— perhaps twenty feet deep and a little less from side to side. There were no inner walls, just bare two-by-four studs showing the green lumber of the siding and, through cracks and knotholes, the outside tar paper tacked to that. The wood was new at least, but the floor was covered by lines of fine sand which had obviously seeped in from cracks in the ceiling during the storm. Little mounds of the stuff had piled up in corners and under the window sill. The only furniture inside were four army cots and an iron potbelly stove.

"There's a window!" Yoshiko exclaimed.

Mitsuko said, "Compared with our old stable, this is almost luxurious. What do you think, Billy?"

"It smells good," he said, twitching his nose.

"Listen to this," Goro said, reading from the instruction sheet he had received with the map. "'Residents are advised not to nail up shelves until construction personnel arrive to install plasterboard walls.' Plasterboard! I had almost forgotten that such luxuries exist! 'Scrap lumber will be available for residents who wish to make furniture, and a committee has been organized to supervise its distribution. Approximately 400,000 board feet of lumber is now available. Hence, there will be no necessity for hoarding or pilfering.' I'm going to turn this place into a decorator's dream!"

The sisters smiled at each other. This was the first sign of life that Goro had shown since his release from Missoula.

"There's more," he continued. "'You are now in Minidoka, Idaho. Here we say Dining Hall and not Mess Hall; Safety Council, not Internal Police; Residents, not Evacuees; and last but not least, Mental Climate, not Morale."

"Wonderful," groaned Mitsuko. "Why don't they just call the place 'Miami, Florida'?"

"It's true," Goro said. "Ever since Pearl Harbor, they have been doing strange things with words. They call us 'aliens,' which we are, but the poor Nisei they call 'non-aliens.' I was always disappointed I could not become an American citizen, but when I heard that strange phrase, I was not so sure. I would rather be a Japanese than a non-alien."

"Goro!" exclaimed his wife, "Don't let anyone hear you saying such things!"

"Don't worry," he answered. "Here, the walls go all the way up to the ceiling."

"No more Sano snoring concerts!"

Billy perked up at that. "I want to play with Frank!" he demanded. Mitsuko promised him they would look for Frank as soon as they had settled in.

21

SOON AFTER THE SUN rose each morning, the chilly night changed into raging hot day. No one in the camp wanted to do anything more strenuous during daylight hours than lie on a cot and sweat while waiting for the next meal to be served. The background babble of voices all but disappeared when the sun was at its strongest. Only after the sun set below Minidoka's flat sand table did the camp begin to stir.

Mitsuko would spend a few hours each evening making toys for Billy from lumber scraps. He had a sizeable collection of cars and trucks, some of which he gave away to the other boys in Block 39. One evening Mitsuko was gluing a wheel onto an axle as Billy watched, Yoshiko worked on her crocheting, and Goro dozed. There was a knock on the door and a grizzled, old man poked his shiny bald head in. Goro slowly sat up on his cot.

"My name is Abé," the old man said with the old-fashioned politeness of the Isseis. "I live in Apartment C just two doors down."

"Hello, Mr. Abé," Yoshiko said, getting up and bowing. "I see your wife in the laundry room. She's the strongest woman in the block."

He chuckled and bowed his head, his rubbery lips opening in a broad, toothless smile.

Mitsuko invited him in and offered him green tea.

"No, thank you very much," he said. "I merely dropped by to say how much I admire the toys you make. You have a real knack for wood carving. Some friends and I do ornamental carving, so I recognize skilled work."

"There's so much scrap lumber," Mitsuko noted, "it's a wonder more people don't take up the hobby."

"We don't use that cheap wood," Mr. Abé sniffed. "It's much too soft. The best wood around here is bitterbrush. It grows out in the desert. It's good and hard and it takes a nice oil finish."

"I'd love to see your work sometime," she said.

"How about right now?" the old gentleman offered.

"I'd be delighted."

Leaving Billy with Yoshiko and Goro, Mitsuko went with Mr. Abé. She was amazed to find out how much he had done in a few short weeks to decorate the cubicle he shared with his wife and daughters. He showed her a wonderfully convoluted pedestal for a flower vase, some bookends and a lamp. There were also combs and mirror housings and brooches among his creations.

"These are beautiful, Mr. Abé. Where did you ever learn to do such lovely work?"

His rubber lips sagged open again. He was utterly unashamed of his toothless gums. "You gotta do something on a farm in winter," he declared.

Mr. Abé gave Mitsuko a chisel and two razor knives that he said were spares. He encouraged her to do more challenging work than the sturdy toys she had been turning out for Billy. He also sent her home with a heavy armload of wood he had collected.

"What is that?!" Yoshiko asked when Mitsuko pushed her way in through their front door carrying the gnarled, dusty-looking pieces.

Billy spent many evening hours watching Mitsuko create shapes out of the twisted chunks of desert growth. She tried her hand at delicate designs in relief and even little figurines. Billy especially liked the horse she made for him.

"Here's a nice, fat piece of wood," she said. "How about an elephant or a hippopotamus?"

"What's a hippapomus?" he asked.

Mitsuko realized with a pang that she had never taken him to the zoo— or much of anywhere other than the church.

Billy said, "Make a goose, Mommy. Just like Nils' goose. We can ride away in the sky."

Even Billy knew that their broad new surroundings made them no freer than they had been at Puyallup. "I'll try, Billy, but I'll have to get Mr. Abé to help me with the wings."

From August into September, the main topic of conversation—when anyone had the strength for conversation—was the temperature: how many degrees over 100 was it today? The second most important topic was the wind velocity: how many miles per hour had the sand been tearing at their thin shelters? They also talked about the fleas, and the rattlesnakes lurking in the shadows of the barracks.

By the middle of September, summer was on its way out, and a few residents began to publish a camp newspaper, the *Irrigator*, which provided more dependable weather reports than word of mouth. Mitsuko already knew that conditions were becoming less oppressive as the constant background chatter penetrating the barrack's thin walls grew louder with people up and doing things.

The *Irrigator* called for volunteers to participate in the increasingly complex organization of camp life. Workers were needed in the co-operative store, the accounting office, the fire brigade, the hospital, the kitchens, the Relocation Bureau, the Internal Security Patrol, the Fair Labor Board, and the Japanese language section of the *Irrigator* itself. At one point, the labor shortage grew so acute that the fire brigade accepted nine women volunteers.

The more she read of this burgeoning social structure, the more Mitsuko came to identify the hum of voices with definable activity and to wish that she could be a part of it in some way. Goro finally roused himself from his lethargy and joined the Internal Security Patrol, while Yoshiko kept busy with the United Protestant Church. Mitsuko wanted to do something useful, but she also wanted to continue spending as much time as she could with Billy.

And so when she heard that schools would be opening on October 19, she felt anxious about being apart from Billy but looked forward to contributing to camp life. Five hundred children living in Blocks 21 through 44 would be attending "Stafford Elementary School," named in honor of the kindly camp director Harry L. Stafford. At least the school would be close by, in Block 32, at the curve in the road.

Billy, too, seemed apprehensive about the opening of school. He wanted to go there with his friends from the Block, he said, but there were other children in camp, some of the older ones, who made fun of his blond hair and called him names. "Can Frank go to school with me?" he asked. The Sanos lived in Block 40, just across the road.

Mitsuko laughed and hugged Billy. "Frank is *much* too big to go to school. Don't worry. The teachers will take care of you just as well as Frank did."

But Billy stayed quiet and gripped her hand as they walked through the dust to Block 32 that first Monday morning, increasing her own apprehensions. To the mass of children and parents assembled outside the school barrack, a cheerful-looking woman introduced herself as the principal, Mildred Bennett. She told them of the accomplishments she hoped for in the coming school year, and announced that parents of kindergartners and first graders could accompany their children to their assigned classrooms. Billy turned his frightened blue eyes up to Mitsuko as the crowd began to stir, and she hugged him encouragingly.

In the classroom, just another bare room in the barracks, were rows of little desks and chairs. The school furniture was badly worn and covered with carved initials—discards from a nearby school district. An American flag hung at the front of the room and patriotic posters had been tacked to the walls between studs: "Don't Waste: It Pleases the Enemy," "Young and Old Can Save," "Save All You Can," "Carelessness Aids the Enemy." Mitsuko wondered if the teacher, Miss Pollock, a petite, sandy-haired woman, was nervous about confronting a roomful of little enemies. And she worried how Billy would fare if he became the white teacher's pet. Mitsuko stood at the back of the classroom, sending hopeful glances to Billy as long as she could, but when Miss Pollock signaled the parents to withdraw, she walked outside.

Standing at the curve in the road, Mitsuko hesitated. She could spend the day in their room waiting for Billy, or she could plunge into some camp activity. For one, the *Irrigator*'s Japanese page had enough grammatical slips to suggest that it could use the help of someone who had not been living outside of Japan for forty years. Then she noticed the brick smoke stack of the hospital towering over the far western end of the camp. There she could bring comfort to the sick Isseis who had been cruelly snatched away from a lifetime of work in this country.

She worried that the hospital was far away from Billy, while the newspaper office was in Block 23, just a few hundred yards beyond the school. Frank Sano was working there with some of the other college-educated Niseis. She walked over to the office.

Frank himself stood to greet her. He introduced her, and the rest of the newspaper staff welcomed her enthusiastically. She started that day.

Each morning, Mitsuko walked with Frank and Billy as far as the school, then continued on with Frank to the *Irrigator* editorial offices. Her duties were to translate articles into Japanese and inscribe them onto mimeograph masters. Much of what she translated had to do with the weather. Minidoka went directly from scorching summer to freezing winter. On November 15, Mitsuko described the gale that snatched off the garage shed and carried it fifty feet. "The camp," she wrote, "seems to be at the center of a never-ending blizzard."

On the evening of December 1, Mitsuko, Yoshiko, Goro and Billy were huddled around the pot-bellied stove, faces bright red with the heat while the cold stabbed them from behind. Suddenly the door opened and there came the familiar old-country greeting, "*Gomen kudasai*"—"May I please come in?" After thirty years in this country, Mrs. Abé could not bring herself to do anything so American as to knock on a door. She was a wiry little woman with stark white hair and a sharp chin. Always a bundle of nervous energy, she seemed especially on edge tonight.

"I'm sorry," she said. "I thought my husband might be here. He's not with any of the usual bunch—the old geezers he carves wood with."

Mitsuko smiled at the term she used for her husband and his friends. "I haven't seen him for days."

"He was going to go hunt for wood, but no one's seen him all day."

"You mean they let him outside?" Goro asked, wide-eyed.

"He told me they would. The weather wasn't so bad this morning, but now ..."

Goro left with the old woman to check with the Internal Security Patrol. He came back shivering an hour later, after Billy had been tucked in bed and the fire in the stove had died down.

"Nobody knows a thing. I think he's out there somewhere," he said, waving toward the chilly blackness. "His wife acts tough, but she's worried sick."

Mitsuko spent the next day bundled up and running back and forth from the *Irrigator* office to the Abé apartment to the security headquarters and the hospital and back again. She did not want to believe what seemed undeniably true. A truckload of guards was sent out into the snow fields, but they returned at twilight having seen no one.

The truck pulled out again early the next morning. Mitsuko was working on a new masthead for the Japanese page of the *Irrigator*, trying not to think about Mr. Abé, when Goro burst into the office.

"They found him! It's horrible!"

"No!" Mitsuko shrieked. "He can't be dead."

"They took his body to the morgue. Frozen stiff. I've never seen anything like it. All curled up like a baby ..."

Mitsuko grabbed her coat and dashed out into the burning cold air. She could hear Goro padding in the snow far behind her, calling her name, but she could not wait for him. The wind tore at her face as she ran half the length of the camp to the hospital area. She was turned away at the door of the morgue. "Mrs. Abé's with the body," a sandy-haired young woman in a striped pinafore told her. "She just sits there, not making a sound."

Mrs. Abé maintained her silence when they buried her husband in the desert that had killed him. A wailing teenaged daughter on either arm, she stared straight ahead, hardly blinking. It had taken two days for the workmen to dig the hole in the frozen ground.

Mitsuko could not rid herself of the feeling that she had been at least partially responsible for Mr. Abé's death by helping to deplete his supply of bitterbrush. It only made her feel worse to hear from Yoshiko that Mrs. Abé, once such a flinty old bird, seemed suddenly to have shriveled up. A week after her husband's burial, she was admitted to the hospital.

Finally, though, Mitsuko knew, the blame for such a terrible death would not rest with her. Nor was it the fault of the camp administration, which had been trying to allow the old man to enjoy his favorite pastime when it gave him permission to hunt for wood. The blame lay with far larger forces that had dragged them all out here to the desert against their will.

The approach of the Christmas season brought this home to her through an argument that erupted among the *Irrigator* staff. The problem started when Editor-in-Chief Kenny Kawachi asked Frank Sano to write a "Letter from Santa" for the children of the camp.

"Boy, you couldn't have picked a worse candidate!" Frank protested. "First of all, I was raised Buddhist. And second of all, I don't even believe in *that* crap anymore, let alone Santa Claus."

"Hell, Frank, nobody past the age of five believes in Santa Claus," said Kawachi, his slender hand slashing the air. "It's just a seasonal thing we ought to have in the paper."

"Yeah, calm down, Frankie boy," said the paper's portly cartoonist, Jerry Yamaguchi.

"But don't you see what you're doing?" retorted Frank. "Mindlessly preserving a tradition of mindlessness that accomplishes only one thing—keeps people in their place."

"Here we go again!" groaned Yamaguchi, rolling his eyes. "The camp philosopher."

"This camp damn well needs a philosopher. It needs somebody to think about why we're spending the winter in this desert out in the middle of hell somewhere. If it weren't for Santa Claus, we probably wouldn't even be here!"

Yamaguchi threw his head back and let out a howl. "Whoo-ie! Let's hear this one!"

"Just think about it," continued Frank. "Kenny, you yourself said not even kids believe in Santa Claus."

Kawachi nodded.

"Then what the hell is Santa Claus for? He's a decoy, that's what. He's been set up for children to learn to *dis*-believe in, to deflect any doubts they might have away from the grown-ups' God. The grown-ups set up this decoy, this straw man, this obviously unbelievable father figure to contrast with the 'real' God-father. Compared with Santa Claus, God seems as real and tangible as this desk." He pounded the desk top with his fist.

Mitsuko was enjoying Frank's passion.

"Just think about it," Frank went on. "Santa Claus is an ingenious invention. People encourage their children to believe in him wholeheartedly when they're little so that, when they learn the truth, they can feel proud of graduating to belief in the 'real' God, the adults' God. But of course, God is just as make-believe as Santa Claus."

"Now, wait a minute," protested Jerry Yamaguchi, who was not smiling anymore. "Now you're going too damn far."

"See what I mean?" cried Frank. "I'm in taboo territory now. You don't want to graduate from your 'real' God. And President Roosevelt doesn't want you to either. He wants you to be good. To behave yourself. To do what the 'real' grownups like him and General DeWitt tell you to do. They want you to leave your homes and belongings behind? Fine! They want you to waste your life away in the desert with blizzards blowing all around you? Fine! You're a good, well-behaved little Jap! And why? Because 'He's makin' a list, checkin' it twice, gonna find out who's naughty or nice. Santa Claus is coming to town!'"

"Man!" shouted Kenny Kawachi. "I have never heard such a total crock of—"

"Hey," interjected May Eto, a petite young woman who did most of the paper's typing. "Don't forget there are ladies present."

May smiled at Mitsuko, who nodded back to her in halfhearted affirmation. But Frank's bombast had struck a chord with her.

Frank had another opportunity to sound off three days later when the *Irrigator* received the results of the most recent Gallup Poll on attitudes in the five westernmost states toward the evacuated Japanese. Asked, "Do you think that the Japanese who were moved from the Pacific Coast should be allowed to return after the war is over?", only twenty-nine percent said they were willing to see all Japanese return to their homes. Twenty-four percent said they would allow only American citizens, and thirty-one percent thought that none should be allowed to return, with sixteen percent undecided. Those opposed to allowing the Japanese to return were asked, "What should be done with them?", to which more than two-thirds responded that they should be sent "back" to Japan, while the rest thought they should be kept in the inland areas where they were now interned. Altogether, ninety-seven percent agreed that the Army had done the right thing in evacuating the Japanese, while only two percent disapproved and one percent were undecided.

"God-damned racists!" bellowed Frank when the piece was read aloud to the gathered staff. "Do they think we're animals to be put in cages? Let them try to lock me up in this place after the war is over and they'll have a rebellion on their hands!"

Another blast of wind rattled the flimsy siding that enclosed the editorial office, and, even seated by a burning hot stove, Mitsuko felt a chill go through her at the prospect of spending the rest of her days here in the desert. For her, the thought of returning to a defeated Japan was far preferable to dragging out her existence here—especially if she was destined to lose Billy in any case. But when she looked at the grim faces of the Nisei staff who were trying to digest this overwhelming rejection by their own countrymen, she felt her heart go out to them.

Mitsuko told Goro and Yoshiko about the Gallup Poll report that night after Billy was asleep.

"Ninety-seven percent against us," said Goro. "They really hate us, don't they? Maybe we *should* go back to Japan."

"I hardly remember what Japan looks like," said Yoshiko. "What is left there for us?"

Goro said, "True. I would never really go back. But if they tried to keep us locked up here after the war …"

"They could never do that," declared Yoshiko.

"Not to the Niseis, perhaps," observed Mitsuko, "but what about *us*?"

"Why not the Niseis?" Goro asked. "They were so sure of their constitutional rights as American citizens, and what did it get them?"

Mitsuko said, "I remember once, Yoshiko, you said we didn't have to worry, that they would treat us all alike. I'm afraid you were right. We're all the same to them: Japs. We're all as guilty as the ones who dropped the bombs on Pearl Harbor. It's just as Frank said—racism, pure and simple."

"Young Frank Sano?" Yoshiko asked.

"Yes, you should have heard him sounding off at the *Irrigator* office," Mitsuko said with a laugh. She recalled the fire in his eyes, and she found herself admiring him in many ways.

22

SCHOOL STARTED AGAIN on January 4, and another bone-piercing wind was blowing. Billy announced to Mitsuko that he wanted to walk home alone. She tried to convince him that there would be plenty of time later in the year for him to show what a big boy he was. "Pleeease!" he begged with his cutest smile.

"Really, Mit-chan," argued Yoshiko. "The traffic patrol system is working fine. The other parents are satisfied. Why can't you be?"

"Fifth- and sixth graders? You call that a system? We may have a fence around us, but there are 10,000 people inside this place."

"It's true," Goro said. "You can't tell one tar-paper shack from another, and kids are getting lost all the time."

"Please, Mommy," Billy started in again. She finally gave in, but just before school ended, she left the newspaper office and secretly followed him until she saw him enter their barrack door. When she arrived home an hour later, he leaped into her arms and boasted, "I came home all by myself!"

"Good boy," she said. Still, she kept up the routine for the rest of the week.

The following Monday, Mitsuko watched as the clock moved past school dismissal time. She told herself that Billy would be all right. Besides, this issue of the *Irrigator* had to be out by tomorrow and she had to translate and edit job listings, lost and found items, and George Nakashima's endless commentary on some vaguely defined world spiritual crisis. It was nearly six o'clock before she finished squeezing all the articles onto two mimeograph masters.

"Mitsuko, wait a minute, I'm just finishing up here," Frank called to her as she was putting on her coat. He hurriedly straightened the papers on his desk and followed her out into the cold.

Hard crystals of snow jabbed at her face as she hurried through the darkness. Frank was grumbling about the latest Gallup Poll figures. She paid little attention to his remarks, but it was good to have him to walk with through the dark alleys of this government-built slum. If his words were of little interest to her at the moment, the deep rumble of his voice was comforting. By the time they passed the darkened schoolhouse at the bend in the road, however, she realized that the only sound was of the hard-packed snow crunching beneath their feet.

Frank stopped. "Mitsuko," he said, his voice now strangely thick.

She knew she must not stop.

"Let's hurry, Frank," she said, but her pace slowed.

"Mitsuko," he said again, and this time she stopped and turned to face him. No longer did she feel the piercing cold of the wind. With a few swift strides, he was standing before her. He wrapped his strong arms around her and brought his face to hers. How simple it would be to let him hold her, to let him kiss her. But there was Billy, and there was Frank himself to think about, this young American scarcely out of boyhood. She struggled to avoid his lips, but his hot breath grazed her throat and sent a thrill coursing through her body.

"Frank," she said, "I'm ten years older than you. I'm a married woman."

She wrenched herself away and began to run. For a moment, his footsteps were just behind her, but they stopped, and she was running alone. She looked over her shoulder to see Frank's silhouette under the bare bulb of the street lamp at the bend in the road. She slowed to a walk, her breath coming now in labored gasps, the freezing air cutting deep into her lungs.

Nearing Block 39, she saw that there was no light leaking around the edges of the door to their cubicle. She started to panic and then chided herself for being such a mother hen—everyone was in the dining hall.

She washed off quickly at the lavatory and plunged into the noisy swirl of the large, brightly lighted dining hall. More interested in Billy's whereabouts than food, she bypassed the line and nearly bumped into a waitress holding a steel pitcher of hot tea. The roar of conversation was deafening. She saw Yoshiko at their usual table, and Goro was with her—but not Billy. Yoshiko waved to her, smiling, and formed the words on her lips, "Why so late?"

"Is Billy with you?" Mitsuko asked silently across the black sea of heads.

Yoshiko nudged Goro's shoulder and he turned away from the man with whom he was talking. The two of them left their seats, hurrying to where Mitsuko stood.

"I thought he was with you," Yoshiko said.

"You *know* I let him start walking home alone last week."

"But you were watching him."

"I know, but—"

"Never mind that now," interrupted Goro. "We've got to find him." He forced his way through the crowd to the head of the dining hall and, pounding on the bell, he brought the crowd to silence.

"Billy! Billy Morton! Are you here? Has anyone seen Billy?"

Three of Billy's classmates said they had seen him at school. The silence began to disintegrate, and Mitsuko caught a few sniggering references to "blondie."

Goro asked for help and a few men and women stood and volunteered to join a search. Goro wanted each person to run to as many dining halls as possible, and they would meet back here, in exactly one hour, at 7:30. Yoshiko, he said, should wait in their apartment in case Billy showed up. Goro would go to the security office.

"Will you be all right?" Yoshiko asked her husband anxiously. He was even more emaciated than he had been upon his return from Montana, and he tired easily. He gave her only one brief look of annoyance.

Mitsuko said she would retrace Billy's route home and check all the places she knew he was familiar with. Running toward Block 32, she barely noticed the freezing cold and snow. No one was outside in this weather, and she found the school barrack locked. She pounded on the doors and windows, calling for Billy, but there was no response to her frantic cries.

Suddenly, she heard a woman calling, "Mrs. Morton! Mrs. Morton!" and she ran out to the road. The shadowy figure introduced herself as Mrs. Tonoyama and began apologizing for her son without ever saying what it was he had done. Mitsuko stood listening impatiently until, at last, it became clear that Mrs. Tonoyama's boy and three other fifth graders had been picking on Billy after school today. They had chased him into one of the blocks between school and home and had not seen him since.

"Which block was it?" Mitsuko demanded, but the woman did not know, and she said her son did not remember, but it was probably somewhere between the school and Block 42, where the Tonoyamas lived.

"All right," said Mitsuko. "You start looking in Block 42 and I'll start from here, and we'll meet in the middle."

"But I can't. I have to get back to my children …"

"*Your* children? Your son is the one who started all this! Now, do as I say!"

"What gives you the right to order people around? If you hadn't brought that little white devil in here to begin with—"

Before she knew what she was doing, Mitsuko raised her hand and slapped the woman's face. Mrs. Tonoyama screamed and ran away.

Mitsuko hurried to the middle of the block, where there were laundry rooms and toilets where Billy might have hidden. The smell of the women's latrine was suffocating, and she imagined Billy lying in a dark corner somewhere, overcome by the fumes.

She called out for him at the entrance to the men's latrine, and when there was no answer she dashed inside. There was an old man squatting above a toilet, his feet resting on some kind of homemade boxes he had placed on either side. He grabbed his dangling private parts and shouted at her to "Get the hell out!" but she did so only after making a circuit of the place.

She ran to the recreation hall. Billy was not among the children playing there.

In the next block she repeated her search—laundry room, latrines, recreation hall—with the same results. Just as she was racing across the road to Block 35, she heard Frank calling her name. Her first thought was to avoid him, but he might be helping with the search.

"Here, Frank!" she called, but the huge, cold night swallowed her voice. She called again. A moment later, a dark figure came running toward her down the road, trailing clouds of steaming breath.

"We found him," Frank said, halting at a discreet distance. "He was hiding at my place."

"Is he all right?" she asked.

"He's fine. I left him with your sister."

There was an awkward moment of silence.

"I'm sorry for what happened before," he said. "I promise, nothing like that will happen again. I don't know what got into me."

Mitsuko could only mutter, "Never mind, it's all right."

He saw her as far as the barrack door.

She stepped inside, and Billy ran into her arms. She undressed him by the stove and examined him from head to foot. The worst he had to show for his ordeal was a bruised shin. But he still looked frightened.

Both for Billy, and to prevent any repetition of the incident with Frank, Mitsuko decided to leave her job on the newspaper. The next morning, she told Yoshiko and Goro of her decision.

"You can't," said Yoshiko. "It's the best thing that's happened to you since " She glanced at Billy.

"I know," answered Mitsuko. She had made it clear that she didn't want anyone tearing down Billy's father in his presence. "But I saw this coming. People are turning ugly here, and it's working its way out through the children. I should have known better."

"It is not your fault," Goro said. "Nobody has time for children anymore. The families are being torn apart. Do you know how many juvenile delinquents I have to deal with every day now? When did Japanese children ever misbehave before they locked us up?"

"I am not going to let Billy be a victim. I'll camp outside the school if I have to."

"Be reasonable, Mit-chan," said Yoshiko. "We all need something to do in this place. Goro has his police work, and I am busy with the church. We both have the Sunday school as before. You need something, too. You have been in such good spirits since you started to work. How would it be if I promised absolutely that I will pick Billy up every day after school?"

"That's it," chimed in Goro. "I'll help, too. We'll make up the Billy Morton Security Force."

Mitsuko knew that waiting for Billy all day would drive her mad. Even if she quit the paper because of Frank, she would have to find another job. "All right," she said at length, "I'll have to make sure I don't work late anymore. But I would still like you to come to school, Yoshiko. Both of us will walk him home."

Yoshiko said, "I think you're overdoing it, but I will meet you there."

———

Frank did not come for Mitsuko and Billy in the morning. She guessed that he had gone on ahead to the *Irrigator* office, but Billy kept asking for him and looking around nervously for the "mean boys" as they trudged through the snow. On the way to the office, the sight of the hospital smokestack reminded her of caring for the sick and elderly, but she arrived still not knowing what to do. When she saw that Frank was keeping busy with his work, she began to think that perhaps nothing had to change as long as Billy was safe.

Mitsuko spent the next week trying to sort out her feelings, with little success. She found it frustrating to realize that "sorting" her feelings meant finding a ranking system for the objects of her anger. Who deserved to occupy the head position? Tom? God? White Americans? General Tojo? The emperor? General DeWitt? President Roosevelt? Japanese-American parents who taught their children to hate? And what of her own friends and family in Japan? Did they exult at the news of Pearl Harbor? Were they praying for their sacred Imperial troops to annihilate this country and all the white devils who lived within its borders—or were they being forced to mouth such prayers by the threat of prison and torture?

Toward the end of the week, word came of an opportunity for Mitsuko to find out where she stood. Japanese nationals in camp were being called to meet with an emissary from the Japanese government. She told Yoshiko and Goro that she was planning to attend the meeting on Saturday.

"It would be suicide," cautioned Goro. "You shouldn't have anything to do with the Japanese government. The authorities are just trying to test our loyalty. And if other camp residents found out about it, there's no telling what they might do to you."

"I'm simply not ready to cut myself off from Japan," Mitsuko insisted, and nothing they said could make her change her mind.

———

On the evening of January 16, Mitsuko went to the dining hall of Block 23 near the center of camp expecting to see a Japanese official. Seated behind a table with Mr. Stafford, the project director, were a sandy-haired man and a mustachioed individual in an unfamiliar uniform. Perhaps a hundred camp residents had gathered by the time the meeting started.

Wearing his usual gray business suit, and grinning in that sheepish way he had, eyes set wide apart behind rimless glasses, Stafford introduced a Mr. Bernard Gaffler of the State Department. He in turn introduced the man in the uniform, Captain Antonio R. Martín, who had come from the Spanish embassy in Washington, D.C. as an official representative of Imperial Japanese Government interests in the United States.

Captain Martín stood, his epaulets shimmering in the dining hall light, his moustache a black bar across his olive-complected face. He was slight of build and not much taller than Goro. First he conveyed official greetings from the Imperial Diet to all Japanese nationals being held in enemy territory, but when he announced the nature of his mission, Mitsuko felt her face grow hot.

"I have been sent with a list of names of individuals whom the Japanese government has specifically designated as acceptable for exchange with United States nationals presently being held in Japan. They and other Japanese citizens such as yourselves who care to apply for repatriation can return to your home country some time in the next few months."

Members of the audience groaned and shifted in their seats. Mitsuko felt challenged. He made it sound as simple as buying steamer tickets and packing a trunk.

"Last June," Captain Martín continued, "some fifteen hundred Japanese took the neutral Swedish ship Gripsholm from New York to Lourenço Marques in Portuguese East Africa, a mid-point between Japan and the United States. There the Gripsholm was met by a Japanese ship carrying

Americans, and passengers were exchanged between the two ships. Anyone in Minidoka who would like to be considered for exchange should inform me now, and I will come back to camp later in the year to make final arrangements. Are there any questions?"

Audience members looked at each other. When it became obvious that no one was going to speak, Mitsuko stood slowly and raised her hand. "Do we have to make a final decision now?"

"Not at all," said Captain Martín. "At the moment, I am collecting names of interested parties so that the Japanese government can see what kind of numbers might be involved. You would not be committing yourself to repatriation if you gave me your name now."

"What about the list you brought?" she asked.

Captain Martín said that he had checked the list against the names of Minidoka residents and found only two living here, and they had already been contacted. He held up a small sheaf of papers that was lying on the table. "Please feel free to look at it after the meeting."

When Mitsuko sat down, one old woman stood to ask how long the roundabout journey to Japan required. She and several others sighed loudly when Captain Martín replied that it took three months all together. No one else rose to ask questions. Captain Martín pointed out a sign-up sheet on the table, and Mr. Stafford concluded the meeting.

Mitsuko did not know what to do. Standing here in the same room with a man who could put her on a boat to Japan, she began to see images of home—the straw-thatched roofs, the cedar grove, the narrow mountain road winding with the river down to the sea, the soft roundness of her mother's face: it was as though this Spanish officer had unlocked a treasure chest that she had stored somewhere in the recesses of her heart and nearly forgotten. How wonderful it would be if she could board a ship with her darling Billy and take him to the hills and streams she loved so much!

Captain Martín had said that signing now would commit her to nothing, but even taking that tentative step would mean turning her back on her adopted home, the little son who might, somehow, be hers, and the sister with whom she had shared so much grief. And what if, as Goro had suggested, word were to spread throughout the camp that she had betrayed this country? The Niseis, so eager to prove their loyalty, would no doubt turn on her. What would it do to Billy? To Yoshiko and Goro? And she wondered, too, how Frank would take the news.

Mitsuko approached the front table, where a dozen or more people were signing. Instead of joining the line, she picked up the list of preferred exchangees, leafed through it, and saw "Mitsuko Fukai." She felt momentarily dizzy. Of course—to the Japanese Foreign Ministry, she was still a functionary of the Seattle consulate. It was as though the Japanese government refused to recognize her marriage to a man of impure blood. To them, her name would always be Fukai. She resented this government that rejected her marriage to a man who had rejected her himself. Whichever way she turned, she would face only unhappiness. Unless she was ready to take Billy and plunge into the desert, she would have to choose among the least of the evils that surely awaited her. Heart beating wildly, she stepped to the table and signed: "Mitsuko Fukai Morton."

Yoshiko and Goro were horrified. Mitsuko refused to talk about it and went to bed. But the flow of images from home kept her awake. She glided upstream, following every bend in the river deeper and deeper into the mountains. She swayed on the fragile rope bridge that was the village's only connection with the outside world. And even as she saw the images in the darkness before her wide-open eyes, she was aware of the faint white presence of Billy's hair on the nearby cot.

She wanted to pray, to reach out to something in the darkness. But God, Tom's God, had vanished from her heart. He had been her God, too. He was the God of Yoshiko and Goro, of Reverend Hanamori and of all those loving people in the congregation. But no god kind enough to have given her Billy could be cruel enough to take him away.

She opened her eyes to find the night dissolving into softened gray. Already the voices were beginning to stir, and soon the desert's vast emptiness would hum with the presence of humanity. As quietly as possible, she rose and dressed and stepped out into the freezing dawn. Past black, looming walls she hurried through the snow to the rear of the block, where the camp's eastern edge gave way to unbroken spaces.

The desert floor lay open to the glowing sky, as calm and trusting as a child in sleep. Mitsuko watched the sharp upper edge of the sun's red disk cut through the horizon, and a shaft of light shot toward her across the rolling, snow-covered dunes. Her hands came together, but silently today in their heavy winter wrappings, and she bowed to the only certain source of light and life.

23

"**QUESTION 27**: 'Are you willing to serve in the armed forces of the United States on combat duty wherever ordered?'"

Frank's voice was shuddering with rage.

"And listen to this. Question 28: 'Will you swear unqualified allegiance to the United States of America and faithfully defend the United States from any or all attack by foreign or domestic forces—'"

"Come on, Frank, there's nothing wrong with that," interrupted Jerry Yamaguchi, the *Irrigator*'s cartoonist. "I would defend America from a Japanese attack."

"Wait. You haven't heard the worst part: 'Will you forswear any form of allegiance or obedience to the Japanese emperor, or any other foreign government, power, or organization?'"

"The emperor can go to hell for all I care," said Jerry. "Sure, I'd sign that."

"So you are loyal to the emperor now?"

"Didn't you hear me? What are you talking about?"

"If you 'forswear' your allegiance to the Japanese emperor, that means you've been loyal to him up to now but you agree to turn your back on him. Don't you see what those lousy bastards are doing to us? They want us to prove they've been right all along—that we *are* loyal to the emperor, that we're all emperor-worshiping Japs."

"Wait a minute," said Jerry.

"He's right," interrupted the paper's editor-in-chief, Kenny Kawachi. "What do you think this is going to do to our parents? How can they forswear loyalty to Japan? All these years, this country tells them they're not good enough to become citizens, and now they're supposed to throw away their Japanese citizenship. They won't be citizens of any country!"

"And why do they call this thing 'Application for Leave Clearance?'" asked Frank. "It's just a way of getting us into the Army so we can 'faithfully defend' the white man's paradise. You know who's going on leave, don't you?—us,

right straight into some kind of segregated combat unit. My friend Dunks
Oshima was right: they must take us for idiots. First, they classify us 4-C as if
we're aliens who can't be trusted to carry a rifle, then they run us out of town
and lock us up, and now they tell us we can volunteer for their goddam suicide
squad so we can go out and get killed to defend their goddam democracy.
They've got brass balls, the whole bunch of them! (Sorry, ladies.) But it's
true: Roosevelt talks about the 'right of every faithful citizen, regardless of
ancestry, to bear arms in the nation's battle.' We all know what that means: Jap
boys now have the right to go out and get shot."

Mitsuko had never seen the *Irrigator* office in such an uproar. And the
commotion continued everywhere she went. In the dining hall, parents and
children shouted at each other in public, the sons declaring that they wanted
to prove their loyalty to the United States, the parents convinced that the
government was simply trying to break up Japanese families. Once their sons
were gone, the government would dump them onto the streets of Chicago or
New York after having robbed them of their means of livelihood. Mothers
with tear-stained cheeks went down on their knees, begging their children
not to turn them into welfare cases, pleading with their sons not to commit
suicide by joining the Army and destroying everything their parents had
worked for in this country.

"I thank God for once that he never gave us any children," said Goro as
they sat by the stove in the evening. "Until now, I had secretly questioned
His divine wisdom where that was concerned, but now I see why He did it.
Imagine what those poor families must be going through."

"But what are we going to do?" Yoshiko asked.

"We'll do whatever it takes to stay here. I've made my life in this country,
and I am never going back to Japan. We will both answer 'Yes.'"

"Mit-chan, what will you do? I told you you shouldn't have signed
for repatriation."

"I wish I knew."

The quiet hours Mitsuko spent carving bitterbrush were more and more an escape from the camp's turmoil and from her increasingly politicized work on the *Irrigator*. Near the end of February there was a big debate among the staff over whether or not to publish rumors about a mysterious experimental plane that had crashed into a meat packing plant near Boeing Field in Seattle, killing twenty or more employees. In the end, those who were afraid of the camp administration prevailed, and nothing appeared in print.

Through the rest of February and into March, Japanese cordiality and cooperation disappeared as the Minidoka population became divided into warring factions. Rumors flew that it was no longer safe to go out alone at night: there were gangs roaming the blocks armed with sticks and baseball bats. Fights broke out in the shower rooms and the work places. Young men taunted each other as "traitors" or "cowards." In the recreation halls, friendly games of *go* and poker and shuffleboard erupted into bloody brawls. Gradually, the population of young men began to dwindle. Those who were proud to serve their country and eager to prove the loyalty of the Nisei departed for Camp Shelby in Mississippi with noisy celebrating. Others, more ambivalent about Army service, slipped off quietly. News soon began to reach Minidoka of the rigors of training being undergone by the "Japanese-American Combat Unit," as it was called.

For Mitsuko, the greatest surprise came when Frank showed up at the *Irrigator* office one morning wearing a white *hachimaki* band around his temples emblazoned with a blood-red rising sun. He was now a "No-No Boy," he explained, and his friends were calling themselves the Black Dragon Society and wearing the hachimaki. They had all taken the step of answering "no" to both Questions 27 and 28, and they damn well wanted people to be aware of it. No, he would not defend this lousy, God-forsaken country that had jailed him and his parents; no, he would not forswear his allegiance to the emperor: didn't his yellow face prove that he was loyal to Japan?

"But what if they deport you?" she asked. "Would you renounce your American citizenship? Would you go to Japan? You can hardly speak a word of the language. How would you live?"

"I haven't thought it out that far," he said. "The important thing is to let the government know what it's doing to its citizens."

Thanks to new outcries from Congress, the government decided that it was not doing enough to its citizens. Workmen came to electrify the fence at Minidoka and to begin construction on guard towers, the absence of which had helped to soothe inmates' feelings. Gangs of all political persuasions united to sabotage that project, stealing lumber and tools at night, until a twenty-four-hour-a-day armed guard was posted at the construction sites. Then, in May, as if in grim celebration of a year wasted in the desert, an eighty-year-old Issei who had wakened from a dream and wandered out to the fence, calling the name of his long-dead wife, was shot and killed by a tower guard.

This seemed to snap something inside of Mitsuko. Here was an opportunity to deal in some small way with the lingering guilt she felt regarding the death of old Mr. Abé, the wood carver. She resigned from the newspaper that day and presented herself at the hospital.

Maxalyn Evans, the chief nurse, a blond woman in her early thirties, gave her a suspicious look and asked, "Have you ever done hospital work before?"

"No," said Mitsuko, "but I feel this is where I can do the most good. I want to take care of people, not fight with them."

Mrs. Evans softened a little. "A lot of what we do here is not very pleasant," she said.

"I especially want to work with the elders," Mitsuko replied. "I tended my grandmother on her deathbed. I know what is involved."

Mrs. Evans smiled sadly and said, "All right, if you think you can handle it." She showed her to the nurses' station in Wing 12, where the hospital's only other registered nurse, Mrs. Suzuki, took charge of her. Mrs. Suzuki gave her a white blouse and a striped pinafore with huge pockets. "This is what the aides wear," she explained. "They're mostly high school girls, but you can probably wear the same size they do."

It was true, Mitsuko realized. She must be several pounds lighter now than she had been when she left Seattle.

The halls and wards of the hospital were painted a bright white, a nice break from the dull barracks. And despite the seemingly endless number of bedpans she had to empty, Mitsuko came to look forward to her duties.

———

Soon the harsh Idaho winter gave way to the harsh Idaho summer. A year of living on the desert floor had toughened the people of Minidoka, and they did not collapse in defeat at the onslaught of the sun. A crew of resident volunteers cleared land and made a beach in the natural cove behind the warehouse area—a strip twenty feet wide and some two hundred feet long.

On her days off from the hospital—when there were no sandstorms— Mitsuko brought Billy to swim. The water was up to nine feet deep, and the canal had a treacherous undercurrent, but residents patrolled the beach in "Minidoka Lifeguard" T-shirts. Frank Sano was one of these, and Mitsuko could not help admiring his handsome sternness as he patrolled the beach with his white hachimaki across his forehead.

Toward the end of June, Billy found a new playmate at the beach. It was Brooks Andrews, the Reverend Emery Andrews' little boy. The entire Andrews family had moved to nearby Twin Falls so that the reverend could see to the needs of his congregation, performing weddings and funerals, and running frequent errands for them to Seattle. They brought Brooks into the camp on weekends to play with his friends from the Japanese Baptist Church. He and Billy were almost exactly the same size and age, and when the two little blond boys got together, they were an unusual sight amid the Japanese population.

Mitsuko carved some wooden boats for the boys to share, and she enjoyed chatting with Brooks's big sister while they watched the boys running races in the shallows, splashing and making motorboat sounds. When the girl looked past her and fell silent at one point, Mitsuko turned to see that the current was slowly dragging the boys away from shore. They were so engrossed in their play, they had no idea what was happening to them. She leaped to her feet and started running toward the canal, but Frank had already spotted the problem. With the powerful strokes of a trained swimmer, he shot across the stream and lifted the boys up before they even noticed they were in trouble.

Mitsuko felt all the more grateful to Frank when she heard later that day that an eleven-year-old boy from Block 24 had become the canal's first victim. She walked across the road after dinner to tell Frank how much she appreciated what he had done, but only his parents were home. Mrs. Sano promised to convey the message to her son, but she seemed unusually curt, and Mitsuko wondered if she had offended them in some way.

The Sanos' strange behavior was still on her mind as she was preparing for bed. The stillness of the night was broken by a knock on the door. Goro was away on his rounds, and Mitsuko and Yoshiko looked at each other uneasily.

"Who is it?" called Yoshiko.

"It's me—Frank Sano."

Yoshiko slid open the wooden bolt that Goro had installed on the door.

"Come in, Frank," said Yoshiko, but he stood at the threshold, glancing uneasily from Yoshiko to Mitsuko and back again.

"No, thanks," he replied, looking at Mitsuko. "I just wanted to talk to your sister for a minute. Outside."

Mitsuko hesitated, but then she thought that Yoshiko was sure to be alerted by too obvious a show of indecision. Besides, nearly six months had gone by since that night in January.

"I'll be right back," she said to Yoshiko. She slipped on a shawl around her shoulders to ward off the chill of the desert night.

"Just be careful, Mit-chan," Yoshiko said.

"Don't worry," Mitsuko replied, pulling the plank door shut as she stepped outside.

Yoshiko slid the bolt into place with a loud clunk.

They walked as far as the end of the barrack. "You're not wearing your hachimaki," Mitsuko observed.

The desert sand was still releasing the heat it had stored during the day, but a cool breeze had picked up.

"I can't be angry all the time," he said with a grudging smile. "My mother said you came to see me."

"I wondered if she would give you the message. She seemed a little cold."

Frank said nothing, but he gestured to the right, where the road led out past the ball field and the water tower to the residents' farm acreage.

"Maybe she's heard us talking," he said at length.

"'Us'?" Mitsuko asked.

"The Black Dragon Society. We're a pretty fierce bunch," he said with a soft chuckle.

"Japanese racial purity and all that?" she asked.

"You've heard? There has been a lot of tough talk about women who ..."

"... are married to white men?"

"Yes."

Away from the barracks and the street lights, there was nothing to obscure the enormous, black canopy of the sky, and handfuls of the warm sand underfoot seemed to have been scattered, sparkling, far overhead.

"I was disappointed to see you join a group of super patriots. They bring back ugly memories of Japan," Mitsuko said.

"You were disappointed in me? Does it matter to you what I do? I thought, after that night last winter ..."

"I have always liked you, Frank, you know that. I ... I wanted you to hold me."

"Then why did you run away?"

"I was worried about Billy, first of all. And I am so much older than you. There would be no future for us."

"You're not saying anything about your marriage."

"Who knows what is left of that? If my husband wanted me, he could have gotten me out of camp. Other women married to Caucasians have been released."

They were standing at the edge of the field, where a narrow stream gurgled in the night. They appeared to each other as little more than shadows.

"I want you so badly," Frank said.

Wordlessly, she turned to him and raised her face to his in the darkness. Then her arms were around his neck, and he bent to kiss her. His lips tore into hers, and his strong arms pulled her against his powerful body, all but crushing the breath out of her.

He took her hand and stepped down from the road into the field. In a moment, he was naked and spreading his clothing on the ground for her, and before she knew it, they were together, struggling desperately beneath the cold dome of stars.

Afterward, they lay huddled together, Mitsuko's skirt and shawl thrown over their clinging bodies.

"I don't suppose you'd like it," Frank began somewhat hesitantly, "if I asked about your husband."

"I don't mind," she said. "Not anymore."

"It amazes me that a man could let go of someone like you."

She laughed softly. "Thank you," she said. "That's very nice."

"If you were mine …" He held her more closely. "Why did you ever marry him?"

She searched for an answer.

"I'm sorry," he whispered. "If it's too painful …"

"No," she said. "I was just wondering myself. He was so kind at the beginning. He was not my first husband, you know."

"No, I didn't know."

"My first husband was an officer in the Japanese Army. He treated me very badly. I came to America to forget, but I was still feeling hurt and lonely when I met Tom—Pastor Tom. I had never known a man like him before. He was gentle, and he had such faith in his work. I was swept up in his enthusiasm. And he was Billy's father. I had lost a child in Japan, a boy, and it seemed as if Billy had been sent to me to take his place. I wonder if I would have married Tom if he had not had Billy. Yoshiko tried to warn me about that but I wouldn't listen."

"You love your sister very much, don't you?"

"We were never that close at home. She is ten years older than I am. But we have been through a lot together these past few years."

"You don't go to church together, though."

"It's strange. When I was persecuted for my religion in Japan, I fought to keep it. I thought that America was a country that prayed to the one true

God and I was so happy to become the wife of a man of God. Now it all seems so hollow."

"That's perfect, then," he said. "We're members of the same religion."

"I thought you were an atheist," she objected.

"That's what I mean," he said with a laugh.

"Oh no, Frank, I am not an atheist. I still believe in something. In life …"

"Atheists believe in life," he declared, pulling her close. "Atheists believe in love. Atheists believe in trust and nobility and honor and beauty. Only children should need the threat of punishment to behave themselves. I have no trouble telling good from evil. But I refuse to let God tamper with my life in any way. If all I had to do to pay homage to the supernatural was stick my finger in the air, I would refuse. Do you realize that whoever wrote the Bible's story of creation thought the world was flat? I don't have any use for a god who doesn't know the actual shape of the world he supposedly created."

"I wish it weren't so dark and I could see you more clearly now," she said. "I remember how handsome you looked that day in the newspaper office when you were talking about Santa Claus."

He laughed and kissed her throat. "I meant what I said just now," he whispered. "I do believe in love."

24

THE VERY NEXT DAY after Mitsuko's night in the field with Frank, a letter arrived from Tom as if there had been some malign telepathic communication. The envelope contained a form written in legalistic jargon, but the letter itself left no doubt as to its meaning. He had filed for divorce, and unless she chose to contest it, it would become final as of September 1. On that date, he intended to come for his son. He wanted her to prepare Billy for his departure and leave him with the project director. He did not wish to see her. He was prepared now to "set up a new household," he said, and he did not want her to stand in his way.

"Are you going to contest it?" Yoshiko asked when they were alone in the barrack.

"It's hopeless," Mitsuko replied. "No American judge would ever see it my way. I'm going to lose Billy. That's all. A legal battle would only hurt him."

"I'm so sorry, Mit-chan. I wish I could do something."

"No one can do anything. I've got two months left."

Mitsuko met Frank that night at the east end of the barrack, away from Yoshiko's eyes. She told him the news as they walked out to the field.

"I know how much you love that boy," he said. "I've got a real soft spot for him, too. But maybe it's for the best. It had to happen sooner or later."

It became Mitsuko's new habit to "take a walk" each night. She was less ashamed of her clandestine behavior than afraid of hurting Yoshiko.

"I've got my own news," Frank told her on the night of July 24. "They just announced that the Tule Lake camp in California is being converted from a relocation center to a segregation center for 'disloyals'—No-No Boys like me."

Mitsuko inhaled sharply. First Billy, now Frank.

"Come with me," he implored as they lay together beneath the open sky. "They'll be moving us in September or October. Billy will be gone by then, and we can be together all the time."

"You make it sound so easy." And perhaps he was right: perhaps she deserved to have this eager, young lover after all she had been through. Lying in his arms, she could forget the pain, the cruelty. Even the impending loss of Billy could be blotted out for those few moments when their bodies melted perfectly together.

"It is easy," he said. "Just say yes."

———

The hours she spent with Billy were more precious now than ever, but they foretold the emptiness that was to come. She would look at the little bitterbrush toys and figurines she had carved for him and wonder if Tom would be heartless enough to destroy them all when he repossessed his son. Now she was carving a small mirror housing to take with her as a memento of the months she spent with Billy under the scorching desert sun. The hard, desert-tempered grain of the bitterbrush yielded to her knives and chisels a round, dark sun whose edges streamed with fire. She hollowed out the other side to accept a round mirror the size of a silver dollar.

"Put in a goose," said Billy, who lay beside her on the hard plank floor, chin propped on hands, watching her shape the wood.

"Where? Right here in the middle of the sun?"

"Yeah! Make his wings stretch out."

True, the circular disk would be very plain without some ornamentation. She liked its round simplicity, but she liked the idea of superimposing on it the soaring bird of freedom even more.

When the mirror was nearing completion a few days later, the shining glass ready for insertion, Billy surprised her by asking if she would give it to him.

"Oh, Billy, I made this for myself. Whenever I look at the goose, I'm going to think of you."

He gave her a puzzled look. "But you can just look at me to think of me," he said.

Perhaps she should do as he asked. Perhaps Tom would let him keep what she had made for him.

"All right," she said at length. "I'll make two—one for you and one for me."

"Oh, goody!" He clapped his hands.

She saw her own reflection in the glass and wondered if Billy could sense the storm of emotions that had left her looking so much older.

But she was not alone. The upheavals of the past few months were taking their physical toll on all the Minidoka residents. Goro's vitality was visibly dwindling. Hardest hit were those Isseis who were having their grown children snatched away from them by the Army or lured away to the cities of the East. The hospital wards were filled to overflowing, and Mitsuko worked later each day. The hospital's substantial architecture provided the camp's best relief from the summer sun, but when the windows had to be closed during sand storms, this could also trap foul smells inside.

Her late departures from work brought Mitsuko out of doors when the sun was down and the cool evening breezes had begun to move across the sand. One evening she took the short cut past the warehouses and through the open area by the bend in the canal. She could see the gleam of the dark water reflecting the sky's last glow, and if the breeze was rather less than she had hoped for, at least the gentle gurgling of the canal seemed to have a cooling effect.

Just beyond the bend, in the broad stretch between Block 32 and the bank of the canal, Mitsuko saw some bushes or boulders arranged in a semi-circle on the ground. She had never noticed them before, but she kept walking. Suddenly one of the shapes moved. It was a man, and now she could make out a light-colored band up around the forehead. He must be one of Frank's Black Dragon cohorts—perhaps even Frank himself.

"Who's that?" an unfamiliar voice growled across the few yards remaining between Mitsuko and the man. She drew to a halt. The other men stood up.

"I'm taking a short-cut. I live in Block 39. I'm on my way home."

"Like hell," said the voice. "You've been listening to us. Tell me your name."

"I am sure you don't know me. I'm Mitsuko Morton."

"*Morton?* The white man's whore. Now I know you've been spying on us."

The other men began to grumble threateningly.

"You're spying for the administration. The whole white bunch of them are probably screwing you."

Mitsuko strained to see through the darkness, hoping that Frank was there. She wanted to cry out his name, but was afraid the men might turn on him.

The man took a step in her direction and the others began to move.

"Keep away from me!" she shouted in a shrill voice she barely recognized as her own.

"I've got just what you need," said the man, "right here between my legs."

"All right, Charlie, that's enough. Let her go."

It was Frank's voice, she was sure.

"Let her go? Shit, I haven't even got her skirt up yet."

"You heard me, Charlie, stop it."

Mitsuko whirled and began to run back toward the bend in the canal, but rough hands caught her around the neck and waist.

"Let me go!" she screamed, but she felt herself being lifted off the desert floor and slammed onto the sand. A sharp pain pierced her side. Hands were pulling and tearing at her, ripping her clothes. They panted and snorted all around her, their hot breath searing her face, the smell of sweat and saliva filling her nostrils.

"Frank, help!"

Suddenly everything grew still. For a moment, the only sound was that of labored breathing. Then she heard someone yell, "Traitor! Kill the bastard!" Some fireworks exploded, and something hard slammed into her head.

Mitsuko woke in a white glare, her body stiff with pain. She felt as if she were up in the air, then she realized she was in one of the high, pipe-frame beds in which the Isseis lay when she was tending them. She could barely open her eyes.

"Thank God," she heard Yoshiko saying. "She's waking up."

Mitsuko groaned.

"Mit-chan, I thought they had killed you!"

The bed was jostled slightly, and she heard Yoshiko's muffled sobbing.

"What about Frank?" Mitsuko asked. "Is he all right?"

"Doctor Neher is with him now in Wing 7," said Goro, who stood by her bed looking gray and haggard.

"Wing 7?" she gasped. "That's surgery."

"He has some internal hemorrhaging," Goro said.

"He saved my life. Please find out how he is doing."

Goro limped away. Yoshiko sighed and turned to her sister.

"Oh, Mit-chan ... out there ... Is that where you and Frank ... ?"

"You knew? And you did not try to stop me?"

"I knew that God would understand. You have had to endure such loneliness."

Mitsuko reached for her sister's hand, and for a long time they did not speak.

"What happened?" Mitsuko asked at length.

"They beat you," said Yoshiko. "They almost ... "

"I know," she said. "I mean, what happened at the end? Did the fireworks frighten them off?"

"Fireworks? There were no fireworks. The guards heard the noise and started shooting. They could have killed you. I think they must have hit someone. There was blood in the sand."

"Don't they know who did it?"

"No. Do you?"

"No, but if anything happens to Frank ..."

Huffing from the walk, Goro came back with the news that Frank's bleeding had stopped but that Doctor Neher was not ready to commit to a prognosis. "The Sanos were there, too, but they wouldn't talk to me," he added, shaking his head.

Mitsuko had suffered a cracked rib and other scrapes and bruises, but she was well enough to leave her bed the next day. Frank, meanwhile, had come through the surgery and was resting in Wing 10. Mitsuko felt as if her back and sides would crumble if she moved too much, but she tiptoed down the corridor and entered the long ward.

Beside one bed far down on the left she could see Mrs. Sano's familiar black-and-gray frizz, but when Mitsuko approached the bed, Frank's mother stood as if to block her view and demanded that she leave immediately.

"It's all right, Mom," groaned Frank from behind this resolute guard. "Let her by." His voice sounded strained, as if it were being forced out through a constricted tube.

Mrs. Sano stood aside, stroking back her wild strands and fixing Mitsuko with an angry stare. Frank waved her away, but she went no farther than the end of the ward, out of his line of vision.

Instead of his *hachimaki*, Frank now had a bandage wrapped around his head, and his right eye was a swollen purple fruit. Against the white bandages, the sharp curve of his nose stood out prominently.

"Frank, I'm so sorry!"

"It's not your fault. What was I supposed to do? Stand by and watch them tear you apart?"

———

Mitsuko was discharged from the hospital the following morning, and after a day's rest, she was ready to go back to work. Yoshiko pleaded with her not to push herself. "You look so pale and thin, Mit-chan. Mama would be angry at me if she knew how badly I've been taking care of you."

"I'm fine," she said. Frank was in the hospital, and she wanted to be near him. In contrast to the old Isseis, who recovered from their ills slowly if at all, Frank made rapid progress. "Come to Tule Lake with me," he pressed her.

"I'm afraid, Frank. The Black Dragons will be there. All the Black Dragons from all the other camps will be there. We would live in constant fear."

"It won't be that bad," he insisted, "We'll be together. Isn't that the most important thing?"

"I'm not sure it is," she said with brutal honesty.

"Not sure? I love you, Mitsuko. I want to marry you. You have to come with me."

"I don't know, Frank. Let me think."

Mitsuko did not tell Frank that there had been an announcement: today, August 10, the Spanish envoy, Captain Martín, would be visiting Minidoka again in the evening. Although no details had been given out, Mitsuko felt certain that tonight she would be asked to make her final decision for or against repatriation.

Yoshiko pleaded with her not to go, but after dinner, she headed once again for Dining Hall 23. The tables and chairs were arranged as they had been in January, but the size of the crowd had dwindled to perhaps half. There was a different State Department representative at the head table with Captain Martín. Project Director Stafford introduced him as Ralph Blake, and Blake in turn introduced Captain Martín.

As before, the Spanish officer opened his remarks with a greeting from the Imperial Diet, which had passed a resolution of sympathy for those Japanese nationals incarcerated in enemy countries. But this time, there was nothing preliminary or tentative about his mission. The Gripsholm would be sailing from New York on September 1, he said, and tonight he needed to have the names of all those in camp who wanted to be on it. Departure from Minidoka would be on August 29 via the train station at Shoshone.

Mitsuko could hardly breathe when she heard these immovable dates. She had only nineteen days—less than three weeks—before Billy would be torn from her life. Yes, it was coming one way or another, but to have it confirmed by this somber Spanish captain was more than she could bear. And yet, what choice did she have? Tom was coming on September 1, backed by all the power of his country's government.

And there was Frank. "I love you," he had said. "I want to marry you." But had he ever asked her if she loved him? How tempting it was to follow him, married or not. But what awaited them in Tule Lake, where the government would bring together all the smoldering resentment it had created? For her, it mattered little what the future held, but what right did she have to inflict suffering—perhaps even death—on a man she did not love with her whole heart? She recalled how the eyes of Mrs. Sano had glared at her in the hospital—the eyes of a mother filled with hatred for a woman who dared to harm her son. Mitsuko knew that she herself would be equally capable of hatred in the face of a threat to Billy.

Half conscious of her own movements, Mitsuko drifted to the table and signed the official application for passage to Japan. Never had she imagined when she left her native land that a decision to return to it would entail such inner turmoil. Now, every moment she spent here would feel like her last.

———

That night, in the shower, she washed Billy with special care, covering him with mounds of the lather he enjoyed so much. Her washcloth found every little fold and wrinkle of his skin—the funny hollow at the top of his right ear where the cartilage dipped in; the white elastic ball of his tummy, so perfectly round and smooth it was impossible to imagine there were intestines and a stomach inside; the springy, little penis that moved languidly from side to side like a blind lizard with a life of its own; the space between the solid, little buttocks which he had finally learned to control for himself after endless coaxing.

The moonlight set their matched yukata aglow in the night as they walked slowly back to the barrack, hand in hand.

"Sing Odoma," said Billy. "You don't sing Odoma anymore."

It was true. She had been leaving him so often in Yoshiko's care these days that he had been going to bed without his lullaby.

Holding his hand more tightly, and looking up at the moon, Mitsuko sang in her low, plaintive way: "*Odoma Bon-giri Bon-giri, Bon kara sakya orando ...*"

"Don't stop, Mommy."

But Mitsuko could not go on. The words were true, she realized: "I'll be here until Bon, and when it's over I'll be gone." O-Bon—the festival of the dead—was little more than a week away. And eight days later, she would be gone. It was as if she had been singing this lullaby to him night after night for the past four years in preparation for their final parting. The moon dissolved in her tears, and her throat was convulsed with sobs.

"What's the matter, Mommy?" asked Billy. "Why are you crying? Did you hurt yourself?"

She knelt down and held him tightly to her breast. "No, no," she said at last. "It's just that ... I don't know ... I was thinking how much I love you. Sometimes ... when you love someone very much ... it can hurt inside. It feels so good, it hurts."

"You're silly, Mommy. Sing Odoma."

Mitsuko wiped her tears on her sleeve and, sniffling, she stood up. In a tremulous near-whisper, she sang, "*Odon ga shinda chuute, Dai ga nyaate kuryo ka, Ura no matsuyama semi ga naku*"—"Who will cry for me when I am dead? The cicada on the pine-covered hill."

"No!" Billy protested. "Sing the real words."

"Oh, Billy, those are the real words. I never sang that part for you before. Do you think you can learn the new words?"

"No! I want you to sing Odoma."

"All right," she said. "Come. I'll sing to you in bed."

Nineteen more times she would sing for him. Nineteen days until she was gone. Nineteen days, and then what?

25

"YOU SIGNED WHAT!" Frank shouted. "I can't believe this!"

Sleeping bodies stirred and eyes focused in this direction all up and down the ward.

"I had to do it, Frank. I can't stay in this country any longer," Mitsuko said quietly but firmly.

Mrs. Sano charged toward them, jaw set. She stopped short when Frank waved her off.

"Frank, if you don't lower your voice, I will have to leave."

"What the hell difference does it make?" he muttered. "You're walking out on me anyway."

"It is for your own good."

Again Frank gestured to his mother, who backed off.

"The only thing that's good for me is you," he said.

"I will tell you another thing," Mitsuko went on. "You must not go to Tule Lake. They will kill you."

"So let them kill me."

"Don't be such a child," she said. "If you change your 'no-no' to 'yes-yes,' you can stay here. Some men who do not want to go to Tule Lake are changing their answers."

"And then what? They get sent to the Nisei combat unit."

"Not necessarily. You do not have to volunteer."

Suddenly Frank reached out and grabbed her wrist. "Well, I will," he growled, his eyes full of anger.

"What are you talking about?"

"If you won't come with me, I'm going to join the 442nd. They call it a suicide squad. That's perfect."

"Stop talking like a little boy," she said, wrenching herself free.

"Please, Mitsuko, you're all I want. Come with me!"

"You have no idea how much I would love to, but it wouldn't work for either of us. Can't you see that?" There was nothing more she could say. She hurried down the long alley of beds while Frank called out to her.

"I'm sorry," she whispered to Mrs. Sano, as the frantic mother, hair and clothes flying in all directions, stormed past her.

———

Frank was still in the hospital ten days later, the night of the Bon dance.

"I want Frank to pick me up on his shoulders!" shouted Billy, trying to be heard above the din of drums and bells and the high, squealing voice blaring over the loudspeaker.

Mitsuko herself could hardly see a thing besides thousands of arms held aloft and swaying back and forth to the pulse of the music. The entire field behind the administration building was swarming with dancers in yukata rotating around the ten-foot-high roofed music platform in the center. Gathered together here, in the American desert, having brought their Bon dancing styles from all parts of Japan, the crowd moved with none of the uniformity of Bon dances that Mitsuko had known, but the vigor was there. Thousands of stamping feet raised clouds of dust that shone yellow in the light of the hundreds of paper lanterns strung up around the field. The dancers' familiar, glazed look of joyous abandonment to the hypnotic beat gave Mitsuko a delirious sense that she had made the crossing to Japan with Billy and the war was over.

Her arms were aching from the effort of holding Billy up. "I wish Frank could be here, too," she said. "But he's still sick."

"I wanna go up *there*!" Billy pointed up to the water tower in the corner of the field, where several dozen men had climbed the tower framework and hung precariously, surveying the lively scene. Even from here, their unsteady clinging to the framework suggested that several of them had managed to buy or make themselves liquor in violation of camp rules and were having a more authentic celebration than they were supposed to. A few of them were wearing the white hachimaki of the Black Dragon Society. Mitsuko hated to think of what might happen if some of those men were to descend from the tower and see Billy.

"Time for bed," she told him.

Billy pouted. "I want to dance more."

But now the thought of plunging into the crowd again had become a little frightening to Mitsuko. "I've got a present for you," she said teasingly.

"Let me have it!" Billy cried. "What is it?"

Holding her hands behind her, pretending to hide it from him, Mitsuko shuffled through the thick dust underfoot, moving backward, away from the crowd. Billy ran after her, snatching at her concealed treasure, but she twisted her body away each time his hand shot out.

Finally, at the edge of the field, she showed him her empty hands and confessed, "It's not here. I have it in the room."

"Let's go!" He started running, pulling her yukata sleeve.

"Wait. Slow down. We don't have to run."

For a few minutes, they walked silently, hand in hand, listening to the metallic singing drawing into the distance behind them. The deep thump of the huge drum continued to shake the desert air, and Mitsuko felt as if it were passing through her heart.

"Billy. Mommy's going to give you a going-away present," she said when she could no longer stand the wait.

"Are we going away?" he asked.

"I am going away first," she said, "and then Daddy is coming to take you home to Seattle."

"Then you'll come, too?"

"No, Billy, I am going far away."

"I'll go with you," he said, his voice unsteady. "Then, we'll come back to Seattle to be with Daddy together."

"I would love that very much."

"But you have to," he said nervously, his grasp tightening on her hand.

Her voice would no longer come. They approached the bend in the road.

"I want to give you something to help you remember me," she said at last.

"No! I'm going with you! I don't want that kind of present!"

He pulled his hand from hers and began to back away. "I don't want it!" he cried again. Then he turned and ran toward the field of dancers.

"Billy, come back!" Mitsuko tried to hurry after him, sandals flapping against her heels, but the loose sand caught the front edges of the sandals, slowing her down until, in frustration, she kicked them off and ran barefoot.

Billy plunged into the swaying crowd just ahead of her, ducking under hands and elbows, squeezing between tightly packed hips wrapped in yukata and *obi*. To Mitsuko, the crowd was almost as impenetrable as a wall, and she heard curses as she pushed her way through. She felt as if she were swimming across a swiftly flowing stream, the current always threatening to carry her away to the right. She broke through to the hub of the vast wheel of bodies just in time to see Billy duck under the legs of the music platform and out the other side. Again he plunged into the flow of bodies, and again Mitsuko dove in after him, her yukata in hopeless disarray. Now the stream at the top of the wheel was moving left. Mitsuko lost sight of Billy among the dancers. When she emerged from the other side, there was no sign of him between the crowd and the barracks at the other end of camp.

A flash of white disappeared between the barracks of Block 10. She dashed ahead and through the block just in time to see Billy swallowed up in the darkness of the no-man's-land beyond. He was heading straight for the fence.

"Billy, no! Don't go out there! Billy!"

But it was too late. The beam from the watch tower swung around to catch the small figure flying toward the fence, and a shot rang out. In the glare of the search light, Billy crumpled to the ground.

"No! No!" Mitsuko screamed, "Don't shoot! He's just a boy!" but the words torn from her throat seemed to die as they were sucked into the emptiness. Under the harsh, blue-whitelight, she could see a red stain on Billy's yukata. Skirts flying, she ran to him with all her strength, hoping that the guards would kill her, too.

Before she could reach him, a khaki form darted into the light, taking up a position between her and Billy, a rifle like a bar blocking the way. But stopping was out of the question. She collided with the wild-eyed soldier, knocking him to the ground.

Doctor Neher told her that the bullet had passed cleanly through Billy's thigh about four inches above the knee: in the back and out the front, without hitting any bones. There would probably not be any permanent muscle damage, but for a few days, they had to be on their guard against infection.

"A few days?"

"Without complications, he should be out of the woods in ten days or less."

"I don't have ten days!"

Mitsuko spent most of the time remaining to her in Minidoka in the hospital, sponging Billy's forehead and making him as comfortable as possible. At first, whenever he came around, he wouldn't look at her or speak, but soon he began to forget himself and smile. On the fourth day, he gave her a sly, knowing look and said, "You're not really going away, are you? You were just kidding."

"Don't worry, you just get better. I won't go right away."

He began to toss wildly in the hospital bed, swinging his arms, pounding the mattress with his fists, kicking with all his strength against the sheets.

"Billy, don't! You'll make it bleed again."

She stood and pressed his shoulders down, but he continued to struggle.

"All right, Billy. I won't go. I won't go."

The pitching stopped. His heart pounded beneath her hand, and his breath came with the quick gasps of a frightened animal. He looked at her, his little nostrils flaring, and she knew he was waiting for her to tell him her comforting lie again. She had never told him anything but the truth, and now, when she wanted to be closer to him than ever, the need for deception seemed to be driving them apart.

"What I meant was," she said, pronouncing each word slowly and carefully, struggling to find a way to bridge the gap between truth and falsehood, "I was not kidding, but now I can stay." Yes, she could stay; she would refuse to be repatriated. The others could leave without her on the twenty-ninth, and Billy would go with his father on the first. He would have three extra days of healing that way. It was worth it. What difference did it make when she got to Japan? All that mattered was that Billy should recover.

When Billy was napping that afternoon, Mitsuko went to see Richard Dawson, the assistant project director who had been handling the repatriation. When she told him her change in plans, he turned bright red.

"You can't back out now!" He rose to his feet, towering over her. "Everything has been arranged with the Japanese government and the Spanish embassy."

She explained her desperate need to stay in camp just three more days, which only made matters worse.

"You're crazy! We're not going to embarrass ourselves so you can hang around for three lousy days. You signed that thing and you have to stick to it."

"I want to talk to Mr. Stafford."

"You can talk to anybody you like. It's not going to do you a damn bit of good. You wanted to go back to Japan, and that's where you're going, come hell or high water."

He was right, she *was* crazy. What kind of suffering was she sentencing herself to by remaining in this country? Was it really for Billy's sake she wanted to stay? Wasn't it just a way for her to postpone the inevitable for a few more days? Now was the time to be strong, to face what was coming and help Billy to face it.

That night Yoshiko came to see her in the hospital. She told her that twenty-two people had been brought into Minidoka today from Topaz: six families and five individuals. They would be combined with the forty from Minidoka who were choosing repatriation.

"Please, Mit-chan, don't go with them."

"It's too late," said Mitsuko. "I tried today. They told me I have to go."

"You tried? Then you don't want to go! I knew it! Goro and I will come with you tomorrow. We'll make them keep you."

"No," sighed Mitsuko. "I don't have the strength to fight anymore."

Yoshiko left in tears.

On the morning of August 29 it took Mitsuko little more than an hour to sort her things and pack. Repatriates were allowed two suitcases, but she could barely fill one.

Slipping the mirror from the brocade case she had sewn for it, she polished the little circle of light, then held it before her. How sunken and dark her eyes had become. She saw in herself the faces of the Isseis who had died in their hospital beds, and she half hoped that death would be coming for her soon as well.

Leaving the suitcase by the door, Mitsuko trudged across the baking desert sands to see Billy one more time at the hospital. The sun was burning through the shoulders of her blouse, and several times she mopped the perspiration from her brow.

"What's wrong?" Billy said immediately when she approached his bed with tear-filled eyes. She did not have the courage to tell him. Yoshiko had agreed to make excuses for her until Tom arrived on Wednesday.

"Nothing," she said, trying to smile. "I think I may be catching a cold."

"Oh," Billy replied, but he did not return her smile.

"I brought you something," she said, sitting on the edge of the bed with her feet dangling above the floor.

"It's not a going-away present, is it?"

"No, it's just a present."

She drew the mirror in its case from the pocket of her dress and handed it to him. He did not reach for it.

"What is it?"

"Something you like. See for yourself."

At last, he stretched his hand out and took the case, working the flap loose from beneath the narrow band that held it closed. The mirror slipped easily into his small hand.

"The mirror?" he asked, holding it at arm's length.

"That's right," she said. "Look at yourself."

He brought it closer to his face.

"Now look at the back."

"The sun," he muttered, touching the carved figure.

"And Nils' goose. Just what you wanted."

He did not reply, but he turned it in his hand, running his fingers over the wood and studying his image in the little circle.

"You keep it," he said at last. "I don't like it."

He tried to thrust it into her hand.

"No. I want you to have it. I made one for myself just like it. We can both have one."

"Take it back," he whimpered. "I don't want you to go away."

Before she could lie to him again, he flung the mirror across the aisle. It clanged against the pipe frame of the bed opposite, and dropped to the wooden floor with a crash of glass.

"Don't go, Mommy, please don't go," he wailed, wrapping his arms around her neck.

She held him tightly, praying with all her might. Let the sun explode. Let it wrap the earth in its blazing embrace. Let it fuse this hate-filled globe into a single, molten mass, ending war and parting and suffering forever.

PART FIVE:

1959

JAPAN

SCALE OF MILES

0   50   100   200   300

Railroads ———

26

THEY USUALLY MET at midnight, after Bill finished work at the restaurant. They would go to quiet places, where Frank would wander back freely across the years, his black, intense eyes staring out into the night. The year was no longer 1959 but 1942, when Frank first met Mitsuko at Puyallup, or 1943, when Frank left his hospital bed in Minidoka to find that Mitsuko had returned to Japan on a repatriation ship.

As Frank led him through the dark passageways of the past, Bill could almost hear Mitsuko singing to him, but it was as if they were on opposite banks of a rushing stream. Her lips were moving. The song was for him. But the melody never reached him.

Frank could do nothing to help him hear it. "We were living in that tiny vacuum world in Minidoka. It was only after I started looking for her that I realized how little I actually knew about her."

"When did you start looking for her?" Bill pressed him.

"Not for several years. I was angry with her, angry with everything. That's why I joined the 442nd. I figured I'd just go out there and get killed and it would be all over. They sent me to Bruyéres. That's where this happened." He patted the empty sleeve. "After the war, the government paid for me to finish school. They paid me for my arm, too. I had some pretty good cash for a while. Bought myself a fancy car."

"The DeSoto?"

"The DeSoto." He smiled. "A lot of the other guys bought cars, too, but they frittered their money away. There was a lot of anger. The government had locked up our families and sent us out to die, but when it was all over, it was the same old story: no jobs for Japs. So I went back to school. Majored in economics at the U.W. Then I tried working for Boeing for a while, but I didn't have the engineering background to go very far with them. Besides, I wasn't too crazy about the military side of things at Boeing. I started investing on my own. I did all right for myself. Even got a pretty wife."

"You're married?"

"No, not anymore."

"Oh. I'm sorry."

"Yeah, so was I. When my marriage went sour, I realized I hadn't ever gotten over Mitsuko and started looking for her. By then, it was already 1953 and I hadn't seen or heard anything about her in ten years."

"Nineteen fifty-three," said Bill. "I must have been fifteen then. That's when I saw you at the bus stop, isn't it?"

Frank nodded. "I had almost nothing to go on. I knew her sister and brother-in-law—"

"She had a sister?"

"Her name was Yoshiko. Husband was Goro Nomura."

"Doesn't ring a bell."

"I figured they would have come back to Seattle, but they weren't in the phone book. I knew both the husband and the wife had been active in the Minidoka protestant church, but that was some kind of united church and I didn't know which one they had actually belonged to in Seattle. I tried calling a few and asking for them, but no luck. A couple of the Japanese churches never got off the ground again after the war. You know—their people went East or the Issei members died off."

"Issei?"

"First-generation Japanese in America, the ones who immigrated. I'm a Nisei—second generation, but the first generation born here. A lot of the ministers were old, and some of the Issei just didn't make it through the winters or summers in the desert. That's what happened to the Japanese Christian Church. I'm almost certain that's the one the Nomuras would have attended. It's still over there on Terrace, all boarded up."

"What a shame—for them and for us."

"The more churches they close, the better if you ask me," Frank spat. "I'm amazed anybody could have come through the war thinking they had any kind of god watching over them."

"It's not that easy to give up something you've always lived with," Bill said.

"You just have to think about it with an open mind. It takes about ten seconds to see what nonsense it is."

"Yes, but ..." Bill was not sure enough of where he stood on these matters to become involved in a debate. His father had seriously shaken his faith, and what Frank had been telling him dealt it another blow. But still, doing ministry work in Japan seemed like a good idea—all the more so since he now knew that Mitsuko had gone back there. Bill said, "You were talking about your search."

Frank looked at him and chuckled. "Sorry," he muttered. "Religion's a sore spot with me. Still, it's got something to do with my search, too, because next I went to see your father."

Bill had to look away, but Frank went on speaking as if he had noticed nothing.

"I really hadn't wanted to approach your father except as a last resort. I figured I could at least learn the name of his old congregation and get in touch with those people. He was easy enough to find in the phone book, so I went to see him in Magnolia. He didn't want to tell me anything. He practically threw me out."

"I'm not surprised," said Bill with a scowl. "He didn't want to be reminded of what he'd done."

"As long as I was in Magnolia, I thought it might be some consolation if I could get a glimpse of you. You were a great little kid. I always liked you, so I drove over there and hung around outside for a few hours. Finally it dawned on me you weren't a little kid anymore, and I wasn't going to see you except coming or going to school. I tried again the next morning early. The weather was bad, so I had to drive right up to the curb. Sorry. I must have scared the daylights out of you."

Frank spent a whole evening describing to Bill a fruitless two-week trip he had made to Tokyo after failing to turn up anything in Seattle.

"I don't know why I went," he said. "A kind of sentimental journey, I suppose. I didn't know her last name—she was Mitsuko Morton, as far as

I knew—and it wasn't likely she would have kept the foreign name in Japan. I tried the American Embassy, but they couldn't help at all. About the only thing I had to go on was the name of her sister and brother-in-law, but I can't read the language, and my spoken Japanese is a mess, so I hired a girl to go through the Tokyo phone book and try calling all the Nomuras. You should see how many Nomuras there are in the Tokyo phone book—and that was back when not many people in Japan had phones. None of them knew Goro or Yoshiko. Of course, maybe they weren't even in Tokyo. Talk about looking for a needle in a haystack!"

One of the few mementos Frank still had from Minidoka was a brittle, yellowed copy of the camp newspaper, the *Irrigator*, with a Japanese section that had been written by Mitsuko herself. Holding the fragile sheet, Bill felt he could almost touch the hands of the woman who had inscribed the graceful characters.

"She designed the masthead, too," Frank said. "She was a very talented lady. Used to make you toy boats and things. I don't suppose you've got any of those hanging around."

Bill shook his head. The Japanese masthead was like a little woodblock print, with a meandering stream and cattails, a water tower and some low buildings sketched in behind the two vertically-written words "Minidoka" and "Irrigator." Oddly, the name of the camp was spelled "Minedoka" in Japanese. Maybe it just sounded more natural that way.

Turning back to the English section, Bill said, "Here's an article on a Gallup poll." He could hardly believe the figures. "Thirty-one percent were opposed to letting *any* Japanese-Americans come back to their homes after the war! That's incredible!"

"It still burns me up to think about it."

"What hatred there must have been! But at least the relocation camps weren't as bad as the Nazi concentration camps," Bill offered hopefully.

"How do *you* know?" Frank shot back, dark eyes burning past the sharp curve of his nose.

"Well, they didn't gas people."

"No, but *we* didn't know that at the time. And the Jews didn't know they would be gassed. We went just like the Jews—docile, cooperative, good little Japs. We were plain lucky General DeWitt had his superiors to answer to. If he'd had his way, he'd have buried us all out there in the desert."

The more he learned from Frank, the more impatient Bill became to get to Japan. Now he had a real reason to go there, and preaching the Gospel was not it.

"Don't be in such a hurry," Frank said. "If you really want to go and find her, you'll have to know a lot more Japanese than I do. I was lost."

"I've picked up a fair amount working at Maneki."

"Don't make me laugh. You need more than a few set phrases. And you've got to learn to read and write. I see you've picked up a little of the phonetic script, but you have to memorize thousands of characters if you want to read anything. It's murder. After I got back here, I tried to brush up my Japanese and learn the writing system. I took a course at the U.W. but I gave up after a couple of months. I've got to work for a living, I don't have time for flash cards. And even if I did manage to get enough language under my belt, I can't go and live there for months at a time. You're not going to find her in a week or two."

"I can't wait, though. I'm ready to quit school now, forget about graduating, and just go."

"Well, how are you going to pay for it? Ask your father for the money? Have you got a trust fund socked away?"

"I could get a job once I got there."

"I suppose so, teaching English. But that's all you'd be doing all day. You wouldn't have time to study Japanese or do any searching. No, I'm telling you, there's only one way: learn the language here before you go, and get a scholarship to support you while you're there."

"How long would that take? More than a year, I'll bet."

"Way more than a year. Four or five, I'd guess."

"Four or five years? I want to go *now*."

27

TO BILL, THE UNIVERSITY of Washington had always seemed a hopelessly large, hopelessly secular institution. It was where the scientists labored to disprove the word of God, where the communists held their secret meetings, where beer-swilling fraternity men tortured and debauched new inductees into their dens of iniquity. He recalled having once driven through the sprawling campus in the back seat of his father's car. They had kept the windows closed tight the whole time.

Since then, he had had no occasion to visit the university. The assumption had always been that he would attend Cascade-Pacific College, and he had gone there without question. Now that he thought of it, it seemed as if his entire life had been spent within walking distance of home. Occasional excursions across the Ballard Bridge to Clare's neighborhood hardly counted. As he pulled into the broad mall of the main entrance on 45th, it struck him that a mere ten-minute drive was all that separated his closed, little world from this unknown territory. The university campus was a cool, green park, filled with drooping pines.

At the registrar's office, he tried to register as a "transient student" in the university's beginning Japanese course but was told he had to be tested before he could be admitted to the course's second term, the winter quarter, which would start after New Year's. He found his way to the office of a Professor Tatsumi, who immediately began speaking to him in Japanese when Bill told him why he had come.

Professor Tatsumi was a soft-spoken man in his early sixties with no more than a few wisps of hair running in straight lines across his shining pate. He wore tortoise-shell glasses that seemed to have trouble clinging to his broad, flat nose. His first question to Bill in Japanese was "What is your name?"

Professor Tatsumi chuckled—in a restrained, courtly sort of way—when Bill gave his name, and by the time Bill had replied to two or three more questions, the professor was shaking with laughter.

"Where did you learn your Japanese?" the professor asked in English.

"Is it really that bad?"

"No, actually it's surprisingly grammatical. And your pronunciation is pretty good, too, which is the main thing we've worked on this quarter. I'm tempted to let you in if you think you can catch up with the others. Buy the textbook and work on it over winter break. We'll bring you up to speed next quarter. One last question, though: why do you want to study Japanese?"

He wanted to answer simply, "I need to go to Japan to search for my mother," but he was not ready to answer all the questions that would raise. "I'm studying for the ministry at Cascade-Pacific, and I'm thinking of doing missionary work in Japan."

"That's nice, I guess," the professor said.

"You guess?"

"You seem so motivated, you'd probably make an excellent graduate student. Let's see how you do next quarter. Our literature program's pretty good, if you're looking for an area of study to apply your Japanese."

———

As his senior year went by, Bill began to imagine that he was a kind of Paul Bunyan, trying to gain a foothold in two parts of the city at once. The foot at Cascade-Pacific was planted firmly on hard ground, while the one at the university skipped nimbly from log to log in a gushing river of language that never slowed down.

At Cascade-Pacific, he knew where he was. Sometimes, on the small campus, he had the feeling that he knew all too well where he was, especially when he would bump into Clare or her friends. Gradually, he began spending more time than necessary among the university's anonymous hordes, where the work he did was endlessly exhilarating. Scheduling conflicts made it necessary for him to petition the college dean to excuse him from daily chapel attendance, a privilege rarely granted at Cascade-Pacific.

Toward the second half of winter quarter, his grades in Japanese began to decline somewhat, and nothing he did seemed to remedy the situation. Bill took his worries to Professor Tatsumi.

"Most students would be perfectly satisfied with grades like yours," he said.

"I'm not just earning grades," Bill protested. "I want to learn the language inside out."

"That's very admirable, but you're going about it all wrong."

"What do you mean? This course is like a monster. It's eating up the time I need to devote to my course work at Cascade-Pacific, and still it's not satisfied."

"But the difficulties you're having are not language difficulties," Professor Tatsumi observed. "Students come to me constantly with the same misconception. They think they can 'learn the language' as though it were some kind of abstract skill that existed in a vacuum—like learning algebra. Language doesn't work that way. Language is immersed in culture. You just don't know anything about the country and its culture—the 'background' knowledge that everybody *inside* the culture can safely assume everybody else knows without further explanation. If you really want to learn Japanese 'inside out,' you're going to have to learn about Japanese culture inside out."

"But—"

"Now, wait a minute, I was just getting to my pitch." Professor Tatsumi smiled broadly, his tortoise-shell glasses riding up on the wide bridge of his nose. "You're one of the best students I've had in years. Why don't you apply to do graduate work here?"

"You mentioned that possibility before, but I'm going into the ministry."

"I remember. But you'd make a first-rate academic."

"Thanks, Professor. I will think about it."

Bill had never imagined that a compliment could cause him such distress. He had been taking his calling for granted so long now that the appearance of another alternative was forcing him to question why he was going into the ministry when serving God had dropped to his second priority. The cause that lived closest to his heart was the search into his past, and it was to this that he was now devoting the greatest portion of his energy—not that it was yielding tangible results. But the more he learned, the closer he felt to his memory of Mitsu.

Bill was called into Dean Foster's office at the end of April. He could only imagine that the dean was going to reprimand him for lack of interest in his courses at Cascade-Pacific. Instead, he stared in disbelief when the cherub-faced dean declared that, owing to his outstanding academic record and his avowed goal of missionary service, Bill had been chosen to make the Robert L. Houston Memorial Address at the graduation ceremony this June.

"Thank you, sir … thank you very much. But I can't do it," he replied, astonished himself to realize the truth and finality of his own words.

Dean Foster's face flushed a bright pink. "Now, see here, Morton, this is a great honor. I've already informed your parents and they're tickled to death."

"I don't know what to say, sir. I never imagined …"

"I'd say that makes you all the more suited for the honor. A sign of true humility."

"Believe me, sir, it's not humility. I've changed my plans. I don't think I will be doing missionary work."

"You don't *think* so? You're not sure, then."

"No, I'm not going to. I'm definitely not." He was smiling now, and he felt his heart pounding.

"This is a very serious business, Morton. I do wish you had informed us earlier of your decision."

"But I couldn't. I made it just now."

"Do you mind telling me why? I was under the impression you had been studying Japanese at the university specifically to prepare yourself for missionary service."

"I was."

"If this is some kind of whim …"

"Call it a flash of insight. Something has happened to my faith over the past year, something I haven't quite worked out for myself. I only know I have lost some of the certainty it takes to make believers out of non-believers."

"In other words, you've been accepting a 25% ministerial discount on tuition, and now that you're about to graduate—"

"Please, Dean Foster, it's nothing as crass as that. I'm just not sure what I want to do anymore."

The next day, Bill submitted his application for graduate study in the university's Department of Far Eastern and Slavic Languages and Literature. When he gave the news to Professor Tatsumi in the hall afterward, the professor let out a loud "Yes!" that echoed up and down the marble-floored corridor of Thomson Hall and brought him startled glances.

"Too bad you didn't decide sooner," the Professor said afterward. "We could have gotten you a fellowship."

When Bill took his final exam in Biblical Theology on June 9, workmen were beginning to erect the tent framework in front of Bander Hall for the graduation ceremonies on Saturday. Some of the other students came dangerously close to violating the college rule against dancing in public when they witnessed the hubbub.

At Maneki, the boss's wife, Kumiko, chattered endlessly about the "great future" he had in store.

When graduation day came, the sight of the red-and-white candy-striped tent in the morning sunshine meant only that he would have to endure a few more hours with his family, who were seated inside. He watched his father shake hands with Dean Foster and introduce Lucy and their sons Kevin and Mark, both of whom had inherited Lucy's bright red hair.

He spotted Clare standing with her friends jabbering away. She never once looked in his direction.

Precisely at ten o'clock the processional music started, and the faculty began to file into the tent. When it came time for him to march down the center aisle, he noticed a small, dark-haired woman in the audience.

After he had taken one or two more strides ahead, he glanced back to make sure. Yes, it was Kumiko, her eyes shining in his direction, looking as proud as any mother in the assembly. For the first time, he experienced the sense of fulfillment he imagined the others in the graduating class to be feeling.

President Shelton climbed to the podium. "Welcome to the sixty-sixth annual commencement on this glorious eleventh day of June 1960. This has been another wonderful year in the history of our college. Academically, we have seen definite enrichment of the curriculum and increased interest on the part of both faculty and students in genuine scholarship, research, and world service. Along with this growth has been equal progress as a Christian institution."

At that point, the air began to rumble, and President Shelton looked up, smiling sheepishly, as a huge silver plane without propellers thundered across the sky. It was one of Boeing's new jet planes on a test flight. The audience waited patiently for the roaring to die down and the speech to resume.

"Society, everywhere, needs the penetration of the spirit of anointed Christians. God has a program for each of you, our graduating seniors. How you react to His divine call will finally constitute your biography. And now, when the words 'under God' have been added to our national Pledge of Allegiance to the flag, it is all the more incumbent upon us, as representatives of the Northwest's only evangelical Christian liberal arts college, to respond to the world's need for Christian leaders. Let us join in renewed dedication of heart, mind and energy, under God, in making Cascade-Pacific College throughout the years ahead a dynamic influence in the lives of increasing thousands of young people to the end that they, too, shall accomplish God's will for them. To one and all I say, 'Fare-you-well.'"

Had Bill graduated a year ago, the president's remarks would have fit in perfectly with the benevolent rhetoric he grew up hearing and might have remained immersed in for life. Now, he was standing outside it, wondering what it meant, wondering what it really and truly meant for him. More than anyone else, his father had represented the unquestionable reality of this world. If a man so wholly dedicated to these comforting words was capable of harboring such a terrible secret, how much could they mean to anyone?

The same doubts assailed him as he listened to Colin Ashwood, the Houston Memorial speaker. Bill wondered how he himself could possibly have stood up there speaking of "the inspiration of the Scriptures," "the efficacy of Atonement," or "the personal return of the Lord Jesus Christ."

After the ceremony, the Morton men—Tom, Bill, the fourteen-year-old Kevin, and Mark, twelve—posed together in the spring sunlight as Lucy aimed the camera at them. Tom grumbled to Bill, "That could have been you up there. Dean Foster told me."

Before Bill had a chance to answer, he heard an all-too-familiar voice. "Here, let me, Mrs. Morton. You get in the photo too." Clare, in the black, red, gold and white of academic dress, her long, blond tresses released from the mortarboard now, practically snatched the Brownie Hawkeye from Lucy.

Looking down into the box camera's viewfinder, Clare called out, "Say 'cheese,' everybody!"

"Cheese!" cried the others obediently, but still she did not press the shutter.

"Come on, Bill, smile!" said Clare. "I see your Japanese girlfriend came to watch you graduate!" She swung the camera in Kumiko's direction. "She's right over *there*!" Her thumb came down on the shutter button with a loud click.

Kumiko stiffened when the entire Morton family turned their gazes on her. She slipped behind a row of arborvitae.

Bill broke from the ranks and strode toward the gloating Clare, yanking the black box from her grasp. "I never meant to hurt you, Clare. That was uncalled for."

Without looking back, he lunged through the crowd in search of Kumiko, but she had disappeared.

"What was that all about?" his father demanded when Bill returned with the camera.

"Never mind," Bill muttered. "Let's get out of here."

"What about the picture?" cried Mark.

"Forget it," said Bill, but when Lucy and Mark insisted, he resumed the unwelcome pose.

"I want a full explanation at home," muttered Tom when they were standing side by side again.

"There's nothing to explain."

"Come on, now!" cried Lucy. "Where are those smiles?"

They drove to Magnolia in a two-car caravan. Bill wanted to have his car available. Lucy rode with Bill.

"I only pray," she said to him when they were alone in the front seat, "that today you and your father can put behind you whatever it is that has made things so difficult over the past year."

He glanced at her. The last few times he had seen her, she had been wearing large curlers, but today, with her face framed in soft, red waves, she looked lovely—if a little sad.

"I'd like to straighten things out with him, too, but I don't have high hopes."

"That's a terrible attitude," she said.

"I'm afraid it's the only one I have right now." He could see from the corner of his eye that she was looking at him, but he refused to take his eyes from the road.

"And who was that blond girl?" she asked.

"She ... we used to see a lot of each other. She didn't take it well when we broke up at the beginning of the school year."

"Well, why *did* you break up? She's a very pretty girl. Did it have something to do with that ... that Japanese woman?"

"Indirectly, I suppose. Not really."

"She was acting like a jealous woman. I hope there was nothing to that remark of hers about her being your 'Japanese girlfriend.'"

Bill paused. "It's a complicated story," he said finally.

"Oh, Bill! I've tried so hard to be a mother to you, but you've never let me!" Her voice cracked, and her questioning stopped. Before long, they pulled up to the house on the bluff.

Bill felt as if he had not seen the place in years. He could hardly believe that he had actually lived behind those dark walls. Inside, Lucy stripped sheets of wax paper from the platters arranged on the dining room table, revealing a spread that seemed too lavish to be in his honor. No one else seemed to notice his presence, either, at first. He might just as well have been at some convention where strangers mill around the hors d'oeuvres, trying not to look at each other's bulging mouths.

The boys immediately grabbed handfuls of chocolate chip cookies and Lucy brought in refrigerated platters to fill the few bare spots on the table. Bill put a deviled egg and a small mound of tuna salad on his plate, then stood staring out through the patio door. He could hear his father munching on celery sticks, but neither said a word.

Lucy joined the glum, little gathering, "Let's have a toast!"

She poured lemonade into the glasses lined up on the table and held one out for him and one for his father. They were forced to approach each other in taking the drinks from her, and she raised her own in salute.

"Congratulations, Bill," she said. "We're proud of you."

The three clinked glasses. Both men looked down at the small, nervous redhead, and then, at long last, faced each other. Only now did Bill realize that his father had aged, his leathery skin become worn and wrinkled. Bill found it impossible to smile, but Tom managed to say, "Yes. Congratulations."

"Thank you both," Bill said and sipped his lemonade. His parents looked at him, waiting for him to say something else. He wished that he could slip out unnoticed, as one does at a church function that has gone on too long. Unfortunately, though, he was the guest of honor and he had to be here to respond when his step-mother remarked how fortunate they had been to have had such nice weather for the ceremony, and weren't the floral displays beautiful, and the girls looked so lovely and the men so handsome all decked out in their academic robes and singing so fervently. She had noticed little groups of girls afterward, hugging each other and crying, and it had reminded her of her own high school graduation.

It dawned on Bill that if he could keep the conversation confined to the graduation ceremony or to highlights of his college career, avoiding any talk of the future, everything would be all right. He mentioned Dr. Sweeney, the scholar with whom he had studied medieval history, and how pleased he had been to see the dear, old man at the ceremony today in his robes, whiskers fluttering in the breeze. "He pretends to be such an old curmudgeon," he noted, "but I saw tears in his eyes today."

While he spoke, Bill saw Kevin glancing at him from across the room. Fourteen now, Kevin was taller than his mother, his body slim and wiry.

"Why don't you join us, fellas?" Bill called to Kevin and Mark, realizing that they, too, could provide topics for conversation that would fill the time until he could decently excuse himself. Even the twelve-year-old Mark might have something to say about his own coming graduation from elementary school.

"Looking forward to going to McClure next year?" Bill asked with as much enthusiasm as he could muster.

"Kind of," said Mark, scratching his nose.

Bill wondered what to say to Kevin. The freckled redhead always became sullen when his elder half-brother was around. He still had a scar above his right eye from a fall over the bluff across the street. Bill had tried to grab him at the last moment, but had succeeded only in accelerating his fall. Bill could never convince Kevin that it had been an accident.

Lucy excused herself to heat some pastry. As soon as she was gone, Tom looked at Bill and said, "Come into my study."

The boys glanced at each other, and Mark, hunching his shoulders, muttered, "Uh-oh!" Bill followed his father across the living room to the heavy, dark-brown door that he had always tried to avoid passing through.

"I was going to ask you what that little scene on campus was all about, but the more I think about it, the less I want to know," Tom said as soon as the door had closed behind Bill.

"I'm sorry about—"

Tom held up his hand to cut him short. "I have paid over a thousand dollars this year so that you could finish college, and I would like to know what I am getting for my money. You haven't said a word about what you plan to do with your life. Well, now I want to hear it."

Bill's eyes wandered over the holy books that lined his father's shelves, grazed the sacred images upon the wall, then settled on the burning blue eyes that could be avoided no longer.

"I'll be entering graduate school at the U.W. this fall. I'll be studying Japanese."

"I told you, you'll be wasting your time. Any mission to Japan is doomed to failure."

"I won't be going as a missionary."

"I don't understand," Tom said.

"I'm not ready to commit myself to the ministry."

"You mean to tell me that after four years of study, you're not even going to enter the ministry?" His voice rose with each word.

"Not yet. There are too many questions in my life that need answering." Bill struggled to remain calm, but his hands were beginning to tremble.

"Questions? You know as well as I do where all the answers to all the questions are to be found."

"No," Bill said, his voice struggling to escape his parched throat. "The Bible says nothing about a woman named Mitsuko."

Tom sagged back against a tall bookcase.

"She was your wife, wasn't she?"

"That's a lie!"

"I have no reason to lie," said Bill. "Just tell me the truth. That's all I've ever asked of you."

There was a tentative knock on the door, and Lucy poked her head inside. With a strained smile, she said, "It's not very polite to disappear from—"

"Leave us alone!" Tom shouted, blasting her out of the room.

"Shall I tell you what I know?" Bill said.

"I don't want to hear the filth that others have been telling you."

"I want to hear the truth from my father's own lips!"

"I wouldn't profane myself with this evil."

Lucy burst into the room. "What is happening with you two?" she wailed.

"Lucy, stay out of this room!" Tom shouted, but she stood her ground.

"Coward!" shouted Bill. "You're afraid of the truth! Doesn't 'atonement' mean anything to you? How can you live with yourself?"

Suddenly Bill was slammed up against the wall, the wind knocked out of him. He fell to the floor with Kevin's knees on his chest. "Take it back! Take it back!" Kevin screamed, pounding Bill's face and body with his bony fists. Bill shielded his face, but the boy kept flailing wildly, and his knuckles stung. Lucy tried to restrain Kevin from behind, and Bill grabbed the boy's wrists. The scar over Kevin's right eye was bright red. "I hate you!" he screamed. "Get out of our house!"

With Lucy's help, Bill managed to drag himself from underneath the squirming Kevin. He stumbled out through the door of the study, nudging past Mark, who stood there frozen, and made his way across the living room. Throwing open the front door, he lunged into the warm spring sunlight.

28

c/o Niiyama
Ogikubo 1-124
Suginami-ku
Tokyo, Japan

November 15, 1962

Dear Frank,
        You are probably wondering if the earth
has opened up and swallowed me since I left
Seattle almost two months ago. Let me assure
you first of all that everything went off as
scheduled. The Fulbright people met a planeload
of us at Haneda Airport, brought us in to a fancy
hotel called the New Japan, and proceeded to
"orient" us to the Orient for three solid days
under hermetically sealed conditions. The only
indication I had that I was in a new country
came the first day when I noticed that the whole
building was swaying. It was my first earthquake
and it came as quite a shock (no pun intended).
There have been several since, and now I take them
very calmly.
        Perhaps I ought to mention one other
little shock I received during orientation. By the
second day, I was thoroughly fed up with seminars
and hotel food and I decided to launch out on my
own. I left the hotel and walked down a narrow
street to a main thoroughfare clutching an old
Occupation Army map of Tokyo in my hand. (It did
me no good whatever, and I have since discovered
that the only way to find your way around is with
Japanese maps printed in booklet form with each
spread showing a particular ward of the city.) In
contrast to the artificial calm surrounding the
hotel, the main street had trolley cars screeching
back and forth and motor scooters and tiny cars
roaring past, kicking up clouds of dust. There was
a seedy, little restaurant facing the street, with
plastic models of food displayed behind its dusty
windows. I immediately recognized katsudon from
Maneki and went in and ordered a bowl. I was glad
to find that the Japanese I learned in Seattle
really does work, though the "real thing" is still
something of a shock. (I keep writing about these
"shocks" I've been getting, but, if anything, I'm
not using the word enough. This shock is not the

shock I said I was going to tell you about. That
comes in the next paragraph.)

So, anyway, I left the restaurant,
feeling at last that I had arrived in Japan, and
the feeling only increased when I climbed a green
embankment running parallel to the narrow street
I had taken from the hotel. I followed a dirt
path on the embankment that was lined with little
pine trees twisted into all sorts of interesting
forms, as if walking through a life-size bonsai
tray or through some of the Sesshu landscapes
I had seen in Professor Fleming's art history
class. Down at the far end of the path, I saw a
man who looked as if he had been standing there
since the Meiji period. He wore nineteenth-century
Japanese clothing top and bottom--which means he
was in skirts and had a cape on his shoulders.
He was somewhat bent over and leaning on a cane
and when I drew closer, I could see that the felt
hat he had on was old and battered, though not
at all shabby. He looked like Nagai Kafu or one
of those other great Meiji writers who had been
to the West but returned to find their Japanese
roots. I knew for sure that I was in Japan, and I
was filled with an overwhelming desire to talk to
him and thus to commune with the Japanese past.
Still holding my Occupation map, I approached him
and, in the most exquisitely polite Japanese I
could muster, said, "Excuse me, sir, but could you
please be so kind as to tell me the name of the
street down there below the embankment?"

He looked up at me through his old-
fashioned, round wire-frame glasses and said,
in equally exquisite Americanese, "Hey, Mister,
you from the States? I used to sell peanuts on
Coney Island." And he went on to tell me how, for
decades, he had traveled up and down the East
Coast selling peanuts and popcorn on beaches and
in amusement parks. He was a dear, old fellow, but
I doubt if he had even heard of Nagai Kafu. And he
never did tell me the name of that street.

The Fulbright people got me connected
with the University of Tokyo, and I have been
attending a seminar there on my specialty, the Noh
plays of the fifteenth century. I've also been
going to the theater a lot to see what Noh looks
like in the flesh. Actually, Noh hasn't got a lot
of flesh, it's so austere and restrained. Let's
face it, at the U.W. I was so overwhelmed with
Professor McCracken's encyclopedic knowledge of
and enthusiasm for the subject that I was sure it
was what I wanted to study, too. It seems that I

spent my two years in graduate school living in the fifteenth century, and I'm still trying to acclimatize myself to twentieth-century Tokyo. If I have a few more shocks like the one with the peanut seller, the transformation should be complete before too long!

A couple of the advanced graduate students at Todai (short for the University of Tokyo) have taken me under their wing. Haruo Nishino, the more scholarly one, knows almost the entire Noh repertory by heart, and he will chant lyrics at the slightest provocation, which usually means at bars. (Yes, I go to bars now. Imagine that! Next time you and I drink together, I might have something stronger than orange juice. Then again, I might not.) The other fellow's name is Keiichi Tashiro. He is probably the gentlest, kindest person I've ever met—until he gets a little alcohol in him. The two of them are so courtly at school, and they turn into feuding sailors when they've been drinking. I like them both, though, and we go everywhere together. My Japanese is improving by leaps and bounds.

I must confess that I have been enjoying all this immensely. The country is neither an Oriental paradise nor is it completely Westernized. (Actually, I shouldn't be talking about "the country" at all: I have yet to set foot outside of Tokyo, and I keep hearing how much stronger traditions are elsewhere.) Just when you think you might as well be in downtown Seattle (no, that's crazy, no part of Tokyo could ever be confused with Seattle—downtown or otherwise: you've never seen such crowds! The sheer volume of humanity here is probably the biggest shock of all, and, let's face it, the city is plain ugly. It wears its modern machinery out in the open: viewed from an elevated train or a tall building such as my hotel, it looks like what space you find under the hood of your car—hoses, wires, tanks, nuts and bolts, but, as I was saying before I started this parenthetical detour), you run across some little pocket of culture that has survived from the days of the shogun and the samurai.

I don't know how long this is going to last, though. Tokyo is in a fever getting itself ready for the 1964 Olympic Games and you're constantly hearing about how this or that has to be cleaned up or covered over or gotten rid of before the foreigners start pouring into the country "only" two years from now. There are new

subway lines being put in, and every other day the
work has to be stopped for some new archeological
find. (Sometimes the "archeology" only goes back
as far as 1945 when lost air raid shelters are
found and people are "reunited" with long-dead
relatives.) The amount of construction everywhere
is just breathtaking—almost as breathtaking
as the amount of destruction accompanying it.
Sometimes it feels as if the whole city is being
built up and torn down at the same time.

The government is also pursuing a
campaign urging people to clean up certain
kinds of behavior before the games start. The
Japanese are known for their extreme attention to
cleanliness, of course, but you'd be amazed to
see what litterbugs they are, casually dropping
old newspapers anywhere they happen to finish
reading them, discarding lunch wrappings and used
chopsticks and empty disposable tea pots on train
seats, smearing the ground with gobs of phlegm (no
wonder they take their shoes off at home!). One
of the most disgusting sights is that of drunks
sprawling on the benches of the commuter trains
at night or vomiting anywhere the urge happens
to hit them—over the edge of train platforms, on
the platforms, and not infrequently inside the
trains themselves. People usually look the other
way. Apparently, drunkenness is viewed as a valid
excuse for all sorts of anti-social behavior.
One more example of male grossness is acceptable
even without such an excuse (though no doubt the
drinking contributes to it): urinating in public.
You know how energetic the Japanese are supposed
to be, and I would say the image is a true one,
to the point where I have formulated a rule (call
it Morton's Law): No matter what time of day or
night, if you see a Japanese man standing still,
he is in the act of emptying his bladder. If this
is traditional behavior, then I'm all in favor of
doing away with it!

I am glad to say that most encounters
with Japanese tradition are pleasant surprises.
I'm still amazed when I'm walking through a fairly
modernized neighborhood and I run across a little
tatami shop with the owner sitting there cross-
legged, usually in a T-shirt and laborers' pants
something like riding jodhpurs, and sewing thick
floor mats with a huge needle.

Speaking of tatami, I am living in a
small, two-room arrangement that is half-Japanese,
half-Western. The family that owns the house had
converted these two upstairs rooms to wood floors,

but I paid to have the larger room re-converted
to a six-mat tatami room, though I haven't gone so
far as to sleep on futon on the floor yet. I sleep
on a bed in the narrow, wood-floored Western room,
off of which there is a wash basin and mirror.
This is the entire second story of the house, so
you can imagine how small the house is. When I'm
at home, I spend most of my time in the tatami
room.

The Niiyamas are nice people, but
they both studied in the States as Fulbright
students (of course, the Fulbright office got
me the connection) and speak excellent English,
which makes practicing Japanese with them very
difficult. For that reason, I don't see a lot of
them. I usually eat at restaurants rather than
with them—which must sound very extravagant, but
prices at local restaurants are so low that it
puts no strain on my budget. In fact, at 360 yen
to the dollar, nothing puts a strain on my budget.
I'm rich here, living on an American student
budget. A ride on the National Railways train that
comes out to this rather suburban part of the city
costs only ¥10. That's about three cents! And the
most beautifully printed books can be bought for
a dollar. My library has expanded dramatically!
There's an amazing section of town called Jimbo-
cho, where you see almost nothing but book stores
for block after block. I tend to get lost there
for days at a time.

One small but unexpected expense here
is the bath. Rather than try to fit my schedule
in with that of the family, I have been going to
the public baths, which is where most ordinary
Japanese go to get clean. You give your ¥17 to the
old lady who sits in her perch overlooking both
the men's and women's sides, undress right there
in a wood-floored locker room, and step through
sliding glass doors into a steaming cavern full
of naked men and boys crouching on little stools
and scrubbing themselves as if they're determined
to get down to the third and fourth layers of
skin. After they're through rinsing off, they
soak in scalding hot tubs until they've turned
bright red. The people in my neighborhood bath
have finally gotten used to seeing this big, blond
American going through the same routine, and I
find I have some of my most pleasant conversations
while soaking in the tub. It made me a little
uneasy when some of the men I met there offered
to scrub my back, but I guess it's a gesture of
friendliness and I see people doing it all the time.

I'm probably giving you the impression
that I spend all my time with Japanese, even to
the point of avoiding people who speak English.
It's true, there are Americans living here who
never see a Japanese or learn a word of the
language, and I would avoid people like that if
I had any occasion to meet them, which I do not,
since they are mostly in business or the Army and
they stay in their little enclaves. I have become
very good friends with some Americans who live
next door in a house rented out by the Niiyamas.
Their name is Green: David and Martha Green and
their little son, Peter. They have been here
almost three years on a work visa (except Peter,
of course, who was born here). David teaches at an
English conversation school called ELEC (English
Language something-or-other: there are hundreds
of these places) and he has become an authentic
national celebrity. The rage for learning English
is so great in this country that NHK, the Japan
Broadcasting Corporation, has TV English courses
at all levels, and they hire foreigners to
appear on them to provide accurate pronunciation
models. David's name even appears in the daily TV
listings, and I have been with him when people
have come up and asked for his autograph on their
textbooks. At 6'1", like me, he is very tall here,
and if that weren't enough, his bushy walrus
moustache makes him extremely easy to spot. He
has suggested that I go on the show some time to
give the audience a little variety, but I've been
resisting.

Back to food again. I thought I had
gotten to know Japanese food pretty well in
Seattle, but the quantity and variety available
here is simply overwhelming. I'm now a confirmed
raw fish addict. I even went with Haruo and
Keiichi down to the Tsukiji fish market at four
in the morning to see the day's supply for the
city being delivered and sold. You would be amazed
at the sight of the huge, tin-roofed concrete
slab covered with sparkling tuna. Haruo and
Keiichi took me to one restaurant, though, where
I encountered my limits as a Japanese gourmet.
The fish was not raw there, though I found myself
almost wishing it were. The name of the place is
Komagata. It has a long history going back into
the Edo period, and it is located in the lively,
old merchant class section of the city called
Asakusa. (Of course the building itself is not
that old. This part of the city was virtually
flattened by fire bombs during the war.) Their

specialty is a little fish known as dojoh which
is not much bigger than a minnow. I looked it up
later and found it is called "loach" in English
and it lives in mud, which I can easily believe.
When they're cooking at the table, arranged like
the spokes of a wheel in round, iron, gas-fired
cookers, they look like mud, and even drowned
in soy sauce, they taste like mud. There is
one method of cooking them that is especially
horrifying. The little creatures are served to
you live, swimming in an earthenware pot around a
cake of tofu floating in cold water, and the pot
is set on the fire. As the water heats up, the
dojoh become frantic and try to save themselves
by burrowing into the cool tofu. Finally, you're
supposed to eat the tofu after it's cooked through
with all these poor dojoh embedded inside. They
call this dish "dojoh-jigoku," which means "dojoh
hell." I absolutely refused to eat it. I felt
queasy for two days after I left that place.
        Some of my most successful culinary
discoveries have not involved Japanese food at
all. Tokyo is remarkable not only for its mixture
of new and old Japan but for the availability here
of all the world's culture. I'm eating Chinese,
French, Russian, German, Hungarian and Italian
dishes that I had never heard of in Seattle. I had
to come to the Far East to learn how little I know
about the West. I'd guess the average Tokyoite
is exposed to more Western high culture than
the average American. Sometimes my ignorance of
classical music or European history makes me feel
like a real country bumpkin.
        I suspect you're finding this all
very frustrating and you want me to get down to
business. Believe me, I am just as impatient with
myself. It is only now, when I am learning about
the real Japan, that I am beginning to understand
how I was able to immerse myself so completely in
my studies. Noh and the other arts of the medieval
period are very otherworldly. Instead of bald
realism, they rely on suggestion, indirection
and mystery because they are based on a Buddhist
belief in the unreality of the everyday "real"
world. They suggest that what is real and true is
something transcendent. Obviously (it's obvious
to me now, though it was not so obvious when I
started graduate school in 1960) these ideas
appealed to me as a kind of substitute for the
religious feeling I had come close to losing then.
When I began to learn the truth about my father,
it shook my spiritual life to its foundations, and

I am still wondering if I will ever recover. I almost never go to church anymore, and when I do, it's mainly as a tourist. I've been to a Catholic church, a Greek Orthodox, the old Protestant church on Reinanzaka, and a few others, where I mostly sit and look. But the process of discovery has been a painful one for me, and I can see, now, that I have been using my studies not only as a way to realize my goal but also as a way to hide from what I must do.

To put it simply, I am afraid. The more I learn about this country--the more I learn to find my way around here--the less excuse I have for postponing my search. But what am I going to find? As much as you were able to share with me, it was so little! And it was your experience. How much of that can become mine, I do not know.

There is also the practical matter of my having almost nothing to go on. I am looking for a woman named Mitsuko and her sister, Yoshiko Nomura. I couldn't have picked more ordinary names to work with! Once I feel confident of my ability to begin scouring the countryside, how am I to go about it? Of course, I can use the lack of facts as an excuse for doing nothing at all. But I will not do that, I can assure you. When the time comes, I will not hesitate.

In the meantime, my dear friend, please be patient. It meant a great deal to me to have you see me off at the airport, and you must not think that I have forgotten about you or our search. (I haven't forgotten about Maneki, either. Please say hello from me to Kumiko and the Bosu-san and to Norman Miki and the guys.) After two months, I am just beginning to get my bearings. I will let you know when I have made any progress, and, if you don't mind, I will write from time to time simply to share some of my new experiences with you. If you can find a spare moment or two, please drop me a line.

      Yours,
      Bill

29

THE RIVER OF JAPANESE people flowed on and on, covering every square inch of the gravel crunching underfoot. The New Year's Day crowd carried Bill and the Greens down the Meiji Shrine's broad, tree-lined avenue. The river took a sharp left turn beneath a towering Shinto shrine gate. Far ahead, it made another sharp turn, this time to the right, where Bill imagined the main shrine building must lie. The orderliness of the crowd was remarkable—and indispensable: panic would have been fatal in a situation like this.

"This is the biggest wooden *torii* in Japan." David Green pointed up to the huge wooden cross-pieces towering fifty feet above them as they passed underneath. The gate's giant pillars straddling the crowd would have been impossible for a man—perhaps even two men—to put their arms around.

"I believe it," Bill said, but David was grinning for a woman staring at him, his walrus moustache stretching from side to side. She was another of his TV fans, no doubt.

Martha, walking between them, was beginning to struggle carrying Peter on her shoulders. Almost six feet tall herself, she held Peter high above the crowd. She had dressed her sandy-haired son in a necktie and wool vest under a brass-buttoned, navy blue blazer. He looked like Little Lord Fauntleroy.

"C'mere, Pete!" Bill called, holding his arms out to the boy, whose desperate arm-hold around his mother's forehead threatened to send her black-framed glasses down to be trampled by the relentless horde. At first, he seemed reluctant to leave his mother, but Martha leaned toward Bill, who caught him under the arms and raised him up until he could straddle Bill's shoulders. Now Bill had to walk with two short arms wrapped tightly around his head.

"I needed that," Martha groaned. "Thanks."

"Half of Tokyo must be here today," Bill said.

"All ten million!" David laughed. Talk to anybody tomorrow, and they'll tell you they were here."

"But why?" asked Bill. "Is the cult of the Emperor Meiji still so deeply rooted?"

"Don't be ridiculous, it's just a tradition. Nobody's thinking about the Emperor Meiji."

"That's hard to believe," Bill said. Something more than "tradition" had to be behind the turnout of this many people. And if they weren't thinking about the Emperor Meiji, what were they thinking about? The puzzle only deepened for Bill as he neared the main shrine. People were tossing coins into the wooden grille of the offertory box, clapping their hands together and bowing briefly before the austere wooden building upon which no images were displayed, and in the depths of which could be discerned nothing but gloomy empty spaces. He had heard that the Meiji Shrine was one of the holiest pilgrimage sites in the country, but the "pilgrimages" being performed here were so swift and simple that there could be no time for what he had always thought of as "praying." Whatever these people were experiencing, it was wordless. And yet, undoubtedly, it was every bit as real as the elaborate masses he had been observing at Saint Ignatius or the Nicolai Cathedral. It was a moment of reverence—to what, or for what, it didn't seem to matter. With little Peter on his shoulders, he stepped forward and bowed his head, bringing his palms together and closing his eyes.

In the few seconds he stood there, the tiny person on his back seemed to grow enormously heavy, as if the power of gravity had suddenly increased or the boy's flesh had unexpectedly doubled or tripled in density and begun pressing down upon him. He had to plant his feet more firmly upon the earth to support this burden of flesh. And he knew that, if it cost him his life, he must continue to support this infinitely precious burden, this palpably holy child who had been entrusted to him.

Then everything was as it had been. Casting one last glance into the empty building, he moved away from the railing to follow David and Martha into the broad, stone-paved courtyard, where the press of the crowd relented and people were standing in small groups, taking each other's pictures or milling about aimlessly.

"Down!" ordered Peter, who must have spied the other children dashing back and forth among the adults now that they no longer had to fear being crushed to death.

"Let Daddy take a picture," said David.

Peter fidgeted on his shoulders while Bill waited for the click.

"All right," said David when it was done, and Bill set Peter on the ground.

"Let me take a picture of the three of you together," Bill said. After snapping the family portrait, he walked up to the Greens, put his arms around David and Martha, and practically knocked them all off balance with a big hug. "I can't tell you how glad I am you brought me here today," he declared, smiling. Peter squirmed his way out from among the six long legs that caged him and the three of them stepped back, laughing.

Bill felt a new kind of joy, a euphoria he was aching to share with the Greens, if only he could find the words. "Today I learned the meaning of 'holy infant so tender and mild,'" he said, smiling broadly. "Peter is one of those."

"Uh, sure, Bill," said David, rubbing his moustache.

"No, I'm not kidding. It's wonderful, let me tell you."

"You should try changing his diaper sometime. You've heard the expression 'holy shit,' I presume?"

Martha shrieked and swatted David on the back with her purse. "Let's buy some arrows," she said, pointing to a small stand where shrine workers were frantically handing out long, white "demon-quelling" arrows and collecting money from outstretched hands.

Bill followed the Greens to the stand, still searching for the words he could speak to them that would say what he felt and not make him sound like an absolute idiot. But it was true—Peter was a holy infant. All the hundreds of thousands of people pouring through the Meiji Shrine today—all the people who had ever felt the warmth of the sun —had been holy infants. And they all needed to eat and to urinate and to defecate and die. Century after century, men had been too stupid to see the miracle of this. They told themselves fairy stories of virgin births and gods-become-men and visitations to and from heaven in a vain attempt to make what was already holy seem holier, and all they had succeeded in doing was blinding themselves to the miracle of life. Today he had seen it. Carrying a genuine holy infant on his shoulders, he had flowed with the river of humanity, seen thousands upon thousands of the sons and daughters of man come to worship the fountain of holiness: the life throbbing within themselves.

"This is not Shinto," said Bill, still frustrated at the nonsensical sound of his own words.

"You're right," said David, "it's Mass at St. Peter's. That guy over there selling arrows is the Pope."

"I mean, nobody here is thinking about Meiji or the sun goddess Amaterasu, or how Izanagi and Izanami created the earth, or any of that stuff."

"And?"

"Being here doesn't have anything to do with your other beliefs."

"Who ever said it did? Bill, are you all right today?"

"I'm fine, really fine."

"I'm just here to see the sights and to wish for a Happy New Year like everybody else," David said. "You seem to be worried that coming in here compromises you as a Christian, but the Japanese learned long ago that you can practice Shinto and any other religion without conflict. It's hardly even a religion—not since it was taken out of the hands of the militarists after the war. They distorted it into a big state cult, but now it's more what it always used to be, just a generalized feeling of gratitude for the nice things in life. It leaves all the problems of death and guilt to the Buddhists and a few Christians. But even they bring their babies to their local shrines, and weddings are usually Shinto or at least have some Shinto elements. I'm no less a Quaker because I just clapped my hands and bowed at a Shinto shrine. The trouble with Westerners is we've gotten into the habit of thinking if you believe in one thing, you can't believe in anything else."

"That's just what I was saying."

"Oh, yeah? I would never have guessed it. I thought you were going to start singing 'Silent Night' for all the folks here."

Bill threw his head back and laughed at the top of his lungs.

Until New Year's Day, Bill had tried his best to avoid the trains at the most crowded times, but after his experience at the Meiji Shrine, he almost welcomed the prospect of riding at rush hour. Sometimes, squeezed in among the warm bodies until he could hardly breath, he would imagine that, indirectly, he was in touch with his Japanese mother again. Perhaps someone he was touching was touching someone who was touching Mitsuko. He would try to catch the eyes of women in their late forties or early fifties, hoping Mitsuko would recognize him after twenty years and throw herself into his arms. Mostly he succeeded in making a number of permanent-waved matrons nervous.

Fantasizing chance meetings was going to get him nowhere. For one thing, women of any age had good reason to be nervous on Tokyo trains. More than once, he had seen the *chikan* in action—the molesters who exploited the jam-packed conditions of the trains to run their hands over women's bodies. This was one shock he had not been prepared to describe in his letters to Frank. The first time, he had watched in horrified silence as an ordinary-looking, bespectacled man had thrust his hands under the coat of a girl no more than twenty, indulged in some heavy breathing, then relied upon the press of the crowd to keep himself standing while his eyes rolled back in his head. Bill had considered intervening, but no one else seemed to notice. It occurred to him that the girl, who uttered not a peep, was perhaps enjoying it. But the two had parted when the crowd poured out at Tokyo Station, and Bill had seen her rubbing at a stain near the front of her coat, eyes full of tears. When a similar event occurred a few days later, he reached out over the crowd and knocked the man in the side of the head, expecting to be cheered by the other passengers and thanked effusively by the maiden in distress, but everyone—including the girl and the molester—pretended as if the whole thing had never happened.

Although it was not more likely to work than hoping for a chance encounter on the subway, contacting all the Nomuras in the Tokyo phone book seemed the only avenue open to him. Frank had tried it when there were fewer phones in the country. Perhaps Bill would stand a better chance.

He found twelve pages of Nomuras in minuscule type but only a few Goros and Yoshikos. After those were exhausted, he went back to the top of the list, systematically phoning ten a day and delivering the same speech each time in his politest Japanese: "Excuse me, but I am an American named William Morton. I am searching for a Mr. and Mrs. Goro and Yoshiko Nomura who used to live in Seattle, Washington, in America, until about the year Showa twenty or twenty-one."

Most people would allow him to deliver his introduction in full, then apologize for being unable to help him. Others hung up as soon as they heard the word "American," and he worried that it was precisely those reacting strongly who were most likely to be the ones he was searching for. He imagined the person at the other end cutting the connection on impulse, then regretting the rash act but having no way to re-establish contact once it was broken.

More time-consuming were those people whose curiosity was aroused by the strange caller and who wanted to hear whatever bizarre tale it was he had to tell, but who, in the end, could offer nothing. One man speaking a crude street argot that Bill could hardly understand offered to lead him to the Nomuras for a fee, and that time Bill was the one who hung up. A woman whose hoarse voice suggested that she was the right age asked him to meet her at a coffee house in Sugamo. He waited for her with a mingled sense of anticipation and dread, but his heart sank when he saw the diseased street woman in her twenties. Some of the most heart-rending calls ended in hysterical denunciations of all Americans for having killed "my husband" or "my whole family." Bill wished that he could do something to heal the wounds still festering from the war.

And then there was the obvious objection, which his landlady, Mrs. Niiyama, never tired of pointing out to him (though he paid her ¥10 for each of the calls and was careful to return the telephone book to its proper place when he was through with the day's allotment), that the Nomuras he was seeking might not even be in Tokyo.

On one particularly frustrating day, he tried escaping to the Noh theater with its refined lyric plaints of cherry blossom spirits and court ladies in distress. He and his friends Keiichi and Haruo went to see *Obasute*. One of the loftiest plays in the ancient repertoire, "The Abandoned Crone" was an astringent exercise in detachment and abstract beauty with its cool, silver imagery of the moon and the ghost of an old woman left to die on the mountain. As the play drew to its climax and the traveler left the stage, the white-robed ghost turned in perfect synchronization with the traveler, who was abandoning her in death as she had been abandoned in life. She intoned:

> O give me back
> My autumns of yesteryear,
> To them I cling,
> To memories implacable
> The night wind cuts
> Through me, the past
> Is all I ask for now,
> Upon this mountain of despair
> Alone, deserted, aged crone!

Bill's chest tightened with sorrow. Was the woman that he sought alone somewhere, abandoned, growing old and bitter, perhaps on some mountaintop far from the city with its trains and telephones?

The spectators filed out of the theater in silence. Once on the sidewalk, however, only inches from the trucks that came screeching around the corner with headlights glaring in the night, Keiichi and Haruo gesticulated wildly in the wind, competing to see who could best express the mysterious silence of the play.

"There's only one way to resolve this," Haruo proclaimed, his eyes shining behind thick, black-framed lenses. "With beer!"

"Absolutely!" said Keiichi, pounding his open palm with a bony fist.

They were going to drag him to a bar again. The three walked from Omagari to Suidobashi Station. In their company, Bill had come to like the taste of Kirin and Sapporo, but also the native rice wine. On winter nights, especially, the comfort to be found in a nice, warm bottle of *sake* had not been lost on him, and tonight, when sharp gusts of wind were whipping up gritty dust from the streets and sidewalks, was definitely one of those nights. Bill could feel the sand between his teeth. Haruo spit into the gutter once or twice as they walked along.

The first dispute that needed to be resolved was which way to go on the Chuo Line—west to Shinjuku or east to Kanda. Bill settled that one by choosing Shinjuku, which was closer to home in Ogikubo. He was less help when it came to deciding which bar in Shinjuku to pick. Haruo preferred Club Funky, which specialized in jazz, while Keiichi maintained that such a place, after Noh, would be a desecration. They must, without question, go to the Furusato, where only traditional Japanese folk melodies were to be heard on the sound system.

Haruo conceded, and they forged into the shadowy labyrinth of Kabuki-cho, the three of them walking arm in arm with the harsh reds and yellows of neon signs splashing their excited faces. No sooner had they entered these intoxicating environs than their steps became unsteady, and their linked elbows yanked each other back and forth, though not a drop of drink had passed their lips.

A huge straw sandal, probably five feet long, hung on the back wall of the Furusato. On the other walls were pieces of traditional pottery in a variety of earth colors, and ancient wooden farm implements such as winnowing baskets and threshing sticks. The ceiling resembled the underside of a thatched farmhouse roof, and to the left hung a large, black hook holding an iron pot over an old-fashioned sunken hearth. Music was coming from loudspeakers somewhere in the corners of the warm, dark room.

Since the bar itself was crammed full, they sat at one of the few remaining empty tables, which was barely large enough for three men to fit their knees beneath. The surface of the small table was done in dark tile—four slate-colored squares, or so they appeared in the murky light. A woman wearing blue-and-white speckled *mompe* trousers and the white bandanna of a farm worker came to take their order. Keiichi and Haruo both wanted draught beer, and Bill asked for *sake*.

"This is a great song," said Keiichi.

The single, thin voice on the record was accompanied by the strains of a shamisen, a three-stringed instrument with a cat-skin head. Much of the singing accompanied by the shamisen sounded to Bill as if it were being done by the cat itself—at the very moment of being skinned. The voice now coming out of the loudspeaker, though, was sweet and frail and lovely.

Once they were settled at the table and the waitress had brought peanuts and tiny rice crackers for them to munch with their drinks, Keiichi launched into his interpretation of why, in spite of the fact that it depicted an old woman—and a commoner to boot—*Obasute* was considered to be such a lofty work. Haruo observed that it was his favorite Noh play—his favorite play of any kind.

Bill tried to concentrate on the ensuing discussion, but the music kept breaking in on his concentration. The woman on the record was now singing the lament of a child who has been scolded and sent on an errand, and her voice was perfectly complemented by the breathy sound of a flute. As the warmth of the sake began to circulate, the literary debate at the table sounded increasingly unimportant, though the effect of the beer on both Bill's companions was to raise the volume at which they offered their profundities to each other.

Bill was sorry to hear the needle of the phonograph clicking in the final grooves of the record, and the next LP started out disappointingly, with lush strings and electronically exaggerated drums and shamisens.

"Listen to that shit," growled Keiichi, his gaunt, bony face flushed with drink. "I hate it when they 'modernize' folk music by crapping it up with all those Western instruments."

"Shut up," slurred Haruo. "S'nice. Sounds like Mantovani."

"Your taste is up your asshole," replied Keiichi.

"What do *you* know?" countered Haruo.

"What is this stuff?" asked Bill, still intrigued.

"Kyushu *minyoh*," answered Keiichi—"folk songs from the island of Kyushu. Isn't it disgusting?"

"You got something against Kyushu?" challenged Haruo.

"Don't be stupid. I love the music. Just listen to what they're doing to it. It's not Japanese anymore."

"All of a sudden, you're a purist."

Bill could side with neither of them. This singer definitely belonged to the most authentic cat variety, but the pounding bass and whining violins imported from the West made the whole even more unpalatable than the real music might have been.

"I'm glad that's over," Keiichi groaned as the first selection ended. But when the next number started, it was in the same style. He violently rubbed his face and grumbled, "Okay, I've had it!" He dragged himself up from his chair and staggered toward the little booth where the turntable was located.

Haruo looked at Bill, wide-eyed. "He's going to make them change the record," he said, laughing raucously.

But Bill was not looking at Keiichi anymore. Instead, he was staring into the dark corner from which the music echoed. Beneath all the moaning saxophones and swishing cymbals, something terribly familiar was coming out of the loudspeaker. The harsh, piercing voice of a woman began to sing, "*Odoma Bon-giri Bon-giri, Bon kara sakya orando, Bon ga hayo kurya, Hayo modoru.*" It was in a dialect that meant nothing to him, and yet he recognized it. More than recognized it. He knew that melody with his whole heart.

Suddenly the bar was convulsed by the amplified screech of a phonograph needle being dragged across the grooves of a record.

Bill turned to see Keiichi leaning clumsily over a low partition that surrounded the record center, his hand fumbling with the tone arm. The bartender, overhead lights shining on his bald pate, rushed in his direction, crying, "Please, sir! Customers are not allowed to handle the equipment."

"Then don't make our ears dirty with that phony garbage!"

Shouts and laughter filled the place.

Stumbling over outstretched legs, Bill fought his way through the crowd, latching onto Keiichi's waist from behind. "Stop it, Keiichi! I have to hear that song!"

"I won't listen to this shit!"

With the bartender's help, Bill lifted his sprawling friend away from the turntable. Apologizing as best he could to the bartender, he begged the man to start the record up again.

"Look, he's ruined it," he replied, holding up the scratched platter.

"Please," Bill said. "Just that one song. I have to hear it all the way through."

The man looked at Bill oddly and mumbled something about "strange foreigners." Then he said, "I can't play a scratched record. It would offend the other customers."

"I'll pay for it." Bill pulled a wad of bills out of his pocket.

"This record cost two thousand yen."

"All right. All right." Bill stripped off three ¥1000 notes. "Just play that one track, and I'll take the record off your hands when it's through."

Keiichi sat on the partition, his mouth agape, observing this incomprehensible transaction. Bill helped him back to his seat while the bartender placed the record on the turntable.

"What was that all about?" asked Haruo as they came stumbling back.

"Just shut up and listen," Bill said, dropping the drunken Keiichi in his chair. Keiichi slumped down on the table, moaning.

Again the overblown orchestral prelude came flowing through the smoky air, and again the meaningless words came screeching out of the loudspeaker. He was surer than ever now that he knew the song, even punctuated by the sharp clicks that resounded with each revolution of the record.

"What is this?" Bill asked Haruo, who was looking at him as though he had suddenly gone mad.

"I don't know, just some folk song. It's a lullaby."

"Where is it from?"

"Kyushu someplace."

"You ignorant asshole," mumbled Keiichi, face down on the table. "Don't you know anything? It's the Itsuki Lullaby."

"What? Say that again?" Bill demanded, but Keiichi simply lay there with his cheek against the tiles, drooling from distorted lips.

Bill shook him until he sat up. "It's the famous Itsuki Lullaby," he mumbled.

"You already said that. Tell me more."

"Later," Keiichi said, slumping down again.

Just then the song ended. Grimacing, the bartender removed the record from the turntable, slipped it into its jacket, and brought it over to their table. Bill let Keiichi flop onto the table and took the record from the bartender with effusive thanks and apologies.

"Folk Songs of Kyushu" said the big, red characters on green background. The rest of the album cover was taken up by a photo of a red demon mask with gold fangs and bulging gold eyes. The booklet inside contained extensive liner notes in tiny Japanese characters. Bill turned immediately to the description of the Itsuki Lullaby.

The song was in the local dialect of Itsuki, which, according to the notes, was a village on the Kawabe River upstream from an old castle town called Hitoyoshi, which in turn was up the Kuma River from the city of Yatsushiro, which, he supposed, must be on the island of Kyushu, hundreds of miles southwest of Tokyo. Isolated, the area was said to have been settled by fugitives from the losing side of the Gempei War in the twelfth century. The song was known by virtually every Japanese.

Bill's heart sank when he read that. If all Japanese knew the song, Mitsuko could have learned it anywhere. But the liner notes held out one ray of hope: the song had suddenly become popular after World War II. She must have sung it to him before the war or while they were in the camp together. Certainly she had brought it with her from Japan long before anyone had dreamed of Pearl Harbor. She must have sung it to him over and over again, not merely because she had learned it by chance but because it was something deeply rooted within her. She *had* to be from Itsuki.

"I've got it!" he exclaimed to Haruo. "I know somebody who lives in Itsuki. I'm going to go see her—tomorrow."

"Tomorrow? What about the seminar?"

"To hell with the seminar! I'm going home!"

30

THE TRAIN CARRIED BILL through an unreal landscape into deepening darkness. The Hayabusa—"Peregrine Falcon"—left Tokyo Station exactly on schedule at 4:45 pm. It trundled across the Tama River, gained speed and left the city behind. The wind-driven gray hiding the sun since yesterday turned swiftly into black.

At 6:30, the express train sped past Numazu and then through Fuji City. He had seen Mount Fuji only once from Tokyo—on a midwinter Sunday, when the factories were pumping less smoke into the air and the elevated train was passing one of those all-too-rare open spaces between the drab buildings that stood shoulder-to-shoulder along the tracks. But now, with the sun fully down and the clouds hovering low over the earth, there was no hope of seeing the legendary peak as the train raced past it.

Not even hunger could lure him from his tiny sleeping compartment. In Shizuoka, he made do with food sold from the platform. Had he gone to the dining car, someone would surely have approached him for English practice or out of sheer curiosity, and he was in no mood for conversation. He had eight hundred miles to cover; he wanted no one intruding on his solitary thoughts.

He was still wide awake when the train stopped in Kyoto after 11:30. This was the city in Japan that he had most dreamed of visiting, the cradle of the Imperial court, a treasure house of temples and museums arranged on the same grid of broad avenues that had been laid out more than a thousand years ago. Street lights revealed the dark silhouettes of a pagoda and a curving temple roof, but from here there was nothing to recall those days when emperors and court ladies traversed the streets in ox-drawn conveyances with bamboo curtains. He promised himself to return to this city someday—perhaps soon—with Mitsuko. They would renew their old ties here, in the spiritual center of her homeland, twenty years and thousands of miles away from the hostility that had torn them apart.

Near midnight, he began to doze, waking briefly when the train jerked to a stop in Osaka. A long, smooth run thereafter permitted him a deeper rest, but the cry of "Hiroshima!" woke him with a chill, and he raised the blind to see the first hints of dawn lightening the sky. The city was still wrapped in darkness; he was almost thankful that there was nothing to be seen.

He dozed fitfully to Shimonoseki, finally rousing himself there at eight o'clock. How could there still exist a place called Shimonoseki in the twentieth century? This was where, at the westernmost tip of Japan's main island, the great armies of the Taira and Minamoto had staged their final battle nearly eight hundred years ago, arrows flying, spears slashing, and the doomed Taira fleet sinking beneath the swirling waters of Dan-no-ura with the infant emperor Antoku. Now the train would be diving beneath those same deadly whirlpools to reemerge in Kyushu, the island of refuge for some of those few Taira who escaped death. He would be following in their footsteps to the hidden core of this wrinkled volcanic mass in the ocean.

The ugly skeletons of industry loomed up around the train when it rose to the light again in Moji. Could this be all that was left of the sacred island where Japan's gods had first descended to earth? But during the three-and-one-half hours until he alighted at Yatsushiro, he saw that much of the green beauty of Kyushu still remained. Still, the same thick, gray layer of clouds covering the rest of the country hung in the sky here, too, brooding over the rolling hills.

Within a few seconds of its scheduled arrival, the big, blue train pulled into the station and he stepped from his cramped compartment onto the bare platform at Yatsushiro. A howling wind tore past the station carrying straw, scraps of paper, and stinging dust.

When the train pulled out, he crossed the tracks with a dozen or so other passengers. After surrendering his express ticket at the gate, he ducked through a peeling, glass-paneled door into the station's waiting room.

The doors and windows rattled in the wind, but at least the gusts could not penetrate here. A wood stove radiated just enough heat to provide some relief from the chill.

Bill placed his small shoulder bag on the nearest bench and sat down to study the chart of arrivals and departures on the wall. Arriving at 11:42, the Hayabusa had deposited him here twenty minutes after the last express left for Hitoyoshi and an hour and a half before the next train, a local, was to come through.

Good. He needed the time to collect himself.

But an hour and a half turned out to be too long. He paced back and forth, freshened up in the washroom, ate a boxed lunch, slowly sipped tea from a little ocher pot, and still there was time to kill.

Finally, an enormous, black engine quaked into the station, hissing and belching and emitting clouds of white steam and black smoke. Behind it lumbered in three dirty red-and-yellow cars. He followed four other passengers to the gate where the ticket-taker punched their tickets.

He entered the hindmost car and sat on the long, empty bench that faced inward. The car was floored in ancient planking, furrowed and pitted and brownish-black from years of oiling. A man in his fifties, wearing muddy rubber boots and a dark green raincoat and carrying a large, cloth-wrapped bundle, came in a few seconds later, glanced impassively at Bill, then proceeded to the back end of the car. After some hesitation, as if the abundance of seating space demanded an especially careful decision, he sat on the opposite bench, placed his bundle on his knees, and closed his eyes.

The train lurched out of the station with much squealing and coughing. It dragged itself alongside a wildly gushing river that cut a twisting gash deep into the mountains. As the train made its stops, passengers drifted into and out of the car in ones and twos. Glancing once again at Bill, the man in the green raincoat finally disembarked at the tiny station that hung over the rapids in Watari.

Bill had been on the train over an hour when it shuddered and bumped its way into Hitoyoshi. Garish billboards on the platform and outside the station advertised an inn called the Nabeya promising the healing powers of the town's natural hot springs. After twenty-two hours of travel with little sleep, Bill would have loved to take a room at the Nabeya and soak in a hot bath, but decided first to check for buses to Itsuki. There were none. The uniformed station attendant explained to him that Itsuki was not a single village but a sprawling district comprising many little hamlets hidden away among the hills. The administrative center of Itsuki was an enclave called Toji.

"How far away is that?" Bill asked.

"Exactly thirty kilometers," the attendant replied.

Thirty kilometers ... eighteen miles. He could be there in a matter of minutes. "When does the next bus leave for Toji?"

"*Saa*," hissed the man, scratching his head. "Maybe another hour."

"Are there any cabs?"

The man smiled, revealing a silver tooth, and gestured toward the corner of the station. Half a dozen cabs were parked there, engines sending clouds of exhaust gas into the chilly air. The driver first in line needed no more encouragement than the station attendant's glance. Gunning the engine, he screeched to a halt at the foot of the station steps, the passenger door flying open automatically.

The dirt road followed the river's twists and turns, some of them dangerously close to the cliffs rising above the water. Bill sat in the middle of the back seat, holding the arm rests on both doors to keep himself upright on curves, and looking at the deep wrinkles on the back of the driver's neck.

Neither driver nor passenger spoke for the first half hour, but Bill noticed the man glancing frequently at him in the rear view mirror. Suddenly he began growling some odd syllables, the gist of which seemed to be "Where are you going in Toji?"

"I'm not sure," Bill replied.

The driver cocked his head and mumbled to himself, glancing at Bill a few more times. Obviously straining to speak the standard Tokyo dialect, he said, "I have never seen a foreigner here before. The Occupation soldiers only came as far as Hitoyoshi."

The man seemed determined to raise as large a cloud of dust behind him as possible on the straightaways. Several times Bill tried to look back at farmers they had passed on the road, some leading oxen, but they were too far away by the time the dust cleared. It was hard to imagine where the farmers could be working, so steep were the hills that came down on both sides of the road. High up on the left, he saw a hill that looked as though its tight, green foliage had recently been passed through by a huge comb. Something was growing there in neatly pruned rows.

The driver asked, "Where should I drop you?"

"How far is it to the village office?"

The driver pointed beyond the windshield to a fork in the road a short way ahead, adding something through the haze of the local accent that seemed to be about a fire. Bill asked him to repeat himself in Tokyo Japanese if possible. This time he grasped that the village office and all its public records had gone up in flames sometime back.

Just then, perhaps twenty yards ahead on the left, a sign for an inn came into view: Itsuki-soh.

"You can drop me there," Bill said. The driver slammed on his brakes, swerved into the inn's driveway and came to a stop in a cloud of dust. He popped the trunk and handed Bill his bag.

A very pregnant housewife showed him to his little matted room and brought him tea, kneeling by the low table at which he sat in the center of the floor. The air in the room was thick with the fumes of an oil stove that sat nearby, smoking. Comfortable with Tokyo Japanese, the woman confirmed that the village office had burned, adding that the new building was still under construction.

"Are you here on official business?" she asked,

"No, I'm looking for someone," he said. "Maybe you can help me. I don't have too much to go on. I'm trying to find a woman named Mitsuko."

The mistress of the Itsuki-soh laughed brightly, covering her mouth but not the red flush of her cheeks.

"My name is Mitsuko," she said.

He smiled. "The Mitsuko I'm looking for is in her fifties."

She cocked her head and rolled her eyes up in thought. "I don't know a Mitsuko of that age. My brother-in-law's sister's little girl is named Mitsuko. I don't even know my brother-in-law's sister's first name. We mostly use the family name in Japan."

"My Mitsuko has a sister named Yoshiko Nomura. She is probably a few years older, and her husband's name is Goro. They all lived in America before the war."

"I don't think anyone from here ever lived in America. The man who owns the gas station at the fork is named Nomura, though. I went to school with him. I think his mother might be named Yoshiko, but I have no idea what his father's name could be."

"It doesn't sound very hopeful, does it?"

She shook her head sadly. "Dinner will be served soon. You look tired. How about a hot bath?"

"That does sound good," Bill said.

When he emerged from the bath wearing the inn's blue and white yukata, the skirts of which came only to mid-calf, he found his meal waiting for him on the table. A teenage girl followed him into his room and remained by the table while he ate, pouring his tea and scooping his rice. A pink plastic barrette in the shape of a butterfly held her thin, lank hair out of her eyes, which she kept firmly focused on the table. He tried to engage her in conversation, but she responded only in monosyllables.

After eating, he dressed warmly in sweater and coat. The wind had subsided, but his breath made clouds in the cold night air. He ambled down the left fork until he came to a short concrete bridge over a gurgling stream. It reminded him of a little bridge in Issaquah, where you could watch the salmon struggling upstream. This must be the Kawabe River the cab had followed up from Hitoyoshi. He stood at the bridge railing, staring down into the blackness, wondering if Mitsuko or Yoshiko had ever stood in this spot doing the same thing. Perhaps if he waited here day after day, they would eventually happen by and find him. Or possibly this whole thing was a waste of time and they were living thousands of miles from here.

The gas station seemed deserted, but a man in his thirties popped out of the room in back at the sound of Bill's footsteps. He was chewing something as he stepped into his sandals and began to walk toward Bill, but he stopped short when their eyes met. When Bill said he was looking for a Yoshiko Nomura, the man said his mother's name was Sawa, but perhaps she could help him. He called into the house for his mother.

The woman was also chewing something when she came to the door. Mrs. Nomura invited him in, but he thanked her and stayed at the threshold, where the gas station joined the house. Yes, of course, she said, she knew several Yoshikos her age, but none named Nomura. Why was he looking for her?

"She used to take care of me when I was a little boy."

"That's sweet! Have you lived in Japan for a very long time? Your Japanese is so good."

"She took care of me in the United States."

"You mean, this woman was living in America?" Mrs. Nomura asked.

"That's right."

"That settles it. I know everybody here, and I would know if anyone had lived abroad. I'm sorry."

That seemed to bring his search to a dead end. He looked at the woman's son with a shrug.

The man asked his mother, "How about Momigi?"

"But that's so far away," she said. "It's hardly even Itsuki up there."

"True, but don't you remember we heard something about a woman or a family or somebody who came back from America after the war?"

Mother and son launched into a long discussion, their dialect growing so thick that Bill could hardly understand a word.

Finally the son told Bill about the tiny village of Momigi, which was another twenty-seven kilometers north into the mountains. The only way into the village was a bridge suspended over the Momigi Gorge. Neither mother nor son was sure of the American connection, but Mr. Nomura agreed to let Bill take his old Suzuki pick-up to Momigi, asking only that he replace whatever gasoline he used. Bill thanked them and said he would give it a try the following morning.

———

It had rained during the night, and thick patches of mist hung in the narrow valleys on either side of the dirt road. Never having driven in Japan before, Bill had to keep reminding himself to stay on the left, especially when huge logging trucks came tearing around hidden curves, forcing him over to the cliff edge above the river.

Mr. Nomura had told him to go through a place called Shiibaru and, a few kilometers later, turn right at Hakiai, but road signs were either nonexistent or lost in the fog. At Shimoyashiki a shaven-headed priest told him that he had missed the turn and would have to backtrack three kilometers.

All but their massive trunks shrouded in the mist, ancient trees towered over the narrow track to Momigi. A river was surely out there, just past the edge of visibility, but there was no fear of plunging in: with its grassy middle hump and two parallel ruts, the road itself probably would steer the truck even if he did not. He moved along slowly in first gear, the transmission whining, until the road suddenly broadened into a bumpy open space where there were parked an odd assortment of vehicles—two trucks, some hand carts, and three dust-smeared automobiles. He pulled up between the trucks and stepped out into the fog, buttoning the collar of his overcoat. Chilly drops fell from the branches high above, grazing his cheeks.

A path led to the right between two monstrous, shaggy trees. A short way down the incline, two rusty cables were anchored to the ground. The first few planks of a narrow bridge led out into the milky air. He grasped the cable on the right, stepping tentatively onto the first plank, and gave the bridge a good shake. It hardly budged. Mr. Nomura had told him that vines had supported the bridge in the old days, but even the steel cable was not entirely reassuring. For one thing, the railings formed by the cables on either side might be high enough by Japanese standards, but for someone his height they provided disturbingly little protection against toppling over the side.

Crouching slightly at the knees to keep his center of gravity low, he grasped both cables and set his whole weight on the bridge. The bridge swayed with each small step he took, but it was obviously not going to give way. Soon he was moving with more assurance, thankful that the thick mist prevented him from seeing what lay beneath him.

He came to a halt and gingerly looked around to see how far he had come, realizing with a start that he could see neither end of the bridge.

He was suspended in space, the only sound the distant gurgling of the Momigi River far below.

There was a thickening in the fog ahead. He moved toward it, thinking it must be the place where the bridge dipped to its lowest point. The closer he came, the less fluid the thick area seemed, and just as he was beginning to search for other explanations for its presence, it shifted on the bridge, causing the planks beneath his feet to tremble. It was alive, and it had a definite human shape. He took another step, then drew to a halt.

As if in response to the pulse of energy his own movement sent along the bridge, the shape turned in his direction. It was an old woman in a faded gray kimono the color of the fog. The woman's small, angular face was topped by a stark-white mass of hair. Through the mist, her dark eyes focused on him. She looked genuinely startled.

Bill tried to speak, but he could force no sound from his throat. Could this be Mitsuko? She seemed far too old. After a few moments, she spoke to him in English: "Yes? Can I help you?"

"My name is Bill Morton, and—"

The woman's knees buckled, and she grabbed hold of him, all but pulling him over the cable and down into the gorge.

31

BILL GRABBED THE CABLE, and shock waves ran up and down the length of the bridge.

"Billy!" the woman cried, her voice muffled against his chest.

Tentatively, Bill touched her shoulders as she clung to him. He hardly dared to speak as they swayed on the bridge.

The desperate grip around his waist began to relax and she raised her face from his chest. "You ... are so grown up! "

Frank had told him that Yoshiko should be in her early sixties, but this woman seemed much older. The skin draped over her prominent cheekbones was deeply wrinkled, and her straight white hair seemed to belong to a woman in her eighties.

"Do you recognize me?" she asked, looking up at him with tearful eyes. "I am Aunt Yoshiko."

She held her hand out. He took it and followed her from the bridge. She led him up a narrow path along the edge of a terraced rice field. They passed a cluster of small, weathered farmhouses with high, straw-thatched roofs, beyond which lay a field with close-cropped bushes arranged in long rows like giant green caterpillars lying side by side. Crouching amid the rows, two women in blue farm trousers looked up as they passed.

She led him through a small cedar grove, emerging at the other side to find a much larger house. Its thatched roof was battered and pitted, the bare boards of the siding showing signs of rot. With most of its storm shutters closed, the house looked empty, almost abandoned. He sensed that he would not find Mitsuko here.

He helped Yoshiko slide open the weather-beaten panel door that led into a dark, dirt-floored entryway. He pulled the door closed as she stepped out of her sandals up to the polished wooden floor. She turned toward him, bowing slightly, her bare toes peeking out from beneath her frayed kimono skirt.

"Please wait," she said, disappearing into the gloom. He heard the clatter of storm shutters opening, and the house's interior began to lighten. Soon she returned with a lighted oil lamp and beckoned for him to step up to the wooden floor.

The floor felt smooth and cold. He followed her down a corridor and through an open sliding door into a small six-mat room. In the center of the room was a low, square table, a quilt trailing down its sides and onto the floor. Beneath the table there would be a heating device, just like the *kotatsu* he used in Tokyo for keeping warm.

"*Dohzo*," she said, gesturing for him to sit on the floor and slide his legs in under the quilt. When he lifted the quilt, the smell of burning charcoal escaped. His legs fit into a sunken place in the floor warmed by charcoal instead of the usual infra-red lamp affixed to the underside of the table.

In a blue porcelain hibachi next to the table, a cast iron kettle stood on a tripod over glowing coals, wisps of steam drifting up from the spout as the water boiling within produced a tiny, bell-like sound. The wall opposite was dominated by a large mahogany wardrobe. With her back to him, Yoshiko knelt before the wardrobe, yanking open the top drawer and rummaging in among its overflowing contents. She pushed the drawer closed again and turned to Bill. In a formal kneeling position, she reached out toward the table and set a small brocade case before him, its colors faded, and stray threads dangling from its edges. Hands on her knees, she looked at him and at the case.

"Open it," she said.

It was unexpectedly light. He eased the flap back and the object inside slid into his palm. A disk of oiled wood, its dark polished surface glowed in his hand. Great care had been lavished on the carving of a bird flying across the sun. The sun itself was a round disk-within-the-disk, its perimeter surrounded by flames. He turned the piece over on his palm to find a circular hollowed-out area in which the wood was rough, only the outer edge having been rubbed with oil.

"You broke the mirror," said Yoshiko. "You were very naughty. Do you remember?"

"I don't know. Maybe not."

"She wanted me to give it to you."

He swallowed hard and looked again at the carved bird and sun. "Where is she?" he asked. "Is she living here with you?"

"No …" Yoshiko said vaguely.

"Is she in Japan? Don't tell me she went back to the States."

Yoshiko shook her head, swaying the straight, white thatch of hair. "No, not back to America. She was with my parents and my younger brother, Ichiro …"

"She *was* with them … ?"

"In Nagasaki."

So now his search was truly over. He would never see her again.

"I'm so sorry to have to tell you that."

Bill hung his head. He felt as if everything—the waiting on tables at Maneki, the discussions with Frank Sano, the endless hours of language study, the courses on Japanese literature and history and society, the Fulbright application, the flight across the Pacific, the dark journey from Tokyo to Yatsushiro and on to Hitoyoshi, Toji, and finally Momigi—had lost any meaning they might have had.

"She loved you so much," said Yoshiko. "She would have been thrilled to see you."

"I was so sure … especially when I found you …"

"I'm sorry. I don't know what else to say."

"Uncle Goro? Isn't he here with you?"

"He died in the relocation camp. I am alone."

Yoshiko went back to the tall wardrobe, opening the lower drawer, which was as crammed full as the top one. She lifted a large photograph album from the top of the pile and set it on the table. Bound in disintegrating leather, the album began with formal wedding portraits, the young man in a high, stiff collar, the woman in typical Shinto garb, her *tsuno-kakushi* headpiece that supposedly covered the "horns of jealousy."

"These are my parents, Tsunejiro and Somé Fukai," Yoshiko said.

Bill wondered if a search for Mitsuko Fukai would have been any easier.

Yoshiko's brothers appeared next. Ichiro, one year younger than

Yoshiko, was shown in an elaborate robe in his mother's arms being presented at the shrine at the age of seven days. Even Jiro, six years her junior, had beaten Yoshiko into the album. Yoshiko's picture first appeared when she was seven years old. Her parents brought her to the local shrine for *Shichi-go-san*, the "Seven-five-three" festival in which parents with children of those ages present them to the gods with thanks that they have reached these important points in their lives safely. "This was my first obi," she said, pointing to the broad sash around the waist of the happy little girl in kimono.

"What year was that?" Bill asked.

"Meiji forty-one … 1908. Of course, I was only six by Western count."

If she had been six in 1908, then she had been born in 1902. She was only sixty-one now. The years had been hard on her.

Mitsuko was shown at her first *Shichi-go-san*, at the age of three—or two by Western count—in 1914. Sweet and chubby, she could have been any of the fancily dressed little girls he had seen at the Meiji Shrine.

The Fukai children grew up as the pages flipped by before him. Mitsuko was skin and bones after shedding her baby fat, but had wonderfully bright eyes and a happy smile. She was definitely the best-looking member of the family.

The next album started with the bespectacled Goro and Yoshiko's wedding pictures. Mitsuko was still a little girl in the family portrait.

The scene changed to Seattle, and most of the images of Yoshiko and her husband were swallowed up in large group shots taken at the Japanese Christian Church.

"I even remember the address," Yoshiko said. "Nine-oh-nine East Terrace Street. Goro and I were in charge of the Sunday school."

It occurred to him that he hadn't noticed any religious paraphernalia in the house—neither cross nor Shinto god shelf nor Buddhist altar. "You must have been very active in the church."

"Yes, very active in those days." She smiled as if indulging in nostalgic thoughts. "But not anymore."

"Oh? Why not?"

"After I came back here," she said matter-of-factly, "I found out that the Christian god does not exist."

"'Found out'? How did you find it out?"

"I heard it out there," she said, motioning vaguely toward the bridge. "The only gods are the sun gods," she went on. "A new one comes into the world each day."

She spoke of these momentous things as though she might be explaining to him how to cook rice or run the bath water.

In another of the group photos, Bill saw a blond, youthful Thomas Morton towering over rows of Japanese and standing by a banner reading "Japanese Christian Sunday school." Bill had never seen his father smiling in such a genuinely happy, open manner, chin held aloft, his collar button ready to pop with pride. He wished he could have known him then.

Turning the page, Bill inhaled sharply. Not even two years old, he was in the lap of a Japanese woman in her twenties seated on a blanket spread on a lawn. His mouth and fingers were smeared with grains of rice. In the woman's face he could recognize the lively eyes of the skinny little Mitsuko, but here she was a beautiful woman, her long hair pulled back in a bun. She was not looking into the camera but at the child in her lap, and the smile she gave the little boy made the grown-up Billy's heart melt. It was almost unbearable to think that she was dead. He would never see her, never hold her.

Yoshiko let him gaze at the picture for a few minutes before turning the page. The next pictures were of the two sisters posing before tourist sites in Washington: Mount Rainier, the Columbia Gorge, Hurricane Ridge. But in these pictures she wore a touch of melancholy. One shot with the Olympic Mountains in the background clearly showed the double peak of The Brothers. It could only have been taken from one place: the bluff across the street from the house where he had grown up in Magnolia. To think that, as a boy, he had walked on the very patch of ground where she had once stood.

He found no pictures of Mitsuko with his father. Instead, the pages in this part of the album had rough patches, where the paper corners holding the snapshots in place seemed to have been torn away and rearranged. The pictures here showed him somewhat older—perhaps three or four. The last few pages in the album were empty.

"These are all the photos," Yoshiko said.

Just then the house shook as someone struggled to open the front door. Bill leaned toward the window and slid the *shoji* back just in time to see a figure in blue mompe trousers darting away from the house. It appeared to be one of the farm women they had passed earlier.

"Just a moment," said Yoshiko, gliding from the room. A few seconds later, she returned holding a tray with two steaming bowls of noodles, which she placed on the table.

"What a pleasant surprise," Bill said.

"Follow me to wash," Yoshiko said. She led him to a dark lavatory where a rusty pump fed into a slate sink. She pumped icy water for him while he washed his hands and face.

They ate the noodles in silence. The only sound was the soft ringing of the iron kettle on the hibachi. Yoshiko snagged the noodles with her chopsticks and slurped them up in the time-honored Japanese manner. Thanks to the steam and peppery seasoning, Bill warmed up enough to remove his coat for the first time.

"Delicious noodles," Bill said, drinking down the last of the soup. "Who made them?"

"Tsugiko," she said. "A tenant of ours. It's one of her duties."

By then, the mist had lifted, and streaks of sunlight played across the *shoji* paper. He was feeling sleepy.

Yoshiko said, "Why don't you take a walk while I clean up?"

"I could use some fresh air," Bill said.

Retracing their earlier path through the cedar grove, Bill came to the field with the hedges that looked like giant caterpillars. Everything was a rich green now in the sunlight.

"*Konnichi wa,*" he called to the woman working in the field.

She glanced up at him, dipping her head uncertainly.

He stepped down between the long hedges and approached her. "*Tsugiko-san deshoh ka?*" he asked—"Would you be Tsugiko?"

When she nodded shyly, he thanked her for the delicious noodles. He was probably the first foreigner she had ever met, and he was not sure that his Tokyo Japanese was making sense to her. He tried asking about this crop she was tending, and she answered clearly enough that it was tea.

"I understand you are one of Aunt Yoshiko's tenants," he said.

The woman broke into ringing laughter, and her hand came up to hide her mouth. "Did she tell you that?" she asked. "There are no more tenants in Japan. General MacArthur ended all that. This farm is ours now."

"Well, maybe she just said it from habit."

"No, she knows better, but I am sure she still thinks of us as the family's tenants. Her brother sends us money every month to take care of her."

"I hadn't realized there was another brother. I understand Ichiro was killed in Nagasaki."

"Yes, everyone but Jiro. He lives in Tokyo."

Golden in the morning sunlight, Mount Fuji soared above the train, its snow-draped cone more perfect and graceful than he had ever imagined it. But, for all he cared, it might just as well be another slide in Professor Fleming's art history class. The Hayabusa would arrive in Tokyo at 10:30, and then what was he to do? Go to the Noh seminar? Discuss the meaning of the *michiyuki* in *Kanehira*? What was the point anymore? Mitsuko was dead. And poor Yoshiko, aged beyond her years: was she out there now on the bridge, communing with her sun gods?

He had come four thousand miles in search of two sisters who lived in the deepest recesses of his soul, only to find that his country and his father had destroyed them both. They were imprisoned without trial. One buried her husband in the desert sands. The other was betrayed by her husband and blasted to atoms along with thousands of others. Not in the first bombing—which was bad enough—but in the second, the one dropped *after* they had learned the horrible truth of what the weapon could do.

America, America, God shed his grace on thee.

All this in the name of Christian civilization. Of truth. Our truth. "He that believeth on him is not condemned, but he that believeth not is condemned already, because he hath not believed in the name of the only begotten Son of God. And this is the condemnation, that light is come into the world, and men loved the darkness rather than the light, because their deeds were evil." Japan did not believe. Japan was evil. Its women and children had to be incinerated. Whatever good Christianity had brought into the world, that had been far outweighed by the evil it had unleashed by creating the devil. The world would not be safe until men stopped killing in the cause of righteousness.

His first thought on leaving Itsuki had been to cross the Shimabara Gulf for a pilgrimage to Nagasaki, but wandering aimlessly through unknown streets had seemed so pointless. Anything that was left for him now was in Tokyo. Tsugiko, Yoshiko's "tenant," had given him the address of Jiro Fukai, the brother who paid for her upkeep. Perhaps, when the sense of loss had dulled somewhat, he would visit the man to learn what he might know of Mitsuko's end.

32

c/o Niiyama
Ogikubo 1-124
Suginami-ku
Tokyo, Japan

April 17, 1963

Dear Frank,
        I should have written to you over a month
ago, but I have not been able to find the words.
Perhaps it would be more accurate to say that I have
not been able to find the courage to tell you that
Mitsuko is dead. I learned this from her sister,
Yoshiko.
        There should be a gentler way of breaking
the news, and I have been hoping that, if I let some
time go by, I would find the way, but the weeks have
done nothing to soften the blow for me. I simply
don't know how I can spare you.
        I discovered Yoshiko Nomura living
in a tiny village in the mountains of Kyushu. I
recognized a lullaby that Mitsuko used to sing to
me, and I was able to locate her home village when
I learned where the song came from. Yoshiko looks
far older than her sixty-one years, no doubt because
of what she has been through. She lost almost her
entire family--including Mitsuko--when the atomic
bomb fell on Nagasaki.
        Yoshiko's husband, Goro, must have
died in Minidoka after you left. Yoshiko lives in
a large, old house, but perhaps it would be more
accurate to say that she lives in her own, little
world. She keeps her old photograph albums close by,
and I was able to see some photos of Mitsuko, one of
them with me (age two) in her lap taken at some kind
of picnic. I almost cried when I saw that. She was
so beautiful!
        Aunt Yoshiko gave me the wooden backing
from a small hand mirror that Mitsuko had asked
her to pass on to me. She knew right where it was,
as if the thing had been left with her the day
before. She told me that I was the one who broke the
mirror glass itself, though how I did it I never
learned. Since returning to Tokyo, I have had the
glass restored but I keep the mirror in the back

of my closet. It is beautifully made, but I am not
emotionally ready yet to enjoy it as a memento.

There is another brother, Jiro, who pays
for Yoshiko's upkeep. (The family name is Fukai, by
the way. Come to think of it, I am not even sure
whether Yoshiko is living in the old family home
under the name of Nomura or Fukai.) He lives in a
Tokyo suburb, and I am planning to look him up--
probably tomorrow after visiting one of the famous
cherry-blossom viewing spots nearby. I think perhaps
the beauty of the blossoms has been helping me the
past few days.

The Japanese academic year ended shortly
after my departure from Tokyo, and the new one has
just begun, so I have not had school work as a
distraction over the past few weeks. One welcome
diversion has been supplied by my friend, David
Green, who finally convinced me to appear on his
English TV show. It was gratifyingly time-consuming,
what with memorizing my little skit and going in
early to have my face made up and to be coached by
the Japanese teacher who runs the show and does the
interview at the end. Apparently, Tamura-Sensei
thought I did well enough to invite me back again.
Now they're talking about a third appearance. The
pay is all right, but I don't think my visa status
allows me to make a regular habit of this, and once
my seminar starts, I doubt if I will have time for
such things.

My seminar. I wish I could say I was
looking forward to it. You know that I love the
literature, but it is not what brought me to Japan
in the first place, and now that my original purpose
is gone, I wonder if I have enough innate interest
to continue with the work. Odd: a few years ago,
I might have been able to console myself with
the thought that Mitsuko and I would be reunited
in heaven. I can hardly believe that I was ever
so literal-minded. I was brought up to decry
"humanism," but the people who taught me that view
are far more guilty of a humanist bias, as if the
entire universe were designed with the salvation
of us puny human beings its only purpose. No, I am
afraid that the God who put rings around Saturn
was not aware of the moment the lives of Mitsuko
and her family and the other victims in Nagasaki
were snuffed out. The best we can do is to love and
remember each other. It is with that in mind that I
will seek out Jiro Fukai, so that I can learn and
cherish more of the woman who gave so much of her
love to me.

I will write again if I find out anything
worth sharing tomorrow. Please let me hear from you.
I enjoy your letters with their news of the folks at
Maneki. And try to remember that you are not alone
with your memories of Mitsuko.

Yours,
Bill

Musashi-Koganei was only six stops out from Bill's Ogikubo neighborhood on the Chuo Line. Half a mile north of the station were Tokyo's most famous cherry trees, stretching for nearly five miles along the Tamagawa Canal. A similar distance south was Maehara-cho, where Jiro Fukai lived. The blossoms, though doubtless very beautiful, would be mute. The man might have something to tell him.

Bill turned south. He bought a fancy tin of rice crackers from one of the little shops along the main street. With his obligatory gift and his double-sided calling cards (English on one side, Japanese on the other) he walked through the treeless neighborhood dotted with new middle class houses.

As in the older sections of the city, the numbering system designated tracts and blocks, not individual houses, and the parcels of land were numbered in the order of their development rather than their physical location. This meant that his map was useful only to a point, and he hoped to ask people on the street for directions to Tract 1, Block 11. But here, where houses were still separated by undeveloped stretches of mud, there were few people. He followed the narrow, graveled streets to a dead end at a large, fenced-in area where cars were driving around on the artificial lanes of an auto school.

Backtracking, he questioned a housewife carrying a shopping basket and then an old woman walking her dog, who finally showed him the way to a brown house with a small cherry tree of its own in the tiny front garden behind a six-foot cinder-block wall. Embedded in the wall was a small nameplate with the characters for "deep well": Fukai. He opened the gate to find the cherry tree in full flower. The flagstone path and moss-covered ground were dotted by round, pink petals. He had made the right choice: he could see cherry blossoms and meet Jiro Fukai.

Still not comfortable with the Japanese way of opening the outer door of a stranger's house and shouting for permission to enter, he pressed the doorbell and waited, gift in hand.

Nothing stirred in the house.

Again he pressed the button and waited. Now that he thought about it, if Mr. Fukai lived like most Japanese men, he would not be home until ten or eleven at night after a long day at the office followed by enforced socializing with his colleagues. But it was rare for houses to be completely empty. Usually there was someone—a wife, a maid, a neighbor—doing *rusuban* ("absence-guarding"), who could accept a name card and suggest a more appropriate time to call. He tried sliding back the glass-paneled front door, thinking to leave his tin of crackers and a card in the entryway, but the door was firmly locked.

There were footsteps in the gravel behind him, and he turned to see a young woman round the corner of the cinder-block wall and stop at the open gate.

A single petal dropped from the cloud of blossoms overhead, its path through the motionless air a slow, sinuous diagonal. Nothing could stir so long as that pink disk was airborne, as if some ancient, unwritten law demanded that he and the young woman standing before him suspend all movement until the fragile membrane surrendered to the pull of the earth.

She was beautiful, her clear, oval face framed in straight, glossy black. The hair was parted in the middle and clung lightly where the sculpture of the throat began. The lovely, rounded cheekbones marked her unmistakably as a Fukai, but the delicate curve of the nose was something she did not share with Yoshiko or Mitsuko, and the mouth belonged to a face that had never known pain. The lower lip was slightly full and ready to smile.

She wore a blue-gray blazer of thickly woven material over a pale pink sweater, and a narrow, gray skirt. In shoes with a touch of elevation in the heels, she was unusually tall for a Japanese woman. Her right hand held the handles of a thin briefcase, and hooked over her left elbow was a small purse of brown leather.

After the petal floated down to the bed of moss at their feet, Bill bowed properly at the waist. The young woman hesitated for a moment before returning his greeting.

"Excuse me," he said in his politest Japanese, "is this the Fukai house?" He had seen the nameplate, but it was all he could think of to say.

"Yes," she replied. "Can I help you?" Her voice was soft yet confident.

"I was hoping to see Mr. Fukai, but no one seems to be home."

"My father is at work, and my mother was going to go shopping at the Ginza today. Aren't you Mohton-san? I never miss Tamura-Sensei on NHK."

He smiled and said in English, "Then perhaps we should be speaking in English."

"Oh, no," she replied in English, switching immediately back to Japanese. "My English is terrible. But your Japanese is excellent."

"You must be a student," he said, looking down at her briefcase.

"Yes, but don't ask me what I am studying."

"What *are* you studying?" he asked, smiling broadly.

"English literature," she said in Japanese with a little laugh. "I study at Tsuda College. It has an excellent English literature program, but I'm just a beginner in conversation. You're here studying Japanese literature, aren't you? I remember what you said when Tamura-Sensei introduced you."

"That's right. I'm taking a seminar on Noh drama at the University of Tokyo."

"I don't know anything about Noh," she said, then added with a smile, "But I have read all of Fitzgerald's works."

"All I've read is *Gatsby*," he confessed.

"Good. Now I don't feel so bad about the Noh drama."

"Do you mind if I ask your name?"

"It's Mineko," she said without hesitating.

"Mineko. I like that. 'Child of the mountaintop.'"

"Yes, maybe," she said. "*Miné* does mean mountaintop."

"Which Chinese character do you use to write the *miné* part?"

"I wish you hadn't asked me that. It's a little embarrassing. My parents decided not to write that part of my name with a character. They used the *katakana* syllabary. That way it looks like an exotic foreign word. It's actually very pretentious."

"Don't worry," he said. "You are not pretentious at all."

She blushed slightly.

He wished that they could go on like this, talking about each other all day, but she said, "I believe you wanted to see my father?"

"Yes, I was in Itsuki a few weeks ago and got his address from his sister," which was not exactly true, but close enough.

"You met Aunt Yoshiko? I have never met her. I've been begging them to take me to Itsuki for years. What were you doing there?"

Bill wondered where to start, what to tell her, what not to tell her. "It's a very long story. When I was a young boy, Yoshiko's sister Mitsuko used to take care of me, but she was repatriated during the war. One of the reasons I came to Japan was to see if I could find her. I did find Yoshiko, but she told me that Mitsuko died in Nagasaki."

"Yes, it was a terrible thing," said the girl. "All I know about her is that she and Aunt Yoshiko had to go to some kind of concentration camp in America during the war. I never knew my grandparents or my Uncle Ichiro, either. It's amazing that you still remembered a woman who took care of you when you were so young—and that you managed to find Aunt Yoshiko in her tiny village."

"I was hoping I could learn more about Mitsuko from your father."

"You'll probably have to come back on a Sunday. That's the only day he's not at work. Although I wonder if he will talk to you. He ... I'm sorry to say this, but he hates Americans. He blames them for what happened."

"I understand. But I want to see him anyway. I'll come back. Would you be so kind as to give him this?" He held out the wrapped tin of rice crackers, slipping a calling card under the ribbon.

"Thank you," she said, bowing.

Bill looked at the Fukais' cherry tree. "I have time to go see the cherry blossoms now."

"Oh! Do you know about the blossoms of Koganei?"

"I've heard about them, though I'm not sure exactly where they are."

"Wait," she said, smiling and edging past him to the door. She opened it with her key, set her briefcase and the tin of crackers in the entryway, and locked it again.

"I'll go with you," she said.

He felt his heart thump. He knew that Japanese etiquette required him to insist that she not trouble herself, but he was unwilling to risk having her take him at his word. "That would be wonderful if you have the time," he said.

Once they were walking side by side, he could not think of anything to say. Finally he asked, "Have you been studying English long?" Then he realized it was a stupid question. All Japanese children started studying English in middle school.

"Since middle school," she said. Of course. "How long have you been in Japan?"

"Since September."

"And how long will you stay?"

"My Fulbright ends in June. But I may be able to renew it for another nine months."

"I'd love to go to America on a Fulbright."

"Excuse me, I know this is very rude," he began, but stopped when it became obvious that she was trying not to laugh. "What is it?" he asked.

"You're so formal," she said. "Men your age don't have to be so formal with girls my age."

"Now that you bring it up, what is your age?"

"Nineteen. My birthday was yesterday."

"Happy birthday! Nineteen is such a nice age. I wish I had known, I would have brought you a present."

She smiled and lowered her eyes for the first time. Maybe he was being too obvious. "How old are *you*?" she asked, looking at him again.

"Twenty-five. My birthday was last December. On the nineteenth."

"Twenty-five is a nice age, too," she said with a smile. He liked how she smiled without covering her mouth as most Japanese women did.

They crossed the tracks and continued on north past a row of banks and stores along a busy thoroughfare. They walked with the general flow of pedestrians, but more slowly than the others, who kept passing them.

"You were about to say something before when I interrupted you," she reminded him.

"When I was being too polite."

"I'm sorry, my mother is always telling me I have to learn to control myself."

"No, I appreciate it," he said. "Most Japanese people are so reluctant to criticize or contradict. I hope you'll always ..."

"Yes?"

"No, never mind. I was just going to ask you your age, but we've already talked about that."

"We're coming to Koganei Bridge now," she said. "It's the best place for viewing the blossoms."

Bill could not see a bridge, just a mass of people. Soon, moving with them, he and Mineko came to the center of a short bridge that spanned a narrow canal.

Stretching off endlessly on either side of the bridge were masses of pale white blossoms with just the slightest hint of pink. The branches were thick with blossoms that blotted out the sky. Bill and Mineko stood looking up for a while, then crossed to the other side of the bridge.

He led the way along the green embankment beneath the blossoms, moving farther and farther away from the roar of traffic, where the crowd thinned out to the occasional passerby. Now and then, a breeze would sweep past them, and they would smile at each other through a veil of drifting petals. They walked for long stretches without speaking, hearing only the soft gurgling of the placid water in the canal.

"What an odd, little waterway this is," he said.

"It's an aqueduct. One of the Tokugawa shoguns dug it hundreds of years ago. It's also famous as the site where the writer Osamu Dazai committed suicide with his lover."

Just now, Bill could not imagine ever wanting to die.

33

BILL STARED AT THE TIN of rice crackers resting in the ceremonial alcove in his room. As he and Mineko had walked back toward the station, she had grown pensive and again voiced her doubts that her father would see him. Perhaps the best thing, she suggested, would be to take her father by surprise. If Bill showed up unannounced late Sunday morning, say about eleven, her father would be sure to be in, probably puttering about in the back garden, and would not have a chance to think up an excuse for turning him away.

Even more than the idea itself, Bill was thrilled that Mineko had taken the trouble to think of it. He walked back to the house with her, retrieved his gift from the entryway, and returned to Ogikubo. The one bit of himself he left with her was his card, which she promised to hide. Of course when he came on Sunday, they would pretend they had never met.

David Green stopped by on Friday to ask if Bill had made up his mind yet about appearing on television again in a week or two. Knowing now that Mineko would be watching, he accepted, wishing only that he could somehow peer into the camera and look back at her.

As he thought about looking at her, he began to wonder what it was like for her to look at him. He had seen Japanese paintings of the Portuguese monks and Dutch traders who came to these shores in the sixteenth century, and prints depicting the Americans who came to open the country a hundred years ago, and all of them were grotesque as seen through Japanese eyes: deathly gray skin, monkey-like hair and teeth, bulging eyeballs, enormous beaks for noses. Clare had called him beautiful, but to Mineko, his reddish-blond waves might look like wild flames, and his perfectly ordinary nose a gaping ventilation pipe.

On Sunday morning he left the house carrying the tin of rice crackers, its neat wrapping somewhat rumpled. He considered buying something else to go with it, something more appropriate for Mineko, but he was not even supposed to know that she existed, let alone bring her presents.

It was 10:50 when he walked up to the Fukai house in Koganei and rang the doorbell.

"*Hai!*" Slippered feet flapped toward the door. He slid back the frosted glass-paneled door and came face-to-face with Mineko. She wore a white blouse and a simple, knee-length skirt of gray flannel.

After a quick smile, she said in a loud, clear voice, "*Dochira-sama de gozaimashoh ka*"— "Who might you be, Sir?"

He played along, presented his card, and emphasized in his introduction that he was a University of Tokyo student, which should impress her parents. "I have come to see Mr. Jiro Fukai," he said, matching her tone of voice.

She took several steps away and glided around a corner into a shadowy passage to the right. The entryway had a slate floor, and there was a large *geta-bako*, the cabinet for footgear to one side. Three umbrellas stood at crazy angles in a wire stand in the corner, and on another rack were a few pairs of slippers for guests. He hoped that one pair would be placed on the glossy wooden floor for him to step into.

His heart had begun to slow when a slim, graying man with heavy eyebrows and rolled-up sleeves rounded the corner clutching his card. The man's sullen expression told him that the time for playing games had ended.

"Yes?" said Mr. Fukai brusquely.

"My name is William Morton," said Bill, trying to smile.

"I know who you are. You're the son of that American preacher who killed my sister. What incredible nerve you have to walk into my home."

Mineko stepped out from behind the corner, pale and shaken.

Her father spun around in his stocking feet. "Mineko! Go to your room."

"Father, I—"

"You heard me!"

Wavering, Mineko sent Bill a terrified glance.

"You know this man, don't you?" Mr. Fukai shouted. "What has he been telling you?"

"Nothing, just that—"

"Go to your room now!"

Wilting before his eyes, Mineko turned and ran down the hallway. A woman came out of the shadows and followed her. Not until a door slammed somewhere in the back of the house did Jiro face Bill again.

"You're one of the American devils who murdered my family."

"You don't understand, Mr. Fukai, I loved Mitsuko like a mother, and I'm convinced that she loved me more than—"

"Don't talk to me about love! You're as much of a hypocrite as that father of yours, claiming to love Mitsuko. You look just like him."

"You met my father?"

"Yes, I met him, that holy man of God. And I saw you, too. I visited your wonderful city of Seattle where they build the bombers."

"You're absolutely right. My father is the one to blame. I only want to make up for some of the pain."

"What do you know about pain? Have you ever run for your life from a sky full of American bombers? Have you ever seen a pile of black ash on the earth that just might be your whole family?"

"No, I haven't experienced that kind of pain myself. But I have seen Aunt Yoshiko, and it broke my heart."

"You've been to Itsuki?" Mr. Fukai's face became distorted with rage, and he began trembling all over. He went back into the house, striding heavily on the glossy wood. A second later, he was back. He flung the still-wrapped tin of rice crackers at Bill's feet, hurling the crumpled calling card after it.

Bill bent down, picked up the mess, then turned and stepped out of the house.

On the street again, he walked slowly, hoping Mineko would come after him. At each corner he passed on his way to the station, he stopped, looking back, but there was no one. He dropped the mangled gift and card into a waste receptacle.

On the platform, he let two inbound trains go by before admitting to himself that he was alone. But she still had his card, and she could call him when the storm had passed.

He went home and waited in his room. No call came. When Mrs.

Niiyama asked if he would be joining them for dinner, he accepted so as not to be out of the house if Mineko called.

But Mineko did not call, neither that evening nor the following day.

He missed another seminar and Keiichi called to ask if he was sick. Bill thanked him for his concern and cut the conversation short. Whenever Mrs. Niiyama was on the phone, he circled his room like a caged animal.

———

Tuesday morning, he joined the streams of workers filtering out of the houses in Ogikubo, flowing into ever-broader tributaries, and converging in a torrent on the station. Before the rapids could sweep him toward the center of the city, he extricated himself and boarded a less crowded train headed in the opposite direction, toward Koganei. One stop past Musashi-Koganei, Mineko's station, he transferred to the Seibu-Kokubunji Line and stayed on the rickety, little train for two stops, exiting at Taka-no-dai with hundreds of women students. He hurried to the gate ahead of the crowd, surrendered his ticket, then stood there watching every face that passed through.

He had arrived before eight, as he had planned, but obviously she could have come through here long before. After the students from this train had passed through, he found a slightly less exposed position behind a post.

Wave after wave came, none of them bearing Mineko. Between waves, the uniformed ticket-taker would stare off into space, humming to himself. Next to him, the man punching the tickets of boarding passengers kept up an incessant rhythmic clicking with his metal punch, which he barely interrupted each time a rider without a monthly pass held out a little cardboard rectangle in the vicinity of the clicking jaws.

When the morning rush slowed, the ticket-taker got down from his stool and ambled over to a door in the brick wall of the station. Bill heard water running, after which the man emerged with a watering can. He dribbled water on the area inside the wicket. When the can was empty, he systematically scrubbed the whole area with a push broom. Bill watched him accumulate little, black piles of moistened dust and scoop them up with a dustpan. All the while, the other uniformed attendant remained on his stool, punch clicking as if the hand holding it belonged to a robot.

The trains came at longer intervals now, each disgorging fewer passengers. At 10:30 Bill used one lull between trains for a quick trip to the men's room. As he stepped outside again, a policeman approached him.

"Do you have some business here?" the officer asked, his eyes nearly hidden beneath the brim of his hat.

"I'm waiting for a friend," Bill said.

"Let me see your passport, please."

"I'm not a tourist," Bill said.

"Then your Alien Registration Certificate, please."

Bill patted the pockets of his sport coat and thrust his hands in his pants pockets, knowing that he was not going to find the little, blue booklet that he had carried so dutifully during his first few months in the country. Foreigners were never supposed to be without their *Gaijin Torokusho*, but the damned thing was not only useless, it was too big to put into a wallet and too small to keep track of as it bounced from pocket to pocket. The other foreigners he knew left theirs at home, where it was safe, since loss of it was threatened with all sorts of dire consequences.

"I'm sorry, officer, I seem to have left it in my room," he said at last.

"Then you'll have to come with me."

"I have these other things," he started to say, reaching for his wallet, when he heard footsteps coming down the station stairway. A few paces behind a woman in a yellow dress was Mineko.

"Here," Bill said, looking back and forth between his wallet and the station gate, "my business card."

"That's not good enough," the policeman said. "Anyone can have one of those printed."

Mineko was through the gate. Her eyes were downcast, and even if she had looked up, she probably would not have seen him here off to one side behind a post.

Bill pulled out his University of Tokyo student identification card and the National Railways pass he used to commute to campus.

The officer looked at them, grumbling to himself. Bill craned his neck to watch Mineko emerge from the other side of his post and approach the curb.

"Mineko!" he shouted.

The police officer looked startled, then angry.

Bill said, "That's my friend. She'll vouch for me." But when Mineko saw him, she stepped down into the street and started to run.

"Mineko! Come back!"

On the other side of the street, she stopped and whirled around, vigorously shaking her head, then she continued walking off swiftly across a broad lawn. Bill started to run in her direction.

"Stop!" bellowed the policeman behind him. When Bill reached the curb, he felt the policeman's hand on his shoulder. "You're under arrest."

Mineko turned to look at Bill standing on the curb with his arms in the air. She clutched her briefcase in front of her as if in protection.

The officer pushed Bill toward a police box near the front of the train station. Mineko took one or two tentative steps in this direction, then began walking swiftly to the police box.

The police kept them for nearly an hour, interrogating him, examining his identification and Mineko's. After Bill gave repeated promises never to flee from the police again or to leave the house without the all-important Alien Registration Certificate, they were allowed to leave the police box. They walked in silence until they had reached the middle of the grassy field.

"Why did you run away from me?" he asked.

"Don't you know? After what happened on Sunday? You lied to me. I heard what my father said to you. He knew exactly who you are. You're not just someone who was 'taken care of' by my Aunt Mitsuko. Your father did something awful to her."

"Don't you know? Didn't he tell you?"

"My father has never told me anything. All I know is what I heard before he sent me to my room. I was so disappointed in you!" Her eyes filled with tears, and her voice caught in her throat.

"But I didn't lie to you. I explained my connection with Mitsuko the way

I explain it to everybody, out of habit. The truth is something I am not very proud of."

A group of students stared at them while passing by.

Bill asked, "Is there somewhere quiet we can go?"

Mineko looked at her watch. "I'm missing my Shakespeare class. It started at eleven."

"I'm sorry. Do you have any other classes today?"

"English history, at three."

"I've been waiting for you since a quarter to eight, and I'm starved."

She took him to a little café nearby full of carved wooden bears and salmon and other objects made by the Ainu people of Hokkaido. Bill hoped to find unusual dishes on the menu, but there were only sandwiches and other unremarkable fare. He ordered pork cutlet with curry on rice, and Mineko had a cucumber sandwich.

Bill said, "I'm sorry I didn't explain more about your aunt. I suppose your father was right. My father did kill her in a way. I'm only finding out now what really happened."

Bill told her of his longing for Mitsuko and of his shame for what his father and his country had done to her and her sister.

Mineko said, "I know my father has tried to protect me from all that. I had never seen him so angry before. There is so much locked up inside of him and my mother from the war, things they never talk about. I do know that I am lucky to be alive. The house where we were living was bombed when I was seven months old. When I was born, they had almost no medical supplies. I think my mother had trouble giving birth. She was never able to have children again."

"I suppose that's another reason why they're so protective," he said.

"I know that's it. I sometimes think I'm lucky to have such a wonderful mother and father, but other times I want to tell them to calm down, to let me live my life and grow. One thing is certain, though," she added, looking at him intently, "I never want to do anything to hurt them."

34

MINEKO'S DETERMINATION TO spare her parents any pain made it difficult for Bill to see her. Nighttime dates were out of the question, and departures from her college schedule were difficult to manage. The best they could do was lunch once a week in the Ainu café, and on weekends they would take in a movie or stroll through a park. He could not write to her, and she had to be the one to initiate telephone calls.

In the middle of June, the rains came. Day after day, the heavens drummed on Bill's thin metal roof. The only quiet was to be had when the downpour turned into a blanket of thick mist. He complained to Mrs. Niiyama that his leather shoes in the entryway were turning green and hairy with mold. She laughed and assured him that the annual ordeal would come to an end by mid- or late July. There would be a single, huge clap of thunder, the skies would clear, and then he would be sorry that the rainy season had given way to scorching heat.

Without classes to keep him busy, the wait to see Mineko could be unbearable. He was almost gruff with her when she called on Friday after one week of rain to suggest that they meet in Ikebukuro for a revival of "Summertime" with Katharine Hepburn.

After the movie, they went to a café and ordered tall glasses of iced coffee. "I really enjoyed the Venice crowd scenes," she said. "Did you notice one American soldier with round glasses moving past the camera?"

He had barely taken note of the actions of the main characters, let alone such minor details. He hardly spoke while they drank their coffees. When they stood again in the dark under the dripping eaves at the edge of Koganei Station, he embraced her fiercely.

"I love you, Mineko," he said, his voice nearly lost in the pounding of the rain. "You're all I can think of. I want you with me all the time. I want to marry you."

"You mustn't say that," she pleaded. "There are others to keep in mind. We have to control ourselves."

"Is that what you were doing today? Controlling yourself?"

"Must I blurt it out?"

"Just tell me: do you love me?"

"Yes, you know I do," she moaned, pressing against him. "But I'm afraid. My parents would never allow me to marry an American. They think they will have their little girl with them until I finish college, at least. And I was never expecting anything like this to happen. I don't want to grow up so quickly."

"You have no choice," he said. "Don't you feel it?"

She raised her face to his, her dark eyes deeper than the surrounding blackness. The rain tore into the earth, sealing them off from the rest of the world. Again their lips met, the moisture of the steaming night sealing their bodies against each other.

"I will tell them tonight," she whispered when their lips had parted.

"No, I want to be there with you."

"But that would only make things worse."

"I'm afraid of what your father might do to you."

"I am not afraid for myself, only for them. They will be devastated."

"Then let's try our best to do it right. I don't want to tear you away from your parents, but we have to be prepared for that."

She hung her head and tightened her arms around him.

"I'll come to your house on Sunday morning the way I did the first time. Together, we'll bow down to your father, we'll do anything it takes to convince him that we love each other and want to be together."

"He'll never agree to it. He'll tell us to wait until I have graduated."

"If that's what it takes, I am willing to wait."

"Can you wait for me for three more years?"

"I don't want to, but I can. I'll find a way to stay here and make a living. But let's not worry about that now. The important thing is to be ready for Sunday. What you have to do is pack a bag in the meantime and hide it someplace convenient. Because if this backfires, you're going to leave with me right then and there."

He opened his umbrella and walked her to the nearest waiting cab, then stood amid the downpour watching the car's tail lights pull away.

The sheer joy of knowing she was his welled up inside him. Here he was, standing in the rain with an umbrella in his hand, on this narrow Japanese street with bar signs written in exotic characters and shops offering hot noodles and cool sushi, and damned if he wasn't some kind of absurd Far Eastern Gene Kelly ready to kick up his heels and tap dance his way through the sparkling puddles past policemen and startled onlookers! The mere thought of it released a wild laugh from him that reverberated against the stained stucco walls lining the street.

————

Mineko, Mineko, Mineko: the music of her name played in his ears as he sat in the dark on the edge of his bed near the open window. Dressed in a light yukata, he breathed in the cool, damp night air as the fragile house vibrated in the steady downpour. Against the roar of the rain, mere physical sound was helpless. The music had to come from within.

The headlights of a car cut through the rain on the tiny back street below his window. The roof of a cab with its lighted masthead edged past the Niiyamas' gate. Then it stopped and backed up until it was directly in front of the gate. He had seen Mr. Niiyama's shoes in the entryway, which meant that the master of the house was already at home, and it was unlikely the family would be having callers at this time of night. The light went on inside the cab, spilling onto the whitewashed cinder-block wall on the other side of the lane, and after a few minutes the back door opened. Someone seemed to be getting out, but no umbrella popped up, and after the door closed and the car drove off, he wondered if the passenger had thought better about stepping into the downpour.

Bill peered at the space above the front gate where the cab's roof had been. There was something there. If it was alive, it did not move. He had the uncanny feeling that a person was standing there, staring at the house. Straining to keep his gaze locked precisely on the spot, he edged toward the head of the bed and picked up the small reading lamp by the pillow. His hands turned the round shade toward the front yard and snapped on the light.

There were four fingers clutching the top of the gate. He waved in their direction, and the fingers let go. Now a small palm was waving in the feeble rays spilling out from his window. "Mineko?" he said aloud, but she couldn't possibly have heard.

He bolted down the stairs in the darkness, stepping into the entryway where his shoes were waiting. A second later, he was through the door and into the rain, splashing along the front walk to the gate, where he lifted the bar. Mineko threw herself into his arms, shivering.

"My God, Mineko, what happened?"

Without waiting for an answer, he took her by the shoulders—she was wearing only the one thin dress he had last seen her in at the station—and guided her to the door.

They stood in the entryway, letting the rainwater drip onto the concrete. Then he helped her out of her shoes and led her to the stairway on the right, guiding her up the steep ascent toward the faint glow cast by his reading lamp.

On the landing, he turned to look at her. Still neatly parted down the center, Mineko's hair was plastered against her cheeks, and her cotton dress clung to her, the skirts heavy and sticking to her legs. Opening the paper doors of his closet, he found his spare yukata of blue and white for her and dry clothes for himself. Hanging the yukata and its sash on a hook by the wash basin, he gave her his towel and started back down the stairs.

"Go in there when you're through," he said, pointing to the wood-floored bedroom to the left. "Get under the covers."

In the downstairs bathroom, he stripped off his own sodden yukata, threw it on the drain board by the Niiyamas' bathtub, and dried himself with a new towel from the linen closet. He felt himself stir when the towel's rough fabric caught him between the legs. He put on dry underwear, a white shirt and cotton twill pants.

With a rag from the kitchen, he carefully wiped the water that he and Mineko had trailed across the wooden floor of the hallway and the stairs. Mrs. Niiyama might overlook his bringing a woman to his room, but she would never forgive him if he left water spots on her painstakingly polished floor.

By the time he reached the landing, Mineko was gone, the paper door closed. Her dress was a lump of wet cloth in the basin.

The lamp was still on when he slid back the door. Curled up tightly on her side, Mineko made only the smallest mound on his bed. The thin covers trembled with her shivering. He opened the bedding closet and laid a thick winter quilt over her, kneeling by the pillow. The covers came to her chin, her fist underneath pulling on the sheet. She forced a smile, and he kissed her on the forehead.

"Better?" he asked.

She nodded once with a shiver.

He lifted a corner of the quilt and slid in beside her, but atop the sheet and terry cloth blanket in which she was tightly wrapped. Now they were nose to nose, her curled-up knees against his chest.

"Can you tell me what happened?" he asked.

Again she nodded, but another shiver went through her.

"Never mind. I'll wait."

He laid an arm over her shoulder and kissed her nose. It was small and smooth and delicately curved. He brought his hand up and cupped it over her nose, closing his eyes so the size and shape beneath could register against the skin of his hand. Then, eyes still closed, he placed the cupped hand over his own nose—and his eyes flew open with the shock. What a monstrous hunk of bone and cartilage lay in his hand!

She saw his amazement and began to titter. Then she brought her own hand out from under the covers and performed the same examination in reverse. They laughed and kissed.

"Tell me what happened," he said, lifting the quilt to let some of the accumulated heat escape.

"When I got home, all I could think of was Sunday. Each time I tried to imagine what would happen, it ended in a terrible argument. So I started opening my closet and drawers and wondering what I would pack to take with me. And the more I looked, the more I wanted to begin packing right away. So I did."

"Oh, no, don't tell me. Your father came in."

"My mother. She asked me what I was doing. I couldn't think of anything to say. I felt like such an idiot. I literally could not think of anything. All I could think of was you."

He kissed her on both cheeks.

"So I told her exactly what we had planned. It felt so good talking to her about you, I was glad I hadn't been able to lie."

"How did she take it?"

"Better than I had expected. She tried to reason with me. Of course, she said I was too young to be taking such a step. I agreed. I am, you know."

"Believe me, I know."

"I told her you would wait for me."

"Didn't that make any difference?"

"I think it did make some. Things were actually beginning to look a little promising, when my father burst into the room. He said he had been wondering what the whispering was about, and he accused my mother of stabbing him in the back. Of course, she hadn't agreed to anything, but the mere suggestion from her that she was willing to listen had been enough. While they were screaming at each other, I grabbed my purse and ran out. I didn't even think to take an umbrella. I ran all the way to the station to get a cab."

"I'm sorry I put you through that."

"It wasn't all your fault. Besides, now I'm here with you."

"Yes, but, in a way, I'm sorry about that, too."

A sadness came into her eyes.

"I'm not sure I can say it right," he explained. "Try to understand. Having you here next to me like this is probably the one thing I want more than anything else in the world ... and, at the same time, I'm sorry you're here, now ... like this. I don't ever, ever want to take advantage of you—of what I've made you do."

"I'm not afraid. Well, a little. I've never been this close to anyone."

The warmth of their bodies mingled and mounted, and he shifted the quilt away from himself. She had relaxed her cringing fetal position until now they lay together on their sides in perfect alignment.

"Do you feel how my body wants yours?" he asked.

THE SUN GODS

"Yes," she whispered. "And I know mine wants yours."

"I'm trying to think of a good reason to keep them apart."

"I'm sure there are many good reasons."

He pushed the heavy quilt until it slid off the bed and onto the floor. Then he stood while she raised the light summer covers. Still dressed, he slipped in next to where she lay in his oversize robe. Their arms locked around each other, and their lips sought each other hungrily.

They kissed with their whole bodies, long and hard, and then, at the same moment, they pulled away, looking gravely into each other's eyes.

And when they spoke, it was at precisely the same moment.

"Tomorrow," they said together.

And then they laughed.

"It could be terrible," she said.

They would have to face her parents tomorrow, and they would have to do it prepared for the worst. Above all, they would have to do it secure in their hearts that her parents could fling no accusations at them.

He switched off the light, and they lay in each other's arms for a long time, listening to the rain, which had slowed now to a steady murmur.

Eventually, he slipped out of bed, retrieved the thick quilt from where it had fallen, and spread it on the matted floor of the next room, which was separated from this wood-floored room only by sliding paper doors. The quilt would be his mattress for the night.

They kissed one last time, and he stretched out on his makeshift bed under a cotton blanket, leaving the doors open.

The next thing he knew, Mrs. Niiyama was calling to him softly up the stairway: "Mohton-san!"

It was nearly eight o'clock, and the rain had quieted to a misty drizzle.

Mineko was sitting up in bed, looking at him anxiously. He tiptoed across the wooden landing and down the stairs, at the bottom of which he found Mrs. Niiyama waiting, her tiny black eyes in search of trouble.

"Mr. Morton, my husband is very angry," she said, the stray strands of hair around her face waving as she spoke. "He saw the shoes in the entryway when he left to play golf."

Mineko's pumps were still where she had stepped out of them.

"I'm sorry, Mrs. Niiyama, but a friend of mine had an emergency. She had some trouble at home and needed a place to spend the night. I had no idea she was coming here."

"This is a private home, after all. My husband says there are plenty of hotels—"

"Believe me, it's not what you think. There is nothing shameful about this at all."

"My husband is very worried about our reputation in the neighborhood. He wants you to leave before he comes home this afternoon."

"This afternoon?"

"That is what he said."

"And you?"

"I, of course, am carrying out my husband's wishes."

"Mrs. Niiyama, have I ever caused you any trouble before?"

"No. I think you are a very nice boy."

"Then do me—do us—a favor. I want you to meet Mineko—her name is Mineko Fukai. I said she was a friend, but, to tell you the truth, we are planning to be married."

Mrs. Niiyama's pinched, little mouth suddenly widened into a grin, and a hand went up to the bun atop her head. "Oh, my goodness!" she exclaimed.

"We need advice from someone closer to her parents' age. Can the three of us meet down here in the living room in fifteen minutes?"

She nodded and shuffled off in her slippers.

When the two of them came slowly down the steps at the agreed-upon time, Mrs. Niiyama had shed her apron and tucked in all the loose ends trailing from her bun. She sat demurely in an overstuffed chair, motioning the young couple to the couch opposite and offering them tea.

Mineko, having done her best to fit Bill's large yukata to herself more respectably, was blushing bright red. The initial embarrassment of introductions was reduced considerably, however, by Mrs. Niiyama's repeatedly gushing "What a lovely young girl!"

Mineko explained to her with perfect equanimity the difficulty of their situation.

Mrs. Niiyama had little advice to offer other than to urge them to go ahead with their plan to see Mineko's parents today. She was eager to help, though, and volunteered the use of her iron and whatever else it might take to make Mineko presentable. Bill was sent to fetch her wet clothing and then was ordered upstairs again to kill time while the two women, chattering like old friends, set about their business.

As they were leaving the house at eleven, Mrs. Niiyama assured them that she would handle her husband if things did not go well with the Fukais and they had to return together. Mineko repeatedly bowed to Mrs. Niiyama, who stood in the doorway returning the bows. Finally, they got away and, under Bill's big, black umbrella, they walked to Ogikubo Station.

Mineko called from Koganei Station to say that she would be home in a few minutes, bringing Bill with her. "My mother sounded very subdued," she told Bill, "but at least she didn't forbid me to come home."

They walked from the station through the misty rain to give her parents time to prepare themselves. Mineko's tension grew more obvious as they neared her house. Bill felt as if he had swallowed his voice and would never be able to find it again.

When Mineko slid back the front door, her mother was already there, kneeling on the floor above the entryway. The three bowed solemnly to each other. The mother was absolutely expressionless with the long narrow eyes and impassive smoothness of Buddhist statuary. Mineko took after her father. Luckily, she had not inherited her father's heavy eyebrows. From beneath the two dark bushes, Jiro Fukai glowered at Bill when he entered the formal sitting room. Bill uneasily recalled the eyes of Seiji Miyaguchi, the deadliest of the seven samurai in Kurosawa's film.

"Mr. Morton and I will talk alone," Fukai said to his daughter before she could kneel on the matted floor.

Mineko hesitated until Bill nodded to her. She left the room with her mother.

Fukai was seated at the low table with his legs crossed in front of him rather than in the more deferential manner with buttocks on heels. His arms were also crossed, this lordly posture doubtless intended to make Bill feel as little like an honored guest as possible. Bill knew he must play the man's game. He lowered himself to the mats, knees first, and settled his weight on his heels. As much as he had practiced it since coming to Japan, this respectful posture was not one he could maintain for long.

"A father does not like to see his daughter defer to another man's authority," Fukai said when Mineko was gone. "Especially when that man is the father's enemy."

"Mr. Fukai, I am not your enemy. I only wish I could convince you of that."

"Yes, your own father was a very convincing man—though I was never taken in by him."

Bill felt himself reddening. "I am deeply ashamed of my father," he said. "I came to Japan hoping to make up somehow for the terrible wrong he did your sister. Apparently, she told you a good deal about that."

"Your purpose sounds very noble, but all I know is that my family is being torn apart again by a Morton."

"I didn't come here to tear your family apart."

"You had no intention of luring my daughter away?"

"Your daughter? I didn't know that she existed."

"Are you sure of that?"

"Mr. Fukai, I don't see what you're getting at."

"You really didn't know I had a daughter when you came here?"

"That's right. I knew nothing about your family. Tsugiko gave me your name and address when I was in Itsuki. That was all."

"How the devil did you find your way down there if you knew so little?"

Bill told him of the years he had spent with Mitsuko and of the lullaby she had sung to him. As he spoke, the pressure on his legs was becoming unbearable, and he shifted his weight to the side. "I came to this house for one reason only," he concluded, "to learn from you whatever you could tell me about my mother."

"How dare you call her that?"

"Because, for me, that's what she was. That's what she will always be."

"And have you told all this to Mineko?"

"Yes, of course. Everything I have told you, I have told her."

"There is nothing else?"

"What else could there be? I was hoping to hear the rest from you."

"Mr. Morton, I am going to ask you a question that is very difficult for me to ask, and I want you to tell me the truth." He paused, looking straight at Bill from beneath his massive, graying brows, and when he spoke again, his voice quavered. "Have you ruined my daughter?"

"No!" Bill shot back, looking straight into the older man's eyes. "I could never 'ruin' her as you put it. I love her more than I could ever tell you. I want to marry her."

"Americans are so fond of love," he said with a sneer. "That was one of the weaknesses your G.I.s taught to our people after the war. The Japanese have much to teach the white race about patience and endurance. I wonder if your so-called 'love' is stronger than your legs."

Bill's face grew warm.

Fukai called to his wife, who returned with Mineko, and both women joined them at the low table, mother and daughter kneeling side-by-side with the utmost formality. Mineko glanced at Bill as she entered, but he could read nothing in her face. She had become as much the inscrutable Japanese as her mother.

"Mr. Morton, my wife tells me you are willing to wait for Mineko until she graduates from college."

"That is correct," Bill replied, nodding. Again he searched Mineko's face for some reaction, but she kept her eyes fixed on the lacquered table top, hands folded properly on her knees.

"You realize that she will be at Tsuda for three more years?"

"Yes."

"Good. Then, if your love is as strong as you say it is, the four of us will meet here like this in June of 1966. Before then, you will not see her. Good day, Mr. Morton," Fukai said with an air of finality.

"Mr. Fukai, you can't seriously be suggesting that I walk out of here and have nothing to do with Mineko for three years."

"That is precisely what I am suggesting—what I am demanding."

Bill looked at Mineko. Her eyes seemed to be focused deep inside the wood of the table. What had the mother said or done to her to make her so obedient?

"It's out of the question. I was talking about a normal engagement."

"What is 'normal' for Americans is not necessarily normal for Japanese. When Americans speak of 'endurance,' it must be with qualifications, in comfortable surroundings."

"I am trying to be reasonable, sir."

"All right, then, let us be 'reasonable,' as Americans say to disguise their weakness. You will not see Mineko for one year—is endurance for one year within your powers, Mr. Morton?—after which time, if you are still so much in 'love,' you will be permitted to visit my daughter, here, under the supervision of my wife, once each month for the remaining—"

Before he could finish setting out his conditions, Mineko's fists flashed through the air and pounded against the table top. "No!" she shouted, the single syllable reverberating with a power that seemed too great to have come from her slim body. "I won't live like that!"

"Shut up!" shouted her father. "You have nothing to say in the matter."

"You are talking about my life," she continued. "You can't put me in jail. That's exactly what you're trying to do."

He raised his hand as if to strike her, but when she did not flinch, he backed down. Bill watched her in awe, ashamed that he had doubted her even for a moment. Now was the time to make his move. Without a word, he stood and took her by the wrist. "Let's go, Mineko, it's hopeless."

"Go with your lover!" shouted Fukai. "I should have known—it's in the blood!"

His wife looked at him, horrified. "Jiro, what are you saying?"

"Get her out of here. I can't stand the sight of her."

He turned to the wall. She grabbed her husband by the shoulders and shook him. "Stop her, Jiro, stop her now, before she walks out of our lives forever!"

Bill and Mineko hurried down the polished corridor hand in hand. They stepped into their shoes and flew out the front door, pausing only long enough for Mineko to peer from beneath their umbrella one last time at the house where she had spent her girlhood.

"You were magnificent!" Bill said as they hurried toward the station, both holding the umbrella handle. He planted a kiss on her lips, but she backed away.

"What's wrong, Mineko?"

"My poor mother. It sounded as if my father almost betrayed a secret of hers. 'It's in the blood.' I wonder if there was something in her past ... though I can't believe it. My mother?"

But Bill was far too happy to dwell on the skeletons in Mrs. Fukai's closet.

35

WHEN THEY GOT BACK to Ogikubo carrying packages of things they had bought for Mineko, Mrs. Niiyama charged out into the drizzle to shield them under her own umbrella the last few feet of the way.

"What happened?" she demanded, eyes flashing, as she guided them to the front door as if they were first-time visitors.

Once inside, Mineko said, "My parents wouldn't listen. We had no choice."

Bill announced, "We're getting married as soon as possible."

"Wonderful! Congratulations!" Mrs. Niiyama exclaimed. "But I'm also sorry. I couldn't convince my husband to let you both stay here. You can spend the night, and maybe a day or two longer while you look for another place to live. That's the best I can do."

Bill said, "Thank you for trying. We'll begin searching for a house tomorrow."

Mrs. Niiyama helped them carry their packages up to Bill's room and then left them alone.

Bill hugged Mineko, and the warmth of her kisses told him that her earlier misgivings were gone.

After dinner they carried their towels and water scoops, soap and shampoo to the neighborhood bath. The rain tonight was little more than a cooling mist, and he hooked the handle of his closed umbrella over his forearm. He saw her to the door of the women's section and entered the men's side, where he undressed and quickly began to scrub every inch of himself almost as if he were bathing for the first time in his life. Now everything he did would be for her.

He washed and soaked and washed again. In the bank of mirrors, he saw the glow of reborn flesh. He was ready, and he knew that she would be, too. They had not spoken of a time to meet outside, but he was stepping into his sandals when the outer door of the women's bath opened and she emerged, fresh and bright. He took her hand as she stepped down beside him. The rain had stopped, but he raised the canopy of the umbrella over them nonetheless. They glided along in their own little envelope of air. He could feel the warm fullness of her breast against the arm she took.

Tonight, nothing would come between them. Standing in the half-light of his lamp, they revealed their glowing bodies to each other, touching and probing and caressing.

Between the cool sheets, their bodies intertwined with infinite gentleness and then an urgency through which his whole life passed before his eyes. All of it was good and his heart opened to the farthest reaches of light and life. In the beginning was his father, and the spirit of his father moved upon the face of the deep within him. In his arms he held the world. So vast was his love for Mineko that he could not withhold its power from anyone. All was one, and all was forgiven.

When he opened his eyes in the morning light, she was smiling down at him. Again they kissed and touched and shared themselves unstintingly. Slowly, as they lay there, the sounds of the surrounding daily bustle began to rise about them.

"Will you marry me?" he asked.

She nodded, smiling.

"Today?"

Again she nodded.

He sat up. "You know," he said, "I just realized that I don't have the slightest idea how to go about getting married."

"I don't either," she said with a titter.

"I always thought of marriage as something imposed on people by society. Suddenly I feel completely different about it. I want people to know that we belong to each other."

"Maybe Mrs. Niiyama knows about getting married."

And indeed, she did. "It's complicated," she said. "You have to rent a hall and hire a Shinto priest and have the bride fitted for a kimono and headpiece and wig and invite all—"

"No, Mrs. Niiyama, without all those things. Just the two of us."

"Oh, then it's the simplest thing in the world. Just go register at the ward office. It costs forty yen."

"That's it? Eleven cents to get married?"

"That's all there is to it. Oh, I almost forgot. You have to bring a copy of your family register with you."

Their first stop that morning was Koganei City Hall, where Mineko obtained a fuzzy purple copy of the Fukai family register. They gazed at the document's old-fashioned characters while sitting side-by-side on the train to downtown.

Bill said, "It's funny seeing your name surrounded by all this stiff, formal writing. 'Showa ten-nine-year, four-month, ten-seven-day.' April 17, 1944."

As an American citizen, Bill was legally domiciled in Minato Ward downtown, where the American Embassy was located. At the ward office, the five minute transaction took place that made them man and wife, the one proof of which was the cash register receipt showing they had paid their forty yen.

The more complicated procedures of signing and oath-taking at the Embassy brought the reality of it home somewhat more forcefully, but by 1:30 that afternoon, they were married and pleasantly full of sushi.

Visits to real estate agents that Mrs. Niiyama had recommended took up the rest of the day, with discouraging results. None had small enough houses available for rent, and the few apartments they saw faced either railroad tracks or enormous avenues.

In the evening, Bill brought Mineko to meet his friends, the Greens, who woke up their sleeping son with their cheers.

"I thought something fishy was going on!" said Martha, eyes shining behind her black-framed glasses. "We never see you these days. So that's what you've been doing! Maybe you can take Mineko to Meiji Shrine and tell her your discovery about holy infants and—."

"Never mind!" Bill cut her short.

A real estate agent from Nakano called the first thing the next morning to say he had a house that had just been offered for rent. A childless couple being sent to the Paris branch of the husband's company were hoping to rent out their house complete with furniture.

They met the agent, a slim man in his early forties, at Nakano Station. He led them through winding back streets to a place called Momozono-cho— "Peach Garden." The narrow house was squeezed in among its neighbors like all the other houses in this quiet section. It had a Western living room, matted sitting room, kitchen and bath downstairs, plus two matted rooms at the top of a steep, ladder-like stairway. The light poured into the upstairs rooms. It was perfect, but the agent seemed reluctant to close the deal.

"What's the problem?" Bill asked, but he couldn't wring a straight answer from the man.

"Let me try," Mineko said, launching a rapid-fire negotiation in hushed Japanese.

"He doesn't think we can afford such a nice place," Mineko said, turning to Bill with a smile. "He thinks we're too young."

Bill laughed and gave the man his card. "Here, call the Fulbright office. They'll tell you how much they're paying me. It's just an ordinary American student income, but here it seems huge. And they're going to give me an extra hundred dollars a month now that I'm married. That alone will more than pay the rent."

The agent turned bright red and bowed as low as Bill had ever seen anyone bow in Japan, apologizing. "The only problem," he said, is that the house will not be available until July 1."

"That's even better," Bill said. "We're going to take a trip."

"We are? Where?" Mineko asked.

"I'll tell you later."

She gave him a puzzled look.

He had long dreamed of visiting the temples of Kyoto, he told her that night. Once, too, he had vowed to himself to walk those ancient streets with

Mitsuko, and a honeymoon there with Mitsuko's niece would compensate somewhat for the loss of that hope.

"That would be lovely," she said. "On the way back."

"On the way back? From where?"

"Remember I told you I've always wanted to go to Itsuki? Especially now that it's brought you to me, I want to go more than ever."

"Yes, the mountains and Momigi are very beautiful," agreed Bill. "But meeting Aunt Yoshiko might be discouraging, even sad."

"I'll take the chance," she said. "If the years have been as cruel to Aunt Yoshiko as you told me, I might not have much time left to meet her."

After the long trip on the Hayabusa, they waited in the heat and humidity for the local in Yatsushiro. Finally, the steam train arrived, and it chugged lethargically up the river valley. The windows were wide open to catch any breeze, but also let in soot and ash.

They stayed in Hitoyoshi for the night to soak in the bath and make a fresh start early in the morning before the sun grew too strong. They rented a small Honda two-seater sports car for the ride up the Kawabe River to Toji and Momigi.

Morning shadows still lay over the valley by the time they pulled into the parking area near the suspension bridge in Momigi. Leaving their bags in the car, they walked down the path through the trees to the bridge. The forest buzzed with the languid cries of cicadas, and a light breeze moving up the gorge stirred the trees. The mists that had shrouded the gorge in the early spring were gone now. They stopped in the middle of the bridge, and Bill saw for the first time how deep the drop was to the sparkling stream below. The breeze rocked the bridge gently.

"I'm surprised she's not standing here," he said to Mineko, "praying to her sun gods."

"Let's go," said Mineko, leading the way.

He directed her up the path that skirted the terraced rice fields, where heavy stalks now swayed in the breeze that rippled the surface of the dammed-up water. The old, thatch-roofed farmhouses they passed were quiet enough to be empty, and the tea hedges beyond lay open to the sun, unattended. He took the lead through the cedar grove that separated Yoshiko's house from the others, and when they came to the crooked front door, he pulled it open and loudly announced their presence.

The old house swallowed his voice. He looked at Mineko, who could only return his questioning gaze. They stepped across the worn threshold into the dirt-floored entryway.

Before he could call again, however, there resounded a few soft thumps from within. Slowly, Yoshiko came gliding past the pillar at the corner of the hallway to the left. Her face lit up when she saw Bill, but her smile turned into a puzzled frown.

"I've brought someone who wants to meet you," he said in English. "Your niece, Mineko."

Mineko touched his arm and moved closer to him. Yoshiko peered at her a long time, saying nothing. At length, speaking in Japanese, she told them to come in and led the way to her little sitting room.

The corridor of the gloomy house was chilly, and the quilt was still in place around Yoshiko's low table, just as it had been earlier to ward off the lingering cold of winter. The charcoal fire was not burning underneath the table, but the iron kettle on the blue hibachi kept up its tiny, bell-like ringing.

Yoshiko knelt formally before the large wardrobe, bowing her head nearly to the mats. Mineko bowed as deeply in return, and the two exchanged the usual Japanese formalities.

"You have grown up to be such a lovely young woman," said Yoshiko, cocking her head to one side and studying Mineko. "Is it really you? You were so tiny … not even two years old …" She stared at Mineko as if she were trying to bring back a long-lost memory. "Your mother was so proud of you. She was more than thirty when you were born. Jiro was almost forty. They had given up any hope of having children."

"I must confess," said Mineko, "I am not making my mother and father very proud right now."

"Oh? Why is that?" Yoshiko asked.

"Because I took her away," Bill interjected. "We were married four days ago."

Yoshiko's smile faded. "Perhaps I should say congratulations."

"But ... ?"

"These marriages can bring much unhappiness."

"This one will be different," Bill declared. "I promise you."

Yoshiko looked at him and at Mineko. Her eyes lingered on the face of her niece. Mineko lowered her gaze to the mats.

"Why don't we look at the pictures?" Bill said. "Aunt Yoshiko, do you think we could have some tea? I can show Mineko the albums."

Yoshiko motioned toward the wardrobe drawer and left the room.

Bill got out the first album and turned the pages for her. Mineko laughed at the snapshots of her father as a small child. "I'd recognize those eyebrows anywhere!"

When Bill pointed out Mitsuko as a young girl, Mineko said, "That's strange. Aunt Mitsuko looks familiar. Maybe she looks like one of my elementary school friends."

In the later album, Mineko liked the wedding pictures of Yoshiko and Goro. "I didn't know they were such strong Christians. I've never heard of such a thing in the family."

It struck Bill with a sense of liberation that he had joined himself for life to a woman about whose religious beliefs he had never thought to ask.

Mineko flipped quickly past the group shots from the Seattle church, but she stopped short when she came to the picture of Bill in Mitsuko's lap. He expected her to laugh at the little boy with rice smeared on his mouth, but she instead looked fixedly at the image of the woman.

"Yes," she murmured, "I thought I recognized that face in the childhood pictures. This is the woman, the very same woman. Is this Aunt Mitsuko?"

"Yes, of course."

"I know her," said Mineko. "She came to see me once in Tokyo—at my school in Koganei."

"You must be mistaken," Bill said as a chill shot through him.

"No, I'm absolutely certain," said Mineko. "She was a good deal older than this, but still lovely. She had her hair up in this same kind of bun. I remember she had a scar on her lower lip. How could I forget a face like that? My parents always told me not to talk to strangers, but I wasn't afraid of her in the least. She was so kind, and she knew my name. She even knew it was my birthday. I was twelve years old that day. She gave me a beautiful little mirror for my birthday."

Bill grabbed her by the arm. "What kind of mirror?"

"Please, Bill, you're hurting me!"

"Tell me about the mirror," he insisted, releasing his grip.

"You know the mirror I use. You must have seen it a hundred times. What's the matter?"

"Please, show me the mirror."

"All right. It's here, in my purse, where I always keep it."

She set her purse on the table and released the catch. From a pocket on one side, she withdrew a small leather case and handed it to him. She was right, he had indeed seen this case many times without taking special note of it or of its contents, but he knew already from the lightness of it in his hand what he was going to find. His fingers clumsily peeled back the stiff flap, and he watched in amazement as a mirror virtually identical to the one Yoshiko had given him slipped into his palm. He had studied his own mirror enough to know that certain details in the border work were different, but this was unmistakably a companion to the other, with its representation of the sun and the flying goose.

"She's alive," Bill muttered.

"Aunt Mitsuko? I thought you said she died in Nagasaki."

"I don't know how, but she's alive." He got up and reached for Mineko's hand. "Come with me," he said, then called toward the kitchen, "Aunt Yoshiko, we have to go out for a few minutes."

Holding the mirror in his right hand, he grabbed Mineko by the arm and pulled her out of the house, releasing her only when they had staggered out into the sunlight. Almost without thinking, he started to run. He needed to move, to race through the air, to feel the earth flying beneath his feet.

"Bill, wait!" Mineko cried.

He soared past the fields and the houses, and his pace hardly slowed when he came to the bridge. The soles of his shoes began to slap against the moving planks. When he halted at the center of the undulating bridge, he clasped the mirror to his heart.

"SHE'S ALIVE! SHE'S ALIVE!"

His wild shouts echoed and reechoed between the rocky faces of the gorge, reverberating in infinite repetitions of the one truth he knew more certainly than he had ever known anything.

The sweat was dripping from his face. He watched beads of it fly from him and go sailing far below, there to join with the gushing stream that would carry it to the sea. Then Mineko was standing beside him, panting from the run, and they embraced, the sweat of her body mingling with his.

They returned to the end of the bridge, walking arm-in-arm to Yoshiko's house. Beside the house ran an overgrown path that continued up into the hills. Wordlessly, he plunged through the brush, climbing higher and higher above the soaring roofs of the hamlet. The path gave out at a small, rocky plateau where a still, clear pool lay shimmering in the sun like an offering to heaven. Fed by tiny rivulets from higher up, it released its treasure slowly down the mountainside.

He turned to face her as she joined him at the top of the ridge, their breathing labored now, their clothes sodden with the sweat the sun had drawn from their bodies. He all but tore his shirt off, his eyes urging her to do the same. A moment later, they stood before each other naked and glistening. Droplets of sweat ran slowly down the hollow between her breasts. He knelt and placed his streaming forehead there, then he lapped the salt that was oozing from her flesh. The sun beat down upon his back, where her hands began to slide through the liquid sheet that clung to his skin. He pulled her down to the smooth stone bank of the pool, and their bodies melted together in the heat of the mounting sun, its limitless power focused and flowing through him into her—surging, surging, exploding in relentless waves of energy.

Afterward, his arm lay limp along the rock, his fingertips trailing in the cool water. He brought the hand up to her face, touching her closed eyelids, which quivered and opened. She, too, reached down, and they began scooping handfuls from the clear mountain pool, smoothing the cool liquid over each other's steaming bodies. He crept into the water, and she followed him in. Both ducked beneath the surface and came up clear-eyed and fresh.

He reached for the clothes they had left scattered on the rock, plunging them into the pool, then spreading them out on the rock again to dry. They found a sheltered corner where the overhanging rocks provided respite from the heat of the sun. He held her mirror out into the streaming rays and sent them glancing across the water.

"Now, tell me again about the woman who gave you this," he said.

"It happened over six years ago. I saw her for ten minutes, possibly fifteen."

"Didn't she tell you who she was, or say anything about where she lived?"

"No, nothing. She seemed to know me so well, I guess it never occurred to me to ask about her."

"And if you had asked, I doubt that she would have told you anything."

"It's true, she was very secretive. She told me to hide the mirror from my parents and not to tell them how I got it. I never told them. I kept it hidden in a box of souvenirs—sea shells, pretty rocks. I almost forgot I had it until high school. I've carried it with me ever since, and my mother never really noticed."

"This leather case is new, though, isn't it?"

"Yes. How do you know?"

"Because I have a mirror just like yours, only mine came in a little brocade pocket."

"That's it! Brocade! Mine fell apart, so I threw it away and bought this. Where did you get your mirror?"

"Yoshiko gave it to me and said that it was something Mitsuko left with her for me. I think that must have happened before Mitsuko left Minidoka—"

Bill cut himself short, amazed at the sound of his own words. Speaking in Japanese, the name "Minidoka" had emerged more naturally on the tongue as "Minedoka," and he thought of the old, yellowed copy of the camp newspaper in Mitsuko's handwriting that Frank had shown him. As a non-Japanese word, "Minidoka" had been written in the *katakana* syllabary, and it had been spelled "Minedoka."

"Mineko—Child of Minedoka," he said.

"Bill, what is it? You look so serious—especially for someone without any clothes on."

"Didn't you hear what I said?"

"'Mineko—Child of Minedoka.' I thought you liked to think of it as 'Child on the Mountaintop.'"

"Minedoka is written in *katakana*," he said. "Just like Mineko."

She laughed and pulled him close, kissing him on the head. "You've been out in the sun too long."

"No, listen. Your birthday is April 17. You were born in 1944." He counted nine months backwards to July 1943. Frank and Mitsuko. Together in Minidoka. Yoshiko had said that Jiro's wife had almost given up hope of having a baby.

Mineko was not Mitsuko's niece, but her daughter.

Now he saw what had always been there: the long, graceful, athletic body, the softly curving nose, the clear brows of Frank Sano reborn a beautiful woman. He hid his face in his hands. If it was this difficult for him, how would Mineko take it? Perhaps he should stop before it was too late.

"Bill, you've got to talk to me. What is going on inside that head of yours?"

But wasn't it a matter for rejoicing? Mineko was even closer to him than he had imagined—spiritually, a sister; physically, a wife. Her very existence seemed to expiate the sin of his father. Child of the desert. Child of the agony of war and racial hatred. Child of Minedoka. He put his arms around her and held her close.

"You know I love you, Mineko," he said. "And that I'll always love you, no matter what."

She nodded, drawing away to look into his eyes.

"I ... I need to ask you something," he said. "Have your parents ever said or done anything to make you think you were ... different?"

"'Different?' How?" she said with a little laugh. "What are you getting at?"

"I mean, they've always been as loving and protective as I have seen them to be?"

"Too much so, if anything. You know that."

"Yes, maybe. But that love of theirs is all that matters, don't you agree?"

"All right. Now, will you get to the point?"

"I know now why your father wanted to talk with me alone, and why he pressed me so hard for whatever I might have learned about you before I first visited your home." He paused and then said, "Because you are Mitsuko's daughter."

One side of her mouth drew up in a half smile, but that did nothing to diminish the sadness in her eyes. Her head shook almost imperceptibly.

"No, that can't be right. I would have known. I would have suspected."

"Not if your adoptive parents gave you all the love they would have given to their own child."

"It's crazy. You're so obsessed with Mitsuko; it's done something to your mind." She twisted herself away from him and pressed her forehead to the rock.

He touched her arm.

"How can you be so sure?" she cried, raising her tear-stained face to look at him.

"You heard what Yoshiko said. Your mother thought she would never have a child."

"That doesn't prove anything. Lots of women conceive late."

"But why didn't your mother have any more children?"

"I told you, it was a difficult birth for her."

"I don't believe it. No, I'll tell you what happened. Mitsuko came back from America pregnant, and she gave the baby to her brother and his childless wife. Then she went off to Nagasaki to join her parents, but for some reason, they were killed there while she escaped."

"Why didn't she let my father know she was alive? Or Yoshiko?"

"I don't know. Maybe your father can tell us that. What was it he said? 'It's in the blood?' He wasn't talking about your mother, but his sister. He was ashamed of her."

"It all seems so incredible—and so sordid. If what you say is true, there was nothing admirable in what she did."

He wanted to tell her what a decent, honest, handsome man had loved her mother and given her life, but now was not the time. If Mitsuko was alive—

No. She *was* alive. Mitsuko would be the one to decide what her daughter would learn of the past.

36

ONCE THEY WERE BACK in Tokyo, Bill and Mineko worked for two solid days on a letter to her parents.

37 Momozono-cho
Nakano-ku, Tokyo

July 3, 1963 (Wed.)

Dear Mother,
       You will probably not be too surprised to learn that I am married. It happened on June 24. My husband and I have just returned from a honeymoon of sorts and moved into this house in Nakano on Tuesday. I wish that the four of us could have reached some kind of understanding and that you could share in my happiness, but perhaps that would have been expecting too much at the time. I write to you today in the hope that things I have learned recently can serve to bring us together.
       My husband and I spent a few days during the past week in Kyoto, visiting the famous temples. I suppose it was very lovely, but I can hardly remember a thing we saw. All we could think and talk about the whole time was you and Father. It would not be too much of an exaggeration to say that I was preparing myself to write this letter. I only hope that it reaches you while Father is in the office. You, at least, will probably open it, while he might simply throw it away unread.
       I cannot blame either of you for being upset with me for the way I left the house. As happy as I am with my husband, I fear that I shall always regret what happened that day. You must believe me when I say that, as selfish as I have been, I have not forgotten all that my parents have done for me. Gratitude and filial piety are as much a part of me as ever, and they always will be. Even if you should choose to disown me, I will continue to love you as my parents and to honor your memory.
       I emphasize this because I now strongly suspect that I was not born into the world as your daughter. Before we went to Kyoto, our destination was Itsuki, where I met Aunt Yoshiko. On the way

```
back, we stopped briefly in Nagasaki. I know that
you were trying only to protect me from pain when
you chose to hide from me the identity of the
woman who gave me life. And, yes, the truth has
been very painful, but it has not made me love you
any less. Never once in my nineteen years with
you did you give me cause to suspect that I was
anything other than your child. My husband says
that this is the greatest proof of your love. I
believe that he is right.
         The war has left many scars on many
people, and we may be able to begin to heal them
by being honest with one another. My husband and
I both sincerely hope that you and Father will
consent to see us and talk to us about these
things. Please call me here at 381-5779 if you
think there is any way we can make this happen.

Your loving daughter,
Mineko
```

Mrs. Fukai was trembling when she admitted Bill and Mineko to the sitting room that Sunday afternoon. Her husband looked as morose as he had during the earlier confrontation, but in contrast to the lordly air he had adopted then, he greeted them formally, sitting on his heels and bowing. He did not apologize for his earlier behavior, and he nodded curtly when Mineko and Bill apologized vaguely for having been "impolite the other day," as the situation demanded. Then, staring off into the distance, his voice deep and somber, Jiro Fukai spoke of things long hidden.

"We were never informed that Mitsuko was being sent back from America, so no one went to meet her ship when it docked in Yokohama. This was in late November or early December 1943. Had we known, I would have been the one to go. I had been in Tokyo since I entered the university in 1930, and my wife and I had been married for several years. My elder brother, Ichiro, was in Itsuki with our parents, his wife and two children.

"Later we heard from my mother that the secret police kept Mitsuko locked up for several days in Yokohama. Then, after they had determined that she posed no danger to the state, they sent her to Itsuki. My parents did not know that she was coming until she walked through the door at Momigi. My mother wrote to me late in December to tell me all this. The next I heard, the entire family had moved to Nagasaki.

"The war had been going badly for many months, and anyone connected in any way with the enemy was looked upon as a spy. They called them 'dogs.' Everyone knew that Mitsuko had been living in America, married to an American, which made all the Fukais 'dogs,' even the children. No one would speak to them except to curse them. The other children beat Ichiro's sons. The Fukais had long been resented as Christians, and this new evidence of collaboration with the enemy only stirred up those feelings. Unable to bear the hatred, the family went to live near the Urakami Cathedral in Nagasaki— which is ironic, since by then Mitsuko herself had abandoned her religion. I myself leave religious matters to my wife.

"Late in February, I received a telegram from my mother saying that Mitsuko was coming to see us, and she arrived a few days later. In all that time, nothing had been said about her condition. We were shocked to see her. My mother had convinced her to have the baby in Tokyo and give it to us. We had been trying for years to have a child without success, and my mother took pity on us.

"I did not know what to feel. I knew my wife desperately wanted a child, but I was hesitant to have a half-white baby in my home. When Mitsuko promised me that the child would be pure Japanese, I was horrified. I felt deeply ashamed of my sister, who was bearing the child of a man to whom she was not married. She never did tell us the name of the father.

"The baby was born in April—a beautiful, healthy baby girl. When I saw her in my wife's arms, all my misgivings were swept aside. We have loved her with our whole hearts ever since.

"As the mother, Mitsuko wanted to name the baby herself. We approved of her choice, 'Mineko,' but she insisted that it be written in *katakana* like a foreign word. Neither of us wanted it that way, but she refused to listen to our objections. She even went with me to the town hall when I registered her as our daughter, just to make sure that the name was written in that unusual way. She never did explain her intention.

"Mitsuko also insisted on nursing the baby herself. It seemed only natural, and food supplies were already growing scarce then. It would have been a shame to waste her milk. We soon came to regret our practicality.

"With each passing month, Mitsuko's love for the baby grew stronger. At first, she was only going to nurse the child for the first three or four months. Then it was to be five or six. We began to worry that she would change her mind and try to take the child back. My wife would invent errands for Mitsuko to run, just to get her away from the baby for a few minutes at a time. Then the bickering started. Mitsuko would argue that she was eventually going to have to lose her daughter and should be allowed to enjoy her as much as possible before that happened. The tension in the house was becoming unbearable.

"Early in November 1944, the B-29s began to appear above our heads. They came singly at first, flying so high our antiaircraft fire could not touch them. We began to think we had missed our chance to send Mitsuko away. We worried, too, that it might be more dangerous for all of us to stay in Tokyo. We feared for our lives, especially for Mineko. We were worried about the family in Nagasaki. We thought of going there together. No one knew what to do. No one knew where to go. There was no way to tell where the bombs would fall. We became paralyzed.

"Finally, on the twenty-fourth of November, our minds were made up for us. Seventy B-29s attacked and destroyed the Nakajima Aircraft Factory, where I was employed as an engineer. It was located near here, on the outskirts of the city, and we were living in a house close by. The factory was burning behind me, and I was running home when I saw the house take a direct hit. Ours was one of over three hundred houses destroyed by the bombs that day, but at that moment, I saw only the house with my wife and child in it blown to pieces before my eyes.

"The house collapsed, but it did not burn. I rounded up some workers, and we dug furiously at the wreckage. The only sign of life was Mineko's crying. We tore away a section of roof and found Mitsuko lying beside a pile of cushions, her face covered with blood. Her own teeth had gashed her lower lip from side to side, but she was alive. The floor had caved in at that spot, and underneath the cushions we found Mineko half-buried in mud. She was screaming at the top of her lungs, but aside from some dirt in her mouth and a few scratches, she was unhurt.

"My wife and the maid were not so fortunate. A beam fell on the maid and killed her outright. My wife was trapped under the same section of roof, and she had suffered internal bleeding. Her face was gorged with blood and looked twice its normal size. I could hardly recognize her when we pulled her out.

"Even now, it seems incredible to me that anyone survived. If the bomb had been an incendiary type, and not a conventional bomb, I have no doubt that my wife, my sister, the baby, and the maid would all have perished. The women had heard the sirens but had wasted precious time squabbling over who should carry the baby. They ran from the house, hoping to reach the air raid shelter, but by then the planes were already in sight, and they went back inside. Mitsuko was holding the child and took her to the large formal room. My wife and the maid went to the maid's room. Before the bomb fell, Mitsuko covered the baby with the floor cushions kept in that room for guests. This one act undoubtedly saved her life.

"Within ten days, both women had recovered enough to travel. I brought them and the baby to the home of my wife's family in Chiba, some thirty miles from Tokyo, but I myself had to return to the city to resume my work. I was transferred to an engine factory in the delta flatlands of the Sumida River. I lived in a dormitory with other men whose families had been evacuated, but all around us were the wives and children of the poor laborers who had no place to send their families. I used to wonder what would happen to them when the bombs came.

"And we all knew they would be coming. Through December, and into January and February, the number of B-29s over Tokyo steadily increased, attacking day and night. They concentrated on military targets, but many civilians were killed. The Sumida delta provided the perfect combination for a tragedy. That part of the city is crisscrossed by canals, and each block of land, surrounded by water, was crammed with people living on top of one another beside the factories that were making weapons.

"A rumor began to circulate in March that the Americans would choose the tenth, Army Memorial Day, for the biggest raid ever, and nature seemed to confirm our fears. All day on the ninth, chill winds whipped out of the north, and the sky was covered with a thick overcast. It was cold enough so that dirty patches of snow remained on the ground from a few days earlier. The winds grew stronger after nightfall. There was nothing to do but go to bed. For one thing, lights had to be kept to a minimum because of the blackout, and everyone tried to get sleep in case the sirens might wake us, as they usually did, in the middle of the night. Sleeping was also the best way to endure an empty stomach and to keep warm.

"The sirens did, in fact, sound at 10:30, but the all-clear came through and we returned to our mats. The real thing came at fifteen minutes after midnight. It was a night I will never be able to forget for as long as I live. I sometimes think that, at the moment of my death, the last things to enter my mind will be the sights that were seared into my brain that night. The attack lasted no more than two-and-a-half hours, I read later, but at the time it seemed to go on forever, like the eternal punishments of hell. Close to ninety thousand people were killed in the one raid.

"The sky was already burning red and streaked with black smoke trails when I got out to the street. I looked around me and realized I could read the posters on buildings as easily as in the light of day, though not a single street lamp was lighted. People were running in all directions, screaming, but as close as they were to me, I could hardly hear the sound of their voices through the roar of the airplane engines. The bombs came down, tearing through the air, and I could see the flash of the explosions through closed eyelids and feel the ground shake. Winter had suddenly turned into scorching summer. The air was thick and painful to breathe. The wind whipped showers of sparks everywhere like some kind of burning blizzard.

"The B-29s were huge and horrible, flying down at rooftop level, dropping firebombs on every inch of ground. Fire engines tried to force their way through the crowds, but they drifted around aimlessly, sirens wailing. It was pitiful to watch some of the men assigned to the fire brigades trying to douse the flames with bamboo water cannons. These and our fighting spirit were supposedly all we needed to counter the B-29 raids, according to the government. And in case they weren't enough, there was the Air Defense Law, which required Tokyo residents to stay in the city during raids to help fight the fires.

"I decided then and there that I had had enough of doing my patriotic duty, and I was going to get out. To many, it seemed that the only place to go was into the canals, but I was afraid that once I got into the water, I would never come out. The water was red with the reflections of the flames, and heads were bobbing on the surface, as thick as the public bath on a busy night. I heard later that most of the people in the canals suffocated when the flames burned over them, and the others drowned or died of shock in the cold water.

"I survived through sheer luck. No one knew where to run, and I just happened to pick a route that was less devastated by the flames. The hair was singed off the back of my head, and I had a few cuts and bruises, but otherwise I came through all right. It took me three days to make my way to Chiba, but once I joined my family there, I stayed until the war was over.

"My wife and sister had recovered from their wounds by then, but the situation with the baby was worse than ever. The two women never spoke to each other, and my mother-in-law had to set up a daily schedule stipulating who would do what for Mineko at what times. Mitsuko never went back on her promise to give us the baby, but the experience of having saved the child's life in the bombing had only served to increase her attachment.

"Things continued like this for a few more months. Then, near the end of June, a letter made it through to us from Ichiro in Nagasaki. It contained nothing unusual, but it mentioned, almost casually, that my parents were feeling poorly and that Ichiro's wife could use Mitsuko's help with them and the children. It was not a direct request for Mitsuko to come home, more a kind of vague wish that things could be different. But I leaped on it, and from that day on, I wouldn't leave Mitsuko alone. I kept badgering her about her duty to her parents and pointing out that this was the perfect opportunity for her finally to break her ties with Mineko, who was fifteen months old by then.

"The two of us never crossed paths in the house that I didn't remind her of these things. And, frankly, I had never reconciled myself to the circumstances of her pregnancy. I couldn't help feeling that the more she was around the baby, the more her immorality was likely to rub off. She had given us her treasure, and now she was of no use to us. Worse, she might be causing positive harm.

"Having no idea what difficulties she would encounter travelling from one end of the bomb-ravaged country to the other, I sent her out on her own. She left on the seventeenth of July, and we never heard from her again. The bomb fell on Nagasaki on August ninth. After the surrender on the fifteenth, I traveled to Nagasaki, through mile after mile of death and destruction, but when I got there, nothing was left. My family had been wiped off the face of the earth. I found a little mound of ashes where it seemed their house had been, but there was no point in trying to recover it. The ashes could have been anything—other people, a dog, a tree.

"Ever since, I have lived with the knowledge that I killed my sister. In the hopes of consoling Mitsuko's spirit, we have tried to raise Mineko with all the love and care that her own mother would have lavished on her had she lived. Perhaps this has made us even more protective than ordinary parents. I do not know. I can only declare to you, Mineko, that we have always meant well for you and have never forgotten the obligation we feel toward my sister and her memory. I hope you can find it in your heart to forgive us for having concealed the truth from you all these years.

"After what we experienced, it is very difficult for us to reconcile ourselves to the fact that our daughter has chosen to marry an American. Perhaps we will never be able to accept it fully. If, as you say, Mitsuko was devoted to you as a child, perhaps she would not have felt our misgivings. Perhaps we should rejoice that fate has brought together the two children she could not have. If this is truly the case, then perhaps, some day, our hearts will open to you."

All heads were bowed when Fukai finished speaking, his eyes closed, as if reliving the horror and pain. His wife sobbed openly and Mineko wept quietly into a handkerchief. Bill felt a deep sadness that, he knew, would burst forth as tears if he tried to speak. He listened to the sounds of children playing in the nearby fields.

Mineko was the first to speak, thanking her father for having told her the true story of her birth, and assuring both parents that her feelings for them were now, if anything, deeper than before. "But there is something we must tell you—something Bill must tell you, because he feels it with more certainty than I do."

Mrs. Fukai was still too overwhelmed with emotion to do more than glance up at Mineko and bow her head again immediately. Fukai himself opened his eyes and looked at her, then Bill, expectantly.

"Your sister is alive," Bill said with quiet assurance. "You don't know for certain that she was in Nagasaki at the time of the bomb."

"I understand your wishful thinking. That thought haunted me for years, both as a dream and as a nightmare. I kept praying that she would present herself to us in forgiveness, but I feared, too, that she might wish to claim Mineko for herself. It has not been easy living with such conflicting emotions."

"You may not have to anymore. You can be sure that she did not die in Nagasaki."

"Perhaps not. Perhaps she was in Hiroshima on the sixth. Perhaps her train was passing through Kobe when fire bombs destroyed that city. During the confusion following the surrender, it took me only three days to reach Nagasaki. Yes, the trains were in a more chaotic state while the bombs were falling, but she had over three weeks to cover the same distance. I cannot believe she is alive. She would have found her way back to us."

"My husband is telling the truth," Mineko said. "I saw her, Father."

Both her parents looked at her, eyes full of pain and wonder. Mineko took the two mirrors, hers and Bill's, from her purse, and explained where they had come from. Then she showed them the photograph of Mitsuko holding the young Bill, which Yoshiko had let them take. "And when you told us about the bombing of our house, it ended any lingering doubts I might have had," she said. "The woman who came to see me had a small scar on her lip. On the right side, like a red swelling."

"Yes." said Mrs. Fukai. "The impact of the bomb made her bite into her lip. Most of the scar was on the inside. Only one end showed."

"But where has she been all these years?" objected Fukai.

"I don't know," his wife cried, "but one thing is certain: we must find her!"

"We spent a day in Nagasaki," said Bill, "but we came up with nothing. We went through City Hall records, checked the phone books, visited the A-Bomb Museum."

"The Museum was just ghastly," added Mineko with a shudder.

Fukai said, "I would give anything to see her alive. But how? She obviously doesn't want to be found."

"We're not giving up," said Bill. "But first, Mineko, we're going to have to get you a passport."

37

MINEKO NEEDED NOT ONLY a Japanese government-issue passport but a full-sized chest X-ray in order to be admitted through United States immigration in Seattle. She couldn't help giggling as she hoisted the enormous manila envelope over the turnstile.

"It's almost as big as you are," Bill said, grinning, as he put his arm around her.

They were no longer smiling as they pushed open the last door leading out to the airport's reception area. Bill immediately spotted Frank Sano among the crowd of greeters. Frank glanced at him, then locked eyes on Mineko. She clutched Bill's hand and looked at him, her eyes full of fear.

"Don't worry," Bill said. "He's a wonderful man."

Frank was wearing a dark brown suit and glossy gray tie, and Bill guessed that he had spent hours agonizing over what to wear, what to say to his daughter.

The crowd of passengers brushed past them as their pace slowed. Frank took one step in their direction and stopped. He held his hand out toward Mineko, who tightened her grip on Bill's hand.

Bill took another step in Frank's direction, drawing Mineko along. Head bowed, she came to a stop before Frank. Then she looked directly at him and said, *"Musume no Mineko desu. Dohzo yoroshiku o-negai itashimasu."*

Frank seemed to know enough Japanese to realize that Mineko was introducing herself to him as his daughter. He brought his extended hand to his face and pressed hard against his eyes. Then he lowered his hand and said, *"Chichi desu. Aitakatta."*

"Frank, I'm impressed," Bill said.

Frank smiled. "That may be all the Japanese she's going to get out of me," he said with a chuckle. He held his hand out to Mineko again, and this time she took it.

"Let's get our bags," Bill said, "and then we can go someplace to talk."

They went to Frank's spacious apartment on Beacon Hill. Mineko looked at the framed picture of Frank and some of his Nisei buddies in the 442nd Regimental Combat Team hanging over the fireplace.

"That was before Bruyéres," Frank said. "In France. We took Hill C from the Germans, but they took it back again. It's where I lost my arm."

"Did it hurt very much?" Mineko asked.

"Not as much as losing the hill did. But don't get me started."

Mineko looked at Bill. "Get me started?"

"Let's sit down and talk," Bill said. "I'm sure he'll give you the whole story."

Speaking slowly for Mineko, Frank told them about his early life and the wartime relocation and his love and loss of Mitsuko. Bill was thrilled to see the two of them drawing closer, and when the story got into familiar territory, he decided to leave them alone for a while.

"Mind if I borrow your car, Frank? I've got a little errand to run."

"It's no DeSoto," Frank said with a grin.

"I'll settle for the Chrysler," Bill countered.

Frank tossed him the keys and turned back to Mineko, who flashed Bill a reassuring smile.

Bill had driven no more than two blocks before he spotted a phone booth. He had not spoken with his father since the day he graduated from college—over three years now without so much as a postcard. He wondered if his father had heard anything about his graduate career at the University of Washington, or whether he knew that Bill had left for Japan despite his dire warnings.

Half expecting that his father would slam the phone down when he heard his voice, Bill dropped the coin into the slot and dialed the number he still had engraved on his brain.

The phone rang once, twice, three times, and Bill felt his heart pounding in his chest.

"Hello?" The voice was familiar but more weathered than Bill remembered.

"It's me. Bill."

Now was when the crash should come. But there was only silence.

"I'm in Seattle."

"I thought you were in Japan."

"You knew?"

"Of course I knew. Are you coming over?"

"Do you want me to?"

"I think I do."

"I'll be alone."

"Well ... I assumed that."

"I mean, I have a wife now, but I'm leaving her at a friend's house."

"You brought a wife back from Japan? Is she ..."

"Yes, she's Japanese. Her name is Mineko."

"Is she Christian at least?"

"No. And there's not much of that left in me, either."

"I was afraid of that." Another long silence. Then his father said, "I'll be here. Also alone."

The drive from Beacon Hill to Magnolia Bluff ended far too quickly. The Olympics soared over Puget Sound, and as he climbed the front steps of the house, Bill turned to see the familiar double peak of The Brothers. The door opened before he had a chance to knock, and a grim-looking Thomas Morton stood there, looking shrunken and bent. He was only fifty-five years old, but something had aged him terribly.

Bill could not hide his shock.

"I haven't been well," Thomas Morton said. "Don't worry, I'm not going to keel over while you're here. Come in."

Bill had not been expecting humor from his father, even of the gallows variety. He followed his father through the dining room. Bill had last seen the dining table filled with casseroles and plates of tuna salad and deviled eggs and chocolate chip cookies amassed to celebrate his college graduation, but now it was covered with jumbled piles of mail and newspapers, the once glossy wood dull under a layer of greasy dust. The place had a musty smell. In the old days, the house had always smelled of bacon or fresh bread.

They settled in the living room, Bill on the worn red sofa, Tom in the easy chair on the other side of the crookedly placed coffee table, which held more precarious-looking piles of mail and magazines.

As if he knew what Bill was thinking, Tom said, "I'm the only one who lives here now. Kevin's already in his second year at Cascade-Pacific. Lucy took Mark and left me almost a year ago."

"I'm sorry to hear that." He meant it. Lucy had tried her best to be a mother to him, and she had been the bright spot of the household. It was his own fault that he had not been able to respond to her with the affection she longed to share.

Tom said, "I wasn't much fun to live with. She stuck with me through my illness, but I had too many ghosts hanging around me."

"Ghosts?"

"You start to see them when you've got nothing to do but lie in bed all day."

Bill assumed that one of the "ghosts" was the woman he was searching for.

"How long have you been married?" Tom asked.

"A little over a month now."

"I wish I could say congratulations."

"At least you're honest about it."

"I've gotten a lot more honest in my old age. I've thought a lot about you. About you and ..."

"Mitsuko?"

"Yes. Mitsuko." He sighed. "There, I said it. I haven't spoken that name for twenty years. Maybe we would still be married if the war hadn't happened. You would have grown up in a very different household. But I didn't have the strength to resist everything that was going on. This country was so full of hate, and I let it get to me. It took me a long time to see that. I'm still wrestling with it."

Bill had come here expecting his father to be as self-righteous as ever, but what he was hearing now seemed to be verging on a confession.

"Facing death makes you see things in a new light," Tom added.

"You were that sick?" Bill asked.

"It did a job on me, but I'll be around for a while. I just hope ... you'll be my son again."

"I'd like that," Bill said, swallowing hard. "I really would like that."

Beyond the living room window came the cries of gulls flying over the bluff.

"Are you back from Japan for good?" Tom asked.

"No, I still have a lot more to do there. I've been trying to find Mitsuko." He was not ready to tell his father that his new wife was Mitsuko's daughter. "For a while, I thought she had died in Nagasaki."

"Nagasaki? What was she doing there?"

"Her whole family was there. All but her brother Jiro."

Tom looked up at the sound of the name.

"Yes, I met him. He told me he came here before the war. He even remembered me. What was I—two years old?"

"That was a very unpleasant visit."

"So I understand."

"But you say you thought Mitsuko died in Nagasaki, and now you don't?"

"I'm almost certain she survived the war. It's just that we have so little to go on. I was hoping you might have some clue."

"I wish I could help you. As deeply as I was involved with the Japanese community here, I knew very little about her Japanese roots or even about Japan itself. Her name was Mitsuko Fukai, and she came from somewhere in the south of Japan, a little village, I thought. She went to a mission school, and she came here to stay with her sister Yoshiko after a failed marriage. There's nothing more I can tell you."

His father seemed truly sorry that he could not be of any help. For a long time, he sat slumped in his chair, head bowed. Bill had never seen him looking so defeated.

When Tom raised his head, his eyes seemed to be focused somewhere far away. "Let me just say this. If you do find her—and I hope you do—please tell her for me ..."

Bill waited. His father was obviously struggling with something deep inside.

"Just tell her I'm sorry. That's all. I'm sorry. I don't know how to say it any better than that."

"I'll tell her," Bill said. "I promise."

Tom heaved a sigh, and stared off at The Brothers. "You know, before you go back to Japan," he said at last, "you ought to talk to Emery Andrews. The Reverend Emery Andrews of the Japanese Baptist Church. He stuck with his congregation all through the war. He even took his family out to Idaho to live near that camp, Minidoka, to minister to his people. I used to despise him in those days. I was glad to hear the F.B.I. was investigating him for aiding enemy aliens. I can hardly believe it now, to hear myself say that. He was an incredible man, a real servant of God. I'm afraid I've been something far less. But the reason I think you should talk to him is that, after the war, he went to Japan—twice, I think—with the pacifist Floyd Schmoe. They built houses for people in Hiroshima—and in Nagasaki."

Bill stood to leave, and Tom followed him to the front door. Bill turned to say goodbye, and before he knew it he was shocked to find himself in his father's arms. His father never hugged him. Never.

PART SIX:

1963

38

AS THE PATIENTS IN the ward gathered around the television set, the mayor's voice was drowned out in the shuffle of slippers and creaking of chairs. One of the patients said, "Miss Wada, could you please make it louder?"

Miss Wada reached up to adjust the volume, but she barely glanced at the glowing image of the man on the podium.

"World peace," he was saying. "Pray for the eternal repose of the atomic bomb victims," he was saying.

Lord, spare me these platitudes. She walked down to the other end of the ward, looking for something useful to do.

Every August ninth, at 11:02 in the morning, the mayor of Nagasaki and other dignitaries would stand in front of that muscle-bound monument with its finger pointing to the sky. They would say how terrible it had been, and make promises that such a thing would never be allowed to happen again. They would solemnly offer flowers, and there would be songs and prayers, and then it would be all over for another year.

Away from the television set, she stood by the window, watching the traffic sweep past the Nagasaki Citizens' Hospital as if that was what it had always done, flowing freely from the north as if there had never been a mushroom cloud hanging over the Urakami Cathedral, as if the Peace Park had always been a pleasant open space for the people of the city to gather in, not a smoldering heap of ruins.

Then she was in the train again, leaving her baby daughter behind in the green fields of Chiba, shocked in disbelief at a black, broken, twisted Tokyo. No longer did the city's buildings crowd the tracks; instead, the rubble stretched off into the distance, unobstructed.

Such views soon became all too familiar. Long stretches of track were gone in places, and the connections from train to train could only be made on foot, though a few times she was lucky enough to find space in the back of a charcoal-powered truck or a horse-drawn cart. The shabby inns where she stayed along the way could only cook for her the rice from her dwindling personal supply. The cities that the American bombers had visited stretched in what seemed to be an unbroken carpet of smoking black from one end of the country to the other.

She had come back to Nagasaki to help her brother Ichiro's wife take care of their children and her own parents, but now it was clear there was so much more to do. Nagasaki itself had seen raids on and off for a year, the latest on August 1, just two days before her arrival. How much the city had changed since her departure in February the year before! Across the harbor, charred areas were discernible in the huge Mitsubishi shipyard, where the country's greatest warships had been built. The people on the streets in their drab citizens' uniforms moved along slowly, their pale faces reflecting hunger and overwork. More people were on foot than before. The streetcars ran infrequently, and those that did run were covered with passengers clinging to window frames and any other protuberances they could get their hands on.

Hands. All hands had to be free for unaccustomed tasks—and for emergencies. Everyone had a lumpy canvas haversack slung over one shoulder, each person carrying what might be the last of his or her worldly goods—some roasted soy beans in an old tobacco can, bandages, a triangular piece of material for a sling, burn medicine, a bankbook. Here Mitsuko kept her mirror, her last tie with the past. She had considered leaving it with Jiro or his wife for Mineko, but they would have thrown it away. They wanted nothing to do with her, nothing to remind "their" child of her real mother.

On the morning of August 9, she left her parents' house in Matsuyama to offer her services at the University Hospital nearby. She was not a professional nurse, she told them, but she had worked in a hospital and she wanted to help. Volunteers were needed at the twenty-two relief stations scattered throughout the city, they said, but not here. She should try the relief centers that had been set up in the elementary schools in Kozen or Katsuyama downtown—just a short streetcar ride away.

"Yes," she grumbled, "short, if you can manage to get on."

She trudged along beside the tracks, mopping the sweat from her brow.

It was simply too hot to wear her padded air raid hood. The thick morning mist had cleared, and the sun beat down mercilessly. What she would have given to be able to wear a skirt. But any woman not in homely trousers risked mob harassment for lack of cooperation with the war effort.

Passing Nagasaki Station, she followed the streetcar tracks to the left, half-consciously staying with them until she had reached Katsuyama, which was actually somewhat farther from home than Kozen, though easier to get to if she could ever manage to board a streetcar. Standing in the school entrance, she checked her watch. A little after 11:00 a.m. Traveling back and forth between here and Matsuyama was obviously going to be very time-consuming. Today, at least, having come this far, she would see if they had work for her.

A broad-shouldered man wearing spectacles with a cracked left lens was coming down the corridor toward the door. Mitsuko nodded to him, and as she stepped across the threshold, a blinding blue-white flash washed away the building before her. In the next instant, the earth shook her feet out from under her and the building lurched. She landed on her knees, facing forward. From inside came the sound of shattering glass, and the entryway and corridor filled with a thick cloud of fine dust as the mud coating of the walls crumbled to the floor. The building itself remained standing, but through the dust cloud she could see doors leaning at crazy angles. The man who had been walking toward her a moment ago now lay on his back, bleeding from the top of the head.

A bomb!

But it couldn't have been a bomb. There had been no sound of planes or of the bomb rushing earthward. At least, it could not have fallen close by. But to shake the earth like that, it could not have been far away.

Before she could pull herself to her feet, a nurse in a dirt-smeared uniform appeared from out of the dust cloud and knelt by the bleeding man.

Mitsuko stood and backed slowly away from the school building. Her eyes moved up to the roof. Part of it had caved in. All the nearby buildings had damaged roofs, some where a few tiles had been stripped away, others where the peaks had collapsed inward. The entire second story of one building looked as if it had been chopped off. Everything was strangely quiet. There was no sign of a fire nearby. Where could the bomb have hit? This was obviously the center of the blast, but why were there no fire engines or police?

And then she saw the cloud. Up, high above Tateyama Hill to the north. Higher even than the big, green mound of Mount Konpira, which cut the city in two. A swirling white cloud with a burning red core. Again and again something flashed inside the cloud, and each flash was a different color—yellow, red, purple. She had never seen anything so huge and powerful and strangely beautiful. She stood there, mesmerized, as the cloud swirled up and up, flowing over its own top and down again, its bulbous cap rising on a thick gray stalk, like a huge mushroom growing out of the north side of the mountain.

The north side of the mountain! Matsuyama! Her family was over there! She started to walk back the way she had come, sidestepping little piles of roof tiles that lay on the street like the scales of a giant fish. The closer she came to the station, the worse was the damage to the buildings, many of them on fire. There were more people with cuts and scrapes, then more serious wounds, many gushing blood.

At the station, she turned north toward Matsuyama, walking as quickly as she could in the blistering heat. Now the mushroom cloud had changed to a dirty charcoal gray, spreading out toward the east. It continued to fume and boil, growing thicker and blacker. A sick feeling began to gnaw in her breast. The hills no longer obscured her view to the north, and it was clear from the rising black smoke that something far more terrible had happened there than in the rest of the city. A conflagration was enveloping the entire northern Urakami district, including the cathedral and the place in Matsuyama just below it where she lived with her parents.

The farther north she walked, the more wounded she encountered. A few were living pincushions, the "pins" stuck into them slivers of glass. Some were carried on stretchers, others on doors made to serve as stretchers. Soon the wounds were like nothing she had seen before. The skin on one old man's face and head and on the backs of his outstretched hands was ashen gray and shriveled. Blinded, he was being led by a woman who seemed too young to be his wife. When they had passed, Mitsuko turned to see that the hair on the back of his head was black: he was not old at all.

Now almost everyone she met moved along with hands held out, the skin on them horribly seared and oozing. The skin of some had actually slipped away from the raw, glistening flesh and hung down below their arms like tattered cloth. One boy seemed to have a pair of rubber gloves dangling from his fingertips, but the "gloves," she saw, were his own skin.

Most of the wounded were silent and dazed. A few murmured, "Water, water." Now the procession of stumbling ghosts was so thick, Mitsuko had to twist and turn to keep from touching them.

She saw a young man with a gash on his arm who seemed otherwise unhurt. Running up to him, she asked, "What happened? How did all these people get injured?"

"I don't know," he said. "There was a flash, and then everything was gone."

"Where did it hit?"

"I don't know. The Mitsubishi Munitions Factory, maybe. There's nothing left."

"Matsuyama?"

"Gone. Just a bare slope. The cathedral is a heap of stones. The university may be even worse. There's nothing left."

"No, it can't be. Where were the planes? The bombs?"

"I don't know. It just happened. Maybe it's a new bomb like the one they dropped on Hiroshima. Some people saw a plane."

"*One* plane?"

"I don't know."

He moved off with the procession, and Mitsuko stood aside to let the seemingly endless flow of deformed human beings pass her by. Suddenly a slimy hand was on her shoulder, and she gasped when she came face-to-face with a blinded woman, half whose face and hair had been turned into an oozing ball. The woman wore not a stitch of clothing, and her huge pregnant belly was covered with tiny, red slashes. "Take me to a doctor," she groaned. "Please, help me."

Mitsuko wanted to vomit, but she took the woman's uninjured right hand and began to lead her in the direction toward which the crowd was moving. The woman said, haltingly, that she had been working in her garden in Iwakawa, and the next thing she knew she was lying on the ground, naked and blind. A neighbor had told her that her house had collapsed and was burning, her son trapped inside. The man had led her to the street but had gone to find his own wife, and she had groped her way this far south by herself. Her name was Eiko Wada, she added, and she was early in her eighth month of pregnancy. Her husband had worked in the Mitsubishi shipyard but had been killed in a bombing raid there on July 31.

They had passed the station and turned left toward Katsuyama. The relief center in Kozen would be closer, so instead of following the streetcar tracks as she had done earlier, Mitsuko led the woman through the back streets of Kaneya-machi to the New Kozen Elementary School (or People's School, as it had been renamed with warlike zeal).

"I'm beginning to feel contractions," Mrs. Wada said.

"Are you sure?" asked Mitsuko. "It could be—"

"Yes, I'm sure!"

"Just a couple hundred meters now," she encouraged the woman, who was leaning more and more heavily on her, but when they turned the corner, Mitsuko felt her heart break. The throng of wounded at the entrance spilled out onto the street. Those who couldn't stand or had given up were lying in the dusty schoolyard, squeezing themselves into spaces between the piles of roof tiles shaken off by the blast. Patches of the dry earth were stained blackish-red with blood. Some of the people on the ground were lying very still. Mitsuko saw that one man was unmistakably dead.

"What's happening?" Mrs. Wada asked when they came to a halt.

"There's a long line," Mitsuko said as calmly as she could.

"Oh, no! The contractions are getting stronger."

"Wait here," said Mitsuko. She edged her way through the crowd, trying not to touch people. She had handled some repulsive cases in the Minidoka hospital, but this was different. The smell of the crowd was like nothing she had ever experienced before; she imagined it must be the smell of a slaughter house.

She expected curses from the people she had to nudge out of her way, but no one said a thing. They just stood there, those who still had eyes staring vacantly ahead, mouths hanging open.

To a nurse processing people in the entryway, she said, "I have a pregnant woman back there, terribly burned, who is starting to go into labor."

"I'm sorry, she'll have to wait her turn like everyone else." Mitsuko saw that the nurse herself had a bandage around her arm and a long, brown bloodstain on one side of her dress.

"You don't understand. The baby is coming now."

"No, *you* don't understand. This place is full already, and look at the ones waiting to get in. One of our doctors was crushed under a bookcase, and the other one is going crazy trying to do something for all these people."

There was no point in arguing. Mitsuko would have to drag Mrs. Wada through the crowd and force this stubborn woman to look at her. But by the time she made it back through the crowd, Mrs. Wada was clutching her belly and moaning. Her thighs were wet, and the dust between her feet had turned to mud.

"It's coming!" she cried. "It's coming!"

Mitsuko pulled the cloth triangle from her haversack and spread it on the ground. Then, as gently as possible, she helped Mrs. Wada crouch down until her haunches were on the cloth. She felt the woman's loose skin slide atop her flesh. The woman lay back on the bare earth, clawing at the ground, her whole body convulsing with each new contraction, her moans rising to wails and finally to ear-piercing screams.

Tearing at the hard, dry ground, Mrs. Wada's fingernails were soon streaming with blood, and still the baby would not come. "Take it out! Take it out!" were the only words that Mitsuko could catch amid her screams.

Suddenly the contractions stopped, and there was only the sound of the woman's panting. Then, with amazing calm, Mrs. Wada said, "If it's a boy, name it Tsuyoshi after my husband. If it's a girl, call it Tomoko."

"That's for you to do," said Mitsuko.

"Don't be stupid," said Mrs. Wada. "I'm not going to live through this."

Before Mitsuko could find the words to reassure her, the contractions started again. On and on Mrs. Wada screamed, until finally, with an enormous gush of blood, an inert lump of flesh disgorged itself from between the woman's legs and lay in Mitsuko's hands. Almost at the same moment, Mrs. Wada gave a long hiss, and her pain-racked body shriveled up like a pricked balloon. One corpse had given birth to another. The tiny dead creature would have been a girl.

Mitsuko carried the little thing to the side of the building and laid it on some roof tiles in a shady spot. She searched among the waiting victims for someone who might have the strength to help her carry the mother, but most had all they could do to remain on their feet. Wiping away as much of the blood and slime from the body as she could with the saturated cloth, she picked up what was left of Mrs. Wada and staggered to the place where she had laid the little girl, Tomoko, who had never drawn breath. She wished there were something she could cover the bodies with decently, but she realized that in the short time since they had arrived at the schoolyard, several more corpses had joined them on the ground. Mitsuko did her best to drag these out of the direct sunlight, after which she struggled through the pressing crowd to the nurse in the doorway.

"I can help," she panted. "I've worked in a hospital."

"In there," said the nurse, motioning with a jerk of the head.

Mitsuko stayed "in there" for the next two days without sleep and little more than an occasional toilet break, helping the doctor oil wounds and extract glass splinters from eyes—when he could do anything at all for the lacerated remnants of humanity who streamed into the relief center. For a while on the first day, there was some talk that the building would have to be evacuated if the sudden wind that developed were to sweep nearby fires in this direction, but by six p.m. the winds had shifted and the danger of fire was not mentioned again.

The patients who could speak told of the skies burning after sunset, of new fires near the train station, of horrible swarms of mosquitoes attacking the suppurating skin of the victims trying to sleep in the schoolyard. Over and over word came that the area around Matsuyama had been decimated. The Mitsubishi Ordinance Factory had been destroyed, killing all the high school girls working inside. The Urakami Cathedral had been dashed to the ground. The handsome old camphor trees that shaded the Medical University campus had been uprooted or transformed into skeletal stumps, and the buildings reduced to smoking rubble. In some areas, corpses littered the ground so thickly that it was impossible for the living to walk in a straight line. In other areas, the destruction had been so complete that there were not even corpses left. Matsuyama was said to be one such place.

Alarms were sounded when enemy planes passed overhead, but no one seemed to care. All through the night the planes came, at one point in such numbers that the building shook with the roar of their engines, but at least they dropped no more bombs.

Mitsuko was still working like an automaton the next day when an advance party of doctors from the Sasebo Naval Hospital arrived. She put in one more unbroken night of work, during which time the school was being set up as sleeping quarters for the medical teams pouring into the city. Finally, nearly forty-eight hours after the bomb fell, she dozed for an hour in the corner of one "dormitory" room and then set out on foot for Matsuyama.

None of the rumors had prepared her for the totality of destruction that she found where her family had been living. It was impossible to tell where the streets had been laid out. Except for a few scattered stones, the slope was barren as if a gigantic bulldozer had scoured its way from top to bottom. She was almost thankful. How much more terrible it must have been for those people who had been trapped under buildings and slowly suffocated or burned to death. Here, there was nothing to react to. One day, she had had a family; today, they no longer existed. They had all been at home when she left, even Ichiro, who had little more to do in Nagasaki than tend the vegetable garden. Perhaps they had not even suffered.

She stumbled up the hill to see what was left of the Urakami Cathedral, center of the city's Catholic community. How many of the faithful twenty thousand had been killed? How many of the huge, red edifice's six thousand seats had been occupied at the moment of destruction? What did the survivors think now of their God? The few remaining sculpture saints still cast their gazes heavenward as if seeking an explanation for the indiscriminate slaughter and destruction. But up there, in the heavens, lived no God. Up there were only the planes from Seattle, the Boeings, the B-29s, delivering their gifts of hate, as if sent by Tom for Mitsuko herself. Perhaps, between white saints and their white God, no explanation was necessary. Those who had died here had not been Catholics or Christians or even human beings. They were just Japs.

That day, she turned her back on Matsuyama and vowed never to visit this part of the city again. She returned to the relief center and worked long hours doing the only thing she felt there was left for her to do in this world. The best way she could serve her surviving family would be to join those who had entered oblivion. Mineko must never know she had existed. Yoshiko would go on with her life in America, and Mitsuko could never be part of that. Her "family" were those sick, blinded souls who had been pulverized between the millstones of honor and justice.

Almost before anyone had noticed, she had become a permanent part of the medical team. When the tension of those first days had abated enough for people to begin thinking about themselves as individual human beings again, a doctor smoking a cigarette asked her name. She hesitated only a moment before answering, "Tomoko Wada." Through her, the dead child would have life.

As Tomoko Wada, she stayed on in the New Kozen Elementary School when it was taken over as a branch of the University Hospital. The government, in its wisdom, had stopped supporting it as a relief center in October despite the hundreds of patients still desperate for its services. She continued to be Tomoko Wada when the Occupation freshly outfitted and donated to the city of Nagasaki the old Japanese Army Hospital in Tokiwa-machi a few blocks away, moving both staff and equipment there from the school in December. She found a room nearby and spent most of each day in the wards of the new Nagasaki Citizens' Hospital.

It was not the life she would have chosen. She was not what anyone would call "happy." But as she recalled the horrid images, she smiled to herself, glad at least that her anger was still there. It was this to which she had clung—this angry love for the individual men and women and children whose bodies had been broken by the bomb—some hurt so deeply inside that the damage was surfacing only now, eighteen years later.

Yet today those men stood before the television cameras, mouthing words of palliation, words that had nothing to do with the mortification of the flesh of real human beings. Only once had she seen words that came close to capturing the truth. Not surprisingly, the words had been written by a doctor, one who had cared for hundreds of the wounded, who had been one of the deeply wounded himself, and who had looked at the horror with unflinching eyes. The truth had frightened the American occupiers, and they had tried to suppress Dr. Nagai's words, relenting finally in 1949.

"Yes," Mitsuko had said to herself upon reading *The Bells of Nagasaki*, "this is what it was really like." But when she came to the end, her rage boiled over, for after his heroic act of witnessing one of the worst evils ever perpetrated upon man by man, the doctor had betrayed his own anger. After all the blood, all the fire and suffering, he concluded that Nagasaki should be grateful to God for having chosen the city as a sacrificial lamb to end the war. With that inflated sense of self-importance granted only to the religious, he concluded that Nagasaki was the one holy place in all of Japan and that God himself—not the American pilots—had actually directed the bomb to fall on the Urakami Cathedral. None of the other destroyed cities in the world had been a great enough sacrifice for this bloodthirsty god. But when holy Nagasaki screamed with pain, God had gone straight to the emperor and inspired him to surrender. Nagasaki had been a noble and splendid burnt offering to God because of its cathedral. When eight thousand Catholic believers and their priests entered eternal life burning with pure smoke, that had been beautiful and sublime. These faithful had been the only ones in Japan free from sin and worthy to be offered to God.

Here was God at his finest. Only God could justify the incineration of the innocent. Only God could dazzle the mind of a man whose eyes had seen so clearly. Without God, how tortured, how conscience-stricken must be the great killers of mankind. Someday, she knew, the makers of war would turn to Dr. Nagai with gratitude in their hearts for having shown them the way.

No, a blind woman with her skin peeling off was a wounded human being, not a lamb of God. Turn her into anything higher, nobler, purer or holier, and she ceased to be human. She became an abstraction, a symbol without feelings or pain. The eight thousand Catholics burning with pure smoke in Dr. Nagai's fevered imagination surely felt no pain; but to the eight thousand individual human beings—and the seventy thousand infidels who joined them in death—there was nothing beautiful, pure, or sublime in what happened to them. Of course, there was no way to ask them about that. They were dead now. And probably the partial human beings lying in the wards here wished they were dead, too. We, the living, the sinners, could do only one thing for the dead: to mourn them in anger. To love each other in anger. To resist the temptations of an evil God who would tear his children to pieces and command them to be grateful for it.

Mitsuko's own temptation over the years had been her children, one of her body and one of her heart. On days when her love for the victims did not seem great enough to sustain her, she would think of the baby she had left behind in Chiba and wonder what the child looked like, how she was growing, what kind of a person she was becoming.

Only once over the years had Mitsuko weakened. Knowing that Mineko's twelfth birthday was approaching, she traveled to Tokyo to present her the other mirror. Any younger, and Mineko would have been too much her parents' little girl; any older, and too many explanations would have been necessary. Mineko's beauty had been a thrill to her and brought her memories of Frank. Perhaps it had been with Frank that she had first tasted that love borne of anger which had carried her through the pain.

Sheer distance made Billy less of a threat to her peace of mind. Living across the ocean in the home of the Reverend Thomas Morton, he might, like other Americans, have learned to hate all Japs for the greater glory of God. By now, surely, there was nothing left of her inside him. Sometimes, though, she would imagine that Yoshiko had sought him out and given him the mirror, and that, perhaps, lingering reverberations of her bitter love for him had been transmitted from the carved wood through his hand to his heart.

There had been one instance of temptation regarding Billy, too. In 1951, she had been asked to interpret for a party of American pacifists and do-gooders who were visiting the hospital. The staff knew that she had useful English skills and pressed her to guide the group around. They were visiting Nagasaki to build homes for victims of the bombing. She wanted to ask, who had sent them, the president of the United States to lessen America's guilt? But she held her tongue and showed them around, making certain they saw the most grotesquely disfigured patients.

One especially tall, bony man in a white short-sleeved shirt was furiously taking notes on everything he heard. He had a camera slung over his shoulder and every now and then would ask permission to use it. Some members of the group tried to engage her in conversation, but she had all she could do to remain civil, and she barely looked at them. As the group was leaving, the tall, thin man thanked her for her kindness and asked her name. She looked him in the eye now for the first time and caught her breath. He was Reverend Emery Andrews of the Japanese Baptist Church in Seattle. She recognized him from the crowd of well-wishers seeing the busloads of people off to Puyallup. And he was the father of Brooks, the other little boy Frank had saved from drowning at the Minidoka swimming hole.

For a split second, she thought of giving him her real name. Perhaps he knew Tom and could tell her about Billy. Perhaps he could deliver Billy a message, bypassing Tom. In the end, though, she said only, "My name is Tomoko Wada."

"Tomoko Wada," he repeated, scribbling her name in his notebook. "And where did you learn to speak such excellent English?"

When she hesitated again, he looked straight at her. "Are you sure we've never met before?" he asked. "In Seattle? Or Camp Harmony? Or Minidoka? You look so familiar."

How could she utter the word "Seattle"? How could she tell him that she had been the wife of a man who had betrayed her and betrayed the community he served so faithfully?

"Never mind," she said. "My English is not good."

"Thank you anyway, Tomoko Wada," he said. "You have been very kind and very helpful." Before he closed his notebook, she saw him write a large question mark after her name.

The commemorative ceremonies had ended several hours earlier when Mitsuko heard Tomoko Wada being paged over the intercom. She had visitors, the voice said, at the front admitting desk. That was impossible. No one knew "Tomoko Wada" outside this hospital. She practically lived here, and the destruction of records had enabled her to preserve her anonymity for the past eighteen years. Could it be the police? Had she broken a law by adopting the identity of a stillborn infant?

She took the elevator down and turned right into the long, gloomy corridor. As she moved toward the rectangular glare at the far end, three silhouettes moved away from the admitting desk and stood there, facing in her direction. The two outer shadows belonged to men, one very tall, the other less so, and the middle one was a woman about her own size. As she drew closer, and her eyes adjusted to the light, she recognized her daughter, Mineko, now a beautifully grown woman. She stopped short and strained to see the others. The man to the left was surely no Japanese. No, he was blond and resembled the young Thomas Morton. Could this be Billy, standing before her? And the Japanese man to the right? His left arm was missing, but in his intense gaze, she recognized Frank Sano. Before she could recover from the shock of seeing her past arrayed before her, the blond man started moving toward her, holding his arms out.

What could they say to each other, what could they be to each other after all these years?

But the moment he clasped her in his arms, all her doubts were swept away.

"Mother!" he said. "Oh, Mother!"

THE END

NOTE ON SOURCES

This book is a novel, its major characters and events entirely fictional, but the setting of the story is authentic. Characters often appear in situations which actually occurred, or they encounter people who were actually alive at the time. This factual information owes much to the contemporary press (*Seattle Post-Intelligencer, Seattle Star, Seattle Daily Times*); to the relocation camp newspaper, *The Minidoka Irrigator*; to a 1943 publication called "Minidoka Interlude: September 1942 – October 1943," published by Residents of Minidoka Relocation Center, Hunt, Idaho; and to such books as the following:

Audrie Girdner and Anne Loftis, *The Great Betrayal:*
The Evacuation of the Japanese-Americans During World War II
(New York: The Macmillan Company, 1969).

Hiroshima-shi, Nagasaki-shi Gembaku Saigaishi Henshū Iinkai,
Hiroshima and Nagasaki: the Physical, Medical and Social Effects of the
Atomic Bombings (New York: Basic Books, 1981).

Kazuo Ito, *Issei* (Seattle: Executive Committee for the Publication
of *Issei*, 1973).

Richard H. Mitchell, *Thought Control in Prewar Japan*
(Ithaca: Cornell University Press, 1976).

Shotaro Frank Miyamoto, *Social Solidarity Among the Japanese*
in Seattle (Seattle: University of Washington Press, 1981).

Takashi Nagai, *The Bells of Nagasaki*, translated by William
Johnston (Tokyo: Kodansha International, 1984).

Personal Justice Denied: Report of the Commission on Wartime
Relocation and Internment of Civilians (Washington, D.C.:
U.S.G.P.O., 1982).

Katsumoto Saotome, *Tokyo daikūshū*
(Tokyo: Iwanami shinsho, 1971).

Monica Sone, *Nisei Daughter* (Seattle: The University of
Washington Press, 1979).

Yoshiko Uchida, *Desert Exile: The Uprooting of a Japanese-American
Family* (Seattle: The University of Washington Press, 1982).

Jeanne Wakatsuki Houston and James D. Houston,
Farewell to Manzanar (Boston: Houghton Mifflin, 1973).

Michi Weglyn, *Years of Infamy: The Untold Story of America's
Concentration Camps* (New York: William Morrow and
Company, 1976).

In addition to the above sources used for this book, the reader may wish to
consult some of the numerous publications, both factual and fictional, which
have appeared in recent years. A particularly rich source of information is the
web site www.densho.org, the mission of which is "to preserve the testimonies
of Japanese Americans who were unjustly incarcerated during World War II
before their memories are extinguished." A portion of the proceeds from this
book will be donated to Densho, to the Wing Luke Museum of the Asian
Pacific American Experience (Seattle), to the American Civil Liberties Union
of Washington State, and to the Nagasaki Atomic Bomb Museum.

Many friends, family members and colleagues have helped bring this book
to fruition, among them Todd Shimoda, Bruce Rutledge, Rick Simonson, Hana
Rubin, Davinder Bhowmik, Ted Woolsey, Sara Woolsey, Ted Mack, Scott Pack,
Motoyuki Shibata, Brooks Andrews, Jim Peterson, Ted Goossen, and Tess
Gallagher. By far, the single greatest contributor has been my wife, Rakuko,
without whose intelligence, imagination, determination and love, there would
have been no book. She has been my coauthor every step of the way.